"TOADS! TOADS!"

A nameless warrior alerted the field to the problem only a few seconds after the giant sawdust pile erupted in a fury of motion, smoke and laserfire. Elementals leaped clear from where they had been buried, leapfrogging by groups of five. Ten battlesuit troopers.

Then fifteen. Then twenty.

With the five infantrymen from before, that was the full Star accounted for! Getting battlesuit soldiers into range of their short-range weapons was the usual trick. Helmer had managed it by burrowing them into the soft sawdust, masking their presence until Jasek closed to a good range. But for a few seconds, the Elemental warriors were also grouped together in a vulnerable pack. With some artillery, the Elementals could have been chewed into so many walking wounded.

Bombing runs could accomplish much the same thing. And there were four fightercraft already arrowing down on their attack runs.

"Stormhammers," Vandel called out on command override. "Ground and *hold*!"

It was a risky call, ordering the assault force to give up their maneuverability. For five desperate heartbeats the offensive push ground to a standstill, tempting the Jade Falcons with easy targets.

Then artificial thunder shattered the waterfront as a pair of *Stingrays* slashed from backfield to fore, strafing with lasers and missiles as they ignored the remaining VTOLs in favor of the thick cluster of Elementals.

DARK AGE

BLOOD OF
THE ISLE

A BATTLETECH® NOVEL

Loren L. Coleman

A ROC BOOK

ROC
Published by New American Library, a division of
Penguin Group (USA) Inc., 375 Hudson Street,
New York, New York 10014, U.S.A.
Penguin Books Ltd, 80 Strand,
London WC2R 0RL, England
Penguin Books Australia Ltd, 250 Camberwell Road,
Camberwell, Victoria 3124, Australia
Penguin Books Canada Ltd, 10 Alcorn Avenue,
Toronto, Ontario, Canada M4V 3B2
Penguin Books (NZ), cnr Airborne and Rosedale Roads,
Albany, Auckland 1310, New Zealand

Penguin Books Ltd, Registered Offices:
80 Strand, London WC2R 0RL, England

First published by Roc, an imprint of New American Library,
a division of Penguin Group (USA) Inc.

First Printing, August 2004
10 9 8 7 6 5 4 3 2 1

Cover design by Ray Lundgren

 REGISTERED TRADEMARK—MARCA REGISTRADA

Printed in the United States of America

PUBLISHER'S NOTE
This is a work of fiction. Names, characters, places, and incidents either are the
products of the author's imagination or are used fictitiously, and any resemblance
to actual persons, living or dead, business establishments, events, or locales is
entirely coincidental.

BOOKS ARE AVAILABLE AT QUANTITY DISCOUNTS WHEN USED TO PROMOTE PROD-
UCTS OR SERVICES. FOR INFORMATION PLEASE WRITE TO PREMIUM MARKETING DIVI-
SION, PENGUIN GROUP (USA) INC., 375 HUDSON STREET, NEW YORK, NEW YORK 10014.

For Russell and Roberta Loveday,
who never moved so far away
that the Internet could not reach them.
We've missed you.

Acknowledgments

One year I am helping to create The Republic, through articles and character bios for INN, and consulting on back history. The next, I'm doing my damnedest to tear it apart. Sometimes it feels like one of those old military make-work projects. Dig a hole; then fill it back in. Except that not all of the dirt ever makes it back into the hole. It gets scattered around, lost in the grass and clumped into the treads of work boots.

And that's where all of our stories come from—when the pieces do not fit back together quite so nicely as when we took them apart.

I would like to thank everyone at WizKids for their tireless support in this process: Jordan and Dawne Weisman, Maya Smith, and Mike and Sharon Mulvihill, among so many others. Also the wonderful people I have been privileged enough to work with at Roc—Laura Anne Gillman, who will be missed, and Jennifer Heddle, with whom I always look forward to working—and Vic Milán, who wrote one hell of a book and ended up being a hard act to follow.

Best wishes to my agent, Don Maass, and to his office staff for their hard work on my behalf. A hearty thanks to Dean Wesley Smith and Kristine Kathryn Rusch for their continued support, mentoring, and friendship.

Speaking of friends . . . thanks again go to Allen and Amy Mattila, Randall and Tara Bills, Phil DeLuca, Kelle Vozka, and Peter and Cathy Orullian, all of whom help keep me relatively sane by dragging me away from my computer from time to time. And then there are Oystein Tvedten, Herb Beas, Chris Hartford, Chris Trossen, Pete Smith, Chas Borner, and Warner Doles, who always seem ready to drag me back. Special acknowledgments go out to Dave Stansel for his recent efforts, and Mike Stackpole, who continues to keep in touch with everything.

My heartfelt appreciation also goes out to my wife,

Heather Joy, who continues to indulge my selfish need to lock myself away for days and weeks. And to my children, Talon, Conner, and Alexia, who pick that lock all too regularly or not often enough—I can't decide.

And because I would find hair balls on my pillow if I didn't: thanks to Chaos, Rumor, and Ranger, our Siamese cats, for keeping our house in strict order. (And Loki, our dog, for his frequent infusions of happy chaos.)

REPUBLIC OF THE SPHERE

PREFECTURES VIII AND IX

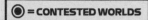
◉ = CONTESTED WORLDS

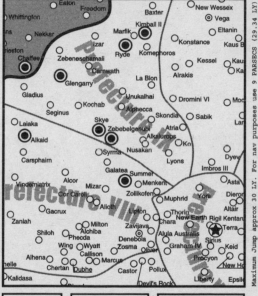

Eaton • Freedom • Baxter • New Wessex • Vega ◉ • Eltanin • Whittington • Nekkar • Kimball II • Marfik • Konstance • Kaus B • ens • Chaffee • Izar • Ryde • Komephoros • Kessel • Kaus • rieston • Zebeneschamali • Carnwath • La Blon • Alrakis • Ka • Glengarry • Kochab • Unukalhai • Dromini VI • Mo • Gladius • Seginus • Alphecca • Skondia • Sabik • Lan • Laiaka • Skye • Zebebelgenubi • Atria • Alkalurops • Ko • Alkaid • Symra • Nusakan • Lyons • Dyev • Carsphairn • Alcor • Galatea • Summer • Imbros III • Vindemiatrix • Mizar • Menkent • Asta • Cor Caroli • Zollikofen • Muphrid • Yorii • Dieron • Gacrux • Alioth • Lipton • Thorin • Altair • Zaniah • Milton • Chara • New Earth • Rigil Kentari • Shiloh • Alchiba • Zavijava • Alula Australis • Terra • Phecda • Denebola • Graham IV • Sirius • Keid • Wing • Wyatt • Zosma • Oliver • Procyon • New Ho • Alhena • Callison • Marcus • Castor • Pollux • Liberty • Epsile • nelle • Chertan • Dubhe • Devil's Rock • Kalidasa

Maximum Jump approx 30 LY. For nav purposes use 9 PARSECS (29.34 LY)

40 PARSECS OR 130.4 LIGHT YEARS

8 PARSECS

Coreward
Anti-spinward — Spinward
Rimward

THE INNER SPHERE
■ REPUBLIC TERRITORY

PREFECTURES OF THE REPUBLIC
IX I II
VIII X III
VII VI V IV

©3134 ComStar Cartographic Corps.

For he owned and displayed such remarkable ability that even as a private person it was spoken of him that he lacked nothing but the kingdom to be a king.
The Prince, by Niccolò Machiavelli

1

Cheops
Seventh District, Nusakan
Prefecture IX, Republic of the Sphere
8 September 3134

Thick, viscous fog shrouded the Willamette Valley, creating the worst whiteout conditions Jasek Kelswa-Steiner had ever seen. It stretched the battlefield into a canvas of thin shadows and brief, pale flashes of fire and lightning. Lasers strobed in snatches of emerald green and angry red. Cerulean beams from particle projector cannon arced back and forth. Occasionally, a bolt of the man-made lightning of the PPC slashed into the shadows, grabbing one in a spectral aura like Saint Elmo's fire, drawing a brief, cold outline around an armored vehicle or a BattleMech.

Jasek could only guess if it had been the enemy, or one of his own.

Violent eruptions of fire slashed a path through the knee-high sward of tall grasses and Scotch broom as a flight of missiles hammered down from the closed heavens. He ducked reflexively, as if he could drag the *Griffin* back by force of will.

Blackened earth pattered against the screen.

Smoke mixed into the fog, tainting the frosted blanket with a gray, dishwater color.

Appearing at nearly point-blank range, two shadows raced forward. Jasek knew they were enemy tanks even before the vehicles opened fire. They probed through the thinning curtain, relying on instruments or instinct. Light autocannon fire *spang*ed off the BattleMech's arms. The dark forms solidified in an instant, showing themselves as Skanda light tanks. Angular lines and their dropped nose marked them certainly as belonging to Clan Jade Falcon.

Bullet-shaped treads chewed up the sward like hungry mouths. They raced to either side of the camera, trading out autocannon for medium lasers and laying in a blistering cross fire. The camera view hitched and swung around, following the left-side Skanda. Return fire came late, scarlet-tinged lasers splashing armor from the tank's rear quarter.

At nearly 120 kilometers per hour the tanks raced off into the fog, disappearing quickly. The scene slowed, catching the Skandas as thin shadows once more, and froze just before they disappeared.

"There!" Jasek threw the remote to his best friend and aide-de-camp, Niccolò GioAvanti. Jasek came out of his chair and prowled a tight box around a kidney-shaped desk. Lean and muscular, the thirty-one-year-old leader had the powerful grace of a stalking cat. "Look at that."

He gestured to the Tri-Vid viewer inset into one of the office's dark, walnut-paneled walls. This compilation of gun-cam footage had been specially edited to give him an overview of an intelligence-gathering raid against the world of Ryde, where one of his Stormhammer units had run into intolerable weather conditions and stiff Jade Falcon resistance. It was showing him a lot more.

"Hauptmann Falhearst's *Griffin* has a Cyclops XII extended-range laser mounted on its right arm. What the hell is he doing, not using it?"

Niccolò GioAvanti rose from his own chair and set the slender remote on the edge of Jasek's desk. His mouse brown hair was cut short and straight across the back and sides except for a family braid twisting down over his left temple. His eyes were an unsettling pale blue and never seemed to blink enough. Wearing dark slacks and a flowing white shirt under a dark vest, he created a stark contrast to Jasek's dusky features and crisp dress-gray uniform. Which was likely the reason he dressed that way.

Jasek watched as his friend squared the remote against a glass-topped holopic base that projected a clenched gauntlet into the air over his desk. Niccolò was obviously stalling, giving Jasek a moment in which to regain his composure. Thankfully, Jasek's noble birth and inherited title did not stand between the two men. Niccolò himself came from a fairly influential merchant family, and twenty-two years of friendship had eroded any formality due a Landgrave and a ducal heir.

"Perhaps if we issued Tri-Vid remotes to our pilots," Niccolò finally offered, "letting them slow the action and review it a time or two before making their decisions."

Jasek glowered. Eighteen months on the world of Nusakan, sitting out a self-imposed exile, had not improved his mood. "Don't twit me over being stuck here, Nicco."

His friend raised an eyebrow. "Who thought Nusakan would be the perfect base of operations?"

"I did. And it was. Is!" He laughed dryly as his tongue tripped him up. "I just thought the key word would be *operations*, not *base*."

Still, the barb stuck. Jasek snagged his desk chair and dropped back into it, testing the springs, which creaked several loud protests. The warm smell of rich leather wrapped around him as he rocked back for a moment, studying the ceiling. The scent reminded him of his father's office, and that memory unlocked the door to so many more.

Skye will never need your kind of leadership.

Shock. And a warm thrill of anger.

We'll see what Skye needs, Father. If you think The Republic will stand on its own merits, you're going to be greatly disappointed.

Obviously not for the first time.

That last conversation with Duke Gregory Kelswa-Steiner, his father and Lord Governor of Prefecture IX, continued to echo through his thoughts. It had angered Jasek in the DropShip, lifting off from Skye. Chased him all the way to Nusakan, where Niccolò offered him offices and support out of the GioAvanti mercantile assets in Cheops. Drawing like-minded warriors to his standard, the Stormhammers, Jasek had stripped Prefecture IX of what little defense it mustered. Then he waited for his father to call him home. To admit to being wrong.

Duke Gregory did neither.

And Skye very nearly fell.

Jasek scrubbed one hand over his face. Opening his eyes, he found himself staring at the clenched-gauntlet hologram projected over its glass-eyed emitter—the symbol of House Steiner and the Lyran Commonwealth. The mailed fist was burnished copper with silver chasing. The background was dark blue, nearly indigo, the same color as his eyes.

A promise, she'd said, giving it to him. He very nearly smiled. *A token of our shared resolve.*

Which, as it turned out, was not all they had shared.

But he couldn't live inside memories, even pleasant ones, for long. Niccolò waited patiently, right elbow braced on the back of his other fist, right hand tapping a knuckle against his chin. Jasek knew his friend would wait as long as it took; he had never outlasted Nicco in any game of patience.

"All right," he finally admitted. "So it's not fair to expect perfection out of the Stormhammers."

He had splashed two fingers of dark whiskey into a tumbler earlier. It sat on his desk, untouched and unwanted. Leaning forward, he reached past the glass and stabbed at the remote, continuing the gun-cam footage. He left the slender wand slightly canted toward the edge of the desk, knowing it would annoy his friend.

On the Tri-Vid, the scene cut to another camera. This one, according to the information tag scrolling along the bottom of the screen, was mounted on a Hasek mechanized combat vehicle. More fog. A shadow grew and coalesced into the *Griffin* that had been under fire only a few seconds before. The fifty-five-ton war avatar showed laser scoring along its left leg and right flank, and jagged armor where its left-shoulder plating had been ripped apart in an earlier engagement. A long-range-missile system sat on its right shoulder. Its lasers appeared intact, stubbing out of the centerline and mounted on the outside of its right arm. The BattleMech's "head" had one of the best range-of-views of any design, Jasek knew, with more than eight square meters of ferroglass curving around the cockpit.

Standing nearly nine meters tall under most circumstances, the BattleMech crouched, twisting from side to side as if expecting another attack at any moment. Jasek tried to imagine what Falhearst's HUD had to look like—a tangle of icons and data tags. What had the MechWarrior been thinking, trying to regroup in the face of a determined assault, cut off from the Stormhammers' DropShip?

Jasek watched as the Hasek disgorged two squads of Purifier infantry. The battle armor troops fanned out in front of the *Griffin*, mimetic armor blending them into the sward with perfect camouflage. Only the bending grasses and scrub brush betrayed their passage as they moved forward to act as an early-warning picket. Slowly, too slowly, the combined-arms lance advanced. He said so aloud.

"This isn't five and six," Niccolò reminded Jasek, referring to The Republic's prefectures that bordered against the Capellan Confederation. "We haven't seen real combat in more than forty years. That much, at least, Devlin Stone did accomplish."

"Yeah, well, where's Stone now?" Jasek asked, not expecting an answer. Niccolò did not volunteer one.

Of course, both men had been raised on Devlin Stone's "accomplishments." His status, perhaps deservedly, as the war hero who saved the Inner Sphere from Word of Blake's Jihad. The campaign to form a new Republic and promote peace through a policy of economically enforced disarmament and the intermingling of cultures.

Jasek had endured such lessons from his father as well as in his formal schooling. Duke Gregory was a true believer, one of Stone's early supporters when the bulk of Prefecture IX had been known as the Isle of Skye. For generations, Skye had sought independent rule from House Steiner's Lyran Commonwealth. Then Devlin Stone dangled the carrot of The Republic in front of them, and Duke Gregory helped lead Skye into Stone's camp. Soon The Republic of the Sphere had gobbled up nearly all worlds within 120 light-years of Terra, humanity's birthplace.

But to Jasek's way of thinking they had merely traded one lord for another, and the grandeur of House Steiner for an upstart with dreams of utopia.

His friend agreed. "For all his speeches of forging a new path," Niccolò had said, "there are still two types of government: republics and principalities. We may style ourselves The Republic of the Sphere, but we are still Stone's hereditary fiefdom. And without him, we founder."

Jasek clenched his jaw as the *Griffin* struggled forward through the fog, sniped at by Jade Falcon tormentors who materialized as half-visible ghosts or simply guessed well based on the Clans' superior instrumentation. A stream of energy from a PPC blasted through the thick curtain and sloughed away a ton of armor in a wide swath across the 'Mech's chest. A Stormhammer *Panther* made brief contact, the smaller 'Mech leading a pair of Scimitar hover tanks and a long line of Cavalier battle armor infantry. For a moment, it looked as if the full unit might reconstitute itself and make a stand.

Then the Jade Falcons hammered into their flank.

A *Gyrfalcon* led, arms thrust forward, alternating between large lasers and medium-weight autocannon. Two Skandas—maybe the same two from before—charged in at its side, challenging the Hasek MCV, with a Kite recon vehicle trailing and adding its SRMs to the hard-hitting assault.

The Cavalier infantry managed to swarm one Skanda, jumping onto its top and ripping away large chunks of armor. They thrust arm-mounted lasers into the crew space and filled the cabin with lethal energy. The Purifiers, by design or just bad luck, ended up in the path of the Kite. Like a lawn mower, the hovercraft slammed through their formation, its nose crumpling. Bodies flew to either side, broken and lost.

The Stormhammers shattered.

Rather than stand their ground, pitting two 'Mechs against the one *Gyrfalcon*, the *Panther* broke left with its Scimitar support and the *Griffin* right. The fog claimed both, separating them as the Falcon MechWarrior hammered the Hasek's nose into unrecognizable scrap. The *Griffin* sliced its lasers at the other fifty-five-tonner, but it lit off jump jets and rocketed up, out of sight, before suffering much damage.

Jasek stood, scooping up his drink and carrying it with him as he walked a slow perimeter around the outer wall of his office.

"I'm tired of waiting, Nicco. I'm done watching. I've sat by while the Jade Falcons tear up our worlds these last two months, and I'm telling you that it's killing me. Skye very nearly fell! I feel like I'm the one lost in that damnable fog, and I don't know where the next blow is coming from."

Niccolò leaned against the side of Jasek's desk. "But look

at how much more we know compared to twelve months ago. Even twelve weeks ago."

Jasek shrugged, looked down into his drink. Amber liquid sloshed back and forth. "We know nothing. We *suspect*. We suspect that other prefectures are having just as much trouble with the loss of the HPG network, and we suspect that the Falcon incursion is more than they claim—this 'hunting expedition' to destroy the Steel Wolves."

Folding his arms over his chest, Niccolò disagreed. "We *know* what worlds the Falcons hold, where they are strongest and weakest. We also know that your father has accepted that Skye cannot stand on its own."

"Granted," Jasek said. A tight smile cracked his stern expression. "At least there is that."

When the Jade Falcon force hit Skye itself, the only reasons the world did not fall were the presence of Tara Campbell's Highlanders and the intervention of Anastasia Kerensky's Steel Wolves. Three rival factions coming together in the face of a common threat: how his father must have hated that. Would he have rather had his son, and the Stormhammers, by him then?

Or was he just that stubborn, to look the other way even in the face of overwhelming odds?

Was it time to find out?

On the Tri-Vid, the scene cut back once again to the *Griffin*'s own gun-cam footage. The fog thinned as the BattleMech slogged its way up a gentle slope, rising above the disturbance. A final, upward jog of broken stone lifted it over a thick blanket of cotton, the camera swinging back and forth with the *Griffin*'s even gait.

The Hasek was lost back in the gloom. Only a limping trio of Purifier infantry remained, scurrying around the *Griffin*'s feet like feeder fish sticking with their shark.

But this shark was wounded, and hunted by predators stronger than itself. Jasek raised the tumbler to his lips, inhaling the whiskey's strong scent, then set the glass back on his desk when he saw the first Jade Falcon 'Mech lift itself from the fog bank, rising up on the same open ridge. A bird-legged *Vulture*, with Elemental infantry scurrying about its feet.

Off to the right side an *Eyrie* also swam up from the white depths, hauling a Kinnol main battle tank in its wake.

The *Griffin* shifted left, the camera finding a trio of Skadi swift attack VTOLs jumping up on horizontal fans, their heavy-class autocannon swinging in search of targets.

Like true sharks, the Jade Falcon forces circled the trapped *Griffin*. The screen washed into a gray haze of static. This, Jasek knew from the report, was when his MechWarrior transmitted the video logs. They had only voice transmissions after that, captured by the DropShip *Noble Son* before liftoff. He didn't have the heart to listen to them again. His warrior had gone down swinging, taking the *Eyrie* and two Skadis with him.

His warrior was dead.

That was what there was to know.

"The Falcons are here to stay," Niccolò said with certainty. Although he was no military mind, his political acumen and advice had never failed Jasek. "You know this."

He nodded. "I do. They came back to Ryde, even after the Steel Wolves beat them there. Which means they'll be reinforcing Kimball. Glengarry, Zebebelgenubi, Summer—they have quite the foothold already, and they'll be coming back for Skye. These Clanners don't leave things half done. They'll be coming back."

"So what will you do?"

Jasek leaned over one corner of his desk. The polished wood felt cold to the touch. "All that there is left to do. Decide the where and when of the final battle. The Archon's Shield is ready, and most of the Lyran Rangers are back from the intelligence missions I sent them on, aren't they?"

Niccolò nodded. "Tamara Duke should make planetfall tomorrow." The way he said it, it sounded almost like a warning. "With the kommandant's arrival, I believe Colonel Petrucci's report will put the Rangers at sixty percent force readiness."

"Orders will go out over my signature today, drawing up whatever we can of the Tharkan Strikers. If we're moving, I want everyone with us. Including you, my friend."

"And where are we going?"

Jasek stared down into his desk's polished surface, at the darker version of himself that looked back out of the wood grain. Niccolò knew, of course. But Nicco also knew that armies did not march except on the express order of their commander. "Home," Jasek said with a sharp breath.

"We're heading back to Skye."

2

Hands tight on the control sticks, worried for every step, Kommandant Tamara Duke limped her beloved "Eisenfaust," her "Iron Fist," into Cheops. The *Wolfhound* BattleMech swayed precariously every time she put weight on its right leg. A grinding screech stabbed into her ears, and her atmospheric system labored to pull the acrid smell of stressed metal from the cockpit.

A pair of VV1 Rangers raced ahead, holding up traffic at each intersection and allowing her to pass safely. Horns honked in a near-continuous salute. People gathered on walks, on building rooftops. They waved to the returning Stormhammers, to her, but she could not afford the distraction of waving a massive hand back at them.

Sprawling full length into the middle of the street would be a very undignified way of returning to Jasek.

Tamara gritted her teeth, leaned left in her seat, straining against the five-point safety harness. She tried not to look at the damage schematic displayed on one of her auxiliary screens. It drew a wire frame of the lean machine. Blackened frames outlined a ruined right hip, and a wide swath of destroyed armor slashed across her Eisenfaust's back. Inside the frame a small icon flashed between black and red, warning her of damage to the massive gyroscopic stabilizer that nested behind and below the BattleMech's fusion reactor, laboring to keep thirty-five tons of metal and myomer upright. If not for the gyro, her Eisenfaust would have been hauled into Cheops on the back of a flatbed recovery vehicle.

Instead, her sideways list was translated through the bulky neurohelmet she wore, turning her own sense of equilibrium into a regenerative signal. This signal was used to calibrate the BattleMech's stride and a natural swing in its arms. It adjusted by the smallest amount her weapons' targeting system in combat. And it formed a continuous feedback loop between neurohelmet and gyro. *Shuffle*-step . . . *Shuffle*-step . . . the gyro's tortured screech and her 'Mech's occasional grinding shudder added fuel to the rage she had held deep and quiet since the betrayal.

Her mission had been fairly straightforward. An intelligence-gathering raid against the world of Towne, one of very few worlds left with a functioning HPG station in this second year of the blackout. Go in, download all intel, and leave Jasek's propaganda message playing on a continuous loop over as many local stations as possible. It was one of several similar missions being conducted by the Stormhammers across several different prefectures, but hers had been handed to her personally by Landgrave Jasek Kelswa-Steiner.

His salute had been textbook formal. His handshake lingered just for a moment. The memory of Jasek's touch had kept her warm through the dull weeks of travel and the tense ninety-three minutes it had taken to accomplish their goal.

Then she had lost it in the confused terror as her own soldier turned weapons against her, nearly destroying the *Wolfhound*.

But she would see Jasek again, and she would have justice. The Stormhammers tank crew who had fired on her was dead, its vehicle left burning on the streets of Towne. The man she suspected of organizing the attempt on her life was right under her sights.

Her targeting reticle actually floated over the outline of the VV1 Ranger, in fact, in which Hauptmann Vic Parkins, her exec, rode as a passenger. Parkins, who never stuck a foot out of line but always seemed to be there whenever anything went wrong. Off the field he fraternized with many of the junior officers. On the field, his frequent repeating of her orders down the chain promoted the feeling that he actually ran the Lyran Rangers' Second Company, not her.

It would have taken only an instant to bring weapons on line and light up the VV1, but the driver might not be complicit. Also, she imagined that Jasek would want to squeeze Parkins himself, rooting out any further treachery in the Stormhammers.

The two of them together, Jasek and Tamara, would eventually form an unstoppable team. She knew this.

First Hill was coming up, and Tamara focused even harder on the task of maneuvering her crippled Eisenfaust. The semisteep slope was not an easy climb, forcing her to lope up in a kind of sideways step with her stronger left leg always lower on the hill. The city of Cheops was laid over three sides of a sculpted mountain. Each of the five Rises had been perfectly leveled and squared, each Hill graded exactly the same as every other. The effect was stunning: to anyone arriving at the DropPort to the south, the city looked like an ancient pyramid. Governor Paulo and Legate Lorenzo, the political and military leaders of Nusakan, had estates on Fifth Rise, at the very top. Jasek and the Stormhammer senior officers had been offered residences up there as well, but their leader had declined. The GioAvanti industrial facilities on First Rise had everything the Stormhammers required, from apartments and cafeterias to corporate offices (now in use as administrative and training facilities) to a large set of warehouses (converted into 'Mech bays and vehicle repair shops).

She angled across an empty parking lot, now the Stormhammers' parade grounds, and straight for one of those warehouses. Giant doors already stood rolled back, and she needed to duck forward only slightly to get inside the cavernous interior. The building still showed signs of its retrofitting, with the second-story floor ripped out of the middle and a series of catwalks and chain falls dropped down from the ceiling for elevated work, but it served.

The VV1 Rangers both peeled away, finding parking slots along one wall. A technician in bright orange coveralls waving two glowing wands directed Tamara to an empty berth, helping her maneuver in the tight quarters with a series of semaphore-style signals. Finally, he crossed the wands overhead, indicating a good position.

Tamara gratefully banked her fusion reactor and instituted shutdown and security procedures for her Eisenfaust, unplugging from the control systems and peeling herself out of the cockpit command seat. Her cooling vest went into a locker built into the back of her seat. The neurohelmet on an overhead shelf. Grabbing a set of breakaway fatigues, she pulled them on over field boots, shorts, and a tube top, which was all she wore in the hot seat. She snapped the legs shut and fastened the cuffs around her ankles, then unlocked and cracked open the cockpit hatch.

The mixed scent of welding and grease assailed her. The techs were slow in bringing her a gantry, so Tamara unrolled the chain ladder from the *Wolfhound*'s head. Scaling it to the ground, she dropped the last meter, landing in a crouch in front of Leutnant-colonel Alexia Wolf.

"Wolf," Tamara sighed, straightening up. Belatedly, she added, "Sir."

Alexia's smile was pro forma. "Welcome home, Kommandant."

The two women eyed each other carefully. Alexia Wolf stood six centimeters shorter than Tamara, with a soft fall of brown hair and an athletic frame. She never wore makeup, which did not detract from her hard beauty and made the colonel even more intimidating. Tamara reflexively reached up to tousle her own black curls, repairing some of the damage caused by wearing her neurohelmet.

"Landgrave Kelswa sent me," the colonel announced, shortening Jasek's name in the most common manner but awarding him his formal title. "I am to take delivery of the data you brought back."

"Are you?" Tamara asked. She felt as if the data wafer, her copy of the intelligence recovered on Towne, were burning in her pocket. The request cut her to the quick and struck her as inappropriate for any number of reasons, not the least of which was that Alexia Wolf was not in her chain of command. "We heard about the assaults by the Jade Falcons. I would think our data would now be of secondary importance."

"Intel is never secondary. Information is ammunition, Kommandant."

Tamara nodded. She recognized the saying as an old Lyran Commonwealth military adage. "Even so, I would rather deliver it in person. I have an urgent matter to discuss with Jasek—the Landgrave."

"You can pass that through me as well," Alexia offered. "If you want a direct meeting, request it through Colonel Petrucci."

Tamara visibly bristled. Alexia Wolf's promotion to commanding officer of the Tharkan Strikers, the Stormhammers' third and least-experienced combat group, had caused a great deal of talk. On the face of it, so far as Tamara Duke was concerned, Wolf had no business in command. She wasn't a member of the former Republic military, as was Tamara and most of the Stormhammers, nor one of the supporters who had rallied to Jasek's call from nearby worlds of the Lyran Commonwealth.

Alexia was a freeborn descendant of Clan Wolf exiles, who had trained as a MechWarrior but failed her Trial of Position. In disgrace, she had left the Arc-Royal enclave and traveled through Lyran space to The Republic. Caught in the blackout, by fate or by fortune she had been on Skye when Jasek's stand against Duke Gregory suddenly opened up a need for warriors.

Watching Jasek elevate the Archon's Shield battalion over the Rangers had been hard enough on Tamara. Seeing a woman who could not cut it in a regular-line military suddenly promoted over deserving warriors due only to her exotic flavor was nearly too much to bear.

Also, Tamara didn't like the looks that Wolf sent Jasek when she thought no one was watching.

"This is very sensitive and of the utmost importance. I'd like to see the Landgrave at once." And let him see her.

The colonel frowned. "The Landgrave is meeting with Legate Carson Lorenzo. I am not going to interrupt them on your word, Kommandant, no matter how good it has proved in the past. You will have to tell me what this is regarding."

Paid a respectful compliment by the woman she saw as a rival, Tamara might have relented, except that Vic Parkins chose that moment to join them. "What *what* is regarding?" he asked, bluntly stepping into the conversation. His sandy blond hair was ruffled from the open-air drive in the VV1 Ranger. "Towne?" No doubt he thought he should be included in any debrief meeting.

If Tamara accused him now, she turned over the entire situation to Alexia Wolf. This was hers. This was personal.

"Kommandant?" Wolf asked.

Tamara shook her head. "I can't."

"Then you can pass along your request for an interview through Colonel Petrucci. Your debrief will happen tomorrow. I cannot spare the time at the moment."

Parkins dipped two fingers into his uniform's breast pocket. "Then you might want this now," he offered, producing a data wafer. "It's a copy of the data we recovered. I thought the Landgrave might want to review it early." He passed it into Alexia's hand with a smart flourish.

Biting down on the insides of her cheeks, Tamara tasted blood. She felt a warm flush building along the back of her neck, and she balled her hands into fists. "With our compliments," she said through clenched teeth.

"Appreciated," the leutnant-colonel replied. Her mind was obviously already looking forward. "Well-done, Kommandant. Hauptmann." She turned on her heel and made for the line of vehicles parked against the wall.

Parkins watched her walk away with obvious male appreciation. "What did the she-wolf want? Prospecting for the Strikers?"

Wouldn't Parkins love that? Shift over to the green-rated unit, pick up another stripe? The man had no loyalty at all. Not to the Rangers. Not to her. Not to Jasek. She waved over two infantrymen, spotting their insignia as the Archon's Shield. Not her unit, and not Wolf's. Safe as could be asked.

"On my authority," she addressed them formally, "you will arrest Hauptmann Parkins on charges of treason."

She wasn't certain which was more satisfying, the expression of pure shock that washed over Parkins' face, or his stutter step stride as the infantrymen dragged him off between them. No backbone whatsoever. Glancing around, she saw the stares sent her way and after Parkins. She nodded, satisfied. News of the arrest would travel quickly.

And that would get Jasek's attention.

3

Rain fell in sheets from a swollen, black sky. Pounding against the temporary roof that spanned the monument's reception area, it sounded to Tara Campbell like premature applause.

She stood at the back of a small wooden stage next to Prefect Della Brown, Skye's senior military officer. A clammy wind swirled beneath the covered area, carrying the fecund smells of churned mud and waterlogged wood. The breeze pulled at a few strands of her platinum hair, which Tara ignored, remaining at a respectful parade rest with hands clasped behind her, shoulders back, and body stretching up to her full 152 centimeters.

The monument remained covered, waiting for the Lord Governor to finish his remarks and hand the podium over to her. The assembled trio represented three of the four groups who had stood up for Skye against the recent Jade Falcon assault. She stood for her Highlanders. Brown commanded what was left of the prefecture's standing army.

And Gregory Kelswa-Steiner spoke for the civilians who had taken to the field in the defense of their world.

Missing was a representative of the Steel Wolves, who had gone back into hiding after the battle. Tara still wasn't certain if that was a good thing or not.

The memorial park sat on a sharp-edged bluff that overlooked Sutton Road and the rain-swollen Thames River and, beyond both, the battlefield where Skye had mounted its desperate defense against Clan Jade Falcon. Reconstruction efforts had not proceeded very far; the land still bore its dark scars. Craters. Blackened earth. A few twisted metal skeletons of 'Mechs and vehicles so badly damaged there was nothing left to salvage. The area would be cleaned up eventually, but right now Tara spent local resources in preparations for the next assault. In fact, if not for the interminable rainfall of a New London winter interrupting one of her more important defensive projects, she might have pushed back this event as well. But she also recognized that people needed closure.

So did she. Someday.

Today, though, was about Skye. Front and center a small contingent of reluctant media representatives recorded the address for later rebroadcast. In the audience wings waited the families of the dead. It was a solemn event, and the polite applause was always—always!—for those who had given up so much. She had been firm about how this would run, and doing it her way had also been required as a means of guaranteeing her presence.

Duke Gregory was nearly finished, she felt. He extolled the virtue and dedication of those brave people who had come forward to help defend their homeland in the face of the Jade Falcon assault.

"Citizens all," he promised, reminding the newsmen and families present that he had awarded Republic citizenship to the family of any resident who had unselfishly joined Tara Campbell's ad hoc "Forlorn Hope" detachment. His bearded visage stared down the media cameras. "Hard times call for great sacrifices by great people. These sons and daughters of Skye will be forever remembered for how they stood by our world. Never shirking or turning away from the call of duty. Our children."

He paused in a respectful silence, and the monument's veil was pulled away.

There were no BattleMechs immortalized in the bronze piece. No regular army vehicles or battlesuit troops. A screaming raptor hovered in midflight, one wing dragging at the air and the other folded back, as if it had been brought up short while stooping down. Below, citizens of Skye lifted spears, warding off the raptor, while others carried the wounded and dying away from the grasp of the sharp talons.

Understated, but respectful. Tara approved.

"Now," Duke Gregory said, "I'd like to bring up the woman who helped lead our valiant defense, and has helped ready our world against further attack. Tara Campbell, Countess Northwind."

Only the driving rain applauded, for which Tara was thankful. She also could have done without the honoraries and titles, but she accepted them, moving forward with a brisk military step and waiting a moment while a few reporters flashed stills of her. Part and parcel of her role as The Republic's media darling, she knew.

"I will be brief," she promised, swallowing against the cotton taste of nerves, "because today should be a day of reflection. When I came to Skye, I nearly despaired. Faced with an impossible choice, I asked for volunteers to fill out the ranks of the *Himmelsfahrtkommando*. These I received."

These she had watched charge a military line in cars and old jeeps and battered trucks, mounting the smallest of weapons or packing along shoulder-weight short-range-missile launchers. The slaughter had been horrendous, but their action bought the military defenders the time they needed.

"Your Exarch can ask nothing more of you, and neither can I. I hope to say that Skye will ask nothing more from you as well."

She scanned the collection of faces. Doubtful journalists and sorrowful relatives stared back. And one that did not belong: hard eyes in an aged, weathered face. "While this remains to be seen," she continued, "we can thank the sacrifice of your fellow citizens for the freedoms you still enjoy today."

He stood several ranks back, in the break between families and media. Elderly, but with squared shoulders and a gaze that could score ferrosteel. Tara guessed his age at eighty. Perhaps older. He stood just behind a still-camera journalist, whom she saw tear the wrapper off a new disk for his camera.

The journalist tossed the wrapper to the ground.

"It was my honor," she said in closing, cutting her remarks short, "to serve with these brave men and women."

She took no questions and the media did not seem interested in asking any. They would take their video and their stills and sound bites back to the office and decide what to make of the news today. Better than average, she was willing to bet. The Republic was still getting a fair shake in light of Skye's defense. The calm, temporary eye inside a hurricane.

Duke Gregory thanked the families for attending while Tara stepped down from the stage and approached the man she had spotted in the crowd. A few mourners pressed forward to offer her their hands and take her condolences.

The photojournalist took her proximity as his chance to slip in one cheap shot.

"Countess. Do you find it appropriate to politicize such events as this memorial service?"

Staring over the journalist's shoulder, she met the gaze of the older man. He had dark eyes and snow-white hair cut very close to his skull. Something familiar nagged at her memory, but she felt certain that she had never met him. He wore a simple, fleece-lined poncho. Warm, and totally appropriate for the wet, winter weather.

"Countess?"

More cameras swung her way, anticipating a reply. Tara had dealt with Skye's media divisions often enough to know that little good could come from answering. But the man's crude manners begged a response.

"That is an interesting question," she said, dragging her gaze back to the journalist, "coming from the man who just littered on the graves of so many citizens of Skye."

The journalist paled as cameras now turned on *him*, as well as the basilisk stares of nearby parents, brothers and sisters, husbands and wives—all of whom had lost someone in the battle. Tara leaned forward ever so slightly. The muscles in her shoulders tightened with new tension.

"Pick it up," she ordered him softly.

He set his chin, and stared blankly ahead. For a moment she thought the man might actually defy her for the sake of his brethren of the press. And he might have, except that the hard-eyed man moved to stand behind him and placed a hand on his shoulder. Avuncular. Supportive. Then he leaned in to whisper something that Tara did not catch, his mouth hidden behind the journalist's neck.

The journalist winced, nodded once. When the stranger removed his hand, the reporter bent down to pick up his discarded wrapper, tucked it into his pocket, and quickly walked away, rubbing his shoulder.

No confrontation, no story. The media drifted back to the main event, and Tara's ally tipped her a slow wink. "That was well-done," he said. His voice wasn't exactly warm, but there was energy to it that most men his age had already lost. "I see where you get your reputation."

"Media," she said, dismissing the recent event and her own sensational reputation all at once. "Once you've dealt with Herrmanns, you've had your fill."

"Herrmanns AG is the media conglomerate that controls a decent portion of Skye's press, and has been giving Duke Gregory, and you, a hard time until late. Very pro-Lyran. I'm surprised you've managed a cease-fire with them at all, quite frankly."

Something told her that this man was not a local, but he clearly was well versed in local politics and the corporate media even so. "Have we met?" she asked, still feeling a sense of familiarity.

"No." He offered her a withered hand full of surprising strength. "David McKinnon. At your service, Countess."

McKinnon! Tara recognized at once the name of one of The Republic's oldest active-duty Paladins, and now saw his rank in his time-weathered face as well. Only four years younger than Sire Victor Steiner-Davion, this man was almost as large a living legend. She froze in midclasp. "Sire McKinnon." Her throat felt tight, and she swallowed dryly. "It's an honor to meet you."

Keeping her hand, McKinnon tucked it into the crook of his elbow and pulled her farther away from the news junkies and crowds. "None of that if we're going to be working together," he admonished her.

"Working together? You're staying on Skye?" Coming back to her senses, she had assumed that McKinnon had new orders for her from Exarch Damien Redburn. The Paladin stayed one jump ahead of her, though.

"Let's just say that you're still getting heavy press coverage back on Terra."

She blew out an exasperated sigh. "Exarch Redburn doesn't trust me," she said.

"You turned down a paladinship," McKinnon reminded her, speaking more freely as they approached one edge of the small covered park. The smell of rain-churned mud was stronger here. "Exarch Redburn understood, but you have to realize that there are forces in The Republic who aren't too happy with your popularity and status as a 'freewheeling faction leader.'" He said this last as if quoting from some source. "Despite," he added, "any claim of yours to support The Republic. Your Highlanders—"

"My Highlanders," she interrupted, pulling her hand free, "have bled for Terra. And for Skye and for a dozen other worlds around The Republic these last several months. Impugning their honor is a slap in the face of many good men and women."

"But will they be enough?" McKinnon asked.

"Enough? Enough for what?"

"Skye. Exarch Redburn asked me to evaluate the chances that Skye can hold. I wanted your word, unvarnished or undistorted by any lines of communication it would have passed through on the way to Terra. Which is why he allowed me to come here and ask you directly." So he did. "Can we save Skye?"

Tara sighed, her anger spent. Could Skye hold? That was the question.

"At what cost?" she asked. "The Jade Falcons have taken a half dozen worlds already, and it's only a matter of *when*, not *if*, they will return. And we're not ready." She let that thought rest with McKinnon for a moment. "My Highlanders continue to trickle in, called from action spots all across Prefectures III, IV, X . . . but they're bloodied and they're tired. And we both know what kind of force readiness the local military was at even before the Lord Governor split with his son."

McKinnon's face was impassive, not about to comment

on the wisdom of an understrength garrison force. Still, he knew. "If you can brace up your people, I might be able to help with materiel readiness. Get some supplies—maybe even a few new vehicles—flowing this way. And Skye has good resources as well."

"Aerospace, mostly. DropShip yards and fighter craft." She ran fingers through her hair. Despite her initial reaction of irritation and anger, she was warming to the venerable warrior. With half a year, eight months, we might—"

"Twelve weeks," McKinnon interrupted. He did not cite his source, and Tara did not ask. "You'll get no more than twelve weeks."

People were leaving now, ducking under umbrellas or dashing for their vehicles. Tara waited while a few of them strolled by, including the photojournalist from the encounter earlier. He stopped and snapped another holopic of her standing off to one side with McKinnon. Then hurried off. The two Republic warriors watched him retreat to a news van.

"If three months is the best we have," she said, "we had better make the most of them. I don't suppose you brought a BattleMech company with you?" He shook his head. "Well, we'll get by, I guess. Tell me, what did you say to him?"

For once she left him behind. "Pardon?"

"The journalist." She nodded after the van. "You seem to have a knack for getting people to go along with you fairly quickly." Or Tara was simply developing a knack for being *handled*. "You certainly convinced *him* to cooperate. What was it you said?"

"Ah. Well. Each circumstance requires its own approach, of course." The Paladin's mouth twitched up into a lopsided smile, but his dark eyes remained granite hard. "I explained to him that he would look very silly on the evening news being fed that camera."

"*That* would help my relations with the local media," she said.

McKinnon chuckled dryly, reached out, and patted Tara on the arm in a very reassuring manner. "Ah, my dear, dear Tara," he said, shaking his head. "I never said that *you'd* get the privilege of doing it at all."

4

Cheops
Seventh District, Nusakan
14 September 3134

Jasek Kelswa-Steiner sat in the highest chair of the three-man tribunal, presiding over the court-martial along with Colonels Joss Vandel and Antonio Petrucci. A slight blush warmed the back of his neck every time he glanced in the direction of Tamara Duke, who rarely took her eyes off him, but fortunately the dusky skin he'd inherited from his mother hid it well. It was the only relief he expected today. His freshly starched uniform chafed at the neck and wrists. The weight of so many stares pressed against him with credible force, shoving him into the padded backrest.

Dozens of military uniforms packed the tiny auditorium, which usually served as a presentation room in the Gio-Avanti, Inc., administrative building. Officers reserved themselves a chair in the short rows of flip-down seating while enlisted personnel and some civilian contractors crowded along the walls. The heavy press of bodies raised the room's temperature several uncomfortable degrees. Some men and women fanned themselves with their military caps. Others silently sweated it out as Hauptmann Vic

Parkins entered the room without counsel or military escort and came to attention in front of the three-man court.

Jasek nodded his own salute. "Stand easy," he ordered Parkins, who tucked himself into a stiff parade rest.

The entire room held its breath. Jasek let them stew a moment.

By toting up unit insignia, the Landgrave saw that Colonel Petrucci's Lyran Rangers counted for more than half of the assembled audience. That was expected, since the Rangers were as large as the Stormhammers' other two combat groups combined. Most of the militia and standing-army soldiers who had followed Jasek into exile filled out Ranger billets, in fact. Hastati Sentinels and Principes Guards. Triarii Protectors. He had kept them together as much as possible. They were a tight-knit group.

They would also be the hardest affected by today's judgment, and he meant to save as many of them as he could.

Alexia Wolf's Tharkan Strikers were the next most prevalent unit. Green troops, mostly, drawn from volunteers and militia castoffs, or recruited directly by Alexia from a few scattered academies, making up in enthusiasm what they lacked in experience.

Very few of Joss Vandel's elite Archon's Shield battalion had bothered to attend. Those who did, Jasek recognized as men and women who had also come with him from Skye or from other "heritage worlds" of the old Isle. The Lyran Commonwealth recruits and the Lohengrin agents "loaned" Jasek by his distant cousin, the Commonwealth's Archon, had better things to do than sit through more Republic squabbling.

As did Jasek himself.

"The charge of treason is a delicate and dangerous matter," the Landgrave began in his best stage voice. "It should never be brought lightly, or with personal animosity, and the investigation never colored by politics, by personal ambition, or by emotion. This tribunal has acted in the best interests of all true citizens of Skye, the Stormhammers, and Hauptmann Vic Emanual Parkins to ensure a fair and impartial judgment."

He spoke slowly and with deliberate enunciation. Jasek's father had taught him the value of ceremonial speaking, among other things.

Weighted words carry farther than the ears. They settle into the minds and the hearts of all who hear them.

Which was why Jasek had named "all true citizens of Skye" first and foremost, referring to the grand *Isle of Skye* rather than Skye as a lone world lost among a census. It was one of his rallying cries, after all, to point out how Devlin Stone had in effect disenfranchised so many citizens of the Isle during The Republic's creation, and it would be good to see something useful come from this delay. Sitting court was not how he had hoped to spend his final days on Nusakan. The necessity of listening to depositions and reviewing evidence had interrupted preparations to fully mobilize, costing the Stormhammers precious time. He'd had to be certain, though, that one act of treachery was not an indication of a deeper conspiracy within his most steadfast troops. And he had owed Tamara a chance to prove her case.

Now he owed Hauptmann Parkins an apology.

Jasek stood, leaning forward on the rail that separated the tribunal from the accused man. Parkins pulled himself up to strict attention.

"It is the finding of this tribunal that no evidence of conspiracy exists to place Hauptmann Vic Parkins in collusion with the personnel who did, with malicious intent, fire on their commander in the recent mission on Towne."

Vic Parkins had already been informed of the judgment in private. Even so, his shoulders slumped with relief to hear it announced.

Several officers surged to their feet, applauding the tribunal's findings. Along the wall, many Lyran Rangers cheered. Not exactly for Parkins, they cheered *with* him. Their relief was obvious. No soldier wanted to suspect treachery within his or her own ranks.

Jasek waved down the excitement. He saw Kommandant Duke rise to her feet as well, holding a stiff military bearing. She also had comrades along the wall, brooding, fearing another shot in the back. The Landgrave had to repair the potential damage if he hoped to salvage both officers.

"At worst," he continued, "Hauptmann Parkins' actions might be considered overzealous and could have encouraged such a rogue action." The implied rebuke was just enough to silence the cheers, and offer Tamara Duke a salve that she had not brought charges without cause. "But the hauptmann's interrogation by machine testing and voluntary administration of truth serum has more than convinced this panel of his lack of guilt. All charges are dropped with the court's apology. Hauptmann Parkins is returned to full, active duty immediately."

More applause, though less strident than before. Parkins stepped forward and traded hand clasps with Colonel Petrucci and Colonel Vandel. He caught Jasek's hand as the Stormhammers' leader came down from the high chair.

"Thank you, Landgrave."

The armor commander had a crushing grip, which at another time might have been a test of strength. Now there was no mistaking the flush of goodwill that colored his cheeks.

"No thanks necessary, Hauptmann. I will, of course, consider any request for a transfer if you feel it is truly needed." He said this as Tamara Duke approached, letting her pick up on the offer.

"Shaking up your lines right before battle is never a good idea, sir." Parkins turned to face Tamara as she joined them. "I believe I can still work within Kommandant Duke's company, if she'll have me. No hard feelings. In her place, I might have done the same."

"And in your place, I'd hope to be as gracious," Tamara said, shaking his hand once, formally. Apology accepted, and given. But it strained the borders of camaraderie.

More work to be done here, Jasek noted, but left it alone for now. "Hauptmann, please see to your unit while I borrow your commander for a time."

Parkins nodded, traded salutes, and moved for the rear of the auditorium. Several officers and enlisted waited there, and accepted him warmly into their company. They moved out in a large group.

Alexia Wolf replaced Parkins, nodding shortly to Tamara as an apology for the intrusion. "They are ready for us," she said. If she said it slightly possessively, Jasek couldn't really blame her.

Or Tamara, for the way the junior officer bristled at the implied dismissal.

Gathered by Niccolò, Petrucci and Vandel were already stealing out a side door of the small auditorium, the only door guarded by a sentry with a sidearm. "I'll be along in a moment, Alex." The familiar address didn't help the escalating level of tension.

With a warm smile the leutnant-colonel preceded them out the side door. It led to a short, wide hallway that ran through a network of executive offices. The faint aroma of gourmet coffee seemed to ooze from the paneled walls and thick carpet. Empty secretarial desks competed in size for prestige. The doors behind them ran contests for the longest, most boldfaced title.

Senior Executive Vice President for Managing Operations was Jasek's favorite.

"I would rather this had been handled quietly, Tamara," he said once the two of them had a moment alone in the hall. It was as close as he wanted to come to a formal rebuke. No press had been allowed into the closed deliberations or for the judgment today, but the story would leak soon enough. Niccolò had promised that it would not break before the Stormhammers left Nusakan. That was something.

Still, "A public arrest does not help us show cohesiveness."

"Landgrave . . . Jasek . . ." She put some strength in her spine, coming to near attention. "I would never do anything to jeopardize the Stormhammers."

"No," he agreed, "you wouldn't."

Tamara's loyalty could never be questioned—she wore it on her sleeve right where he could see it, which was why she had earned the Towne operation. But someone within her own unit had tried to assassinate her. Had that attempt been personal or political? There was no way to answer that question now.

"I'm not saying you didn't have cause. But in situations like this, please leave the public orchestration of events to myself, or Nicco."

"I don't report to GioAvanti," she said with a frown.

"No, but you did not report to Colonel Petrucci either," he reminded her with a touch of steel in his voice. A show of personal displeasure would touch her more deeply than any formal reprimand, he knew. "And the question remains, what do we do with Hauptmann Parkins?"

"I still don't trust him," she said.

"Neither can I," Jasek agreed, smiling thinly at her expression of total surprise. "I said we found no evidence of guilt. There is some gray shading between guilt and actual innocence, though. Like how much Vic Parkins *suspected* he might be influencing your subordinates."

"Then why—"

"We need warriors, Tamara. I can't afford to throw one away—a good one—on what he might have suspected. Or for being ambitious, so long as those ambitions stop short of treachery."

Tamara nodded slowly. "But even if you'd transferred him, it would have undermined his authority. That could turn him toward treachery. Unless you promoted him as well." Her lip curled in distaste at the thought.

"Or," Jasek pointed out, "unless I now transfer you."

"And which of the other colonels would give me a fair shake?" she asked, not believing it.

He shrugged, stopped outside a conference room. Joss Vandel's deep baritone rumbled on the other side of a partially open door. No sentry here. If an agent of The Republic or Jasek's father made it this far into the building, past the best security GioAvanti money could buy, one more man wasn't going to make a difference.

Then, reconsidering, Jasek nodded at the door where Leutnant-colonel Wolf had entered ahead of them. "Alexia has asked about you," he admitted. "She needs experienced people in the Tharkan Strikers."

He figured the chance of Tamara accepting such a post would be the same as that of his father suddenly supporting the Archon of the Lyran Commonwealth, or the Exarch of The Republic voluntarily restoring the Isle of Skye. But long shots were known to come in now and then.

Not this time.

"No." Tamara shook her head. "I know what I have with Petrucci. And with Parkins too, for that matter. I can make this work." She paused, then, "You were going to ask me to keep him from the start, weren't you?"

Her open incredulity made him laugh, which was good. Recent days had not offered much fuel for laughter. He leaned in close enough to smell the scented soap she used.

Her eyes widened at his nearness, and he smiled for her benefit. "Yes, Tamara. I was. But I wanted you to work it through for yourself first."

"Why, Jasek?" She almost sounded as if she were purring, basking in his warmth.

Careful . . . "Because I wanted things right between us before I invited you in on this command-level meeting."

"Invite me in? Now?"

"We're moving toward Skye right away," he told her. "After a quick stop on Zebebelgenubi."

"What? Why?"

"Some Highlanders got themselves trapped there," he said, intentionally answering her question in the most literal way possible, even though he knew what she meant. "We're hoping to pull them out from under the Falcons' claws."

"I meant, why pull me in? Why now?"

He saw it play over her face, no matter how guarded she thought she held her expression. Tamara Duke had nothing on Niccolò GioAvanti for a poker face. Jasek read her easily. The afterglow of his nearness. The sudden shock at being included in a command-level meeting, and then the surge of pride.

And the devotion—the worship—that invariably followed.

After tearing her down, just a little, it was time to raise her back up again and cement the bonds of loyalty that bound her to him. Niccolò called it "personal time." Jasek's father would simply call it leadership.

He knew what it really was, and felt only slightly the heel for taking advantage of her feelings and expectations as he picked up her hand and held it tightly.

"For the same reason I sent you to Towne," he told her. "Because right now, this is where I need you."

With her star-filled eyes and open body posture, if she heard anything other than "I need you" out of that, Jasek would be shocked. He dropped her hand as he opened the door, with no desire to rub Alexia's face in the necessities of command.

From her hard expression, staring at them from the far side of the conference room table, he knew she considered it obvious enough.

5

*When newly acquired states have been accustomed to
living freely under their own laws, there are three ways
to hold them securely: first, by devastating them.*
                    The Prince, by Niccolò Machiavelli

Belletaria
Venicio County, Kimball II
16 September 3134

The *Gyrfalcon* swayed from side to side in its peculiar,
strutting gait as Star Colonel Noritomo Helmer high-
stepped it along the rubble-choked boulevard, leading his
column through the city that had been Belletaria. He remembered a line from one of the ancient texts he had
smuggled into his sibko barracks as a child and hidden inside his mattress. It was a book on mythology.

*And when she opened the box, all the evils of the world
were released.*

He and a sibmate had read such books at night, whispered about them while lying next to each other at rifle
drill or while making camp on extended maneuvers. The
myth of Pandora had been fun to argue. About whether

such a curse could have had any other result. About whether or not Pandora had been an attractive woman.

But one thing they had never discussed was the idea that their Clan would ever visit such a nightmare on an unsuspecting people.

These were not the warriors Noritomo remembered training alongside.

Belletaria had been a medium-sized city on Kimball II. One hundred and fifty thousand people. Large portions of the city had been burned—residential areas, mostly—put to the torch by a determined *Firestarter*. Ash choked the sky, casting a gray pallor over the ruins. A few fires still smoldered, though most had finally burned out or been extinguished in last night's rainfall.

But what the fires missed, Malvina Hazen's handpicked "relief force" had taken apart with ruthless efficiency. Assault 'Mechs leveled the industrial sector, kicking through warehouse walls and wrenching over large cranes used to pull cargo off the barges that plied trade between the river cities. The barges had been sunk. Lifters and trucks were shoved into the river. The assault machines had then joined a couple of modified SalvageMechs and some heavy tanks to raze the downtown area where Noritomo now walked his *Gyrfalcon*. Apartment buildings had 'Mech-sized holes in them where the sturdier machines had simply walked through. Other buildings were nothing better than piles of rubble and splintered lumber. The commercial center of Belletaria, some forty-eight square blocks, had been leveled by artillery fire and then systematically flattened as the 'Mechs and tanks spread out in a line and marched, stomped, and rolled forward in a juggernaut of destruction.

All his fault.

Galaxy Commander Hazen had instructed him to take Kimball II. It was to be the jewel in her crown. A population of nearly two billion *and* the local headquarters for Ceres Metals, this rich Republic world was one of six targeted by the Jade Falcon *desant*. Her "gift" of it to Noritomo was a measure of confidence in one of her senior warriors. But he had made one strategic mistake, and gotten mired in a brutal ground campaign that caused him to miss the rendezvous for the assault on Skye. Malvina Hazen would not soon forgive him that.

Throttling down, slowing the *Gyrfalcon* until he paced to an uneasy stop, Noritomo banked the fusion reactor. "I am stepping outside," he said, the voice-activated mic broadcasting to his battered unit.

Star Captain Lysle Clees argued. "This area is not secure, Star Colonel Helmer. I *don't* recommend it."

Her intentional use of a contraction, debasing the language, had its desired effect. Noritomo paused. Then, "There is no one left to worry about, Star Captain. I will descend."

No one left. It was a desperate salve against the devastation. The Jade Falcon relief force had announced their intentions from orbit, giving people twelve hours in which to begin their evacuation. Perhaps only a few thousand had actually been killed. Perhaps a few hundred. The assault force had moved on to the next city, ready to visit more destruction if planetary leaders did not capitulate at once. Their warning this time was a mere six hours.

Noritomo pulled off his neurohelmet and unplugged his cooling vest from the circulation system. The helmet he left on his seat. The vest he wore for its thin layer of ballistic cloth. Lysle's warning should not be completely ignored.

It was the work of a moment to unbutton from the cockpit and scale down to the ground. Smoke from last night's fires lingered, stinging his eyes, leaving a wood smoke taste in his mouth. Two suited Elementals waited for him. Their hulking forms dwarfed Noritomo. He nodded to Lysle, unable to see her eyes through the reflective faceplate.

Lysle unlocked her helmet, pulled it off, and held it at her side. She was one of the Clans' genetically bred infantry, tall and heavily muscled. The large woman's blond dreadlocks uncoiled in a snakelike mane, like another creature of myth Noritomo half remembered from the book.

"I do not like this, Star Colonel."

Noritomo nodded. "I do not like a lot of things, Lysle." He knew her for one of the more moderate warriors under his command. There were things he could say in front of her that were safe. There were things that were not. He struck out for a large pile of bricks and broken ferrocrete that—he guessed—had been a bank. The two warriors slowly walked around it. "Seven months ago, this seemed like such a straightforward mission."

Seven months. When they were still inside the Clan occupation zone, mustering for the long march under the watchful eyes of Galaxy Commanders Beckett Malthus and Aleksandr and Malvina Hazen.

The Elemental kept pace, taking one long stride for each of his two. "Strike through Lyran space and into The Republic of the Sphere," she said, nodding. One lip curled up in distaste. "Smash the Steel Wolves if we could find them."

"And carve out a foothold for future Jade Falcon operations."

That had been the unvoiced mission directive for the *desant*—what amounted to a large reconnaissance in force. Noritomo had been part of Malvina Hazen's forces, and close enough to both her and her brother to know that they were the true mission commanders with Malthus in place as the Khan's faithful watchdog. He had also been close enough to see the differences in each leader's style. Aleks believed in traditional Clan practices, bidding forces against the local defense and putting into power a provisional government that would honor the Jade Falcon conquest without the need of a large garrison force.

Malvina, as she proved on Chaffee, on Ryde, followed a more violent approach. Terrorize the locals, slash at them with the fear of total destruction, and afterward you could take what you wanted and they would never dare rise against you. Before the advance force ever took a single Republic world, in fact, Malvina's personal affection for the history of the great Mongol khans, for the Chinggis Khan, had bled down into several unit commanders. Restrained for so long by an uneasy truce, held in check inside the Clan occupation zones, their dreams of conquest and glory overrode any sense of moral obligation to the conquered people.

The people of Kimball II understood that now.

"One mistake," he repeated aloud his earlier thought. He crouched down and dug a handful of Republic notes from under a rock. They still had a band around their middle with the bank's seal on it. He tossed aside the bundle of currency. Ahead, the breeze scattered loose bills across a small blacktop parking lot like autumn leaves. "We should have taken Kimball IV and used it as a staging world."

"And still meet the Galaxy Commander's timeline for the assault on Skye?" Lysle asked. She shrugged. "How many military victories are won in hindsight, Star Colonel?"

"If we had applied Malvina Hazen's tactics. If we had struck hard enough to leave the planet reeling." If Noritomo could have brought himself to use terror as a weapon, throwing off twenty-eight years of traditional Clan military doctrine. "'A new age demands new thinking,'" he quoted. "Is that not what Malvina said?"

"Are you trying to convince me, Noritomo Helmer?" Lysle stopped him with a bulky, armored arm barring his path. "Or yourself?" She nodded forward, where two soot-covered teens, a boy and a girl, scrounged through the rubble of the next building. A market. They dug out canned food, mining it like gold, ignoring the currency that blew uselessly around them.

The girl spotted them. Likely she had been the lookout. It would be hard to miss the short line of 'Mechs and armored vehicles halted only half a block over. But rather than flee, hunger and shock drove her to her feet. She hurled a can in the direction of the two warriors, as if they could be threatened by canned produce. It clattered and rolled across the ground a full thirty meters short.

Lysle Clees extended an arm toward the girl. The Elemental suit's built-in laser would reach across the distance much easier than a thrown can. "Malvina Hazen would kill that one for her show of defiance."

Noritomo placed a hand on the weapon barrel. He knew he could never budge Lysle, not even with his full body weight against the myomer strength of the infantry battlesuit. Only his rank let him push aside her arm with ease. "That is not the kind of war I wish to fight," he said.

"Nor I, Star Colonel. But Aleksandr Hazen died on Skye. This may be the only kind of war that will be left for us."

As if Pandora would have listened to a voice of reason. Someone must have told her, "Do not open the box." But she did. She made that decision for everyone, whether they wanted it or not. Was she sorry afterward? The myths rarely went so far as to discuss what happened after. What kind of changes were wrought from such actions.

"Does not matter," he decided, answering Lysle as well as himself. "We have our orders to return to Glengarry. We will see what Galaxy Commander Hazen has decided. Kimball II is no longer our concern."

With the girl staring after them, and the thrown can still lying on the ground between them, he knew this world was going to be somebody's concern. Noritomo doubted that person was going to have an easy time of it, and all because Malvina Hazen had opened the box. Which begged a question from him.

Once opened, could it ever be closed again?

6

New London
Skye
17 September 3134

New London Tower was the small but powerful realm of Prefect Della Brown. Tara Campbell had felt like an intruder the first dozen times walking into the lobby of the slender, twelve-story high-rise, always under the suspicious scrutiny of the military men and women who were responsible for the readiness and defense of Prefecture IX. These were people who knew each other by first name, by unit, by the academies they graduated from and their class standing, by whether their parents were confirmed citizens or unproven residents, and, for professional officers, by how their families had stood on such topics as secession of the Isle of Skye and formation of The Republic.

For a building so devoted in its approach to security, there were not many secrets among its occupants.

She couldn't say exactly when she began to feel less a stranger in this building. Certainly after being "promoted" from her blue visitor's badge and the infantryman escort who had followed her to the most innocuous of meetings. Before the end of the campaign to defend Skye from the

Jade Falcons. Somewhere along the way, the hard-line military presence had breathed a collective sigh of acceptance, and she no longer felt uncomfortable.

If there was one place Duke Gregory might feel the least bit intimidated on his capital world, this was it. The Governor's Palace was his home turf, and he seemed equally comfortable on the Sanglamore Academy grounds, which Tara had taken over as her own offices and the de facto planetary defense headquarters. Which was why she had chosen the Tower for today's meeting with the Lord Governor and Paladin McKinnon.

So far, the two strong-willed men had barely agreed to disagree. McKinnon did not like the state of local defenses. Duke Gregory refused to address most problems raised by the Paladin. It placed her in a bind, mediating between naked aggression and blind patriotism.

Today she hoped to shake things up. To do that, she needed these men uncomfortable, slightly out of their element. But not defensive. To dial back on the atmosphere just one notch, she set up their gathering in the cartography room. It was one of very few rooms in Prefect Brown's secure building not devoted exclusively to the strategic defense of Skye and the prefecture; the domain of a junior captain who rarely visited and three civilian contractors with their bright orange identification badges hung on lanyards around their necks.

"Where's Della?" Duke Gregory asked as Tara cleared the room of civilians.

Her gold badge had a narrow red border around it, denoting temporary status, but it was enough to back up her orders without having to ask Captain Gereine to do it for her. The captain remained to work any equipment they might need. Tara had him pull up several flat-screen maps of Skye. Inside the room's central holotank, she asked for a starfield of Prefecture IX and its surrounding space.

"Prefect Brown is looking into troop movements reported on Nusakan." She didn't need to explain the importance of that to Duke Gregory, but Paladin McKinnon might not be up-to-date. "Nusakan is where we believe—"

"—Landgrave Jasek is based," the Paladin interrupted. He stood near the holotank, where bright stars shimmered in Republic gold, Jade Falcon green, or traitorous blue.

Leaning over the low rail, his shoulder obliterating the world of Seginus, he sighted between two planets as if he might be considering a bank shot on the billiard table. His dark eyes were cold and distant. "The Stormhammers are on the move."

"Or will be soon," she agreed with a curt nod.

But who knew which way they would jump? The latest reports had Stormhammer units striking across three different prefectures on intelligence-gathering raids. What Jasek Kelswa-Steiner was looking for, and how he would act on that information, were anyone's guess. The two warriors spent a few moments discussing the possibilities, drawing Duke Gregory into the conversation almost against his will.

"You are wasting your time," he finally said.

McKinnon shrugged. "I've felt that way ever since arriving on Skye."

Tara placed a calming hand on the Paladin's arm. "Why do you say that, Lord Governor?"

The statesman leaned back against a table, combed fingers lightly through his beard. His posture and his tone said that he thought it obvious.

"If you could predict what Jasek is up to, then so could his enemies. He can't have lasted as long as he has without staying three jumps ahead of everyone else around him. The boy learned his lessons well."

Tara heard a bit of frustration mixed in with that reluctant pride. She thought she knew the reason. After Skye's victory over the Jade Falcons, the duke had mentioned to her renewed attempts to contact his son. Apparently, Jasek was still managing to confound his father too. It made her wonder more about the absent Kelswa-Steiner heir.

"We still need to take him into account," Tara said diplomatically. The duke lapsed back into silence. She shrugged and turned back to McKinnon. "We've had Stormhammers sighted on Ko and Alphecca, and we know they've sent agents to Galatea. Drumming up mercenary support?"

"It's not a bad idea. One we might need to consider as well. Funds are easier to get out of Terra right now than equipment."

"Promises are even easier," Duke Gregory said with a frown.

McKinnon stifled his first reaction. "With the election of

a new Exarch taking place in three months, Damien Redburn is simply being prudent. He does not want to burden
the incoming Exarch with a host of new commitments."

"We also know that a small outfit from Jasek's Lyran
Rangers recently suffered severe casualties on Ryde." Tara
tried to ignore the byplay, keeping the edge of their focus
on local problems.

"What my son wishes to call his deserters is his business," Duke Gregory said. "Those were lost elements of
the Principes Guards who died on Ryde."

Tara shrugged, and the Lord Governor glared at her for
the implied dismissal. "Whatever we wish to call them, we
cannot ignore the fact that Jasek may be looking for some
payback. Also, if Ryde falls, Kimball II becomes vulnerable
again. He may be thinking to add them to his own
resources."

"If he's at all intelligent, he is." McKinnon tugged at a
cuff as if it irritated him. The dress uniform draped over
the elderly warrior's hard-muscled body with flattering
lines, but he would clearly be more at home in a field uniform. Or a cooling vest. "But the Falcons have them now.
And with Glengarry and Zebebelgenubi, and Summer and
Alkaid in Prefecture VIII, they are close to controlling this
entire region of space."

"*Skye* controls Prefecture IX," the Lord Governor proclaimed with indignation. His thinning hair on top gave him
a pronounced widow's peak. Tara saw his scalp flush up
inside his hairline. "Not my wayward son and certainly not
a band of Clan marauders."

McKinnon jumped back at Gregory Kelswa-Steiner with
a cold frost in his voice. "There are eight, maybe ten planets that mean a damn between Yed Posterior and Dubhe.
You are in firm control of exactly *one* of them, Lord Governor. Make no mistake, the Falcons are winning this war."

Duke Gregory shook his head adamantly. "Skye remains
the heart of Prefecture IX. Which is why we must not—we
will not—give it up. Look at what has happened with the
fall of Liao. The Capellan Confederation gutted Prefecture
V. I will not see the same crisis of morale taking place in
the Isle!"

"Now, did that attitude come before or after you drove
away your son and four-fifths of your standing military?"

Long enough! Tara quickly stepped in between the two men with a raised hand and a calm voice. "If Skye can be saved at all, it will only be if we work together, gentlemen. Lord Governor, we need the support of Terra and Exarch Redburn, and of whoever replaces him. Sire McKinnon is a welcome asset." She waited, pressing her will against the petulant Duke until he nodded once, conceding the point and the initiative.

"And Sire McKinnon?" He met her gaze with a defiant stare. "If you have any further criticisms on how things were handled before you arrived"—she paused, giving him the chance to open his mouth—"button it," she ordered. "We will work with what we have, not with what we might have had."

The willful Paladin recoiled slightly, startled at her quick and ruthless move to take control of the meeting. Then he tucked his chin down toward his chest and raised a hand to tip an imaginary hat in her direction. It wasn't a complete accord, but it seemed that in a ruthless grab for the throat, Tara had brokered at least a cease-fire. It was enough.

Now maybe they could all get to work.

"Very efficient," McKinnon complimented Tara later.

After several long meetings, only the first of which was with the Lord Governor and the Paladin, she had retreated onto the local military compound for a measure of privacy. Granted, sitting in the officers' club wasn't exactly putting out a No Trespassing sign, but at least here there would be no press, no mercantile agencies telling her how impossible it was to reassign shipping priorities to her schedule, and no grieving family members wanting to tell her how much they understood her actions in the defense of Skye.

She could sit quietly here, enjoy the bluesy music that the O-club offered, and knock back a few neat whiskeys. Her largest problem was fending off the occasional request to buy her a drink. After her first ten refusals, word got around.

Her easiest victory of the day.

Which suffered a reversal as the Paladin slid into the chair opposite her. His weathered hands gripped the edge of the table with the strength of twin anchors. He did not ask permission to join her. He simply assaulted the private table as he no doubt would any other target. His hard gaze dropped to the table, to the single bottle of whiskey and the tumbler that held a splash of smoky liquid.

Efficient?

"It beats having to wait for the waiter, or making frequent trips to the bar," she said.

"I meant the way you tricked me into playing 'bad cop' this morning, and then managed to shut me down at the same time. If I didn't know any better, I'd say you enjoyed that."

She shook her head. "I didn't. But it was necessary." She had a sense that McKinnon wanted to discuss something else but had decided to lead in with this. All right. She could play that game. "I knew if I got the subject around to the worlds taken, you and the Lord Governor would butt heads."

"How did you know that?"

"I'd expect nothing less from a Founder's Movement supporter." A raised eyebrow was his only response. "I had you checked out," she admitted. "Used a JumpShip relay through Muphrid. Made certain that you were under the Exarch's direct orders."

She signaled for a second glass and, when it arrived, splashed a drink into it for him from her bottle. "Nothing personal."

"And the Exarch included a word or two about me and my associates," he said, nodding. "I'm not the most popular man in certain circles right now. I believe that the borders of The Republic should be held at all costs, and I don't mind saying so." He leaned onto the table. "I didn't get where I am today by being soft-spoken, Countess. And when I see something that needs doing, I'd rather act than jaw it out."

"Is that why you aren't on Terra, preparing for the elections?" she asked. "The first election of an Exarch since Devlin Stone handed over power?"

McKinnon had mentioned them earlier, and it had surprised Tara to realize that Damien Redburn's time in office was nearly up. Soon the Paladins would choose his successor from among their number. That would seem to be a fairly large undertaking by itself.

"Wondering what you're missing, giving up Redburn's offer to be a Paladin? Truth and honor, and more backroom deals than in a Liao Moneylender's House?" McKinnon's smile was not completely without humor. He picked up his glass and sloshed the smoky liquid back and forth. A warm scent of oak and barley wafted up.

"I have people watching over things for me, and the elections are still three months off," he added. Which wasn't so far, given the blackout and disruptions to interstellar travel. "Anyway, Victor Steiner-Davion and his diehards have the election sewn up tight. No one's going to cross him. And I'd rather do something productive than spend my time shouting into the wind. I'll leave that to Kelson Sorenson and to the Pillars of The Republic."

"I don't know that I believe that," Tara said slowly. "Today, with Duke Gregory, you nearly agreed with him once. When he chastised Exarch Redburn for moving more promises off Terra than assistance."

McKinnon's eyes were diamond hard. But he nodded. "Saw that, did you?"

"I can appreciate your loyalty to the Exarch. But a hero of the Jihad, and a man with more than sixty years experience . . ." She shook her head. "He should be listened to."

"I'll have my say when the time is right," he promised. "And they might not like it." He hedged. "Actually, I guarantee they won't like it, but that's just too bad." He chuckled dryly. "In the meantime I'm here, Countess. Here to help."

Tara toyed with her glass, rolling the whiskey around the sides in a perpetual wave. "I'm glad that you are," she admitted. "But . . . victory at any cost?" She chewed on the words, and they left behind a bitter aftertaste. They reminded her of someone else. A person she would rather forget. "The Lord Governor wasn't so thrilled with the idea of hiring more mercenaries off Galatea," she told him, trying to segue into an easier topic. It was one of Duke Gregory's few concessions during the morning's meeting.

If he caught on to the deception, he didn't show it.

"Why not? Taxes can be levied. But Skye?" He shook his head. "It cannot be replaced easily if we lose it."

Tara had her own worries about relying too heavily on

warriors for hire, despite her own unit's history of mercenary service during the Succession Wars. Most of it stemmed from the trouble her Highlanders were running into on half a dozen different worlds, putting down local rebellions backed by mercs bought off Galatea. She voiced as much to McKinnon, who shrugged.

"In this case, since Clanners don't use mercenaries, I think we have the better side of the deal." He finally tasted his drink, and then sat back, pleasantly surprised. "Glengarry Black Label?" Tara spun the bottle halfway around. "They stock that in the officers' club?"

"Not for under two hundred bills—ComStar currency, not Republic *stones*—and the price keeps going up. I don't see the Falcons allowing regular exports off-world. Do you?" A shame. The drink was the closest equivalent she had found to good Northwind Reserve from the Highlanders' home world.

The Paladin finished off his drink with a practiced flourish, tipped the glass over upside down, and set it back on the table. He pushed his chair back, as if to leave, then asked, "Why did you have me checked out? My bonafides were all in order."

And verifaxes couldn't be forged. Tara nodded. "All right. I wanted to ask the Exarch directly for his opinion of you."

"What's wrong with your own opinion?"

She laughed, short and sharp and not with much humor. "Let's just say that my own judgment has been lacking of late." Of course, McKinnon would have seen the report that had gone back to the Exarch. "I let a Lyran agent get close to me recently. Too close." Was this what the grand Paladin had actually wanted to talk about? Rub her nose in it?

"The Knave." McKinnon used the agent's coded identity. "He did us a favor, you know, killing Augustus Solvaig. That man was poison, and would have hurt us a great deal."

"The mission doesn't matter." Through Tara, the agent from Loki had gained access to the highest levels. It came out only later that Skye's chief minister, Solvaig, had been a plant from the fractured Free Worlds League. "It could just as easily have been the Lord Governor, or Prefect

Brown. In the middle of the Jade Falcon assault, any of a dozen different losses might have led to a critical failure of our entire plan."

"Instead, the Knave followed you out onto the battlefield. Even saved your life."

"Skye might have been lost."

"I thought you didn't want to deal in might-have-beens."

"It was a lapse in judgment," she said quietly, forcefully. "And after . . . ," she trailed off, nearly spilling out what no one else needed to know. The man she was still trying to forget.

But McKinnon knew. "Ezekiel Crow," he said simply.

"What? How did—"

"It took some time for the rumors to catch up. As it happens a . . . a concerned Knight looking into the recent actions of Paladin Crow brought them off Northwind."

Tara set her glass down hard. "Great. The scandalvids are going to love this one."

"The scandalvids don't have this, and no reason they should. Exarch Redburn has it. I believe you can rely on his discretion, and mine."

But the wounds were still there, barely scabbed over. Paladin Ezekiel Crow had betrayed The Republic on Northwind, betrayed *her*, working against the state's interests and putting Highlanders at risk. On Terra, shortly thereafter, he had proved what a treacherous man he'd truly been. He'd attempted to assassinate Paladin Jonah Levin, and interfered in the planet's defense against the Steel Wolves. Tara had been so certain she was falling for the man. Hard.

"When he died on Terra, I thought it was finally over."

When Tara had destroyed his 'Mech. Killed him.

McKinnon held back just a heartbeat too long, his face frozen into a hard mask. Deliberating. She spread her hands over the table's slick Formica finish. "He's not dead."

"He's dead," the Paladin said softly, "but not on Terra." He saw her eyes widen. "No, not by my hand either. He ended up on the world of Liao, fighting against the Confederation takeover."

Why? Why would the Paladin dredge this up? It had been his reason for searching her out from the beginning, she knew. The rest had been establishing a rapport, easing into this. "Trying to redeem himself," she scoffed, not wanting to believe it.

"He did, Tara. He did." McKinnon recounted some of the details of Ezekiel Crow's last days. His mistakes and his desperate attempts to make up for them, and the alleged blackmail that had ruined a good man. A Paladin of the Sphere. "You're going to hear more about him as the news filters out. Some of it is worse than you could imagine. Some tragic. But in the end, he was a citizen and a patriot. I thought maybe you should know that."

"Why?" she asked, picking up her glass again.

"So maybe the next time you doubt your own judgment, you'll remember. No man wears a simple white or black hat, Tara." He stood, and gave her a slow nod. "Not even a Paladin." Which sounded as much a warning as a consolation.

It gave her something to think about after McKinnon had left, when the privacy she had sought earlier came rolling back over her like a juggernaut. It did help, she discovered, knowing that she hadn't been the one to kill Ezekiel. That he had died redeemed at least in the eyes of one other. But it also reopened the wounds deep inside, which bled with new grief. For that, she wasn't going to thank David McKinnon anytime soon.

From now on, she resolved, she would put The Republic first and always.

A thrill trembled over her skin and Tara was surprised at the sense of rightness she felt, making that vow to herself. It wasn't just that personal entanglements didn't seem worth the pain and the threat of failure they carried. Whatever the Paladin had hoped to help her understand by talking about Ezekiel, she suddenly understood that the most important relationship she'd developed over recent years had, in fact, been her devotion and loyalty to The Republic. That relationship deserved her attention.

It would be a relief, she decided, to focus all her energy on The Republic. At least for now. But she also wondered, had McKinnon known how deeply his news would touch her?

And had the Paladin truly helped her or not?

7

Alexia Wolf braced one hand on either side of the door-frame and leaned into the control cabin of the S-7A's passenger module. It smelled of warm electronics and sweat. The cabin's twelve square meters was cramped with three pilot's chairs and what looked like enough control circuitry to fly a DropShip. For the shuttle "bus" it seemed overkill. At least to a MechWarrior.

"How much longer?" she asked, seeing only stars through the forward ferroglass window.

"Fifteen seconds more than it'd be if I didn't have to answer your question."

She knew that Leutnant James Richárd resented having to give up his *Eisensturm* fighter craft in order to make this ferry run, but Alexia saw no reason not to tap her best pilot when she wanted a quick and uncomplicated rendezvous. This entire mission had been hastily put together and run at a dangerous, breakneck pace. Only nine days—completed in half the time it would have taken a regular DropShip run from Nusakan to jump point, and jump point back to Zebebelgenubi. Now, with her Tharkan Strikers outbound from their reconnaissance raid, she intended to report in person to Jasek Kelswa-Steiner.

The Stormhammers' leader was incoming from the same "pirate point" her Strikers had used for their own stealthy approach to the world. One of the best uses to which Jasek had put his intelligence units was identifying every nonstandard jump point for every system the Stormhammers visited. There were some dangers in operating JumpShips so deep in a gravitational field, but these were acceptable when weighed against the strategic advantage of fast, stealthy travel.

It did tend to make warriors a bit jumpy, however.

"Just get us there in one piece," she said, "and before they hit atmosphere."

Richárd nodded. Then, without warning, gravity bent onto its left side as maneuvering thrusters fired a long hard burst to turn the bus to starboard. A long curved wall of gray armor edged into view. Jasek's *Himmelstor, Heaven's Gate*. The massive *Excalibur*-class DropShip fell through space scant meters from them. The circular ring of a docking hardpoint was so close Alexia wondered if the front of the bus would scrape against it.

"Rolling," Richárd did warn her this time. Barely.

Attitude jets fired and gravity swam in a sickening direction as the shuttle craft continued to turn but now added a side-over roll in order to expose its belly to the sixteen-thousand-ton vessel. Alexia hung in with hands *and* feet braced in the doorframe, and her stomach in her throat. A second burst from the jets stilled all movement. Then one last shove upward as the bus lowered itself against the *Excalibur*'s hull. Alexia felt her ponytail lift against the back of her neck. A dull, metallic *gong* rang through the small vessel as docking collars mated; a clockwork ratcheting followed as the seal was made.

Now the bus looked back along the length of the egg-shaped *Excalibur*. Twenty meters up from the docking collar, an old insignia had been inexpertly painted over. A dark outline peeked from under the light gray, visible enough to be recognizable as the Roman profile of the Principes Guards. Eventually, the blue shield and cross of the Archon's Shield unit would be painted over it, and The Republic's last claim on the *Himmelstor* would be gone.

Alexia swallowed hard. "You did that on purpose," she accused the grinning leutnant.

"You bet I did," he agreed. "Passengers shouldn't be out of their seats. It's for your own safety."

Richárd liked to use as many contractions as he could manage—a habit most Clan warriors considered lazy, a debasing of the language—as another way to needle his superior. But Alexia was freeborn, and not raised in a strict Clan environment. She could deal with his relaxed attitude, and she could appreciate a joke.

"It's a good thing for you that you're such a hot flyer," she said, making the contractions sound fairly natural. "In fact, maybe I should assign you as our permanent shuttle pilot."

His look of horror was exaggerated, but not by a great deal.

Knowing she'd scored a point, Alexia left him to shut down the shuttle. She swam back through null-gravity to reach the docking collar, already opened by another crewman who stood by to exit the shuttle after her. Alexia crouched, levered herself over the circular hatch, and with a pull on the raised lip she floated slowly down, extending her legs as she fell.

Strong hands caught her around the waist.

The grip tightened into a familiar embrace, guiding her into the ninety-degree turn that would take her from the shuttle's orientation to that of the DropShip. She closed her eyes, easing her shift in equilibrium, and smiled. When she opened her eyes, Jasek Kelswa-Steiner was planting her feet on the DropShip's deck, grinning his best, brightest smile. He anchored her with one of his own feet braced against the deck and the other against the wall, tucked under a low rail. His strength and the angular lines of his face were very, very male. His flawless bronze skin and indigo eyes set him apart from most other men Alexia had known. He looked like a holovid star, but was every part a warrior.

"You're late," he whispered, leaning toward her.

She felt the pull of him deep inside her gut. Alexia winked, then glanced meaningfully toward the hatch where the feet of one of her shuttle crewmen appeared. Jasek rolled his eyes, then spun her to the wall, where she secured herself with one hand on a nearby ladder.

"We'll have gravity in about sixty seconds," he told the crewman. "Get everyone off the shuttle." He returned the man's salute and then gestured Alexia up the ladder.

With Jasek following after her, the two swam into the upper decks of the *Himmelstor*. Warning Klaxons blared a short alarm as they reached officers' country. Standing away from any descending hatches, they clung to the wall and waited as the DropShip's massive drives rumbled back to life in the engineering spaces far below. Gravity returned with the deceleration burn, pushing them down against the deck. Alexia's knees protested under several extra kilograms of sudden weight.

"We'll burn at one-point-two gravities for a few hours to make up for lost decel time," he told her. "You're late."

"It is not like I was on a regimented schedule. Orders to 'go and find out' do not lend themselves to precision planning. But I am fine and all personnel accounted for. Thank you for asking."

Jasek grinned, then laughed. "We've been a terrible influence on you. Your superiors would hardly know what to do with you anymore."

"That was the general idea, was it not?"

After failing her original Trial of Position as a warrior, Alexia had been expected to settle into one of the other pseudocastes on Arc-Royal. Or turn mercenary, if the Kell Hounds would have her. Instead, she had placed herself under *geis*, embarking on a journey to find her true place. Few Clans practiced such a custom anymore, but Alexia had a drop or two of Sea Fox blood in her as well, and that was enough to push her toward a different destiny. Receiving this second chance at a warrior's life, she had paid back every confidence Jasek had shown her, with loyalty and sterling service.

"All right," Jasek surrendered, starting down the corridor again. "I knew you didn't take serious casualties or you would have radioed those ahead. Any wounded?"

"One broken shoulder from a bad ejection. We lost one scout 'Mech, two vehicles, and I think we'll need to send a battlesuit back for complete reconditioning."

Jasek winced. "That's a high price in materiel. I hope

what you brought back was worth it." He palmed open the door to his personal office, adjacent to his shipboard quarters. "The Highlanders are still alive?"

Alexia entered the room, saw that no one waited for them, and collapsed gratefully into one of the bolted-down chairs. Jasek's desk had a map of Zebebelgenubi displayed on the touch-sensitive glass top. Leaning forward, she isolated a stretch of coastal mountains on Zebebelgenubi's northern continent. The map scrolled open to a larger plot. And then again.

"Here," she said, bracing her forearm against the edge of the desk. She took a stylus from its holder and drew blue *X*s in two distinct clusters. "The Highlanders have broken into two mixed lances. As of fourteen hours ago, they have been unable to regroup."

"And the Falcons?"

Producing a data crystal, Alexia slotted it into one of the empty sockets that lined one edge of the desk. "Force estimates," she explained. Then she tapped for a new color—red—and sketched rough lines along the coast and spearheading from an interior highway system.

"Solid lines on both sides, preventing any escape. The Highlanders would be dead by now except for it is all old mining country in there. False positives on magscan make it easy to hide, and there are dozens of old caves to use as base camps. Old-growth forests and treacherous ground. The Highlanders even collapsed an entire cliff face on top of an advancing Jade Falcon column—a classic Twycross Trap."

Jasek studied the topographical map and the enemy force estimates. His level of intense concentration reminded Alexia of a marksman about to fire a pistol. His entire body was taut, breathing shallow. One last breath drawn inward . . . and *hold*. Jasek's eyes tightened with his decision.

"We'll hit from the coast," he said, "and then work our way inward until we find the Highlanders. After that, we'll secure an LZ and call in the *Himmelstor* and your *Star Chaser* for pickup."

Just the two, she noted. And again, there was no one else here for what should have been a mission planning session. "What about the *Eclipse*? Or the *Friedensstifter*?"

Both DropShips were used by the Lyran Rangers on a regular basis. Both should have been available.

"Delayed, and I didn't want to wait another forty-eight hours for them to catch up. I have a lance of the Archon's Shield on board and a reinforced company of Rangers. More than enough for a rescue mission."

"Not if the fighting turns nasty down there. Jasek, I—"

"No, Alex." He didn't even wait to hear her pitch. Moving to a refrigerated sideboard, he retrieved two soft drinks in zero-G bottles. "I know what you are going to ask."

"It should be my warriors leading the mission. We have been down there. We have bled for the information we currently possess."

He shook his head, sipped at his drink. "I sent the Tharkan Strikers ahead because your light-armor company was best suited for an intelligence raid. But you said it yourself. Your people are banged up and down too much equipment. And they're still pretty green. You will stay on station as our reserve force, but I don't intend to let the Falcons take a second bite at you."

"Instead you will give them a shot at the Stormhammers' commander? Where is the logic behind that?" But she knew how much it had pained Jasek to sit on Nusakan, waiting and watching. He was too much a warrior born not to lead the fight now that he was finally able to act. "Do you even have another officer to second you?"

"Tamara Duke," he said with forced casualness.

She shook her head. Of course. Colonel Petrucci *would* dump that snake's nest of problems into Jasek's care. "Well, that makes me feel better."

"It should. She's one of the best officers I have, Alex." He moved behind her, placing lean hands on her shoulders. "What's your real complaint?" He kneaded the muscles that bunched in knots above each shoulder blade.

"In the Clans, we would consider it an honor—and our right—to finish the mission we started." Despite her unwillingness, his hands were loosening the tension in her back.

"You're not Clan right now," he reminded her. "You're not even Lyran, despite your birth on Arc-Royal. You're a Stormhammer. That means you go where we go. And I'm going to use the best resources I have to accomplish any mission. No favorites. No calling dibs."

Alexia shrugged away his hands. "Dibs?" she asked.

"Never mind. I'm simply asking you to trust me, Alexia. I haven't let you down yet, have I?"

"Not yet." She stood, turned to look at him with a coy smile. "But there might be a first time. Maybe you need some more practice?"

Jasek laughed. "We're on a mission, Leutnant-colonel Wolf."

Her frown was only half serious. That was the rule they had set down for themselves. One of the rules, anyway, and hardly the most important one. "It is not because *she* is here, is it?"

"You know better."

"I suppose I do." She sighed. "I'm going to get cleaned up before we meet with the duke and the others, then." Alexia stepped into him, hands coming to his chest as she leaned up to deliver a quick, biting nip on the edge of his strong chin. Then she pushed him back, stepping around him for the door. "You might regret all your rules and discipline some day."

The Stormhammers' leader nodded, already circling around to the far side of his desk, studying the map once again. "So you keep saying," he needled.

"Ha." Her laugh pulled his gaze up from the map. "Wolves are territorial creatures, but I'm not staying with you forever, Jasek. I told you that before."

"You did," he agreed. Her threatening to leave, to continue her *geis*, was a standing joke between them. "But I might leave you first," he reminded her. His usual return volley.

The smile she left him with, playful and just a little bit dangerous, told him exactly how likely she thought that was.

8

Jasek Kelswa-Steiner charged through a wall of flames, then ducked his *Templar* behind a massive tree trunk big enough to hide the eighty-five-ton machine. Autocannon fire and lasers chased after him. One line of bullets tore deeply through the sequoia's bark, splintering and shredding the wood beneath. Red lances of energy cut deeper, burning dark scars into the bole.

Leaning back, Jasek extended his left arm and blasted a pursuing team of Elementals with his functioning PPC. The white arc of lightning chewed one battlesuit trooper into a twisted hunk of ruined metal and man.

The others scattered, leaping for brush, for branches. Two disappeared back into the flames, trusting their armored suits to protect them. Jasek saw one infantryman use his arm-mounted laser to encourage the fire, stoking it with short, scarlet blasts.

Senseless ruin. The Jade Falcons would rather see Zebebelgenubi burned down around them than surrender any fight.

Borrowing time from the besieged Highlanders, Jasek had led his people up from the coast through the old-growth forest rather than along cleared ridges where the Falcons would see them coming. The Clanners had tripped to it too early, though. A line of medium and heavy machines was waiting for Jasek as he tried to break out of the forest, spearheading the drive. They pushed him back under cover of the titanic trees, and then deliberately set fire to the forest in several locations in an attempt to shake up his lines.

Now the fire raged over several square kilometers, choking the mighty forest with a noose of thick, black smoke. Flames chased through the treetops of the giant sequoias, whipped from crown to crown by gusting winds.

Ash and glowing orange embers rained down from above in hellish curtains.

But the real damage and the real risk was closer to the ground, where stunted pines and hemlocks and scrub brush tangled with ivy and wisteria—all tinder-dry thanks to several weeks of arid winter—burned in a true inferno that drove temperatures into dangerous levels and eventually set fire to the massive trees. Even with one PPC out of commission, Jasek's heat scale climbed. Sweat burned at the corners of his eyes, and the sharp scent of greenwood smoke could not be completely filtered out by his life-support systems.

"Such a waste," he whispered aloud.

Then his communications gear crackled to life, shouting static into his ear before parting to reveal Tamara Duke's voice. "Hammer, Anvil is in place," she said.

About time.

Jasek glanced to his upper right to activate his vision-reflex systems and blinked over to his all-hands circuit. "Two-lance, Three-lance, move up on my position now. Flankers, envelop and hold!"

Throttling forward into a moderate walk, Jasek wrenched his control stick over to twist the *Templar* into a sideways lean as he moved from cover. Laser fire stuttered through the tree breaks, gouging wounds into the side of his 'Mech, and molten composite splashed over the ground. He saw nothing through the smoke and flames. Thermal imaging was useless and magscan nearly so. But his targeting computer found something out there it liked, drawing brackets around a glowing icon on his heads-up display.

Jasek levered his left arm forward again and blasted through the fires with his particle cannon. No way to tell if he'd hit something or not.

Behind him, a second Stormhammers 'Mech—Leutnant Gillickie's *Storm Raider*—ran up under his covering fire. Gillickie brought a pair of Jousts and a Hasek mechanized combat vehicle with him, the Hasek's Fenrir infantry already deployed and running on all fours to keep pace with the tracked tanks.

On his right, Jasek caught glimpses through the flames of Three-lance pulling even with him, saw the flash and smoke of missile launch as their JES carriers spread a destructive umbrella out ahead.

"Good to go," he decided, cutting a path straight into the fires ahead. He tied his lasers and TharHes four-pack SRM into his secondary trigger, readying them.

A pair of Elementals leaped at him in the flame, arm lasers probing for weak spots. Jasek cored through one with his pair of medium lasers. The other he simply swatted from the air.

Temperatures soared. Fire licked up from below while burning embers swirled into his face and struck sparks against the ferroglass shield. Autocannon fire pecked and pocked his BattleMech's legs, ringing with distant hammer peals.

Then he was through.

A tangle of burning, low-hanging branches shattered over the *Templar*'s head as Jasek stepped out onto an old backwoods road—all hard-packed dirt and gravel. A Skanda light tank spun around only fifty meters away, autocannon tracking in to hammer more damage into Jasek's right side. There were four more vehicles spread farther along the road. To his left, the road twisted up a rocky hill. A green-painted *Vulture* nested among some moss-covered boulders. Sylph battle armor sprang out from around the sixty-ton 'Mech, like its mechanized young taking to flight.

Sparing a handful of seconds to hammer the Skanda with lasers and missiles, driving it back, Jasek clenched his teeth and tensed for the *Vulture*'s ground-shaking assault.

It did not disappoint. The Clan 'Mech all but disappeared

behind a curtain of exhaust smoke as it staggered out four full spreads of strategic missiles. As the warheads rained down with bone-jarring force, pummeling the eighty-five-ton machine, a pair of red-tinted lasers sliced out from the smoke and carved angry wounds down the *Templar*'s left arm and leg.

"Ne-eed some he-elp he-errre," Jasek stuttered into the voice-activated mic as he was thrown repeatedly against his safety harness. He wrenched on the controls to keep his BattleMech balanced.

The gyroscope screamed a high-pitched protest, but with Jasek's aid the *Templar* held to its feet.

All along the fire-struck road his Stormhammers broke free of the forest. Gillickie exploded through a burning thicket like some fire demon come for vengeance. His autocannon pounded hot metal into the *Vulture*'s side. Kicking in the *Storm Raider*'s myomer accelerated signal circuitry, Gillickie pounded up the road at 130 kilometers per hour, mace held above his head, ready to smash. The Joust tanks clawed their way through more slowly, with a few Fenrirs clinging to their tops like giant armored fleas.

The Sylph battle armor had arced up too high to stop the *Storm Raider*. Instead, they fell onto the Joust tanks, trading weapons fire with the Fenrirs and ripping at the tank's armor and treads.

Jasek ignored the scuffle, staggering forward over the missile-savaged road. His sensors rang new alarms as a *Shadow Hawk IIC* led another pair of Skandas over the crest of a distant hill, but they were too far away to worry about now.

The *Vulture* had to be dealt with before it got off another devastating round. Dropping crosshairs over its outline, his PPC smashed armor into shards and spatters. Lasers worried its right side. Two of his four missiles corkscrewed in to smash at the *Vulture*'s shoulder and head.

The *Vulture* limped out from behind its cover of boulders, gray smoke seeping out of several joints. Lasers stabbed out again, this time drawing in on the advancing *Storm Raider*. Large red lances from each arm and smaller daggers from the paired microlasers in its center torso.

Only one of the large lasers hit, slicing away armor from the *Storm Raider*'s chest, barely slowing it.

A poor second showing. Even against the forest fire, the *Vulture*'s thermal profile stood out as a desperate blaze. Risking all on the earlier, savage strike, the Clan 'Mech had overheated itself, impairing its ability to move, to return fire.

Gillickie attacked it again with his autocannon, then gave it an overhead smashing blow from his BattleMech's hand-held mace. The mace staved in one of the *Vulture*'s missile launchers. His second, cross-body blow drove one of the microlasers back into the torso cavity, and on Jasek's imaging screen a heat spike carved a blue-white streak over the *Vulture*'s profile. Damage to the BattleMech's shielding reactor.

Light autocannon fire and some ineffectual laser shots peppered the back of Jasek's *Templar* as a Skanda and two Kite reconnaissance vehicles flashed by, on their way up the road at better than one hundred kilometers per hour.

Jasek checked an auxiliary monitor—his rear-facing camera—and saw Three-lance finishing off two armored tanks. One of his JES carriers was overturned and burning, with infantry giving the missile cruiser a wide berth. His second carrier launched a spread of missiles up and over his position, showering warheads over the fleeing vehicles as they raced between Jasek's position and that of the crippled *Vulture*.

One Kite took an unlucky hit, spilling air out of its ruined skirting. It swerved right, dug its forward fender into the road, and then tumbled into a death roll that ended when its fusion engine exploded in a golden ball of fire.

The *Vulture* followed a moment later with a much quieter death. It staggered and stumbled as Jasek and the two Joust tanks added their firepower to Gillickie's autocannon.

Another PPC from the *Templar* and it went down, having lost its right leg at the knee.

The *Vulture* wrenched itself up on one side, and its canopy blew away as the MechWarrior inside ejected from his stricken machine. The fiery blast under the ejection seat rocketed him above the sequoias, barely; then a large parafoil spread overhead. With a choice of mountainside or road, both in the control of the Stormhammers, or a burning forest, the Clan warrior chose to take his chances. He wheeled over and ran with the wind, into the building forest fire.

"Crash and burn," Jasek muttered, watching him disappear into a dark curtain of rising smoke.

The Jade Falcons had created the problem. Jasek felt no compunction wishing them the worst of it.

"Hammer, Three-lance. Backfield is secure." A pause. "One Jess is down. Light damage all around."

"Two-lance," Gillickie called out, panting heavily, "The Sylphs have dodged back into the forest and good riddance to weary company." Even his *Storm Raider* looked tired, dragging its mace at its side. "I have a crippled Joust and two dead Fenrirs. And a bum knee." He limped the mace-wielding 'Mech up the road. "Our friends have turned back."

The *Shadow Hawk* and the Skanda. After picking up the retreating vehicles, they had turned back over the crest of the hill, heading forward to link up with the main Jade Falcon line.

Jasek laid it all out in his head as he throttled into a fast walk, moving his *Templar* forward at nearly forty kilometers per hour, heading up the hill. "We're still twenty klicks short of the Highlanders." At best guess. The Falcons are jamming transmissions. "We have that *Shadow Hawk* and whatever else is out here trapped between our location and Tamara Duke's Anvil Lance." They were five kilometers away. "And she's caught between the retreating Falcons and their main line."

As temperatures fell back to somewhat bearable levels, now that his weapons were cooling, a nervous sweat replaced the heat stress. "Not good," he said.

The Jade Falcons had obviously not expected him to push so much force through in a single location. He'd forced them to run too early. Tamara wasn't ready for such a heavy force.

And the Falcon machines were faster. He couldn't catch them in time.

He blinked over to his private channel to Tamara Duke. "You heard?" he asked the kommandant.

Her voice was faint, nearly lost in a crackle of static, but there. "We just stopgapped a pair of Skadi VTOLs," she said, "but another got away. Our secret's out. Get here quick, Jasek. Damn!" She cut away, dealing with whatever problem had cropped up.

"Two-lance." Jasek switched back to his all-hands. "Gillickie. Best speed forward. Take the Hasek and as many Fenrir battlesuits as we have left."

The Hasek was slow, plowing its way from the burning forest, but was soon on the road and powering forward. The *Storm Raider* maintained a good lead on it, managing a kind of limping run that was nowhere near its optimum speed, but it pulled away from Jasek's *Templar* regardless.

"We'll still be late to the party," Gillickie said.

And minutes made a huge difference in such desperate battles. Jasek slowly throttled up to his best running speed. "Just so long as it's still going on when you get there," he answered.

It was. Four minutes spread his forces out in a long, staggered column, and still put him a kilometer shy of Tamara Duke's position when Leutnant Gillickie spearheaded a relief force into the battle. "Cowabunga!" the young warrior shouted.

Jasek took that to mean, "Have made contact with the enemy."

The fire had not spread this far yet, and the majestic forest had thinned out considerably as the Stormhammers pushed into the old mining country. From a final hillcrest, staring across a long valley quarry, Jasek saw the bright, brief glow of lasers crisscrossing with brutal savagery. Missiles rained down, indiscriminately it seemed, blossoming fireballs over the rocky terrain and occasionally throwing down one of the larger machines that stalked the battlefield.

Tamara's *Wolfhound* was easy to find, streaking back and forth on the far side of the valley, doing her best to prevent the Jade Falcons from opening an easy path through her line. She had three vehicles and a handful of Gnome battle armor left to what had started out as a double lance. One downed ForestryMech. Three stilled tanks—one burning.

Jasek hoped that the others were salvageable. Skye was going to need his people in top form.

But just now Tamara and Leutnant Gillickie needed *him*. He found the mace-wielding *Storm Raider* protecting the damaged Hasek on the nearer side of the valley. The Falcons had split their strength, at least for the moment. The *Shadow Hawk IIC* and two VTOLs pressed forward against Tamara Duke's position. An *Ocelot* and a very dangerous Lyran-designed *Uziel* led armor and infantry forces back in a delaying action against Gillickie.

"Any . . . time"—rapid panting filled Jasek's ear—"sir."

With the acrobatic moves he was being forced to make just to keep from being pinned and killed, no doubt the young leutnant was exhausted. His *Storm Raider* crouched, leaped, ran around behind a young stand of alders, then raced forward to snipe at the *Uziel* while trying to dodge its PPCs.

Jasek had left his JES behind with a light guard of Cavalier battlesuit infantry, but one of the Joust tanks had managed to keep up. Together, the 'Mech and tank rolled down the shallow slope. Jasek ordered his man to fade back slowly, drawing the *Uziel* after him, letting it get within range of the stranded Hasek. It was a gamble, tempting the Clanner with a possible kill.

At the last moment, the *Uziel* hesitated. But the *Ocelot* took the bait, thinking it could slip in and out again with its superior speed before the *Templar* made it into range. Jasek surprised it by goosing just a touch more speed out of his machine and relying on his targeting computer to make corrections to his wild, long-range snapshot.

His PPC's lightning strike twisted and snaked in an eyeblinding arc, slashing downrange to blast into the *Ocelot's* right leg. The light 'Mech stumbled, sprawling over the quarry floor with a baseball slide that struck flinty sparks from the ground.

"Hammer that *Ocelot*," Jasek ordered. "Burn it!"

But the Clan 'Mech still had serious teeth. Dragging itself back to a standing crouch, the *Ocelot* used its heavy laser to slash dark orange energy at the advancing *Storm Raider*. Gillickie broke away quickly, his left torso exposed right down through to his gyro housing. Jasek's next PPC shot missed wide to the right.

"There they go!" the young leutnant warned Tamara.

The *Uziel's* MechWarrior had recognized in time that the Stormhammer reinforcements would be only the first of several arrivals, eventually swinging the battle against the

Falcons. Rallying what was left of his armor contingent, he led a quick feint-and-flee maneuver that pushed right in behind the *Shadow Hawk*. The Falcons' *Ocelot* wasn't far behind, and with its leg damage still moved faster than Jasek's *Templar*.

"Let them pass, Tamara." His call went out quick and commanding. "We'll pick up their trail further along. Get out of their way!"

She did, for a moment, falling back and to the side. Her beloved Eisenfaust looked beaten and scarred, but still moved with a kind of lupine grace not often seen in a mechanical battle machine.

It was with that same grace that she charged back into the Falcons' line of march, bounding forward with a determined stride and her laser flaring ruby bright. It brought the *Shadow Hawk* up short. The Falcon pilot had not expected this, his machine outmassing the *Wolfhound* by twenty tons, backed by a solid line of 'Mechs and armor.

A trio of lasers flashed out, burning new wounds into the *Wolfhound*'s side.

Tamara's bite was less savage but still painful as her arm-mounted laser drilled directly into the *Shadow Hawk*'s centerline. Jasek doubted the Clan machine could stand up to another coring hit like that.

But then neither could his warrior. "Tamara, what the hell do you think you're doing? I said get out of their way."

Static crackled in his ear. Then, "That would be . . . a poor host," she said, just as the first Highlander tank—a Bellona—bulled its way into the valley from the far pass.

Followed by a Condor, a second Bellona, and then a limping *Pack Hunter*.

A modified MiningMech and a pair of M1 Marksmen protected the flanks of a *Legionnaire*. A line of ten . . . twelve Gray Death battlesuit infantry and a MASH truck brought up a staggered rear.

Jasek would have been surprised if the Highlanders had five tons of armor to spread among their entire line. These machines looked like hell, limping, slapping broken treads against the ground, trailing smoke from too many engines. But they formed a battle line with disciplined precision behind Tamara Duke. The *Pack Hunter* sprint-wobbled forward to add its PPC to her large laser, throwing a scathing assault against the *Shadow Hawk*.

The Falcons had had enough. The *Shadow Hawk* and *Uziel* took to the air on jets of golden plasma, leaping far afield and then racing up the side of the nearby valley wall, where they could lose themselves in the foothills. The armor broke and ran in half a dozen different directions, most of them bending around to the west and the subjective safety of the forest fire and its blanket of smoke.

The *Ocelot* never stood a chance. Sensing its weakness, Tamara pounced forward, driving it back into the weapons of Gillickie's *Storm Raider*. Lasers flashed, cutting deep and certain. Another severed leg. Another MechWarrior punching out on his ejection seat.

Another salvageable 'Mech.

Jasek slapped his armrest in celebration, then throttled back to an easy walk. His throat parched from fluid loss, he swallowed dryly and toggled in a free-security channel. "We didn't expect to see you this far down the mountainside," he said.

The *Legionnaire* saluted, raising its hand in the general direction of its low-slung head. "Falcon chatter told us that a relief force had landed. It cost us, but we regrouped and punched through for your landing beacon."

Landing beacon? The landgrave looked up into the sky, saw the curls of black smoke rolling heavenward from the forest fire. His mood took a darker turn. "Ah, that. Not quite what we had in mind, of course."

The Highlander's voice sounded dog-tired and bruised. "Just so long as there's a DropShip or two on the other end of that smoke."

"And a JumpShip," Jasek promised. "Twenty-eight light-years to Skye, all the medical attention your people need, and, if reports are still accurate, your Countess Tara Cambell."

He smiled. "Compliments of the Stormhammers."

9

When newly acquired states have been accustomed to living freely under their own laws, there are three ways to hold them securely: [second], by establishing dominion and ruling them in person.

The Prince, by Niccolò Machiavelli

The Acropolis
Tairngoth, Glengarry
26 September 3134

The Acropolis was a testament to Clan engineering. Sitting in the passenger seat of a VV1 Ranger, ignoring the cold silence radiating from the driver, Noritomo Helmer recognized the dome-and-towers configuration from its silhouette while five kilometers away. Though it was no doubt constructed in a matter of days from prefabricated pieces brought by the Falcons to Glengarry, an instant stronghold, there was a permanence about it now in the way it crouched at the edge of the deep canyon overlooking Loch Tay.

The twisting, switchback road they traveled wound down toward the canyon's edge, past new guard towers and old rockslides clumped with purple-blooming heather and dwarf

Scotch pines. A *Shrike* stood solitary sentinel at the final checkpoint, the ninety-five-ton monster tracking the Ranger with heavy-class autocannon and a disdainful air in the way the pilot never turned completely toward the open-air vehicle.

The driver transmitted clearance codes, and they were through.

Beautiful land, Noritomo judged, keeping an eye on the approaching complex but unable to ignore the rugged beauty rolling past him. Crisp, knife-edged mountains surrounded him, slicing at the sapphire blue sky. Everything was verdant and sweet-smelling, if low growing because of the rocky soil. Worlds like this were what had brought the Jade Falcons back to the Inner Sphere from the severe Clan home worlds nearly a century before, more tempting, in Noritomo's opinion, than the promise of battle.

Of course, Malvina Hazen would argue that point. Then again, she also would likely argue his point if it meant a better fight and the possibility of greater honor.

The Ranger pulled to a stop in front of the complex. The large dome, easily one hundred meters across, was the color of wet basalt, all shiny and gray black. Offices. Strategic centers. Training and medical facilities. Ground-hugging barracks capable of sleeping their entire army flanked the dome, and from the south side of each rose up magnificent, slender towers that housed communications arrays, radar and satellite uplinks, and hidden weapons emplacements.

"She is waiting," the driver told him.

Noritomo pegged him as second-line armor crew, to draw escort duty. It did nothing to deflate the driver's superior air, however. He had a swagger and a sneering attitude that the Star colonel was finding all too common among the local garrison troops. Including the way he practically genuflected when speaking of capital-*H Her*.

"Our leader who art immortal," Noritomo mouthed, lips framing the words but without sound, "hallowed be thy name."

Malvina.

It wasn't hard to find her. A sentry-aide at the dome's main doors nodded to him and said, "Dojo."

Training facilities. Left at the main intersection and up one flight of bolted-together metal stairs. Down to the end of the corridor. Noritomo kept his hands clenched into tight fists, his fingernails gouging into his palms, as he steeled himself for the meeting. Hearing the sounds of sparring, he stepped through an open door—careful of the thin mats—and waited quietly behind Galaxy Commander Beckett Malthus and a white-coated doctor while Malvina Hazen finished her sparring match.

She faced another MechWarrior, a man, each of them stripped down to shorts and a tight-fitting shirt. Malvina's opponent was tall and roped with wiry muscle, and moved with a feral grace. He slid in low and fast, coming at her injured side, hands reaching, but was deflected by a swift jab toward his temple.

He ducked away, back on his guard. Malvina Hazen glared after him, furious.

Noritomo took the opportunity to study his immediate commander. Malvina had had a dangerous beauty before. Hard-bodied and intense, she had blond hair and brilliant blue eyes. She'd lost a measure of that on Skye, along with Aleksandr. Pulled from the ruin of her BattleMech, by all accounts Noritomo had heard, she had been more dead than alive. He believed it. Her bionic eye could hardly be distinguished from her natural one, but the scar that creased her brow and curled in toward her mouth remained. Her right arm and right leg were an obsidian black. No vanity involved here. These were prosthetics, and Malvina obviously wanted no part in disguising them to resemble her true limbs.

The Galaxy commander was obviously in a hurry. It would have taken Clan scientists only three months to rejuvenate replacement limbs for her. Another few months for conditioning. A lesser warrior might not have recovered fully, even then. Here, barely five weeks later, she was racing back toward top form. Whatever her impetus, rage or revenge, it spoke of great need.

Or great hunger.

With a battle shriek very much like a hawk's cry, Malvina charged her opponent. She moved with very little grace, hobbled by the dead weight of her prosthetics, but made up for it in savage fury. Her sidearm chop was hard enough to break the man's arm—Noritomo heard the wet snap. She leaped forward, grabbed two fistfuls of his hair, and while still in the air drove a knee into his nose, breaking that as well.

Malvina landed, staggering onto her good leg, crouching into a ready posture.

Her opponent landed hard on his back and lay there, dazed.

"You do not *ever* go easy on me!" she shouted down at him. "I want your best. Always!"

The doctor moved to the injured man, letting him get up on his own and then guiding him aside. Malvina glared after them both with contempt. "Next time bring me an Elemental."

"Easy, Galaxy Commander." Bec Malthus crossed his arms over a thick chest. "You will leave us no able warriors to take Skye."

She scoffed. "What does that matter? We have Star Colonel Helmer. Finally."

Her glare skewered Noritomo as she limped toward them. Her scar burned red and angry. This did not look like the champion being whispered about in reverent tones. Their *Chinggis Khan*—the title that in itself bordered on a betrayal of Khan Pryde, the Jade Falcons' supreme leader.

Then again, with Beckett Malthus backing her, Malvina Hazen could afford a few setbacks and indulge in her dramatics. Malthus was a power in his own right. Some had called him the Shadow-Khan after he assisted in Jana Pryde's ascension. If he had decided to play kingmaker again, Noritomo knew better than to stand in his way. Warriors who tried had a tendency to end up ruined, cast down, and with their genetic material excluded from the Clan's breeding program.

All Malvina Hazen was likely to do to Noritomo Helmer was kill him. She still might.

"All our planning," she said, grabbing a towel from a nearby shelf and blotting the sweat from her face. "All our previous victories. Worthless," she spat. "I *gave* you Kimball II. And you may have cost me Skye."

"The assault did not go as expected," he agreed carefully. "I sent word to you, but my courier was intercepted at Ryde by the Steel Wolves. It was an unforeseeable tragedy."

Malvina wrapped the towel around the back of her neck, held the ends with one white hand, one black. "Losing my brother was an unforeseeable tragedy, Star Colonel. And you do not even have his excuse of martyring yourself for our cause."

"I am sorry for the Clan's loss of Aleksandr Hazen," Noritomo told her. Personal condolences would be improper, no matter how close the brother and sister had been. Everyone served the Clan. "His vision will be missed."

"And I will make the universe pay dearly for depriving us of him," she said in a spate of cold fury.

Malthus shifted carefully toward her, as if cautioning her, and she relented. Slightly.

"Still . . ." Her eyes narrowed into blue slits. She nodded. "We take this one step at a time. Our forces are battered, but not beaten. We control six key worlds in this region of space. We might still accomplish everything we desire, and more. The question becomes, how do we proceed?" She looked at him carefully. "Would you say it is time to call for Khan Pryde and the entire Jade Falcon Touman?"

It was a trap, laid out neatly in front of him and no way to step around it. The two commanders certainly knew of the talk openly spoken among warriors of Clan Jade Falcon's *desant*. The death of Aleksandr Hazen and even their failure to take Skye was ultimately being laid at the feet of Khan Jana Pryde, who had refused to support the long-ranging strike with greater strength from the Falcon military.

When making her decision, Pryde had cited the Clan tradition of bidding the least amount of force necessary to claim victory and therefore the greater honor. But such blind adherence to the old ways had also been a point of contention between Aleksandr and Malvina. Aleksandr followed Clan traditions of bidding for a goal and attempting to take it with the least amount of force—and destruction visited on the target—as possible. Malvina championed a more severe approach. Rip out the spine of all potential resistance up front, and rule through the threat of holocaust.

"I believe that it would be premature to involve Khan Pryde at this time," Noritomo offered diplomatically, searching for a way to slip the noose being drawn around his neck.

Beckett Malthus nodded. "So you agree that we should strike first." It was not a question. It could also be read on many different levels. The Galaxy commander gave nothing away. His eyes were unreadable.

"At Skye?" Noritomo asked, deliberately reading into the question its most obvious meaning. "Of course. Knowing what we now do with regard to its defenders and their tactics, our bid will be that much stronger."

"Our bid," Malvina said, her lips skinned back from strong teeth, "will be all or nothing. We will no longer court failure just to give our enemies a fighting chance. This was Aleksandr's mistake."

Noritomo nodded slowly, but not necessarily in agreement. "Your brother's methods, they worked on Summer and Alkaid." The two worlds taken in Prefecture VIII. "Reports I have seen indicate that their local governments have settled down under our occupation."

"To be lost just as quickly should we show any sign of weakness." Malvina brushed aside his argument with an impatient wave. "Your failure on Kimball II should have opened your eyes to this, Noritomo Helmer. My brother was a great warrior and leader of men, but he believed too blindly in our traditions. He would not recognize that the old ways must give way to the new. And you, Star Colonel. I am beginning to worry about you as well."

"I am Jade Falcon," he offered stiffly. "I serve the Clan."

"Truly?" Malvina sent a glance toward Bec Malthus. "The simplest way for that to be true would be to lay the blame for Aleksandr's death and Skye's resistant stand on your shoulders."

Noritomo had been meant to see that glance. To know that a new alliance had indeed been forged in his absence. A prickling sensation crawled along the back of his neck. He chose his words very carefully, accepting the need for a tactical retreat.

"That would be the simplest solution," he agreed. "But regardless of bidding, it is the challenging battles that still bring the greatest honor."

The implication: such a move would be beneath Malvina Hazen. And though it might very well be in keeping with Malthus' typical behind-the-scenes manipulations, Noritomo suddenly recognized, it would also shift attention back away from Khan Pryde. Would Malvina see it that way?

It was enough that Beckett Malthus did. He raised his chin slightly, acknowledging the move. "In this case," he said slowly, "the challenging battle still looks to be the taking of Skye. Nothing should get in the way of that. You will receive a chance to redeem yourself, Noritomo Helmer.

A new assignment." His green eyes looked through the star colonel as the senior warrior smiled.

"You will take over the garrison force on Chaffee, holding open our lines back to the occupation zone."

A hollow sensation bloomed inside Noritomo.

Chaffee. The Lyran Commonwealth world just outside The Republic that the Jade Falcons had taken and used as their initial staging grounds. It was also the world where Malvina Hazen had tested her terror techniques, using a blistering agent and then sending waves of wounded refugees into The Republic ahead of the invasion as a way to sap local morale.

"At the Galaxy Commanders' will, of course," Noritomo said with due humility, bowing directly between the two senior warriors. They were of equal rank, technically. If he was to have a chance, he would need to keep them both mollified.

For now.

"Then go, Star Colonel." Malvina Hazen had already all but forgotten him. She limped toward the door, turning her back on Noritomo and the entire situation, which she likely considered dealt with. Almost.

At the door, she turned back. "We will review your rosters, and leave you with more than enough force strength."

Beckett Malthus followed Malvina out of the room, leaving the weakened star colonel alone. The dojo smelled of sweat and the plastic mats, but the taste in Noritomo's mouth was cold and bitter. He gave the two military leaders enough time to disappear down the corridor before he allowed his feelings to twist his face with rage.

Chaffee, of course, was hardly important now with Glengarry and so many other Republic worlds in hand. This was their answer, to shuffle Noritomo Helmer aside while stealing away his best troops for a renewed offensive against Skye. He could not stand for that.

But he also knew not to challenge without thought, and careful planning.

"Not even Aleksandr Hazen was able to challenge his sister and make it stick," he reminded himself, smoothing his face back into a neutral mask. If Noritomo hoped to survive, and still prosper as a warrior, he would have to exercise the one trait for which Malvina Hazen had shown no proclivity.

Patience.

10

New London
Skye
4 October 3134

New London's DropPort hid inside a curtain of gray fog. A silvery drizzle made sporadic promises to clear the air, but rarely did more than spatter the large concourse windows. The DropShips that currently sat in their ferrocrete nests of blast deflectors and reinforced pads were little more than great, spheroidal ghosts at the very edge of Tara Campbell's vision. At any moment they might fade from sight.

She didn't want that. Not until her Highlanders were safe, at least.

Desultory droplets speckled the blue glass, chased each other in long trails down to the bottom sill. Tara stood at one of the concourse windows, looking past her ghostly reflection and the rain, out onto the tarmac. The *Himmelstor* was one of those DropShips, grounded as close to the main buildings as safety allowed. A large, hulking outline. An *Excalibur*-class.

She watched as a two-story shuttle bus finally departed the DropShip ramp and made its way slowly across the wide, gray expanse to the lower gate door. Intent on the arriving personnel—wondering who had made it off Zebebelgcnubi, who was lost to the Highlander rolls forever— Tara did not notice at first the security agents taking up silent posts around her. She did wonder briefly at the unnatural calm of the DropPort concourse, but was too busy counting familiar faces by then as they climbed the covered stairs toward the nearby door.

"How many?" Duke Gregory Kelswa-Steiner asked, his deep baritone startling her.

The lord governor waited behind her, half a head taller than she was and staring over her spiked, platinum blond hair. Tara saw that he wore a conservative suit—the kind he habitually wore for a day of closed meetings, rather than the stylish wardrobe he kept for ceremonies and public appearances. Shoulders back, chest out, his bearing wasn't bad for a man who had never subjected himself to military discipline.

He also seemed rather calm, considering.

"Looks like twenty-three men and women," she answered, completing her count.

The first of her Highlanders came through the door. Some limped in, but most seemed fit for duty. A few DropPort staff and some junior liaisons applauded their arrival, welcoming the Highlanders to Skye. The warriors milled around uncertainly, seeing their commander penned in by local security.

"I really should see to them," Tara said, anxious for a formal report. The numbers were better than she'd feared, but not so good as she'd hoped. She started to move past Duke Gregory, who caught her arm.

"This is good news, Countess. Good fortune for Skye." His eyes were alight with fresh resolve. "Please tell your men that we will hold a banquet in their honor." He hushed her with an upraised hand. "I know, it is hardly adequate, but it is a prime media opportunity and we don't get many of those. My coming down to meet them alone should be worth a few percentage points in public approval, which will translate into support for our continuing defense."

The lord governor was far out in front of himself, looking at the political opportunity. Which meant he had not received a full briefing. The loss of Augustus Solvaig reared its head again. "Sir," Tara said carefully, "I think that might not be an appropriate response."

"Why not? Are many of your men hurt?" he asked.

"The ones who made it off Zebebelgenubi seem fine," she said, looking past him at her assembled Highlanders . . . and now also at the man responsible for their rescue. Even though he was clean-shaved and had dark skin, the family resemblance was obvious. As was the warrior's spirit that shone brightly in his dark eyes. "We lost two DropShips and a JumpShip, which hurts, but we'll salvage most of our ground-based equipment."

The duke waved off her concerns. "Transportation is hardly as important as good troops to defend Skye. I'll take all we can get, at this stage."

"Glad to hear some sense out of you, Father," Jasek said, butting into the conversation. Security had flanked him with two agents, but had not held back the duke's son. Rank still owned its privileges. Jasek glanced at the agents, then smiled at his father's flabbergasted stare.

"For a change," he said, adding the caveat like a contract killer might put one extra bullet into the back of his victim's head.

Landgrave Jasek Kelswa-Steiner had inherited his father's strong chin and angular face. His skin was too dark to be just a healthy tan, and Tara had to believe he'd inherited the bronze color from his mother, along with his dark, piercing eyes and the easy warrior's grace with which he carried himself.

Certainly his father showed no casual aplomb, the duke's spine stiffening like it had suddenly turned into titanium.

"You . . . you come back here, now?"

Jasek shrugged as if his father's reaction was expected. "Good to see you too," he said. "We're fine. Oh, and your gratitude for our rescue of the Highlanders is overwhelming."

"I didn't know you had done so," Duke Gregory told him. His face flushed dark, from his pronounced widow's peak to his beard. He shot Tara an accusing glare.

"I found out thirty minutes ago," Tara told him. "They kept it quiet coming in." Now she could see why. Jasek had obviously wanted to arrive in his own way, without a lot of fanfare—or a firing squad, depending on his father's mood. Safer.

"And now that you know?" Jasek asked.

If he was expecting a warm embrace—and Tara doubted that he was—the lord governor disappointed him. His face clouded up like a brewing storm piling thunderheads on the horizon. "I suppose it was the least you could do for The Republic," Duke Gregory reluctantly offered. If Tara had not been standing there, she imagined, he would have had a lot more to say.

Jasek bit off a laugh. "I'm not here for The Republic."

"Then why are you here?"

"To settle our wager. Something about the kind of leadership Skye needed. You seemed fairly certain, once, that it would be found right here." His glance found Tara hanging on every word. "It appears that you had to go looking, regardless."

Tara decided to interrupt the reunion before one of these men went a step too far past the line the other was willing to bear in public. Having Jasek Kelswa-Steiner carted away by security would not help Skye. Neither would the lord governor running his son off again, and with him the Stormhammers' strong military presence.

"We've all had to look for new strengths, Landgrave. Everyone," she said. "The entire Republic."

"Yes," he agreed, never backing down an inch. "And I found mine with the Lyran Commonwealth."

He threw it at her as both a challenge and an entreaty. Tara found herself drawn in by Jasek's strong will, wanting to understand his position, and that surprised her. She had expected to despise this man when she met him. Especially after learning how badly he hurt The Republic's local military by gutting it to form his Stormhammers. Of course, most of the information she possessed she had from Duke Gregory, so it was going to be slanted somewhat off center, but she'd assumed not too far.

Certainly she had not expected to empathize.

"Wherever you found it, you are standing on Skye. Which means we may have at least one thing in common in wanting to keep these people free." And she realized she did want to find common ground.

"Whatever else there is," she said, looking around at the audience of Highlanders, militia, civilians, "might be better served with a *less public* discussion."

Jasek hesitated, then bowed to her in a gesture of respect he had not shown his father. His eyes never left hers as she accepted a warm hand and shook it in agreement. "Whatever else might come between us, Countess," he said sotto voce, keeping it private between the two of them and his father, "I owe you this much, for standing up for Skye when I was not here."

There was something hard in his gaze when he said it. Something that said Jasek was not altogether pleased with her intervention. Neither was he upset, though, and the contradiction intrigued her. As did Jasek's raw magnetism. No wonder so many soldiers had flocked to his banner. This was not something that could be inherited or learned. It could only be something that *was*.

And Tara immediately set her guard against it.

Whatever else might come of Jasek Kelswa-Steiner's return to Skye, he would not gain one inch of ground on her for charm's sake. That much she promised herself.

11

It turned into a parade.

Jasek left the *Himmelstor* on the morning following his arrival in a small caravan of two Force Avanti armored stretch sedans, a single VV1 Ranger leading the way, and a pair of hoverbikes trailing. Alexia Wolf and Niccolò Gio-Avanti rode with him in one sedan. Colonels Petrucci and Vandel, newly arrived this morning, shared the second. They charged down the DropShip ramp, bumped onto the tarmac, and then sped across the wet-black ferrocrete toward a guarded gate on the north side.

Opening a breakfast drink, Jasek toasted the guards from behind tinted glass. It was a thirty-minute drive to the lord governor's palace, given normal morning traffic. Still time enough to chase away the last of the jump-lag left over from a ten-hour shift in his schedule traveling from Nusa-kan to Skye.

He preferred the banana-citrus combination, teasing his taste buds with something that tasted healthy while the hidden caffeine stirred his system awake.

"You really should try morning calisthenics," Alexia said. She'd pulled her soft brown hair back into a severe ponytail. Her face glowed a disturbingly healthy pink. "It really is a better way to start your day."

"If that's your excuse for crawling out of a warm bed at five this morning, you stick to it." Jasek took a long pull at the fruity beverage.

And he almost forgot to swallow as his short caravan charged through a very narrow gap between news trucks and two dozen film crews for the planetary media networks. Flashes strobed and camera lenses swung around to follow the lead sedan. Jasek saw several fingers pointed his way, even though no one outside could possibly see through the reflective tint.

"How do they know?" Alexia asked, putting voice to the same question running through Jasek's mind.

Jasek turned a suspicious eye on his best friend.

"You're big news," Niccolò said with a ghost of a smile. He admitted nothing more.

Jasek swallowed, the fruit taste suddenly losing its appeal. "So it seems," he said, deadpan.

Immediately north of the DropPort, a small industrial center quickly gave way to New London's largest commercial district. Cafés and clubs nestled between malls, museums, and monuments. Two news trucks managed to slip ahead of the caravan, blocking both northbound lanes. Holovid cameras pointed back with dark, unblinking eyes. Jasek looked behind him. Four or five more vehicles followed, weaving around as drivers fought for the best position to let their cameramen shoot out through the forward windshield or while leaning out the side windows. He saw one of the shoulder-mounted recorders swing out toward the side of the street. People on the sidewalk cheered and waved as he passed. More flooded out from the local businesses as news traveled faster than the caravan along the main thruway. Before long the intersections were becoming choked off by spectators, and another ten or twelve civilian vehicles had joined the procession, their occupants honking horns and holding defiant fists in the air.

His father's people had also tuned in on the news, apparently. Roadblocks cordoned off the street that ran by the lord governor's palatial mansion, holding back the press of onlookers as well as separating Jasek's sedans from his military vehicles. Niccolò glanced a warning at him, but Jasek simply nodded, letting them go.

Alexia looked back through the rear window, at the crowd that thronged up to the roadblocks. "I never knew you were so popular. People did not act this way on Nusakan."

"Nusakan has a fairer press corps," Niccolò told her. "The Herrmanns AG media group owns many news outlets on Skye, and they are unabashedly pro-Lyran."

"Be nice, Nicco." Jasek's glance was warm, but stern. To Alexia he said, "He's just bitter because the GioAvanti family lost their minority interest in a local news network in a forced buyout."

"Not bitter. Just jealous. There is a difference." Niccolò's pout was exaggerated. Slightly. It was good for a quick laugh.

Still, as the sedans pulled down into a covered garage, Jasek worried that the media attention would not help put his father in a receptive mood. The duke had yet to accept (and certainly he would never forgive) his son's difference in opinion and allegiance. Jasek had tried to make his father see, but a lifetime of blind devotion to a single man—including three years just to the *memory* of that man—was hard to fight. Even when Jasek proved he had the right of it, when seventy percent of the prefecture's armed forces followed him into forming the Stormhammers, the duke refused to recognize his position.

I do not like to see Skye divided, or improperly defended. Jasek had sent his father this message by courier. Between them, Skye was more than one planet. It was a symbol for the entire region. *It invites disaster.*

I also would not hold you hostage to the situation you find yourself in. If you cannot accept that Skye should stand proudly with the Lyran Commonwealth, at least grant that Skye cannot stand alone in the waning shadow of Devlin Stone's Republic. Call, and we will answer as allies of Skye.

The duke's reply took three weeks to return by courier.

Skye seeks no alliance or accord with those who hold their citizenship or their heritage so cheap. Do not answer. We will never call.

And he hadn't. Not even in the darkest time when the

horror-struck refugees from Chaffee taxed Skye's morale, or when the Falcons actually attacked Prefecture worlds.

Jasek had watched, and waited, and waited.

No more, he promised himself in the elevator and during the short walk down grand, marble-tiled halls. The echoes of their footsteps rang back like distant gunshots. "Skye must survive, even if first it has to die."

"What was that?" Colonel Vandel asked. A frown piled up on his forehead like a building avalanche. "Making predictions?"

"A resolution," he answered with a sharp glance at Niccolò. He hoped his friend was wrong, but planned for him to be right.

The formal meeting between Jasek's Stormhammers and Skye's defenders took place in the palace's east-wing gallery, where portraits of former Skye leaders stared at each other across a wide divide of rust brown carpet and a long, mahogany table. The paintings of Ryan Steiner and Robert Kelswa-Steiner, ancestors of the current line, held places of minor importance on either side of closed terrace doors. Duchess Margaret Aten, another leader from pre-Republic times, had the grand location over the fireplace mantel. Her dark, smooth skin and indigo eyes looked very familiar. They should, since Jasek saw them often enough in the mirror. His mother, the duke's second and last wife, had called Margaret Aten her grandmother.

Facing off against them were the five past lord governors of Prefecture IX: Skye's entire history under Devlin Stone's auspices, not counting Jasek's father, who had—in a rare demonstration of humility—decided that his own portrait would not be added until after he died or was voted from office. A pity. With his ties to the Atens as well as his position as the dynasty heir of the Kelswa-Steiners, a portrait of Duke Gregory would have balanced out the room.

Or perhaps not.

"The 'Salvation of Skye' has arrived," his father proclaimed, holding up the folded newsfax so that Jasek (and everyone else) could see the headline. It must have been warm still from the printer. A holographic picture of Jasek's caravan leaving the spaceport this morning ran just beneath the bold type.

The Duke slapped the sheaf of paper down on the table.

Next to him, Tara Campbell frowned at the dramatics. An aide handed the lord governor another. "And this one, 'The Herald of House Steiner.' How very poetic. Ah, this is my favorite." It had a large holographic pic of some protesters out in front of the spaceport, waving placards. " 'Lyrans Rejoice!' "

He threw the third sheaf onto the table with a measure of disgust. "Herrmanns!"

Legate Stanford Eckard and Prefect Della Brown seemed torn between applauding the duke's condemnation and worrying that Jasek might take his troops and leave. These were military leaders first and foremost, but politics ran a close second in their lives.

The fifth member of Tara Campbell's coalition did not bother to disguise his sour anger. Jasek recognized Paladin David McKinnon from pictures. Jasek also had researched the man's politics, and knew that McKinnon would likely rather see him put up against a wall to be shot for treachery than officially recognize the Stormhammers as a military or political entity.

A tough room. But Jasek felt the wall of strength behind him, his senior officers and his closest adviser, propping him up against the onslaught.

"These are your constituents, Father. They seem to feel that their voices are being ignored."

"I believe their voices are being given weight far out of proportion to their actual numbers by what amounts to a pro-Lyran conspiracy." Duke Gregory held his temper in check, but the vitriol behind his words burned Jasek deeply.

"However," he continued with begrudging reluctance, "it seems that a few people in this room believe that Skye cannot hope to hold against a return by the Jade Falcons without your help. Such as it is. The Countess and Sire McKinnon have convinced me that accepting your return is the lesser of the two evils facing us."

Which Jasek understood as Tara Campbell advocating acceptance, and Sire McKinnon agreeing that Stormhammer involvement was the lesser of two evils. At least, he hoped that was the way it broke down. Tara Campbell was a strong woman and a natural leader. After she had saved Terra from the Steel Wolves, her accomplishment in throwing the Jade Falcons back from Skye had only increased her legendary status. He recognized that. Was it a shock for him to discover that he actually cared about her opinion of him?

Maybe it was just a desire to have one friend in the room that he hadn't brought with him.

"We brought our force strength estimates," Jasek said, stepping up to the table as Niccolò stacked a pile of print-outs on the dark-grained wood. Next to the hard copy, his friend set data wafers and a few crystals.

An aide to Tara Campbell, limping forward with a cast encasing her right leg and a steel crutch braced under one arm, traded Niccolò for the short stack of manila folders she brought with her. While they dealt hard copy around the table, Jasek introduced his senior officers. Antonio Petrucci drew dark glares from everyone but Tara Campbell, who looked askance at Jasek.

"Colonel Petrucci served as Legate of Ryde before he came with me."

Alexia Wolf's brief introduction raised a few eyebrows. Colonel Vandel was roundly ignored. A good trait for a Lohengrin agent to cultivate.

"I already have a good idea of what you have left on planet," Jasek offered, taking a seat at the table. He gave the hard copy a cursory glance, saw a missing unit. An important one. "The Glenowens?" he asked. A storied unit with the local militia, it had been critical in Skye's recent defense.

Tara waved him farther down the file. "They and the Ducal Guard have been folded into the Seventh Skye Militia." She smiled thinly. "It's a motley assortment, but we can wield them as a much larger unit if we keep them together."

An interesting idea. Jasek wasn't certain he agreed, but wasn't about to argue the local politics. "The question is, then, what do we know about the Jade Falcons' remaining strength?"

"They came in with two Galaxies," Prefect Brown stated. She met his gaze evenly, showing no shame to the man who had beat her out for the loyalty of her own soldiers. "We believe the arrayed forces are roughly the equivalent of a mixed regiment. No more than that."

"I think it might be a bit stronger," Paladin McKinnon

offered. He was the only one to refuse a seat at the table, standing over the back of his chair, gnarled hands clamped on to the backrest. His eyes were diamond cutter sharp. "Maybe by as much as half."

Tara nodded. She thanked her aide, who hobbled to the back wall and rested there, staring over Tara's shoulder directly at Jasek.

"Obviously they hit Skye without their full strength last time. The Steel Wolves stated that a large unit had failed to rendezvous from Kimball II. We can hope they were destroyed."

"They weren't," Colonel Petrucci told them. "We put forces on the ground on Ryde right behind the Steel Wolves, gathering intel. We learned that a Star Colonel Helmer saved the majority of his assault force, and that Malvina Hazen sent in a relief force to free him up. Kimball II is under Falcon control now." He waved down the beginning of several outbursts. "But it may be that their hold is tenuous."

"Still." Jasek rubbed his jaw with one hand. A few missed whiskers pricked at his skin. "We have to assume a regiment and a half of troops spread over seven worlds."

"Six," Della Brown corrected him. Her gray blue eyes looked inward, counting them again. "Four in Prefecture IX. Two others in VIII."

Tara sat next to the Prefect. She placed a hand on Brown's arm. "I believe Jasek is counting Chaffee. The Falcons' staging world inside the Lyran Commonwealth."

"Not our problem," McKinnon declared. Then he reconsidered slightly. "Except that it spreads the Clanners a bit thinner. We might be able to use that."

Jasek thought so as well. If the unstable coalition being formed on Skye could move fast enough. But as the morning wore on into afternoon, with arguments over every assumption, every plan, it began to look less likely that an accord could ever be reached. "Look," he finally said, slamming one hand down flat on the table. "We don't need to put every Falcon warrior and his machine in an exact spot. Generalities are good enough for now."

"I agree," Tara said, the constant friction wearing on her as well. She didn't look nearly as polished as she had appeared this morning, Jasek noted. But he was willing to bet that she'd clean up nicely before any press cameras got within fifty feet of her. Alexia Wolf thumped his knee under the table.

Tara missed the quiet byplay entirely. "I'm more worried about our exact force accounting. Even with the mercenaries we hired off Galatea—and I'm not completely confident about their usefulness—I don't believe we have enough strength. Not for a protracted campaign."

Niccolò broke his silence to agree. "Any ruler who keeps his state dependent upon mercenaries will never have real peace or security."

"We had enough military force last time," Jasek's father reminded them. "The people of Skye will never surrender to Clan occupation. In fact, in four Succession Wars *and* the Jihad, Skye has fallen only once into enemy hands, and then not for long." He stroked his beard thoughtfully. "With the kind of damage visited on the Steel Wolves in the first assault, the . . . the . . ." He couldn't bring himself to call the Stormhammers by name. "Jasek's people are a stronger, battle-ready unit."

"That doesn't change the fact that if I could find the Steel Wolves, I'd swallow my pride and ask them to stand with us again." Even that admission had seemed a hard one for Tara to make. Her skin flushed with embarrassment or anger, Jasek couldn't say which.

"Even then . . ." She shrugged. "Several things worked in our favor last time. The Falcons rushed themselves. They fell for several traps, which they will be wary of doing when they return." Her voice took a melancholy turn. "And they were momentarily stunned by the suicide charge of our Forlorn Hope task force. Which they will prepare against, which is why I think we should not attempt to try that again. It would be a terrifying slaughter, and for little gain."

Jasek agreed. Out of the corner of one eye, he saw Niccolò nodding as well. Actually, having reviewed media coverage of the event, he knew that his friend felt the slaughter gained very little the first time. A high cost for a diversion.

But that's what commanders do. They gamble with lives.

Jasek had felt stung by the oversimplification. *I do not gamble.*

No. You are quite the Lyran. You assign a value to each life, and spend them with a miser's reluctance.

He still was not certain if his friend had paid him a compliment with that comment.

"Why do you think that the same tactics will not work the next time?" Colonel Vandel asked.

Jasek took the question for her. "When the Falcons come back, it won't be with the gut punch strategy they tried before. They will strip every occupied world to its minimum garrison. They will land, plant their flag, and stand by it until the end. They will not retreat, and they'll make every victory a costly one for the people of this world. So much so that the population will welcome any end to the fighting."

His father hedged, no doubt imagining his world so hard struck. "What makes you so certain?" he asked.

Tara looked at Jasek. Jasek stared back. Barely perceptibly, she nodded. "Because that is what we would do," she answered for him.

Jasek leaned back in his chair, staring down into the table's dark surface. His exhale was long and weary. "That is how you take Skye."

═══ 12 ═══

New London
Skye
9 October 3134

Jasek had always enjoyed roaming the capital house library as a child and as a young man, losing himself in the labyrinth of corridors and galleries and great rooms lined floor to ceiling with books. The scent of old paper and new print. The feel of leather as he ran a hand down one long shelf of texts after another. The awe-inspiring silence, broken by soft footfalls and scuffs against tight-knit carpet.

Here he read and he studied. He explored with Niccolò GioAvanti and other friends, and together he and Niccolò discovered two secret passages that, by all evidence, had been forgotten even by state security. And standing in just the right archway or corridor, he eavesdropped on whispered conversations and learned as much about ruling and The Republic as he had been formally taught by his father.

Good memories. Happier times.

Still, the musty, paper smell that permeated every room was a welcome, warm embrace and not the melancholy reminder he had feared when Niccolò suggested taking the library as a personal residence and the Stormhammers' command post.

It was a strong political move as well. Under the auspices of previous lord governors, the mansion residence attached to the library was the home of Skye's Steward—an appointed aide who served as liaison to the world governor on behalf of the prefecture's ruler. With strong lord governors, in fact, legislation passed through the offices of the Steward first and to the world governor second. There was no small amount of prestige attached to the local mansion, and the man who resided within. And it had been available. Duke Gregory was one of the rare Republic leaders to hold both world and prefecture leadership positions at the same time, which was a measure of the duke's—and the family's—powerful support within the Isle of Skye region. When Jasek's father had need to appoint a Steward, mostly during times when he traveled off-world, that appointee took up temporary residence at the Governor's Mansion in New Gloucester, which was otherwise treated as the duke's summer offices.

Now Jasek prowled around a long table in the library's Commonwealth Room, the space dedicated to cataloging the latest texts coming out of Lyran space. The banner of House Steiner—the clenched gauntlet—hung below a wide skylight, equal to the mezzanine level that wrapped around three sides of the grand room. Jasek's senior officers worked in busy clusters, updating force strength estimates and designing strategies based on what the Jade Falcons might try next. Junior officers drafted as aides ferried and fetched noteputers, maps, and reams of hard copy at request.

His graceful strides ate up the blue carpet one meter at a time while his eyes scoured a noteputer's amber screen. He tapped in a request for more detail, handed the 'puter off to the team formed around Colonel Petrucci and Tamara Duke, then accepted a thermal-insulated mug of spiced coffee and a sheaf of reports from Niccolò GioAvanti.

He took a sip of the hot beverage, enjoying the cinnamon flavor. The coffee warmed him on its way down, and a hint of cloves rolled out on the aftertaste. The drink was fine, but the intel . . .

"Not good," he said after a cursory glance at the hard-copy material. Jasek had been briefed by Tara Campbell—in her newfound manner of terse, clipped sentences—about what to expect.

"The Highlanders' force readiness is hardly up to battalion-level strength. That's the best they can do?"

Niccolò shrugged. "It's what they have, Landgrave." In public, his best friend always defaulted to the formal address due a member of the nobility. No matter how much Jasek berated him for it later. "The Highlanders have spent a great deal of blood for The Republic lately."

It was hard to fault Tara Campbell for fighting the depre-dations of Steel Wolves, Dragon's Fury, Swordsworn, and any number of other factions rising within The Republic. Her loyalty was beyond question. But the lack of direction from higher up, a lack of support from The Republic's standing army . . . it was like fending jackals off a dying body with a slowly splintering stick.

"What a damned waste of good men and materiel."

Tugging at his family braid, one of his more obvious stall-ing tactics, Niccolò finally volunteered, "Difficulties must never be allowed to persist in order to avoid war. Wars can only be deferred to the advantage of others."

A military maxim that Jasek placed from several old texts. "Isn't that what I've been doing, Nicco?" Jasek was never certain when his friend was being wise or intention-ally witless. "Avoiding war? With the Jade Falcons? With The Republic?" With his father?

He would never ask that last question aloud. He did not have to. Niccolò knew him well enough to understand the demons that wrestled within.

And as usual, when the questions grew toughest, Niccolò defaulted to vagueness. " 'The hereditary prince has less cause and less need to offend than a new one,' " he quoted directly this time.

A roundabout method of reminding Jasek that any strug-gle directly against his father put him immediately at odds with the old worlds of the Isle of Skye. Was his only answer to let Skye fail on its own, and then pick up what pieces remained? He drank deep and hard, barely able to taste, punishing himself with the close-to-scalding beverage. He set the mug down on the table.

"I want a better solution," he told his friend. Louder, he said, "We're chasing the problem in circles, people. Find another way."

"You couldn't have been more interested in another way before you stripped Skye of its defenses?"

The familiar scorn snapped Jasek around at once. Duke Gregory stood inside the double-wide arch at the room's entrance, waiting to be recognized. Some of Jasek's more junior officers snapped to nervous attention. Everyone rose at the table, showing respect for a duke's title at the very least.

New demons stoked the fire burning in Jasek's heart. His blood coursed. "Leaving Skye in the manner I did was 'another way,' Father." He put just as much sarcasm into the two words as the elder man. "Would you care to discuss my other options publicly"—he nodded at the gathered Stormhammers—"or in private?"

"Avoiding public spectacles has not exactly been your way, Jasek." Still, Duke Gregory stepped inside the arch, clearing the way for people to leave. "Perhaps privacy is warranted for what we have to discuss."

A few of the Lyran Rangers, remembering their previous time in the Triarii and the Principes, acknowledged the duke's dismissal with a rapid departure from the room. Jasek noticed that even Tamara Duke took two steps before stopping to wait for Colonel Petrucci, who remained in place. Jasek nodded a dismissal to his senior staff. Colonels Vandel and Wolf, with no ties at all to the former Republic military, were slowest out the door, and only a few paces behind Niccolò GioAvanti.

Alexia Wolf cast one quizzical glance back at Jasek, which Duke Gregory caught, and then was gone.

Security agents stationed outside the room pulled shut heavy doors that filled the archway with golden-stained oak. There was a kind of finality in the heavy thud of their closing.

Alone with his son, Duke Gregory threw formality and carefully studied appearances out the window. He let some of the weight he carried slough away. Slouching into a chair at the head of the table, he spread his hands on the warm, varnished surface, looking for all intents and purposes like a father sitting down to a meal with his family.

The last several months had not been kind to his father, Jasek saw. The extra gray sprouting in his beard and at his temples, the bags that showed more clearly under his eyes when he relaxed the political mask, the weary slump to his shoulders. But the same ardent fire still burned behind the duke's bright, hazel eyes.

"Legate Eckard informed me that you had commandeered the library," Duke Gregory finally said. "Nice maneuver. Confers legitimacy. Your idea, or Nicco's?"

Jasek let the silence answer for him.

The lord governor nodded. "He always was the more politically savvy," he said with a touch of regret. "You," he continued, "you had the military mind, boy, and the drive. And the devil's own charm, which you inherited from your mother. I just wish you had picked up more of her devotion to Skye."

"Perhaps I did." Jasek strolled around the far end of the table, headed back along its length toward his father. He ambled, in no particular hurry, stopping from time to time to rest a hand on one of the empty chairs.

"Maybe I picked up more than you wanted me to. Mother was not the slavish adherent to Devlin Stone's philosophies that you are. She believed in The Republic only so far as it benefited our people." He said "our people" in a way that excluded his father, and an angry flush warmed the old duke's high brow.

"You are going to educate me about my own wife now?"

"Do I need to? Or have you already forgotten the mealtime debates when she pushed back against your enthusiasm for Stone's Republic?"

The duke's hands balled into fists, but Jasek noticed a slight tremble, as if he had touched a raw nerve. "Your mother *never* stood against me," his father said, tight-lipped.

"No," Jasek agreed calmly. "Not like I have done. She tempered you. It was a good match. At the right time in Skye's history." A stab of longing cut into Jasek's chest. His mother was five years passed away. At times, he wondered if she would have accepted his stand against The Republic. "But it is history, Father. Our worlds have come as far as they can under The Republic."

"So now you'd like me to toe the media line and welcome you back as the savior of Skye?" the duke asked. He snorted his disbelief. "I came within millimeters of having you arrested for treason and thrown into a deep, dark hole, with Niccolò not far behind you."

"We both know you can't touch Nicco. The GioAvantis are too powerful an old Skye family."

"Damn the luck," the duke admitted, "or he *would* be arrested. Or worse."

"That was uncalled for." Jasek clenched both hands around the high back of a nearby chair. "Nicco was like a second son to you."

His father levered himself to his feet. "And just as loyal, it turned out," he said hotly. "Maybe if I'd stripped him of favor as a pup, you'd have done better being raised an only child." He calmed himself with visible effort. "But now my prodigal son has returned, eh? Well, I'm not about to kill the fatted calf for you, boy."

Jasek nodded curtly, not having expected such a welcome from his father. The two of them simply could not agree to disagree, and too much tied them together, making a clean break just as impossible. Blood ties. And their mutual concern for the worlds of Skye.

"Not asking it," he replied.

"But you're going to ask me for something," his father said, dialing back on the open antagonism a few notches. He nodded at the table full of documents and glowing note-puter pads. "Four days you've been working in here. You must have some idea of what you want, and how you'll proceed."

Jasek pulled out the chair he gripped, only two seats down from his father, and slipped into it. A tall pile of hard-copy documents rested on the table in front of him. "Skye is wounded," he said, toying with the pile. Slick-panel folders slid haphazardly against each other. "I shouldn't have to tell you that. I know Tara . . . Countess Campbell . . . has kept you informed. But I wonder if you understand how close you are to losing this world."

"I'm sure you'll remind me every day," his father said through clenched teeth.

Jasek let a touch of his ire show in his eyes. "One good push," he said, shoving at the top of the document stack.

The pile tipped and slid apart, scattering files and documents over the polished wood surface.

The demonstration seemed to rattle the duke more than hard words would have. He sat down again. "Think you could take my world with these Stormhammers of yours?"

"Yes." Jasek didn't bother to deny that his people had looked at that. "We could. But it would not solve the greater problem. We could take Skye, but never hold it. Not against the Jade Falcons."

"Fortunate for me that my entire realm is under assault, then."

"It allowed you to accept help from the Steel Wolves," Jasek reminded him. "Surely you can extend the same courtesy to my people."

The duke bit off the first reply that formed on his lips. He thought a moment, putting a bit of steel back into his shoulders as he squared them off against his son. "What do you have in mind?" he asked finally. Quietly. A man backed against a wall, staring down a loaded gun.

Jasek's finger was on the trigger. He folded his hands on the table in front of him, to keep their tremble from showing.

"Tara Campbell allowed that she'd take help from Anastasia Kerensky. With her offer in hand, I hope to bring them back to Skye. Them"—he swallowed dryly—"and any other allies I can rally to our defense."

His father slapped at the table, the *bang* reverberating around the large, empty room. It ricocheted back from the open mezzanine with a tinny echo. "You're talking about House Steiner!" he accused Jasek. "Isn't one enemy at a time enough?"

"The Lyran Commonwealth is not massing on our borders. They did not send in a large military force on some fabricated excuse. But they just might offer us some help if it meant protecting their own interests as well."

"Once they come back, we'll never dislodge them." Duke Gregory shook his head, denying the vision. "I'd rather see Skye burning around my ears."

Jasek recoiled. "Truly?" he asked. He waited for his father to bluster that he hadn't meant his words literally, but the lord governor remained silent. Always a good political move.

"Well, you just might get that wish before this is all said and done," Jasek said. He slid back his chair and rose, leaning over the corner of the table. "And that is an image I want you to hold very, very close to your heart, Father. You have a good champion for Skye in Tara Campbell. I know you have your own plans in motion as well. You always do. But before you make a final decision, I want you to think on one idea.

"That if it comes down to a choice between the Steiner fist and the Jade Falcon raptor," he asked, "which would you rather live under?"

13

New London
Skye
9 October 3134

Following Niccolò GioAvanti down the corridor and around a corner from the closed door and the two security agents, Alexia Wolf quickly and quietly padded up a set of wide green marble stairs only a few steps behind him. The intense young merchant shot her a measuring stare, which she returned with interest. But he said nothing, which suited her as well.

She had no idea what he was up to. Only that she felt certain he would not take to being shut out of the father-and-son discussion. In the short time she had known him, Niccolò had proved himself resourceful, spirited, and utterly devoted to Jasek.

One of Jasek's greatest draws, in fact, was the quality of men and women he kept around him, and his means of doing so. It was the first measure of a leader's intelligence and strength, to see what kind of advisers he kept. Jasek Kelswa-Steiner did not suffer fools or sycophants. He searched out strong-willed people who challenged him.

Meritocracy might be an Inner Sphere term, but it was a concept that all Clan warriors understood.

". . . the devil's own charm . . ."

The snatch of conversation whispered to her at the head of the stairs. She turned her head, searching for more, but if it had been there at all, it was lost now.

Niccolò stealthed ahead of her, down the narrow third-floor corridor, without any reaction whatsoever. Alexia followed, thinking rapidly on what she thought she'd heard. It could have been Jasek's father. Certainly it described Jasek. One glance was enough to cause her heart to pound in her throat and set her skin tingling with anticipation. The duke's son had a raw, powerful magnetism that attracted men and women equally. She recognized this, though that did nothing to prevent her being affected by it. She at least did not confuse it with the self-serving righteousness many of Jasek's soldiers wore like a protective mantle.

Or *love*, which was also an Inner Sphere term but a concept not wholly unknown among the Clans.

More snippets of conversation whispered in her ear as she chased after GioAvanti. ". . . Stone's philosophies . . ." and then ". . . our people . . ."

". . . about my own wife now?"

She was certain this time. Something about the library's acoustics formed an echo chamber, dumping tidbits of the conversation taking place below into this deserted upstairs corridor.

Alexia guessed where Niccolò was leading her even before they passed through a small sculpture gallery and then stepped to either side of a door that opened onto the mezzanine level above the Commonwealth Room. A wide parapet ran around three sides with shelves of books guarding the walls and a balcony rail overlooking the center of the room. The warm scent of so many leather-bound volumes was stronger up here. She tasted paper on the back of her tongue. Staying close to the wall, they were invisible to the lower level, but they had a perfect vantage point for eavesdropping.

Niccolò slouched against a shelf of books.

Alexia adopted a modified parade rest.

The two stared at each other across the open doorway.

It became a kind of game, to see who could react the least to what was being said below. She caught a glimpse of amusement on his pinched face when Duke Gregory admitted that he could not touch Niccolò because of his family ties. Alexia thought he should have been more concerned that Jasek's father saw the merchant as an obstacle to overcome.

And she did not doubt that he noticed her eyebrow twitch when Jasek talked about finding Anastasia Kerensky and her Steel Wolves. Then the conversation turned back toward the idea of Jasek approaching the Lyran Commonwealth.

"I'd rather see Skye burning around my ears," the lord governor gritted.

"If it comes down to a choice between the Steiner fist and the Jade Falcon raptor," Jasek asked, "which would you rather live under?"

Silence followed Jasek's question. Alexia doubted that either man noticed that at this moment, both stood under the House Steiner banner that hung suspended beneath the room's skylight.

The clenched gauntlet was familiar to Alexia from her time with the Wolf enclave on Arc-Royal, but it had never meant much to her until Jasek made it important. This was the reason she had sought him out, followed him to Nusa-kan and now back to Skye. Jasek was a leader, and offered her direction as well as this second chance at a warrior's life. On Arc-Royal, when she failed to test out, it had been because she thought that being a warrior was enough. The end-all of her life.

It had taken a rebellious Republic noble to give her a measure of true purpose. Maybe not her own, not yet, but it was a start.

Finally, from below, Jasek's father answered, "I do not accept your terms. One choice must be to remain under The Republic's banner."

"The Republic sent you a battered command and one out-of-favor Paladin. This does not show a great deal of confidence in the Exarch's ability to protect his own."

"You are selling the Countess extremely short."

"Not at all," Jasek said. Alexia could almost see him shaking his head with adamant resolution. "Tara Campbell has performed miracles. I'm not denying it. But she cannot make the difference all by herself. Even she knows that."

There was something in Jasek's voice when he spoke Tara Campbell's name that tweaked a nerve with Alexia. A depth of respect and admiration that she had never before heard in the young leader, not even in praise of his own Stormhammers. She wrote it off as a meeting of equals—two faction leaders with genuine respect for each other's abilities and strengths. Nothing more, she assured herself.

Jealousy was another Inner Sphere concept. It had nothing to do with her.

"You seem to be the authority these days on what other people know and believe. Would you like to know what I believe, Jasek? That you've chased a childhood fantasy of romantic heroism and Lyran destiny to the point where if you do not make it happen yourself, then you would rather see Skye in the hands of a true enemy. Because otherwise you have to face the failures piling up behind you. Failing your converts. The Republic. Our people. Failing me *and* your mother."

"Leave her out of this."

"You brought her into this, boy. Choose your battlefields more carefully next time. The fact is you were born to privilege, and with that came certain obligations. To serve the people before you served yourself. To honor the family line, and continue it. But you haven't even attended to that, have you? You've thrown over every match we ever tried to make for you. No wife. No heir. No future!"

This kind of argument would not help matters. Worrying about offspring on the cusp of battle? Alexia was freeborn herself, but here again she recognized the superior ways of the Clans, that they had long ago divorced themselves from the need to seek immortality through procreation. Clan warriors distinguished themselves in duty and glory first. And even if they died, their lines were continued through the breeding program.

"The future takes care of itself." Jasek sounded truly angry now. She had heard his temper simmering beneath his words the entire time, but now it threatened to explode. "Isn't that what you taught me? Study the past and work toward the now?"

"And The Republic shall provide," Duke Gregory finished with a wounded snarl. "Yes, I said that. But it won't provide Skye with an heir. Your selfish manner notwithstanding, I'd think that even you could have figured out the political necessities by now."

Personal abuse would accomplish nothing. Alexia moved for the door, looking to Niccolò to see if he would follow. He merely shook his head, slowly. He was obviously going to stay, no matter how uncomfortable the conversation in the room below. His pale blue eyes showed neither avarice for gossip nor the cunning mask of one who looked to turn such knowledge to his own advantage. He was a blank slate, absorbing all he could for later benefit.

Alexia saw no benefit. Not in a military sense, anyway. She shrugged, and stepped back into the adjoining gallery just as Jasek said, "I'll produce your heir with the right woman, not just a politically expedient one."

It was not the banner under which Alexia had thought to meet up with Tamara Duke, who leaned against the wall just inside the doorway.

Tamara's green eyes widened only slightly at her discovery. Or at seeing Alexia come through the door when the only person she could have been able to see from her vantage point was Niccolò GioAvanti. Had she followed them up, or discovered the surveillance point on her own?

How much had she overheard?

"Too bad." The lord governor's voice carried into the room quite strongly, losing little of the sarcasm. "I suppose this means it is too much to even hope that you've sired a bastard along the way? I've seen the way she looks at you."

Which could mean any of half a dozen women who had been in the company of both Jasek Kelswa-Steiner and his father over the last four days. But the way in which Tamara's eyes narrowed accusingly, the kommandant obviously pegged Alexia for it.

Alexia wondered. Tamara Duke wore her feelings on her sleeve, after all. Though no doubt the junior officer thought she was cagey about it.

Jasek did not help. "I don't know who you are talking about," he claimed.

If he didn't want to admit anything to his father, even in their supposed privacy, then both women could only be left wondering.

There was no rank in this room. Not even a moral high ground. Not when both had caught each other listening in on a conversation that should have been private. Alexia met the challenging stare with a blank face. When Tamara Duke stepped toward her with a sharp, determined stride, she tensed the muscles in her calves, her arms, ready for violence.

But the other woman stopped short of raising a hand to her. Staring through her, Tamara simply bit off every word as she warned Alexia, "Stay out of my way, Wolf."

Turning on her heel, Tamara strode from the gallery without a glance back.

Behind her, Jasek maintained his position and his father pressed. Niccolò glanced only once into the gallery, again showing none of his own thoughts. Cataloging. Considering.

Alexia shook her head. In public, in private, in banter or in battle with Skye hanging in the balance. Everyone had his or her own agenda, and she would be well advised to keep a ready eye on her own.

That was not a thought to cause surprise, it was simply a fact of life.

In the Clans, or in the Inner Sphere.

14

An icy breeze blowing in off the distant North Inlet carried a hint of brine and the sharp, acrid smell of gunpowder into Norfolk. In the shadow of a partially completed *Overlord*, Tara Campbell pulled her wool overcoat tightly closed at her neck. She walked the edge of the DropShip's "cradle" with Paladin McKinnon and Legate Eckard, ten stories up, surveying the nearby battlefield and the hive of activity that buzzed through the streets surrounding the Shipil Company dockyard.

It had taken less than an hour on-site for Tara to understand that the dockyards were the reason Norfolk existed. Its industrial center was twice as large as it would be for any similar-sized city. The commercial sector half again as small. There were no office building skyscrapers or highrise apartments. Since nothing could compete with the thirty-story vessel under construction, the massive cradle that surrounded its lower third, or the multifactory complex nearby that required six months to turn out just one interplanetary drive for the mammoth vessels, no architect or construction company even tried.

"A people who know who they are," McKinnon said when she voiced her observations. From the cradle's north corner, they could look west toward the recent battlefield and, several kilometers beyond, the azure bluc waters of the North Inlet, or east toward the low-lying sprawl of Norfolk. His hard eyes narrowed. "And now they know what they are."

"A prime target." Tara nodded.

Yesterday's Jade Falcon raid had pushed no closer to the city than the borders of Shipil Company property, but that was close enough for most of the locals. So many had called in to take the day off from work—laying in provisions or moving their kids to relatives far outside of the city or just plain worried for themselves—that the corporation had dismissed everyone with pay for forty-eight hours.

Very few civilian vehicles moved on the streets. Tara easily counted two dozen Maxim hover transports, patrolling with a hastily scraped-together militia. A Praetorian rolled into the Shipil parking lot, establishing a local command post. A pair of Drillson hover tanks and SM1 Destroyers flanked the mobile HQ.

Tara pointed out a gap in the snow-dusted hills to the west. As she had hoped, the cradle gave them an incredible overview of the surrounding terrain.

"So they came through there in column formation. One *Griffin* leading a short company of hovercraft. The local defenders took a piece out of them just this side of the gap."

Legate Eckard raised a set of field glasses to his eyes, nodded. "Shipil Company keeps a small mercenary force under contract. Last month I supplemented them with a lance of Condors and a Kinnol main battle tank." Eckard was a small man, but had a bodybuilder's shape. There was no mistaking the knuckle-whitening strength with which he gripped the field glasses. "If they had been on the ball, they would have plugged that gap with the Kinnol and shoved the Falcons right back toward the coast."

"While we're wishing," McKinnon said with a nasty edge, "if they had been veteran troops, we'd be counting up Jade Falcon salvage right now."

"So the defenders retrograde back toward the industrial area," Tara continued, keeping the peace by drawing both men back to their purpose at Norfolk: to assess damage and make preparations for any follow-up raids. "They lose a pair of Condors crossing the river." She couldn't see the silver-blue stream they had visited earlier, but a winding cut in the woods to the west gave her an idea of where it was. "And they set loose some Gnome infantry in the forest to slow down the Falcon advance while they reset the lines right out there."

Right out there was the wide-open ground where local tree farms had been harvested only a year ago. Several square kilometers of bare-branched saplings tied up to stakes, blackened craters, and burned-out vehicles.

"More room to maneuver," Eckard said.

Sire McKinnon snorted. "More room for the Falcons too. You can't stay on the defensive against a small, maneuverable force."

Tara watched as a VTOL snaked its way down the river's twisting cut. It dipped down low, beneath the treetops. "And a small force had no hope of taking the Shipil Company dockyards. So was this simply an intelligence-gathering raid? Or did the Jade Falcons hope to accomplish something more here?"

"They had a J100 salvage vehicle. They might be trying to replace some losses of their own." But the legate did not sound too certain himself.

The Paladin turned his weathered face toward the city's main stretch, then turned to look up at the DropShip that towered over them. Not all of its armored hull was in place yet. There were still weapon bays to finish and a docking collar to install, but engines and navigation were intact according to all reports.

"Could be they were thinking of grabbing the *Overlord* and fell back when they saw it wasn't quite spaceworthy. Afraid we'll get it finished and deployed before they make it back in force."

"We will," Tara promised. She wasn't about to let such valuable hardware sit there for the Falcons to claim as battle spoils. *Isorla*, they called it. "We need to advance the manufacturing lines at Cyclops, Incorporated, as well."

It was more a mental note than an opening for a new

discussion. Neither man commented. Sire McKinnon continued to study the DropShip, the towering cranes that rose up from three corners of the massive cradle complex, and the work that would remain unfinished by the crews for the next day and a half. Legate Eckard focused his glasses on the VTOL, which jumped up over the tree line and skimmed above the nearby battlefield. A Cavalry, the craft had sharp lines that pulled back severely from the missile systems that blunted its nose. It thundered straight for the trio, as if intent on finding them, then banked into a long, slow turn that circled it back over the killing grounds.

"Company?" she asked. She shivered as the wind ran icy fingers through her spiked hair.

"Jasek." Eckard waved a dismissal. "Never was one to be content with reports. Della's been complaining about his people in the New London Tower, pulling every battlerom we've collected from the Jade Falcons' first assault on Skye."

Tara could understand that. Prefect Della Brown had a larger grudge against Jasek than anyone had, save perhaps his father. Legate Eckard had lost a handful of troops to Jasek's Stormhammers. Brown had lost nearly the entirety of the prefecture's standing army, and then had watched as the Jade Falcons rolled over worlds unopposed.

"We could do worse than listen to a fresh perspective," Tara said, shading her own reservations with a touch of optimism. A large part of her position here as Exarch Redburn's direct representative seemed to be bridge building. If Skye had any hope of standing free from the Jade Falcons, Tara could not allow demons from the past to set fire to her carefully constructed work.

Eckard lowered his field glasses. "I hear he's been tearing into your plans for a counterassault as well." The legate looked at her with curious brown eyes.

Why should that surprise her? She had copied the Stormhammers on plans she'd put together with Paladin McKinnon, hoping to draft them into her upcoming operation. So Jasek Kelswa-Steiner had some criticism to offer. So what?

So what if she wanted to bridle right there in front of the legate and Sire McKinnon, who now gave her the same careful attention he'd spent on the DropShip a moment before? Studying her. No doubt seeing the parts that lay open, unfinished, with work delayed by circumstances beyond her direct control. McKinnon knew a few of the areas that lay exposed, but he had avoided poking at them again since that evening in the O-club, and he didn't say anything now.

He simply watched.

"All right," she said, not altogether against a debate with the Stormhammer leader, but not eager for it either. But how much of that was personal, and how much professional? He'd make some good points, she was sure. She nodded toward the Praetorian crawler. "Why don't we adjourn to the local command post, then, and invite the Landgrave down?"

Sire McKinnon shrugged. "Why not indeed?" he asked.

Tara couldn't help but feel that she had missed something important in the Paladin's simple question. Was Sire McKinnon warning her, or offering tentative support for her building an alliance with the Stormhammers?

Whichever it was, she knew, he would make his feelings known soon enough.

Jasek jumped down from the VTOL's open bay, feet splashing through icy slush that coated the parking lot's paved surface. Colonel Joss Vandel followed him. The Cavalry's blades hammered overhead, still pounding at the air, but Jasek didn't bother to duck. No VTOL had been built yet that would take a man's head off for not crouching down, and he had always thought it stupid when a soldier worried more about the perfectly safe rotors than he did the battle that waited just ahead.

Which was what he was looking forward to, he felt certain.

Battle.

"Landgrave." Tara met him with a warm handshake and cold, blue eyes. She had a warrior's grip, made more obvious by the hard callus at the base of her thumb that told of her years of experience at the control stick of a BattleMech. "It is good to see you again."

For all her initial warmth when they first met at the New London DropPort, their last few meetings certainly hadn't made him feel particularly welcome. Not that he needed

Tara Campbell's favor. He simply hoped to win it. And that was not likely to happen today.

He quickly reintroduced Colonel Vandel. Tara had certainly not forgotten the Stormhammers officer, but it gave Jasek the chance to break the ice between them with a social chisel.

"I hoped to catch up with you," he said as the three of them walked into the shadow of the two-story Praetorian. Legate Eckard and Paladin McKinnon waited near the command vehicle's armored door. "We'd like to speak with you about your plans to strike back at the Jade Falcons."

"Not one for small talk either," Tara said to Eckard with a tight smile.

Her offhand comment and the legate's frown left Jasek with the feeling he and Vandel had interrupted a conversation. Had she been asking about him? It threw him off his stride for a few seconds. But the dark glower ever present on the Paladin's face helped him snap back quickly. Some things in the universe were constants.

"Since you were hoping to launch at multiple Falcon positions in three days," he said by way of explanation, "there doesn't seem to be much time for dalliance."

The inside of the mobile HQ was warm and well lit, with armored shutters open over ferroglass windows to reduce any feeling of claustrophobia. The command-level officers filed back toward the rear of the massive vehicle, taking over the Praetorian's small but well-equipped strategic office. The room smelled of electronics. Legate Eckard and Tara Campbell slid over bench seats and around to the rear of the holographic display that doubled as the room's only table. Paladin McKinnon stayed at the door, leaning back against it with an air of finality.

Jasek did not doubt that he was stuck in this room until McKinnon decided to let him leave. He also took a seat at the table/display, leaving Vandel to stand at his shoulder. The Lyran officer set himself in an easy, patient stance.

"As you say," Tara finally broke the uncomfortable silence that had followed them into the office. "There isn't a great deal of time. Yes, I intended to strike back at the Jade Falcons. But with this latest raid . . . ," she trailed off.

"It wasn't a raid," Jasek said evenly. "It's a bluff."

"What?"

"It's a bluff. They had no hope of taking salvage or even creating much havoc against Shipil Company. A short company to attack a DropShip? Even an unfinished one? No. What this has done is draw your attention here. To Norfolk. Which means they will ready their play somewhere else."

"New London?" Eckard asked. "We would prepare against them at the capital regardless." Answering his own question, the truth lit up his eyes. "Cyclops, Incorporated."

Jasek shrugged. "That would be my guess. Cyclops manufactures the Drillson and the Maxim, as well as weaponry for the *Wolfhound* and *Banshee* BattleMech designs. That's the kind of prize they need to further their goals against other worlds."

Tara tapped a thoughtful finger on the glass tabletop. "Which means they are readying their next assault." She considered, nodded. "Our plans, as you've seen them, involve a series of simultaneous strikes. None would force them from a world they currently control, but they would throw them off-balance and hopefully push back any timetable for a new assault against Skye."

"This has been in the works for some time, I take it?"

Tara nodded hesitantly. "Sire McKinnon and I consulted with Legate Eckard weeks ago. We agreed on the need to buy Skye more time." She paused, obviously considering, then, "But it wasn't until your arrival with the intelligence gathered by your Stormhammers that we had all the data needed for such a plan. We didn't"—she shook her head—"*I* didn't inform you at first, as we were adapting earlier plans made in your absence."

The politics of alliances. Jasek knew that game.

"I noticed that you did not make use of my Stormhammers in your plans," he said, conceding the point easily, as he did not particularly care about the late notification. Only the results. "Your Highlanders will be spread very thin. You plan to hit three worlds in simultaneous strikes?"

"Ryde," Paladin McKinnon said from the door. His voice was as abrupt as his manner. "Zebebelgenubi. Glengarry."

"Glengarry is the most important world, naturally," Eckard elaborated. His tone held a touch of conciliation. "We know that is the world the Jade Falcons are using now as their staging grounds."

"But they were using Chaffee," Vandel reminded them. His voice was deep and broken, like a rusted gate. "It is a redundancy."

"We don't intend to throw the Falcons off Glengarry regardless," Tara said. "We only want to shake them up a bit, and make them burn time. Weeks. Hopefully months. Skye can use whatever we can purchase."

"Then allow me to chip into the account," Jasek said, warming to the idea.

He caught himself leaning in toward Tara Campbell, and pulled back reluctantly. He had to keep things professional, with a wary eye on how they would use his people. Tara's divine reputation aside, he never doubted she was for The Republic first and foremost.

"I think you should modify the target worlds, and pull back some of your Highlanders in exchange for most of my Stormhammers."

"Which worlds would you change?" Tara asked.

"Trade Summer for Zebebelgenubi." Jasek's first recommendation was his easiest sell. "We just hit Zebebelgenubi, so they are on high alert and spoiling for another fight."

"Summer isn't part of Prefecture IX," Eckard said.

No. It wasn't. Summer sat just over the border into VIII. "Why should that matter to you?" Jasek asked Tara directly. He glanced at the Paladin. "It's still part of The Republic."

McKinnon thought about that for all of three seconds. "Maybe the better question then is why should Summer matter to *you*?"

But Tara knew the answer, Jasek saw. She leaned forward, intent on his face, which he held impassive. "Because Summer is a world of the old Isle of Skye. Isn't it?" No need to answer. "If your Stormhammers land there, and the people rally to them, you could throw the prefecture borders into dispute."

Jasek shrugged as if the thought had never entered his mind. Niccolò had bet him a gentlemen's wager that Tara Campbell would see through that play. He was ready to pull it from the table in exchange for a stronger position on his next move.

"Also," he offered, "thanks to a quick and nearly bloodless conquest, Summer's docile population is settling in under Jade Falcon reign. The garrison there is complacent and can be severely hurt, which might inspire some of the local population to rise against the occupation."

Tara hesitated. "He makes a strong case," she said. She weighed in Eckard's and McKinnon's vote by glance. "What if we use the Highlanders for Summer?"

Jasek had not counted on Tara's so easily volunteering to shift her own forces away from Glengarry. But that played as well. "Then you don't have to worry about any pro-Lyran uprising," he said. "And I'll support the Highlander drive on Glengarry as well."

"Why not simply give Glengarry to your people?" Eckard asked. "Why spread the Highlanders so thin if you are truly on board?"

Jasek smiled. "Well, you should give Glengarry to me, since my people know it better than any outside force. But regardless, it will take us both, since I have one more target I'm putting on the table." He had their attention. "It is my intention to hit Chaffee as well. By stirring up the Falcons on both their staging worlds, inside and outside of The Republic, we can hope to accomplish more toward setting back their timetable."

A flicker of interest sparked behind McKinnon's dark eyes. "Doing favors for the Steiner court?" he asked, measuring his gaze between Jasek and Colonel Vandel.

"Opening a bridge to the Commonwealth is not the same as handing over Skye to House Steiner," Jasek pointed out. "Let's at least keep the option on a future alliance. That's just good business." He saw a wary look in every eye, and decided to raise the pot. "Plus, I'm going to hit it with or without any formal blessing from Skye. If you're so worried about me, have my father put his stamp on it."

Tara's dark glance told Jasek that he had forced her into a corner, and she didn't like it. But he knew there was only one way out, and that was his way. Or *their* way as everyone did, in effect, get what they were after.

Compromise. Again, the politics of alliances.

"It might work," she finally admitted. "But we counted on at least some of the Stormhammers remaining on Skye to guard against a new Jade Falcon raid. We'll be spread very thin with just the Seventh Skye Militia, a few Highlanders, and mercs."

"I'll leave at least a third of my people here," he guaranteed her.

She frowned. "That's an awfully light force left to you for hitting two stronghold worlds. Even with my Highlanders assisting on Glengarry, you are going to need more troops."

"I'll get more," he assured her.

There was that wary look again. "Where?" Tara asked. Almost an accusation.

Time to play his trump card. His ace in the hole, which he had saved in the last week for just such an occasion. "I have my resources," Jasek said breezily.

But seeing that the others would never be content with that, he leaned in toward Tara as if spilling a confidence. Maybe she had drawn him in, despite his best preparations to ensure the Stormhammers held themselves as an independent party. But she couldn't see everything. And that gave him an advantage.

"I know where the Steel Wolves are hiding," he told them all.

15

*When newly acquired states have been accustomed to
living freely under their own laws, there are three ways
to hold them securely . . . [the third] allows them to
live under their own laws, taking tribute from the new
rulers who are friendly to you.*
                    The Prince, by Niccolò Machiavelli

**Longview
Cowlitz County, Chaffee
19 October 3134**

The maddened warrior came right for him.

Noritomo Helmer waited in a ready crouch, his back to
a cement-slab monument commemorating the founding of
the city of Longview, and ignored the spectators who
waited around the edge of the city's small central park. His
combat boots found ready purchase against the cement
patio, anchoring him in place. He controlled his breathing.
His focus centered on the other man's midsection, watching
for a telltale shift of weight.

At the last second, Noritomo raised one knee as if planning to spear-kick the charging warrior.

The other man leaped into a flying kick. It was exactly as Noritomo had planned. He ducked low and crabbed forward, getting beneath Star Commander Gregory. Grabbing the other man's folded leg, he thrust up and backward and threw Gregory sideways into the monument.

There was a sharp *crack* as Gregory's lower arm broke against the slab's corner. His face left a smear of blood and skin down the rough side. He landed poorly but kept to his feet with one arm braced against the upright slab.

Noritomo stepped back. He waited, facing his staggered opponent and the dark gray monolith.

The city's central park boasted of little more than this simple monument and a few concrete paths poured between fresh-cut lawns and sparse flower beds, but it was quickly becoming known as "Warrior's Park" as challenge after challenge was decided here. The round patio made for a perfect Circle of Equals. Many trials had been fought before his arrival—before his banishment to Chaffee—as a new pecking order shook itself out among the Jade Falcon castoffs. This was Noritomo's fourth challenge in a week. He'd killed the first two, as object lessons. The third he merely knocked unconscious, hoping to preserve a good warrior.

Gregory he'd yet to decide about. The man was hot-tempered and shortsighted, a poor combination of genes that told of a Roshak blood heritage. An armor commander *and* a freeborn warrior, Gregory began with an inferiority complex when comparing himself to a trueborn MechWarrior like Noritomo.

If that had been Gregory's motivation for this Trial of Grievance, Noritomo would have already planned to kill him. Now he waited for any sign that the man—and the warrior—could be salvaged.

Nothing so far.

Spitting out a tooth, Star Commander Gregory stalked forward more cautiously this time, closing with his garrison commander. He held his broken arm carefully to one side, protecting it.

Noritomo deflected an eye-gouging fingertip strike and a kick at his groin.

A punch glanced off his shoulder. Another bruised his left chest.

The next he trapped and *pulled*. Gregory stumbled into

Noritomo's elbow strike, catching it in his jaw. A hammer fist to the center of the forehead staggered the armor commander back again.

And when the pain cleared, Noritomo saw doubt and frustration at war in the other man's eyes. There was no cold-blooded arrogance in the other man, not anymore. He looked trapped. Already beaten. But Clan warriors did not simply surrender. Having called out the challenge, he could not in good face call it off. Honor drove Gregory forward the third time.

Which was why Noritomo decided to let the man live.

This time he did spear-kick his opponent, stopping Gregory dead in his tracks with a foot planted into his gut. Air rushed out between Gregory's teeth. Noritomo stepped down, chopped at his opponent's broken arm, then slipped one leg behind Gregory's knee and delivered a final ridge hand to his temple.

In a tangle of limbs, Gregory fell back. Unconscious.

Star Captain Lysle Clees broke the circle then, stepping onto the paved patio. Even unarmored, the woman was impressive: more than two meters tall and solid with muscle. A tangle of blond dreadlocks swept down past her shoulders. She motioned forward two warriors from Gregory's Star. The tank crewmen approached warily, which was good to see.

Helmer dismissed them with barely a nod.

"Wake him. He walks to the garrison post from here. I accept his *surkai* if he makes it without passing out." Fifteen kilometers with a broken arm. Was that enough to salve the man's honor? Lysle raised an eyebrow. "He will have it reset without pain meds." The large woman nodded imperceptibly.

With everyone's honor intact, Noritomo headed for the nearby city hall, which the Jade Falcons had commandeered. Lysle fell in next to him.

"A good choice. The man is stupid, but not necessarily untrainable."

"We will have a hard time reconstituting a new cluster if I keep killing off warriors," he agreed. "If I had seen one ounce of the same arrogance I measured in Malvina Hazen . . ." He let the thought trail off, not wishing to step over the line, even in front of his longtime friend.

"Galaxy Commander Hazen is a strong leader." Lysle grabbed the door for him, held it open, and then ducked beneath the header to follow him inside. "She will bring the Jade Falcons much glory."

Armed guards secured the corridor, and the two lapsed into a determined silence until they reached Noritomo's commandeered office. It was on the second floor of the two-story building. A fully suited Elemental stood watch in the upper lobby. The armored infantryman traded nods with Lysle Clees. It had taken Lysle only one Trial after their arrival to establish dominance over the battlesuit soldiers. Noritomo envied her calm acceptance.

Safe behind his office door, he shoved aside a collection of data crystals and laid his hands atop the smooth, polished metal surface of his desk.

"If she can accomplish our goals quickly enough," he reopened their conversation, "perhaps. But look at Ryde and Glengarry. Look at what we have had to deal with here. Nonstop aggravation from the populace. They are afraid of us, yes. No one wants to provoke another blistering-agent attack like Malvina used to 'soften up' Chaffee before our first assault. But neither do they respect our rule or work for the betterment of the Clan. They will turn on us the instant they see an opening."

There was no chair into which Lysle Clees comfortably fit. She remained standing. "Relations have settled down in the last week since your arrival," she noted.

"Because I do not occupy their capital or pretend to be a replacement for their world governor. I appoint a new governor whom the people can respect, and who now owes his position to me and relies on my force of arms to keep his newfound power. It is an imperfect solution, but long term it will work."

"You have been reviewing the reports off Alkaid and Summer." She flicked a large finger at the pile of crystals, scattering them.

Noritomo nodded. "Aleksandr Hazen had the right of it," he said, speaking of Malvina's twin. Such a tragic loss to the Clan, that he was the one who fell on Skye. Rescuing his sister, no less. "He took those worlds with hardly any losses, following Clan custom of bidding the lowest amount of force needed and then honoring the local government so long as they abide the Falcon occupation. Over time, they will grow dependent on us."

"Or they will appease us only so long as they can find no opportunity to assassinate us in our sleep." Her tone told him how little she thought of Inner Sphere honor. "Star Colonel, you know you have my loyalty, but what do you hope to accomplish here that even Aleksandr Hazen was unable to do? He fell on Skye. By Clan ways, he is proved wrong. You will fight the Way as well as the Eye?"

The Eye of the Falcon. Meaning Malvina. If ever there was an argument against allowing a cult of personality to grow up around a Clan warrior, even one so accomplished as her, this was it.

"Was Aleks proven wrong?" he asked. "Galaxy Commander Malthus has laid several of our failures at his feet, his and Khan Pryde's. But we were not there, Lysle." He glanced down at his desk, and chose a dark blue data crystal from the scattered pile. "These are interviews I have conducted on Glengarry and here on Chaffee. As it turns out, we have several warriors who served with Aleksandr Hazen, fought with him on Skye. While careful not to call Beckett Malthus a liar, they have some interesting tales to relate."

He pushed the crystal toward her. "Take it. See what you think."

She picked it up, the small crystal looking lost in her large hand. "I do not need recounts of the battle to know that Aleksandr Hazen fought bravely and died with honor." She closed her massive fist. "But I will use this to form an opinion on the warriors who survived and are currently with us. We need to work this motley group into a coherent unit, Star Colonel, and we need to do it quickly."

He agreed. Malvina Hazen would not be delayed long on Glengarry. When she moved against Skye again, they had to be ready to follow. Somehow he would redeem his honor, lost on Kimball II. Somehow he would be in place when, not if, Malvina stumbled.

"Find me four good warriors," he instructed his friend and adviser. "The best we have. We will build them into the core of a new cluster, and we will show Malvina Hazen and Beckett Malthus that the pride of the Jade Falcons does not extinguish so easily."

A ghost of a smile turned up the corners of Lysle's mouth. "The last man who tried to teach our distinguished leaders anything wound up a martyr to their cause," she reminded him.

All too true. And if there was an immortal life beyond that granted by the Clan breeding programs, Aleksandr Hazen must be livid with fury. "Review the data, Star Captain. If you believe I am wrong, that this is not a cause worth fighting for, I will temper my approach." But he would not abandon it.

Noritomo Helmer would live as a true Clan warrior, or die trying.

He doubted that Malvina Hazen would give him a third alternative.

16

DropShip Himmelstor
Venite DropPort, Seginus
23 October 3134

Jasek watched as the Shandra scout vehicle sped up the *Himmelstor's* main ramp with little regard for caution. Anastasia Kerensky stood in the front passenger seat, hands braced on the windshield's upper edge, riding tank commander style, her dark red hair streaming behind her. The vehicle's front end bounced as it hit the deck of the DropShip's main bay, working the suspension to its limit. A sharp jag to avoid a pallet of munitions, tires grinding against the deck's nonskid surface, and another as the driver swerved around a disassembled Gnome battlesuit being serviced inside an area roped off with yellow tape. Then the vehicle powered to a short, abrupt stop.

He did not think it an accident that the missile rack atop the Shandra ended up pointing directly at him and Paladin McKinnon.

"Cocksure little bitch," McKinnon growled.

With good reason, Jasek knew. Despite serious battlefield losses in the last year, Kerensky had kept a firm grip on the Steel Wolves. Not an easy task for an outsider, come to

The Republic from Clan Wolf to challenge for the faction's leadership. Having watched Alexia struggle with her peers in the Tharkan Strikers, Jasek knew how accomplished this woman had to be. Even her position here on Seginus, trading her services as planetary defender for local support, argued in her favor.

Of course, she had some serious history behind her name to help back her play.

"Find me a descendant of Aleksandr Kerensky and the Black Widow who *can't* hold her own," Jasek said, "and I'll be impressed."

"Find another one who is even half as predictable as the weather," McKinnon cut right back. "It's a large gamble for risking half of your strategy."

More and more Jasek regretted being saddled with Sire McKinnon. The man was an incredibly strong personality. He had the damnable habit of being right far too often, and self-righteous whenever the facts were open to debate. Already he had rewritten half of Jasek's battle plans for Glengarry. Though not for Chaffee—any mistakes Jasek wanted to make outside of The Republic seemed all right by the venerable Paladin.

Which included Anastasia Kerensky.

Kerensky had not bothered to duck back into the Shandra's open cabin. She simply levered herself up onto the side frame and rolled off the top of the vehicle as easily as a child might fly down a playground slide. The warrior-leader had long legs that efficiently absorbed the short fall. Instead of a formal uniform, she wore black leathers with red piping down the arms and legs and a high mandarin collar, emblazoned with a red hourglass across her flat abdomen. The mark of the Black Widow—a nod to her ancestor, Natasha Kerensky, who had been one of the best warriors of any generation.

Except for a few welding arcs, sputtering against the armored side of a nearby Kelswa assault tank, most work around the DropShip's bay had come to a halt. Officers and enlisted stared, some in open hostility, others in frank interest. Anastasia Kerensky knew how to make an entrance—that was certain.

Without waiting for the man who slid out of the Shandra after her to catch up, she struck out toward Jasek. Colonel

Petrucci and Tamara Duke had been talking near the feet of Tamara's *Wolfhound*, only a few meters away from where the Shandra had come to its final stop. They stepped forward, partially into her path, but she blew by both of them without a word. There was no telling how she recognized Jasek, but quite obviously she did.

She also had to be aware of several weapons pointed her way from surprised—or simply cautious—infantrymen. Alexia Wolf, on the far side of the bay, had slipped into the turret of a Demon to cover the Shandra. A full lance of Stormhammer BattleMechs stood silent guard over the large DropShip bay. In her position, Jasek would be concerned that an assault force had managed to drop on-world with only a few hours' warning. The Seginus system had a twenty-eight-day burn time—very strong gravitational fields creating a great defensive barrier. The Stormhammers' ability to calculate a nonstandard jump point had to have her worried.

But he saw not one hint of hesitation or concern in her determined stride. In a way, she reminded him of Tara Campbell. All duty and poise.

"You are interrupting my day," she said without preamble, still several meters away but closing the distance with long strides. "Get to it."

So much for poise. Jasek blinked away his surprise at her condescending tone, and put a restraining hand on McKinnon's arm. "You have a lot to do here on Seginus, do you? Local merchant spacers on liberty call giving your Steel Wolves a hard time?"

She stopped an arm's length away. Hands on her hips, leaning in toward him. Open and aggressive. Her grin was half feral. "Legate Hateya did not tell me you had a smart mouth." Which explained how she had picked him out of the crowded bay. It was a piece of information freely given.

Be careful, she was saying. *I know things.*

"That's funny. It was one of the first things Tara Campbell told me about you."

So it was a small lie. It got his point across: Jasek knew things as well.

It backed her off somewhat. She glanced back as her man sidled up, late. He had blond hair and a secretive smile, and wore an old Republic uniform stripped of its regular insignia. He kept his hand well away from the Sunbeam laser pistol strapped at his hip.

Petrucci and Tamara Duke had accompanied him, helping close a tight box around the two Steel Wolves.

"Campbell pointed you here?" Kerensky asked warily, turning her back on Jasek's officers. She seemed not the least bit worried at her position.

"I found you on my own. Rumors floating back along the shipping lanes. Legate Hateya requisitioning armor and actuators for a local militia with only a few modified IndustrialMechs. Plus"—Jasek smiled easily—"*one* jump out from Skye *and* Glengarry? Able to strike in either direction? It felt like a choice you would make."

She folded her arms, supporting each elbow with the opposite hand. "How would you know that? We've never met."

"You haven't exactly kept a low profile, Tassa Kay." It was a name she'd used before, just one more fact the Stormhammers' intelligence-gathering raids had uncovered. He shrugged. "And the Countess provided background as well."

That seemed to satisfy the Steel Wolf leader. She relaxed ever so slightly, settling back off the balls of her feet. "Did she provide the Paladin as well?" she asked. It was her first recognition of McKinnon. With it, she gave him a small bow of respect.

"This is Sire—"

"I know who David McKinnon is and I know why you are here," Kerensky cut him off, never taking her gaze off the venerable warrior. To him she said, "I have studied your exploits from the Jihad. The raid on Terra. The last stand at Krupp Armaments." There was a measure of envy in her voice, but a sly look in her green, predatory eyes. "And I have heard about the Founder's Movement. If you are working with the Stormhammers, Skye is in trouble. Again."

Whatever his personal thoughts of contacting Kerensky, McKinnon revealed nothing that would jeopardize Jasek's plans. "Was there any doubt the Falcons would come back for it?" the Paladin asked.

"Not really," the second Steel Wolf answered for Kerensky, joining the conversation. "Star Commander Yulri," he introduced himself directly to Jasek, then shrugged. "I was not on Ryde or Skye, but Tassa filled me in on happenings. A blind surat could have seen this coming."

Kerensky nodded. "But since it was made very clear that it was not our problem, we left there. Now we are here." She sounded very final.

Jasek had no intention of giving up without a fight. "I would think the Black Widow would want to be wherever the action is." As taunts went, he thought it not too bad of one.

Until Kerensky bit into him with a glare. "Let's get one thing clear right now. I am not the Black Widow." She brushed a hand over the red design on her abdomen. "I wear the hourglass as a tribute to my gene-mother, but I'm my own warrior."

Natasha Kerensky's *daughter*? That was one for the history books. "And your father?" he asked, instantly curious.

"Is my business," she said, bluntly evading the question. "Let us say that I have a lot to live up to, all right? I do not need more baggage from you. Quaiff?"

He nodded, gaining a slight measure of understanding for Kerensky. And understanding could lead to persuasion. "Aff," he said, answering her rhetorical question in Clan fashion. Then, "Very much, aff. I know something about trying to live up to a legendary heritage."

She hesitated. Jasek didn't think he was meant to see it, but he caught the brief flicker of interest in her eyes. He knew how to play it too. Strike a very calm and confident pose. Wait.

"And what have you discovered?" she finally asked.

"You can't do it. Ever." He let a smile build on the corners of his lips, spreading slowly as if he shared a secret with Kerensky. "But we still try, don't we?"

It was as if no one else existed in the conversation for a few brief heartbeats. McKinnon and Yulri were forgotten. Tamara Duke chewed jealously on her bottom lip, but was held back from comment by Petrucci, who put a hand on her elbow.

Anastasia Kerensky nodded slowly. "We're not given much choice."

They might have been defeatist words, but Jasek heard the pride in her voice and thought he understood it. She looked at those expectations and saw the challenges to overcome, and the glory there to be won. The desire for personal accomplishment did not burn quite so hot in his blood, but the duty he held to the people of Skye filled its place nicely.

And like Kerensky, "I would not have it any other way."

She chewed on that for a moment, face held in an impassive mask. He saw her decision come with a light behind her eyes. One edge of her mouth turned up in a seductive smile.

"All right," she agreed. Not so much chipping away at her icy exterior as she was smashing it with one blow. "We can talk."

17

Recalled from Glengarry's capital of Dunkeld with news of the midnight raids, Malvina Hazen crouched within the Skadi's small passenger compartment as the VTOL turned above her Acropolis and then thundered over Tairngoth's rolling hills for another two kilometers before it circled in for a landing. The craft's landing skids bumped against the ground and a side door rolled back with a metallic grind. Night still clung to the Tairngoth area like a funeral shroud, damp and chill with the promise of coming rains. Malvina Hazen promised herself she'd pull that shroud around several Republic warriors before morning.

Beckett Malthus met her as she jumped down from the VTOL, the tall warrior standing defiantly beneath the still-thrashing blades. Running lights washed his face in amber and emerald, and his stormy eyes showed a hint of anger in them.

At her, or reserved for the attacking Republic troops?

Malvina did not care, and she did not bother with much

more than a curt nod as she surveyed the impromptu staging area with a critical eye.

Her *Shrike* and an accompanying *Shadow Hawk IIC* stood guard, their three-story profiles backlit by elevated banks of fluorescent lights. A maintenance vehicle lifted two technicians and a half ton of missile reloads up to the back of her 'Mech. Two short columns of vehicles warmed up nearby, stagger-parked against each other like a row of broken chevrons. From the air she had noticed that they pointed more or less in the direction of Glengarry's false dawn—where Dunkeld's lights reflected against the heavy cloud cover. And eighty kilometers beyond that, Malvina knew, the sky would cast back a reddish-orange glow as the Argonaut Munitions Depot blazed in a fire too hot for even the toughest firefighters. She imagined the taste of ash and burned gunpowder that would be choking the air around the fire.

Well, she'd be tasting blood before the night was through, if Beckett had readied everything according to her orders.

"You have an Alamo missile standing by?" she asked without greeting.

He frowned at the lack of courtesy, but Malvina was not about to play formality games. Not this night. Beckett had pledged himself to her.

"With reservations," he admitted, pacing her on the short trip between VTOL and BattleMech. "We have exactly three of the nuclear-tipped missiles. I am not so certain this is the best time to use one."

Malvina unzipped the wrists on her jumpsuit, then paused to raise one foot and then the other to loosen her ankle zippers as well. "Here or on Skye," she said with a shrug. "If we can destroy a large number of Republic troops, it will be well spent. I have no intention of letting this pitiful excuse for an assault rob us of honor."

Malthus nodded, and Malvina decided to accept that as the Galaxy Commander's full agreement. She felt the night's clammy touch on her left arm, and also climbing the exposed skin on her left leg. Her right side . . . nothing. Neither warmth nor chill. Her prosthetic replacements reacted to nerve firings, imitating the function of real limbs with a full range of motion, but the sensory details coming back the other way were limited. She could sense pressure, and would feel simulated, low-grade pain if the replacements took severe damage, but not much more. That was the trade-off for a hasty return to combat status. For not waiting while the scientist caste vat-grew true limbs.

That was the trade-off for getting back to Skye as soon as possible.

Only Skye had come to her this time. Several companies, striking at a wide range of targets meant to harass her local defenders. Summer and Ryde had reported heavy raiding assaults as well over the last week, and the loss of too many standing garrison troops. That would not happen here!

"We push them back to their DropShips," Malvina told him, waiting for technicians to clear the lowering gantry. "With one Alamo we might bring down a *Union*, or an *Overlord*. Cost them a full company or two in mixed forces. Let them take that back home as the cost of such a foolish venture."

She struggled into the gantry's cradle, still not as coordinated with her replacement arm as she might wish, but unwilling to wait for the lift to lower completely to the ground. The cradle reversed direction, lifting her toward her cockpit.

"Stand ready," she ordered Malthus.

If he thought to argue the point any further, he decided to wait until she had fully suited up for battle. Malthus turned for a Tribune mobile HQ that waited at the head of the vehicle column. Malvina Hazen beat him into position by clambering quickly into her cockpit and stripping out of the jumpsuit, pulling it off over her combat boots. The jumpsuit went into a locker built into the back of her command chair, traded for the thin cooling jacket that would keep her body temperature down in the strain of combat. The jacket had abbreviated sleeves, stopping just above her elbows, and was made from black ballistic cloth in case she was forced to eject (again) onto a live battlefield. On each shoulder was stitched an emerald eye, like the false eyes under a cobra's hood. Aleksandr had had them sewn into the cloth after both of them made the rank of Star colonel.

It was one of the few physical reminders of her lost twin that Malvina kept.

Sliding into the waiting seat, she reached up for her neuro-helmet, which rested on an overhead shelf, and settled it over her head with a snug fit, careful that the receptors made good contact with her scalp. She stuck two telemetry pads to the inside of her left thigh and above the left wrist. Her replacement bionics had built-in telemetry. Finally, she threaded a braid of three cables through the loops on the front of her cooling jacket, and connected the single jack into the socket at the neurohelmet's base.

The technician who had walked the ninety-five-ton *Shrike* to the staging area had left the fusion engine on hot standby and her computer on. What was left for her was to release weapons and full gyroscope capability, and remove the speed dampeners that locked into place while in maintenance mode.

On the ten-key pad at her left hand, Malvina keyed in her personal cipher. The computer awoke with several new lights flashing for attention. She toggled them all on.

"Identify," a synthesized and vaguely feminine voice directed her.

"Galaxy Commander Malvina Hazen."

The computer processed that for several long seconds, comparing her voice patterns with those stored on a secure storage device. Finally, the computer prompted, "Proceed with secondary protocol."

Because the technology existed to fake voiceprints and crack number ciphers, most BattleMechs carried a second authorization key that was necessary to turn over complete control to the MechWarrior. This was a private code that could be known only to the warrior. Malvina had lifted an obscure line from the Jade Falcon Remembrance, the living prose that told the entire history of her Clan back to its founding.

" 'Let the Falcon take flight in a new generation,' " she quoted. " 'Let the stars be its hunting grounds.' "

As status lights cleared from amber to green, Malvina throttled forward into a ground-hammering stride that pushed her *Shrike* toward the front of the waiting column. Nothing would slow her now.

This was her generation.

And it was time to hunt.

18

Chauncy Plateau
Tairngoth, Glengarry
4 November 3134

Alexia Wolf tensed over the controls of her *Uziel*, unable to shake the jangling nerves that often plagued her in combat. The examiner in charge of screening freeborn applicants for Clan Wolf had promised her it was nothing. The trembling of a hunter scenting blood. Alexia knew only that the prickling sensation crawling over her scalp had been at its worst just before she failed her Trial of Position, when her testing partner turned on her, and had never once heralded good news.

"Here they come." McKinnon's voice was dry and leathery, and calm for a man about to step into the teeth of battle.

It was all the warning she received from McKinnon or her own nerves. The *Shrike* they had detected moving up on their position—waiting between Dunkeld and the local Jade Falcon military reservation—was coming fast with only a pair of Nacon armored scouts as company. Stormhammer spotters had a vehicle column and a *Shadow Hawk IIC* about a kilometer back, also looking for the open plateau on which the Tharkan Strikers waited. With Colonel Petrucci hitting three targets within close proximity, McKinnon had judged—correctly—that the Jade Falcons would push units from their Acropolis base toward the city. In an audacious gamble, the Paladin pushed far ahead of the main strikes to counter any reprisal by the Jade Falcons. Alexia brought her company along for support.

The plateau was a backdoor route into Dunkeld. It was also the site of an old battlefield, where some now-forgotten mercenary command had fought against occupying forces. Rusted hulks littered the landscape for a dozen kilometers in every direction, creating a background magnetic-resonance disturbance where a company of Stormhammer machines could hide itself. Their angle of attack wasn't the best, and in short order the Falcons might overwhelm their position, but at the moment the advantage belonged to the Skye forces.

Alexia caught an electric blue flash out of a stand of scaly firs, recognizing the capacitor discharge of a Gauss rifle. A silver blur smashed into the *Shrike*'s left shoulder, shoving it around. Stabbing lances of red energy followed as McKinnon threw chivalry to the wind and followed up his ambush with lasers. His *Atlas* shouldered aside tall trees as if they were young saplings, and strode into the open.

"Striker Team One." Alexia opened up communications, switching her sensors from passive over to active. "Advance and fire."

A light *Pack Hunter* broke cover from a nearby quarry, leading out a Kinnol and two Hasek MCVs, which staggered into a line-abreast foreign formation. Alexia stood her *Uziel* away from a pile of rusted vehicle frames. Her PPCs had enough reach to throw some additional damage at the wounded *Shrike*, but not until McKinnon cleared her line of fire.

A lesser MechWarrior would have fallen under the Paladin's savage ambush. The *Shrike*'s pilot was apparently made of sterner stuff. Staggering to one side, the ninety-five-ton machine quickly got a solid stance back beneath it. Turning, it levered forward both of its ultra-class autocannon and belted out extra-long pulls from each. Slugs tipped in depleted uranium hammered at the *Atlas*, ripping long gashes through the assault 'Mech's pristine armor.

McKinnon spent another Gauss slug at the Clan machine, but this time the *Shrike* was ready. It lit off jump jets, spoiling the Paladin's aim with a short, sideways hop.

Landing, it again chewed through nearly a half ton of ammunition, spraying out high-velocity streams of death. The razored metal sliced away tons of armor from the *Atlas'* front, raining it down around its feet in shards and impotent splinters.

Alexia powered into a run, trying to clear McKinnon's *Atlas* and grab an angle of attack on the *Shrike*, but not soon enough. The *Atlas* staggered. Unbalanced from the hard-hitting assault and losing several tons of armor in a handful of seconds, the lordly machine could not hold to its feet, even under the masterful touch of a veteran warrior. It fell, crashing back into the same stand of firs from which it had emerged.

Which left Alexia head-to-head with a machine that outclassed her by forty-five tons!

Her nerves rang loudly as the *Shrike* turned its full attention to the *Uziel*. Not only that, but the Nacon scout vehicles were throwing themselves into the fight, buying time for the Falcon MechWarrior. One Nacon peeled away as a brace of particle cannon from the Haseks crisscrossed argent streams in front of it. The other took a scalding strike from the Kinnol main battle tank, leaving globs of molten composite burning between Caterpillar tracks.

Alarms screamed for Alexia's attention as missiles spiraled in on her position, blasting holes into her armor protection. An offhand stream of autocannon fire picked at the *Uziel*'s lower torso as the *Shrike* walked its fire from the downed and struggling *Atlas* over to her.

"That warrior has skills," Sire McKinnon warned her over the command frequency they shared. "Wary."

She had no time for wariness. But a little good fortune was always appreciated. Twin blasts of argent lightning slashed out from her PPC barrels, coursing across the field, snaking into a tight braid until one stream of energy could hardly be distinguished from the other. Both carved into the *Shrike*'s left arm, burning deep through the damage already caused by the *Atlas'* Gauss rifle.

The arm hung limp and silent at the *Shrike*'s side.

It bought Alexia Wolf a reprieve from the same debilitating fire that had scoured McKinnon's *Atlas*, though for not much more than a moment as a pair of Jade Falcon Skadi VTOLs jumped above the tree line and added their fast-flying autocannon to the *Shrike*'s reduced firepower.

One of the VTOLs buzzed her backup line, worrying the Kinnol MBT, which had a hard time returning fire. Gnome battlesuit troops spread out from the Haseks, but they could do little except take cover as well.

The second VTOL chipped at McKinnon's *Atlas*, now back on its feet and limping forward to join Alexia in pressing the retreating *Shrike*.

The Jade Falcon column had gained the plateau, and the enemy MechWarrior throttled into a reverse walk to close ranks. The *Shrike*'s ultra-class autocannon hammered more of Alexia's armor into useless scrap. An arriving trio of Skanda light tanks sniped from long range, more hot metal spanging against the side of her machine. They ran defense for a pair of SM1 Destroyers and a late-arriving *Shadow Hawk IIC*.

Alexia toggled for an all-hands broadcast, but McKinnon seemed to sense it and whispered, "Wait for it," over their command frequency.

A Tribune command vehicle lumbered up from the back of the Falcon column, bringing a Kelswa assault tank and a handful of hoverbikes with it. They looked to be the last of the enemy forces. It was hard to tell, with the magres interference and her HUD a jumble of overlapping signals. The interference working in favor of the Stormhammers now also worked in favor of the Falcons.

"But we were here first," Alexia Wolf whispered to herself.

She gave herself a soft count of ten, just to be sure. Then, engaging her voice-activated mic, she ordered, "Striker Team Two, slam the door!"

From a shallow valley leading off of the plateau, a second lance of vehicles stormed up and into the right rear flank of the advancing Falcons. Two JES missile carriers, spreading warheads about them right and left, led the charge. A pair of Condors followed, adding in their own missile packs and challenging the Destroyers with medium-class autocannon.

For a moment, the plateau was a tangle of chaotic firefights. Missiles rained down on both sides of the Jade Falcon line, geysering dirt and rock and scorched brush into the air. A few fireballs blossomed over a line of Elementals, scattering the infantry into hiding places.

Lasers slashed back and forth.

A Gauss slug from McKinnon's *Atlas* smashed into the front of a Skanda, crumpling its slanted nose and crushing the barrel of its light autocannon. Another Gauss shot clipped a hoverbike, sending it end over end in a death roll.

Alexia combined her long-reaching PPC fire with more from the Haseks, sending bolt after bolt of man-made lightning snaking across the flat ground to open a hole for Team Two, which continued to pound on the Destroyers.

The SM1s were no pushovers, though. Powering about on a cushion of air, the assault hovercraft drifted backward, turning their twelve-centimeter cannon against the lighter Condors, smashing back with raw force. In a display of devastating unity, both Destroyers concentrated fire on a single Condor. The hammering streams of metal ripped open the crew compartment, cutting through men and materiel both, then reached deep into the engine to rupture the fuel tank.

Greasy flames erupted back through the compartment, finishing off any crew missed by the hail of slugs. The Condor slewed around to the left, out of control, and piled into a short stack of boulders.

The vehicle flipped over onto its side and was still rocking back and forth when a secondary explosion finally tore it apart.

"Welcome them home," Alexia called out, and every one of her units turned its firepower on the Falcon line right where the Jessies and the remaining Condor would cross. The Destroyers, still drifting backward in their own retrograde maneuver, sailed right through her sights. She pulled the crosshairs over, waited for a solid lock on one, and sliced another pair of PPCs across its skirting.

Air spilled out from beneath the SM1, and it settled hard against the ground before the lift fans shattered and spun the entire vehicle back up into the air and around in a violent pirouette.

The three remaining vehicles of Team Two skated through the hole and raced home to their brethren.

"All units, prepare to withdraw."

McKinnon's *Atlas* had advanced far enough to retake point position against the *Shrike*. "We aren't done yet," the venerable Paladin reminded her.

No, they weren't. The Falcons were massing behind the assault 'Mech and the *Shadow Hawk IIC*. The fight wasn't out of them by a long shot. And the *Shrike* was too damned fast for an assault machine. If the Stormhammers withdrew now, it would catch them and deal some serious hurt.

As if summoned by thought, the *Shrike* leaped forward on jets of plasma, bringing its medium-range weapons into range and hammering again at the *Atlas*. One of the Skadi swift attack VTOLs followed after it, but a spearing laser blast from McKinnon severed its tail rotor. The craft cork-screwed into a steep bank, erupting into a ball of orange fire.

Still, the *Shrike* came on.

Jasek's Stormhammers weren't so numerous they could spend their forces casually. But Alexia recognized a tactical necessity when it kicked her in the teeth. McKinnon had called this play and she'd backed him, and the Jade Falcon assault 'Mech was determined to call the bill due.

McKinnon had closed down her fire lane again—wanting the *Shrike* for himself or simply trying to push her toward backing up her own people first, it was hard to say. Well, maybe it wasn't, given the old Paladin's opinion of non-Republic troops. But his *Atlas* was limping, which put him already at a disadvantage and would slow the Strikers down on their coming retreat. She would not leave McKinnon behind, no matter if he would or wouldn't return that favor personally.

She knew what she had to do.

"Team One, advance by pairs and alternate fire at your best target. Team Two . . ." She bit down hard on her tongue for a few heartbeats. It wouldn't be pretty, what she had to ask those hovercraft to do. "Two, slide back around. Try to isolate the *Shrike* and by the Great Father, watch your backs in there."

She pushed her own throttle to the forward stop, racing the *Uziel* ahead at better than ninety kilometers per hour. She followed an oblique line after the *Atlas*, trying to get a clear shot past McKinnon.

The *Shrike* worked its own angle against her, shaving the *Atlas* down one ton of armor at a time while keeping the awesome machine between them. The Kelswa assault tank crept up in the shadow of the Falcon *Shadow Hawk*, both machines ready to add their larger weapons into the fight. McKinnon had to see his danger.

Didn't he?

Twin Gauss rifles on the Kelswa flashed with their capacitor discharge, ramming a pair of nickel-ferrous slugs into either leg on McKinnon's *Atlas*. The *Shrike* fed several laser blasts into the maelstrom, then walked a flight of missiles up the assault machine's body. One warhead clipped the side of its head. McKinnon's progress stopped dead, as if his hundred-ton monster had struck an invisible wall. It teetered back, seemingly on its way back to the ground, but then rocked forward in a smooth hunching motion that most MechWarriors could only dream of pulling off in such a heavy machine.

Still tipped back on its heels, the mighty BattleMech looked as if it had managed a perfect balancing point. With a cross-body shot, McKinnon punched a Gauss slug into the side of the Kelswa, shattering armor into fragments of its former strength.

Then he bent one knee, drawing his *Atlas* forward into an easy crouch that let Alexia see the advancing *Shrike*.

It wasn't the cleanest shot she'd had today, but it was the best she was going to get at the moment and her instincts knew it even if her brain hadn't quite caught on. The leutnant-colonel speared both arms forward, blasting out twin forks of azure lightning that passed to either side of the *Atlas*' head, giving McKinnon one hell of a show no doubt. The spitting arcs drew into the side of the *Shrike*, feeding into previous wounds to reach deep, deep into the left torso.

And found the ammunition magazine for the autocannon.

Striking approximately five tons of heavy munitions with several kilojoules of rampant energy had the kind of effect one might think. Several thousand rounds cooked off in less than a second, and thousands more a fraction later as a chain reaction ate up the machine's entire left side. Special construction channeled a great deal of the horrendous violence out through prepared blast channels, but Newton's laws were still in effect. The *Shrike* pitched forward and around, slamming its left side into the plateau's hard earth and digging a deep furrow with what was left of its shoulder. A twist of soot-laced smoke rolled out of the 'Mech's ruined back.

Alexia could only imagine the cement mixer treatment the feedback of such a large internal explosion had visited on the MechWarrior inside.

Not enough to put the assault machine down for good, unfortunately. The *Shrike* moved almost at once in an effort to regain its feet.

McKinnon was up and backing away, using his last few Gauss shots to worry the fallen MechWarrior about the possibility of a lucky head hit. Alexia Wolf called off Team Two before they tried to pounce on the struggling assault 'Mech. They would have found the Kelswa assault tank too close for comfort, and ready for them.

"I think we've given them enough to think about," McKinnon said on their private channel. His *Atlas* veered away from the Falcon line, attracting the JES missile carriers and the remaining Condor to its side. The *Shadow Hawk IIC* tried to rally a new drive, but a gut-punching Gauss hit took most of the fight out of it.

Alexia wrestled her *Uziel* around, planning a rendezvous with Team One. "We can hope." She panted for breath, waiting for her cockpit temperature to fall back toward nominal levels. "It is still a long way back to the DropShip."

But the Falcons seemed content to gather protectively around their wounded giant. Temerity? From Clan warriors? Or had she come across someone a bit more important than she realized? "Who do you think is in that monster?" she asked.

"The *Shrike*? That was Galaxy Commander Hazen, unless I miss my guess. A bit off her game from the battleroms I've reviewed, but still pushed it too close for the oddsmakers."

Malvina Hazen? "You might have said something." And what? Alexia would have traded a few of Jasek's followers for a shot at the Falcon leader? Maybe.

"I didn't want you distracted." The Skye forces had

gained nearly a kilometer from the battlefield and the Falcon warriors. They could begin to relax. "If she had given us an opening, I would've taken her."

"You're welcome," Alexia said in clipped tones, not caring for the insinuation that she would have been unable to make the same judgment, or the same effort. Jasek had warned her about him when they divvied up on Seginus. "Not that you needed a helping hand or anything."

"It was a nice brace of shots." The beginnings of a compliment, and as far as the Paladin was willing to go apparently. "Just goes to prove that we're part of a brave new world."

"How is that?" Alexia asked, wary.

"In my younger years, Lyrans couldn't shoot that straight if their own lives depended on it." She heard the mocking smile in his voice. "Give them both hands and a map—they'd still manage to wound themselves in the foot."

"I am not a Lyran," she said hotly. But she wasn't Clan either. Not anymore.

McKinnon seemed to pick up on that. Lumbering his *Atlas* after her, he asked, "Well, what are you, then?"

Letting his question hang unanswered, Alexia lapsed into a determined silence. One she planned to hold for the next several kilometers, and maybe even all the way back to Skye. It was a serious question, and it needed answering, she knew. But there was no need to discuss it with McKinnon. She barely had been able to dance around the subject with Jasek.

What was she?

That, she thought, was what she was still trying to decide for herself.

19

*The two most essential foundations for any state . . .
are sound laws and sound military forces.*
                    The Prince, by Niccolò Machiavelli

Longview
Cowlitz County, Chaffee
6 November 3134

Longview's industrious river port was a near-perfect training facility, even if it smelled of stagnant water and wet sawdust. A warehousing district. A lumber mill. The dockyards. It was wide open enough for BattleMechs to move unhindered among vehicle formations. Stacks of logs that had been floated downriver and the most monstrous piles of sawdust Noritomo Helmer had ever seen provided cover for smaller ground forces. The buildings—some larger than 'Mech hangars and all constructed to demanding local codes—could take more than their fair share of abuse. Emergency vehicles stood by to put out any accidental fires from errant lasers, and Noritomo had offered good terms to repay any permanent damage from Clan coffers.

Not only were the local politicians getting used to Jade

Falcon aegis, they welcomed it as a new source of income for the sagging economy.

From a command vehicle parked dockside of the lumber mill, Noritomo sipped at a citrus-flavored energy drink and judged the Star-on-Star battle taking place along the waterfront. The simulated battle was going well, with Lysle on the ground directing a mixed Star of Elementals and converted SalvageMechs against a mechanized striker unit—two M1 Marksman tanks supported by a trio of Demons. So far the Demons were doing a good job harassing her Elementals, herding them away from the center of their line. The M1s had a rougher time of it, intimidated by the SalvageMechs, which continued to pound away at them with light autocannon.

In a real battle, those vehicles would be scrap metal by now and the crew nothing better than hamburger. A poor showing.

He hadn't expected a great deal more. The M1 crews were all new arrivals on Chaffee, more weeding out of the *desant*'s standing forces. Not a Bloodnamed warrior among them, and several were freeborn "orphans." The only upside was that Malvina Hazen's comments—attached to their codex—lacked the same fire with which she'd banished Noritomo to this secondary staging world. Cursory and curt, she'd reposted the crews to Chaffee to be "trained and readied." Which meant she had some idea of what he was up to, and even approved. If that was the case, he saw no reason to let up now.

"Another week," Noritomo said to Lysle as he canceled the exercise. He held a wireless headset up to the side of his face rather than wearing it. "Double-duty rotations which will include refresher training in how to match against IndustrialMechs."

The Elemental jumped up onto a tall pile of lumber, taking a commanding view of the waterfront's blacktop. She waved her acknowledgment with one arm lifted above her head, then paused.

"Is that Bogart?" she asked, her voice deep and strong even through the transmission.

It was. Noritomo turned away from the ferroglass windows and checked an auxiliary monitor. The Star colonel's staff had failed to see the VV1 Ranger, which slalomed carefully between some nearby cargo containers, sneaking up on the blind side of the command vehicle.

He very nearly smiled. The freeborn tank commander was one of the rare finds Noritomo had made while putting together his new battle Cluster. A loner who had left his real name behind him, taking a one-name moniker as did many freeborn when trying to make their way in a Clan's trueborn-dominated military, Bogart had a knack for delivering stopping-power assaults just when you were ready to write off his light armor as a mere diversion.

"Light him up," he ordered a nearby warrior, who slid into the gunner's seat. The warrior tracked the command vehicle's lasers around to drop crosshairs over the Ranger's front grille. The high-pitched whine of target lock would be twice as loud inside the Ranger.

Standing in his seat, Star Captain Bogart bowed his surrender to Noritomo. The VV1 pushed forward at a regular pace now, weaving rapidly between the last few containers and breaking into the open.

"He is early with the dailies," Noritomo said, glancing at a nearby display on which glowing red numerals read as a twenty-four-hour military clock.

The "dailies" were his intelligence briefings, brought back from Glengarry on one of five commercial JumpShips dragooned into his service. They actually came in every other day on a very simple rotation. A JumpShip leaped into the Glengarry system, recharged at an expedient pace, then picked up whatever intelligence Beckett Malthus saw fit to share before it jumped back to Chaffee. Without a working HPG, such a "pony express" system was the only way to keep up on Jade Falcon movements.

"Perhaps our friends have pushed forward more quickly than we thought."

He frowned, unused to sarcasm from Lysle. "You mean the forces sneaking in-system? They are still two days out. Our aerospace forces will hit them tomorrow."

"They could increase their rate of approach."

They could, but Noritomo doubted it. You did not rush to battle when you had the superior force. IR signatures had indicated that at least three JumpShips had breached the Chaffee system using a nonstandard pirate point only four days out instead of the usual eight days it took to reach the zenith or nadir jump points. Three vessels. Republic or Lyran, it hadn't much mattered to him. If he assumed an average carry of 2.5 each, the assault force would bear down on him with between six and nine DropShips. His aerospace fighters and two assault DropShips might cut the margin down somewhat, but he fully expected to be at a disadvantage against whatever landed on Chaffee.

War so often came down to a simple numbers game.

"We had better find out for certain," he told Lysle, calling her over as he dropped down to the command vehicle's door. He finished his drink in a pair of large swallows and handed the empty container and his headset to an aide. "If the JumpShip is back early," he said to himself, "it cannot be good news."

It wasn't. Meeting Bogart and Lysle outside the command vehicle, returning the man's salute and accepting the verifax from him, Noritomo pressed his thumb to the reader and waited while a DNA check unlocked the datafiles inside. It took him two minutes, scanning through the datafiles, to see the new mess The Republic had created for him.

"Idiots. *Stravag* incompetents. What did they hope to accomplish?"

Reading over his shoulder, a feat not too difficult for a woman her size, Lysle scrunched up her face with distaste. "Ryde. Summer. Glengarry. One planet taken: Summer. Two factory lines and a munitions depot destroyed. The loss of three Stars' worth of vehicles. I would say they accomplished quite well."

"In a purely tactical appraisal, that would be correct." In fact, if Malvina had not cost the raiders a *Union*-class DropShip, knocking it out of the air with an Alamo, the balance would tip even farther into The Republic's column. By one way of thinking, it was too bad she caught it on the way down, not on takeoff. Adding a Stormhammer company to the totals might have made for a solid Falcon victory.

A numbers game.

"But why sting at us with raiding assaults?" he asked. "What is the reason behind them?" He did not ask out of confusion, but to make his officers think. Think like the enemy.

Bogart caught on first. "Factory production and stock-piles," he mused, tapping a meaty finger against a square chin. The freeborn commander was a very short man with bronzed skin, large, wide shoulders, and a shaved head. Slender at the waist but with oversized legs and arms, he reminded Noritomo of a shortened version of a mythological beast—the Minotaur. "Delaying tactics?" he asked.

"Exactly. They hope to buy more time to ready Skye against Malvina's return."

Lysle shrugged, accepting the noteputer from him. "I still fail to see the problem, Star Colonel. We salvaged Ryde, according to these reports, with heavy losses to both sides. Glengarry is a wash. Summer . . ." She read the file again. "It looks as if we have given up Summer to reinforce Zebebelgenubi."

"Which means that Malvina Hazen does not plan to wait. Zebebelgenubi is more important than Summer only for its proximity to Skye and targets deeper within Prefecture IX."

He paused, thinking it through. "She will see this assault as an insult. A personal affront, given that her own 'Mech was so badly damaged in a short battle. She will launch for Skye sooner, not later." He shook his head. "She will strike without us, and use every terror tactic at her disposal to break the spine of Skye once and for all."

Pandora's evils, unleashed. With their ill-conceived raids, the Skye defenders had sealed their doom and ruined his plans. Noritomo needed more time. Now he was not going to get it.

"She might yet summon us up," Lysle offered.

"With enemy forces inbound? She will wait to see how we conduct ourselves."

Bogart shrugged, a gesture that used most of his upper body. "Then we smash these Republicans. And we charge for Skye as soon as Galaxy Commander Hazen calls us."

Yes, definitely bull-like. But the freeborn warrior had said something that struck a chord with Noritomo. "Aff, we can only ready our defense and show our leaders that we are still worthy of battle. Smashing the inbound force— Lyran or Republic—will go a long way toward accomplish-ing that goal."

"They are Republic," Bogart said, sounding very certain

of himself. Too certain. "And if we truly wish to shock them, we should ignore their batchall, *quaiff*?"

The question struck Noritomo like a closed fist. "What did you say?"

"Their batchall? It is in the datafiles." He nodded at the noteputer held in Lysle's large hands.

There was a file he had not opened, and it was not linked through the menu of daily reports, which was why he had missed it the first time. And it was labeled BATCHALL, which was the formal bidding practice used between Clans to limit the waste of war materiel. With all the trouble Noritomo had wrestled because of using Clan traditions, here an Inner Sphere faction was recognizing the wisdom of Clan ways? It seemed too good to be true.

He opened the file. Appended to a simple, direct question, which was the entire body of the main text, was a personal bio of the sender. Landgrave Jasek Kelswa-Steiner. Stormhammers, commanding.

There was even an abbreviated list of his accomplishments, arranged in a similar fashion to a Clan codex: *Champion of Nusakan. Victor at Zebebelgenubi. Defender of Skye.*

And if there was any doubt that Kelswa-Steiner understood Clan practices, the short message was even written in the same formal fashion that began most Jade Falcon batchalls: *With what forces does Clan Jade Falcon defend its interests on Chaffee?*

Noritomo Helmer smiled. This was just what his people needed.

20

**Longview
Cowlitz County, Chaffee
8 November 3134**

Pushing along the river's edge, gaining a foothold on the blacktop-covered dockside, Jasek anchored his *Templar* against the water's edge and quickly called up his Archon's Shield battalion to cement the Stormhammers position. After chasing Noritomo Helmer's troops for half a day, Jasek had every intention of forcing the Clanner to abandon his hit-and-fade tactics, and to stand and fight for the city of Longview.

This certainly looked to be it. A double line of Falcon tanks held the center of the waterfront complex, flanked by a pair of modified SalvageMechs. The light autocannon replacing their left arms belted out a few long-range shots that picked and pecked at the forming Stormhammer line. A fifty-five-ton *Gyrfalcon* and a light *Stinger* teamed up at the water's edge, directly ahead of Jasek's position. They stood in front of a trio of Demon medium tanks.

Jade Falcon VTOLs buzzed over the lumber mill, weaving around in a complex dance to disguise how they might break away at a second's notice to strafe the ground-bound troops. Fortunately, Jasek had been able to peel away two two-fighter elements from the air battle raging above the cloud cover. They would arrive in moments. When they did, his line had better be set.

"Colonel Vandel. Dress up our backfield and push those Kelswas up onto our right flank. Buy the Steel Wolves some time to deploy."

"That's some valuable coin we're risking," the Lyran officer warned him over a tight command circuit.

"They're good for it."

At least, Jasek hoped so.

So far Anastasia Kerensky had held to her word, following his strategy so long as he gave her complete tactical freedom. Her parallel push to his had caught several Jade Falcon warriors unprepared, even though he had bid her forces into the batchall fairly, if under the name of the Stormhammers. She was responsible for rolling up the western wing and he had opened the way into Longview. Even-up.

Now, on the far right, an *Eyrie* was already trading close-in blows with Leutnant Gillickie's *Storm Raider*. But as the Kelswa tanks moved up with their 'Mech-killing Gauss rifles and the Steel Wolves after them, the *Eyrie* fell back among two Behemoths and the only Elemental forces that Jasek had yet to see of Helmer's bid Star.

Joss Vandel's mobile HQ crawled up into the seam that separated Stormhammer from Steel Wolf. "If we had kept Third Company and not left them with the Steel Wolf auxiliaries guarding our DropShips, we'd slaughter the Falcons."

Jasek rarely minded being second-guessed by his colonels, and gave Vandel more latitude than most because of his ties back to the Lyran Commonwealth, and Lohengrin. The first judge of a man was the company he kept.

Just so long as they kept it on private channels.

"This isn't about slaughter," he reminded his senior officer as the *Gyrfalcon* prodded at him with its ultra-ACs.

A hail of fifty-millimeter caseless rang into his shoulder, with a few ricochets *spanging* into the side of his head. He cast one stream of particle energy across the blacktop, slashing at the *Gyrfalcon*'s leg.

The Kelswas launched a double-Gauss broadside, pushing the Jade Falcon back as Anastasia Kerensky's *Ryoken II* led a double Star of Steel Wolf survivors in from the southwest.

"These warriors have to acknowledge us as fair and worthwhile enemies for this to work."

"Doesn't matter how you take a world," Vandel said.

But it did if you didn't want to waste valuable resources in a garrison.

The Kelswas' broadside had pummeled a Skanda into scrap and finally cracked the Falcon reserve. Now the Clanners rolled forward with smooth coordination. Not charging in an all-or-nothing gamble nor showing doubt in a hesitant march. Textbook maneuvers, with 'Mechs leading and vehicles flanking and infantry protected in the pocket behind.

Did Noritomo Helmer practice that on a daily basis? It was parade ground perfect.

"Pick them up and push them back," Jasek ordered, throttling into a sidelong march that left the river to his salvaged *Ocelot* and angled his own *Templar* toward the center of the allied line.

More autocannon fire converged on his position, and missiles arced up and fell in well-spaced waves from the Falcon JES carriers dug in near one of the huge sawdust piles. Fireballs blossomed in a line across his Maxim heavy hover transports, cracking one open like an egg and spilling out several Gnome battlesuit troops.

The VTOLs pounced, augering in with their nose-mounted cannon spitting fire and lethal metal. Two slid across the spoiled infantry line and rained destruction on one of the Kelswa assault tanks. But too close, too close.

Anastasia lit off her *Ryoken II*'s jump jets, rising one hundred meters over the waterfront blacktop on streamers of glowing plasma. Torso-mounted particle cannon smashed out with their lightning-style streams of energy, gutting one VTOL as it tried to bank away. The second craft turned inward, maybe thinking to beat the minimum effective range of the PPCs. Anastasia swatted it out of the sky with one backhand chop into its main rotor.

She landed in a ready crouch, lasers and cannon alternating in perfect rhythm.

The two VTOLs landed in explosive wreckage.

"Worthy of your namesake," Jasek said, toggling for an open frequency.

"Wish I could say the same," the commander of the Steel Wolves shot back as a Gauss slug opened a new crack in Jasek's armor, right over his fusion engine. Still, her tone sounded more pleased than put off by his comment.

Whatever it took, Jasek intended to keep Kerensky's attention, and her cooperation, for as long as possible.

The Jade Falcon center flagged, slowed by the ponderous gait of the SalvageMechs and the crawling speeds of JES II carriers and M1 Marksman tanks. As the flanks bent around, they welcomed the encroaching Stormhammers in a hot embrace. Jasek saw the encirclement beginning but did not worry about it yet. Especially with his aerospace fighters finally blipping onto long-range sensors far behind the allied forces. He welcomed the chance to chew the middle out of Helmer's line, especially as the solid centerline force also protected the Clan's command vehicle—an older Praetorian. Though smart money put Star Colonel Helmer in the *Gyrfalcon*, not some behind-the-lines armchair. No disrespect to Joss Vandel intended.

Especially when the Lyran colonel saved Jasek's ass not thirty seconds later.

"Toads! Toads!"

A nameless warrior alerted the field to the problem only a few seconds after the giant sawdust pile erupted in a fury of motion, smoke, and laser fire. Elementals leaped clear from where they had been buried, leapfrogging by groups of five. Ten battlesuit troopers.

Then fifteen. Then twenty.

With the five infantrymen from before, that was the full Star accounted for! Their thick-necked profile and the ninety-meter hops that first gave them the "toad" nickname more than eighty years ago were real attention getters. Most Inner Sphere battlesuit designs were based on the Clan originals, and were never quite as deadly as the real thing.

Getting battlesuit soldiers into reach of their short-range weapons was the usual trick. Helmer had managed it by burrowing them into the soft sawdust, masking their presence until Jasek closed to a good range. But for a few seconds, the Elemental warriors were also grouped together in a vulnerable pack. With some artillery, if Jasek had been willing to use the Paladin defense system near a city (he wasn't), the Elementals could have been chewed into so many walking wounded.

Bombing runs could accomplish much the same thing. And there were four fighter craft already arrowing down on their attack runs.

"Stormhammers," Vandel called out on command override. "Ground and *hold*!"

It was a risky call, ordering the assault force to give up their maneuverability. Few of them realized yet the danger facing Jasek and the Stormhammer center. So it was a good indication of unit discipline that not one 'Mech took another step after that order, and all vehicles killed their forward momentum. For five desperate heartbeats, the offensive push ground to a standstill, tempting the Jade Falcons with easy targets.

Then artificial thunder shattered the waterfront as a pair of *Stingrays* slashed from backfield to fore, strafing with lasers and missiles as they ignored the remaining VTOLs in favor of the thick cluster of Elementals.

Eisensturm followed, the heavy fighter craft again shaking the ground in a high-speed nape-of-the-earth run that blistered a fiery trail through the Elemental wall and made the *Stingray* run look kind.

Knowing that four fighters were all he'd called forward, Jasek preempted Joss Vandel by yelling, "Go, go, go!" and spearheading a new drive into the midst of the momentarily stunned Jade Falcons.

He heard metal-suited infantry land on his legs, his sides, clambering around for purchase. A pair of Scimitar hovercraft skated in quickly, dancing around their commander, using their missiles like marksman pistols to carefully pick off the Elementals one by one.

Two converging lines. One busted trap. The battlefield quickly dissolved into a free-for-all slugging match as vehicles tried to re-form on their 'Mech leads and infantry regrouped to use combined-arms force. A pack of Gnomes cracked open the crew quarters on a Falcon Skanda, letting in a hunter-seeker engineering team who quickly took control of the crew and vehicle. Elementals ran roughshod over their smaller cousins, driving them away from two other targets and unseating a pair of Steel Wolf hoverbike drivers at the same time.

Back near the waterfront, the Stormhammers' *Ocelot* traded on its superior speed and one heavy laser to slice armor from the *Stinger*. JES tactical carriers slipped up to the wounded BattleMech and peppered it with short-range missiles; a lean wolf brought down by hounds.

Then the *Gyrfalcon* abandoned its place at the river for a direct run at Jasek's *Templar*. Autocannon and large lasers cycled in alternating salvos, chewing through armor and splashing away more of the same in fiery mists of molten composite. Jasek let Helmer worry his left side a moment as he tried to finish off one of the troublesome SalvageMechs, which kept clawing for purchase with its salvage arm.

Finally trading it off for the more dangerous man, he let one of the Kelswas move up to threaten the Salvage while he hauled his eighty-five-ton machine around for a full-on broadside against the *Gyrfalcon*.

An unlucky Elemental tried to jump-scoot between them, maybe angling for a crippled Joust or looking to put some pressure on the *Ocelot*. Instead, it took one of Jasek's PPCs. The lightning ripped him apart, smashing in his faceplate and ripping the arms off the suit. Jasek's remaining PPC, his medium lasers, and his four-pack missile system all dumped their loads into the *Gyrfalcon*'s chest. The forward-leaning 'Mech pulled up short, staggered, but held to its feet by sheer force of will.

Another full salvo as Jasek continued to trade against the *Gyrfalcon*'s lasers and autocannon. His *Templar* staggered backward. Temperatures in the cockpit soared as the fusion reactor spiked under the heavy power draw, straight through the yellow band and into the red.

Sweat stung at Jasek's eyes, and his vision swam for a moment in the ready-made sauna. Only the chilled coolant passing through the tubes of his cooling vest kept his core temperature down enough. Kept him from heatstroke.

His breath came shallow as Jasek tried to not pull the scorched air deep into his lungs.

Then he adjusted his aim, threw his heat curve to the Fates, and traded full salvos with the *Gyrfalcon* again.

*   *   *

Something had to give.

Noritomo Helmer had recognized that when taking up his final defensive stand for Longview, and Chaffee by proxy. He had hoped it would be the Steel Wolves, at which he'd thrown some of his strongest forces throughout the day. But Anastasia Kerensky's reputation seemed well deserved. She'd thrown some of her best back at him.

So had this Jasek Kelswa-Steiner. The Stormhammers had even stood strongly in the face of Lysle's Elemental blitz, and then shoved it right back down his throat with the aerospace fighters.

Why hadn't he seen that coming!

At best, he'd achieved a draw so far. Which was still worth a measure of honor considering the shape in which he'd found these cast-off warriors. The truly incompetent were long gone now, tempered from the unit in trial by fire. The best of his warriors remained. But even a finely edged piece of steel could dull if battered against unyielding rock, which was the danger of pushing a bad position.

Something had to give.

Him or the enemy commander, he decided.

Stunned and nearly dropped to the waterfront blacktop by the *Templar*'s blistering assault, Noritomo wrenched his control stick to lever both arms forward and trade new fusillades with Jasek. His autocannon belted out hundreds of rounds in their extra-long cycles, and lasers cut with ruby efficiency. Jasek's answering combination of particle cannon and lasers could not match the *Gyrfalcon*'s impressive damage profile, but the Stormhammer leader had far better armor and a serious advantage with an advanced targeting computer that grouped his shots into deadly clusters.

Both machines staggered back from the blistering trade-off. Jasek with a gimpy knee, limping his *Templar* counterclockwise to Noritomo's position. The Star colonel read his damage schematic with a practiced eye, and counted four warning lights on his left arm. Mostly actuators.

He sidestepped, turning more of his right profile toward the other man. He slashed at Jasek with his lasers again. And again.

Jasek pushed forward into point-blank range. His short-range missiles smashed two warheads into the side of Noritomo's *Gyrfalcon*.

The battle ground nearly to a halt around the two BattleMechs as both sides recognized the honor match between their commanders. Kerensky's *Ryoken II* physically restrained a Kelswa assault tank by holding a foot over its crew quarters. A pair of Steel Wolf Destroyers parked themselves nose to nose with the Stormhammers' Praetorian mobile HQ.

Noritomo dialed for a common, unsecured frequency. "You will let this be decided by you and me now?" His lasers cut angry wounds into the *Templar*'s flank.

"Jousting hasn't quite . . . gone out of style in the Jade Falcons, eh?"

The man had a polished voice and a speech giver's cadence, but lazy grammar. He also sounded a bit winded. It had to be an oven inside his cockpit. His return fire came in staggered waves now, alternating between the two particle cannon.

"So be it. You and I."

"Bargained well and done," Noritomo formally accepted, and pulled into another savage alpha strike.

His autocannon hammered at a crack in the centerline of Jasek's armored chest.

A tongue of flame licked out of the wound, and dark gray smoke from burning insulation drifted up into the *Templar*'s chest.

But Jasek had worked himself into optimum firing range for his entire weapons load-out as well, and by alternating fire between PPCs had lowered his heat curve back to reasonable levels. The barrels on his particle cannon glowed with a nimbus of energy; then new lightning arcs snaked their way between the two machines. One missed wide, but the second smashed away the last of the armor protecting the *Gyrfalcon*'s right flank.

Lasers and missiles probed for critical components.

Missed.

Not a second time, though. Short-cycling his weapons, damning the *Templar*'s heat curve and risking an automatic, heat-driven shutdown, Jasek blasted Noritomo with everything he had. The *Templar*'s targeting computer grouped it all into the *Gyrfalcon*'s savaged right side: The cascade of energy sliced through myomer and foamed-titanium supports.

It ruptured actuators.

Cut into the physical shielding on the 'Mech's fusion reactor.

Heat sinks exploded and jets of greenish-gray coolant spurted out of the wounds like arterial blood.

The raw kinetic force of so much damage delivered in such short order threw the *Gyrfalcon* roughly to the ground like a man struck by lightning (twice!). The machine came down on its left side, crushing the last of its good armor against the blacktop. Noritomo shook against his seat restraints, feeling the harness buckle digging into his abdomen, his teeth clacking together hard enough to chip enamel.

He pulled in one arm and rolled the BattleMech over onto its chest, thinking to push himself back up as quickly as possible. But the *Gyrfalcon*'s right arm would not support any weight. And there was Jasek Kelswa-Steiner. One foot planted near his shoulder, the other next to his *Gyrfalcon*'s hip, and a host of deadly weapons pointed at the back of Noritomo's head.

"Yield."

It did not even come in the form of a request. Jasek knew he had the Star colonel in bad shape, prepared to decapitate the *Gyrfalcon* and turn Noritomo's cockpit into a ready-made crematorium. Still, the Clan warrior almost said no just to throw the harsh demand back into his face.

Fortunately, a few seconds' pause was not enough to prod Jasek into firing. "Yield, Star Colonel. And I will offer your forces *hegira*."

Hegira. That put a new face on things. Completely. A Clan term, *hegira* offered the disadvantaged side of a conflict the option of honorable withdrawal from the battlefield. Whoever had been instructing Jasek Kelswa-Steiner on Clan traditions had not been wholly deficient, it seemed. Noritomo suspected Anastasia Kerensky and her Steel Wolves.

"I accept," he said at once, "if your offer allows us to retain possession of all equipment and materiel." Noritomo had spent too much time building up this force to let any man gut it for war spoils. He would rather let his warriors fight to the death. Jasek had to know that.

There was a slight pause. Then, "Any machine that can move under its own power may be removed to your DropShips. One third of all supplies and materiel not already aboard a DropShip can be taken with you. Chaffee, and the balance of your stockpiles, fall to us."

It was a strong bargain. A tough one to swallow, which meant that Jasek had dealt harshly but not unfairly. Noritomo approved. "Done," he said, transmitting in the clear so that his people would hear in his agreement the order to stand down.

"Bargained *well* and done," Jasek replied. "You have saved a good many lives today, Star Colonel Helmer. That is not something to be ashamed of."

No. Noritomo was not ashamed. And he would see that his warriors felt no great sting to their pride. The battle had brought them together, forging them into a coherent force from a rabble of so many individual warriors and units. They had acquitted themselves well, and they were mostly intact. Meaning that the core of a strong Clan battle Cluster would survive and be ready to assist Galaxy Commanders Hazen and Malthus in the campaign that truly mattered.

Noritomo's warriors were not retreating.

They would be heading for Skye.

21

Norfolk
Skye
18 November 3134

A few days earlier, Countess Tara Campbell had watched as a newly christened *Overlord* fired off its massive drive engines for the first time, lifting itself free of the dockyard cradle that had supported it during construction. The ground shook. The thirty-story DropShip trembled with pent-up power. Then, slowly at first, the *Star Runner* began to rise into the air, as if a titan's invisible hand had reached down to uproot a skyscraper, pulling it out of Norfolk's skyline.

Shipil Company had protested her order to launch early, citing all the work left to complete on the weapon systems, the sensor array, the finishing touches yet to be applied to the many offices and living quarters. When pressed, though, they admitted that it was work that could be completed out of dry dock, even if tradition demanded that a new vessel not leave its cradle without all defensive systems on line. So the order stood.

The drive flare had looked improbably bright, especially when it washed over the dark walls of the large facility.

White golden fire that hurt to stare at. Even from half a kilometer away, Tara felt the backwash of heat on her face and the backs of her hands. She smelled flash-dried ferrocrete, like damp tarmac baking under an early-morning sun.

Maybe the local humidity bumped up a point or two.

Maybe it was her imagination.

But the *Star Runner* continued to lift and to roll, and eventually was lost to sight as a faint morning star in an expansive blue sky.

That had been three days ago. And as impressive as the first liftoff had been, Tara could only marvel at the feat of precision piloting being displayed as a different *Overlord* reversed the process, thundering down out of a cloud-drifted sky like one of the vengeful air spirits that House Liao probably worshipped.

The ovoid shape hung like Damocles' sword over Shipil Company's Norfolk complex, a crushing weight that had to sit heavily on the shoulders of those technicians who had drawn the short straw and worked the ground below. The *Fanged Terror* drifted into place, sitting atop a pillar of golden fire. Then as gently as a feather—a massive feather, nearly ten thousand tons in displacement—it lowered itself over the open cradle. Fusion-driven flames licked down over the carbonized ferrosteel supports and speared the bull's-eye of the landing pad nestled within, and the DropShip lowered itself as easily as if it had come in on laser-point guidance. With a tolerance of only 2.3 meters—considered the maximum vibrational drift on a launching *Overlord*—the *Fanged Terror* threaded the cradle's eye and set itself down perfectly within the Shipil complex.

It was a few minutes' drive in a Shandra scout vehicle to get Tara back to the complex and through the series of security checkpoints put in place by Shipil. Leaving the main supply tunnel, her driver took her out under the cradle's maze of bowed girders and flex-joint couplings, and then up the lowered ramp to meet with the DropShip passengers.

A squad of Elementals met her at the head of the ramp, blocking off deeper access into the main 'Mech bay. Tara disembarked from the Shandra, ignoring the towering infantrymen as she caught sight of her opposite number with the Steel Wolves. Anastasia Kerensky.

The other woman looked angry. Then again, Tara remembered very few meetings between the two of them where Kerensky did not look angry at something or someone. It came with the territory, she imagined, being raised in a warrior society, always having to look over your shoulder for the subordinate with an itch to prove himself.

Physically, it would have been hard for the two women to look less alike. They did share a similar height, but Kerensky's frame was athletic, while Tara was slightly more curvy. Tassa Kay, as she sometimes styled herself, had long, dark red hair, cream-complexioned skin, and green, predatory eyes. She moved with loping strides, as if ready to jump for the throat at a second's notice. The countess carried herself with a noblewoman's easy grace, and if her platinum hair spiked short up top was not quite traditional (or regulation), it was a trademark of hers these days and had inspired many new hair fashions across The Republic.

They were different women. Different warriors. Tara held no illusions on that score. But she also owed a debt of gratitude to Kerensky and her Steel Wolves that Tara perhaps didn't fully articulate at their last meeting. She decided to rectify that at once.

Holding out her hand, accepting Kerensky's challenging grip, she said, "Commander Kerensky, you are welcomed back to Skye."

"Am I?" Kerensky looked around, as if missing someone. "Last time it took three of you to throw me off-world. Where is Duke Gregory and his lapdog prefect?"

The hint of a Germanic accent colored Kerensky's voice very subtly. If Tara had not known that the other woman had come of age on the Lyran Commonwealth border, she might have missed it.

"I would rather set politics aside for the moment," Tara finally said. She crossed arms over her chest. "This is about survival."

"It was last time as well."

"Last time you were hardly invited to Skye," Tara reminded her. And last time the enemy hadn't shown a newfound tendency to throw nuclear weapons into the mix. The two women turned away from some nearby hot metalwork. The acrid stench burned Tara's sinuses. She held up one hand to shield her eyes from the bright cutting flare.

"In fact," she said, turning them in a short walk back toward the DropShip ramp and her vehicle, "we weren't certain at first that you weren't here to follow up the Jade Falcon assault with an attack of your own."

"Wolves are hardly scavengers, looking for the Jade Falcons' battlefield leavings. And I am sure you have seen reports from Seginus by now, so you know how much we gave to the effort on Skye last time and the service we have provided for Legate Hateya since then." Anastasia looked out at the cradle's framework. From here, it looked remarkably like a cage. "We did not expect red-carpet treatment, but you could have allowed my warriors the honor of being received in one of your main DropPorts. Not sneaking into the outback like pirates."

"I would not call bringing your main DropShip in at Skye's largest shipyard facility 'sneaking in,'" Tara said. At least, not in the way that Kerensky meant it. "We cleared this area specifically for you."

"Why?" The woman was full of suspicions. Just one of the things that kept her alive.

"Because I felt that you would be able to bring your vessel down here without causing damage."

Kerensky nodded approval as her nearby Elementals stiffened to attention as they passed. "A nice evasion."

Tara sighed. They would get into that soon enough. "Let's just say that there have been some changes since you were here last. It's a different war we're fighting."

"But with many of the same allies, it seems. We almost didn't make the trip, but Jasek seems to believe that we have something about us which is needed here." Did Kerensky notice the way Tara startled at Jasek's name? "At least"—she smiled thinly—"by him."

Was it her taunt or the familiar use of Jasek's name that warmed the back of Tara's neck? She caught her discomfort in both hands, and throttled it.

"I'm sure that Jasek made his desires clear."

"Very," the other woman said, layering several meanings behind her simple reply. "I have to admit, I find his boldness very refreshing. Unusual in an Inner Sphere leader. He's a fascinating man, don't you think?"

There was no doubt now that Kerensky had caught her hesitation. The mocking tone. Her sudden informality. Tara flushed.

"No, I don't think," she said crisply.

"Easy, Countess. No autopsy, no foul, quaiff?" She held her hands apart. Shrugged, as if to say it did not truly matter to her at all. Though obviously it did. "If you have some kind of prior claim . . ."

"I do not."

"Truly? Well, some of his warriors seem to. There was one who I think was most upset that she was sent on to Glengarry while my Steel Wolves accompanied Jasek to Chaffee."

"Tamara Duke," Tara said at once, nodding. But Kerensky only smiled cryptically. What was that other one? The commander of the Tharkan Strikers? "Alexia Wolf?" she asked, frowning. The smile did not reach Kerensky's eyes, and Tara realized that she was being baited. For a woman who was supposedly disinterested . . . damn her!

"I imagine several of Jasek's officers were displeased with the division of forces."

Kerensky hedged, as if balancing between desires to continue teasing Tara and to shift over to more serious matters. Serious won. "They were," she admitted. "Though Paladin McKinnon could not seem to make up his mind whom he'd rather be stuck with." Her face darkened. "And I hear that the Stormhammers had a hard time escaping Glengarry."

News of the nuclear weapon had flashed across Skye with dramatic speed after the return of the Glengarry raiders. Not surprising that the Steel Wolves already had it. "It was a tactical nuke. Caught the *Freedom's Fist* on descent. With the *Friedensstifter* taking off, fully loaded, we think there was a mistake in targeting. It could have been much, much worse."

Not that it wasn't bad enough. As it was, Tara would be responsible for informing Jasek of the loss of a *Union*-class vessel, fourteen crewmen, and a dozen embarked technicians. If the leader of the Stormhammers ever returned from Chaffee.

"Where is Jasek, anyway?" she asked, forcing the conversation over to practical matters.

Kerensky pursed her lips. "He sent us ahead almost as

soon as he accepted the Jade Falcons' formal surrender. We had to repair and refit en route. By the time we jumped from Chaffee, he was repairing what units he could from the salvage and stores left behind by the garrison, and after our share." She shrugged. "Quite honestly, I expected him only a few days behind us. He must have been caught up with something."

"And Star Colonel Helmer? What of him?"

Now it was Kerensky's turn to frown. No doubt she thought that her report, transmitted ahead of her arrival, had covered that. "Helmer jumped out of the Chaffee system three hours ahead of us. I would assume to return to Glengarry."

Tara let Kerensky stew in her assumption a moment. It was a petty revenge, perhaps, for her earlier goading about Jasek, but it would also serve to put the other woman on the defensive, turning her strategic thinking toward the larger problems at hand.

"You would assume that. So would I, in fact. But we have intelligence out of the Glengarry system that is less than a week old, and as far as we can tell no retreating forces from Chaffee have arrived there." She leaned back against her Shandra. "So the big question is, where did they go?"

If one thing could be said about Anastasia Kerensky, it was that no one put her on the defensive for very long. She waved a hand at Tara. "That's still a little question," she said dismissively.

All right. "So what is the big question, then?"

Anastasia Kerensky's smile widened into a predator's grin, showing the teeth behind. The question, when she asked it, sent a chill through Tara Campbell. The Countess knew that the Steel Wolf leader had the right of it.

She also knew, without a doubt, that they were fortunate to have her back on Skye.

Tassa Kay blew on her fingertips, flexed the hand like a gunfighter preparing for a speed draw.

"When will they be here?"

22

Refusing with a sharp shake of his head to leave the bridge of the *Himmelstor*, Jasek weathered Kaptain Goran's pointed stare and belted himself into the chair normally reserved for the ship's executive officer. The DropShip's command center was a beehive of activity as they approached atmospheric insertion over Hesperus II, with crewmen manning the different stations, calling out time checks, attitude adjustments, and range to target on a contact that Jasek would feel better forgetting was even there.

"And I can't convince you to go below," the kaptain said, his voice rough and gravelly from decades of calling out orders. Thick-necked and heavy-browed, Eduard Goran was a fourth-generation spacer with family ties back to the Lyran Commonwealth.

Jasek gripped the arms of the command-style chair. "I will if you will," he said easily.

The Stormhammers' leader had had enough of "below" after four days under a high-gravity burn, ramping up and holding at the equivalent of 2.5 Gs. Except for short low-gravity periods where a skeleton crew made their rounds and everyone was allowed to eat or take care of personal ablutions, Jasek had been confined to quarters and strapped into bed, feeling as if his spine were threatening to snap in half. Hammered until his joints ached and every muscle felt bruised.

A "suicide sled" run, that's what Goran had called it when Hesperus authorities approved Jasek's request for a fast insertion lane. A Lyran *Scout* jumped the *Himmelstor* to a special Lagrange point in-system, near Hesperus III. Then the trial began.

After barely an hour of the rough treatment, Jasek could think of it only as a necessary evil.

Even with his personal JumpShip fitted out with lithium-fusion batteries, able to make the double-jump transfer from Chaffee's Lagrange point to the Hesperus system in less than a day, this was the only way he hoped to get in and out fast enough to do Skye any good. Using a closer set of nonstandard jump coordinates was out of the question. Jasek had been willing to risk it—anything to save himself the eighteen-day insertion time—but Goran had flat refused. There were things worse than a deep gravity well protecting Hesperus II from unwanted trespassers.

And thinking of which . . . "She's going to come down our port ventral side," the ship's sensor officer called out, and if it was possible to ratchet tension on the bridge up another few degrees, that did it.

Goran grunted. "Roll five degrees starboard. Bring her up on the main screen."

There was no ferroglass viewport on an *Overlord* bridge. No "weather deck" bulkheads at all, in fact. The command center was nestled safely and securely in the DropShip's centerline spaces where only a naval-class missile might hope to penetrate.

And if there hadn't currently been a half dozen launchers capable of throwing such a missile at the *Himmelstor* already locked on to them, Jasek might have felt fairly safe.

The screen, which had been filled with black space and bright stars a moment before, switched camera angles and found the fast-approaching world of Hesperus II. Dun-colored with streaks of dark brown, the planetary surface had a craggy, unfinished look about it with very little vegetation to soften the knife-edged mountains that divided the main continents. Jasek knew that with mean equatorial temperatures up to eighty degrees Celsius, the world was habitable only in the far northern reaches, and most of the population preferred to live under atmospherically controlled domes.

He knew a lot, in fact, about this world he had never visited. Hesperus II was a storied world in the Lyran Commonwealth. One of perhaps twelve worlds about which legend had it that if you knew their history you knew nearly everything important to know about the Inner Sphere. It was here that House Steiner learned of BattleMech designs when an ancient ancestor of Jasek's, Simon Kelswa, raided the Terran Hegemony world in 2445. Hesperus II eventually became a Lyran holding, and was attacked more than fifteen times in major assaults by Houses Kurita, Marik, even Davion. But the world never gave up its allegiance or its secrets again. The 'Mech factories, so important during the Succession Wars and the Jihad, were built beneath the Myoo Mountains and essentially impenetrable to an outside force. Even in this time of downsized militaries coming off a golden age of peace, the factories at Hesperus II continued to turn out 'Mechs at a pace that most other worlds considered reckless.

And this was one of the reasons for Jasek's hastily planned visit.

"The Myoos," Kaptain Goran said, using a laser pointer to scribe a fast circle around a particularly wrinkled range of mountains in the northwest section of the planet's northernmost continent. With a practiced spacer's eye, he found the gray stain that was the only city on the planet large enough to be recognized as such from space. "Maria's Elegy. Put Defiance Peak about here, then." He speared a large mountain with the pointer, seemingly at random.

Defiance Peak. Home of the local Defiance Industries factories. Duke Vedet Brewster, the world's hereditary ruler, would have his capital at Maria's Elegy, which was also where House Steiner's personal ambassador would reside.

Yes, Jasek was interested in those landmarks.

Then a gray-black veil swept over the planet, hazy in its

eclipse. Jasek felt a sharp thrill run through him as Goran ordered his technicians, "Scale back. Bring her into focus."

Coming down the *Himmelstor*'s port ventral side. That's what the sensor officer had said. But no one had adjusted the camera's eye—configured to take in space travel distances that usually ran to hundreds of thousands of kilometers—for close-up viewing.

Now he did, and the gray veil hardened into an angular wall. It dropped back to show a DropShip docking collar and a pair of heavy naval particle cannons guarding the approach. Another level of magnification removed, and the thick-waist profile of a Lyran battle cruiser cut across the planet's profile.

"The *Yggdrasil*," Goran said with an appropriate touch of awe.

Mjolnir-class. Displacing more than 1,200,000 tons, it was one of the valiant Lyran WarShips to survive the Word of Blake Jihad. Thought lost several times over its active life, it was placed in orbit around Hesperus II in 3084, underscoring how important the local factories were to House Steiner, even if Devlin Stone had wanted to pick the world up in his grab for a new Hegemony.

"Never been moved again," Goran said, as if sensing Jasek's thoughts. "Some say it can't be taken out of system. Burned out its KF drive in the last jump it made to arrive here."

"You believe that?" Jasek asked. He shifted in his chair, easing tired muscles, and tried to distract himself by counting the weapon bays visible as dimpled shells and long-barreled turrets on the *Mjolnir*'s side. At least nine naval-class autocannon in its overlapping broadside arcs, he saw. Several particle cannon. And, yep, there were the AR10 launchers. Each one with a set of Killer Whale missiles that could crack the *Himmelstor* like an egg.

Goran cocked his head in what might have been a shrug, or only a pause to think. "What I believe and what I'm careful about ain't always the same thing, Landgrave."

"Good advice," Jasek decided. "And speaking of being careful, you'd better call Colonel Vandel up here."

"More mud sloggers cluttering up my bridge for no reason," the kaptain groused.

"You may be right," Jasek acknowledged. "The Brewsters have never been enemies of Skye or the Kelswas, after all, and I *believe* Trillian Steiner will give us an audience and vouchsafe us regardless of the local duke's attitude." He shrugged. "But she *knows* Joss Vandel. And that monster of a ship will be holding position above Hesperus II, which means we have to come back up past it. How careful do you want to be today?"

Goran picked up his all-hands mic and dialed for shipboard announcement, calling Joss Vandel to the bridge.

Jasek was careful not to let the crotchety spacer see his smile.

23

The universe had compacted down to a single pinpoint. A glowing pearl, hovering in Malvina Hazen's mind's eye. Cold and bright, it pulsed in time to her heartbeat.

Then the jump was over, and her *Nightlord*-class WarShip reentered real space at the zenith jump point above the plane of Skye's solar system. The glowing gem exploded around her in a riot of sound and color, rebuilding the universe in broad strokes around her consciousness. Her body, imperfect but strong once again. The *Emerald Talon*'s bridge with several dozen crewmen still bent to their prejump tasks, now taking their next breaths and their next thoughts. And outside the large ferroglass wall—the ultimate hubris in locating the main bridge of a WarShip against hard vacuum—a galaxy of bright stars unfolded once again against the dark blanket of space.

"Fleet status!" she ordered at once, turning her bionic eye on Star Admiral Binetti. The cold replacement stared, unblinkingly fixed on the elder man's back.

Technically, Khan Pryde had put the Jade Falcon flagship under the command of Beckett Malthus. Her blessing on the undertaking, and a way to exude her own measure of contribution to the task of invading The Republic of the Sphere. But like most warriors who now answered to Malvina as if she were the Khan herself, Dolphus Binetti knew how to sail with the solar winds. He bowed respectfully and set to his task.

It took a few seconds of sensor readings being relayed up through the chain of command, but within the moment he said, "Seven emerging JumpShips. Fleet present and accounted for, Galaxy Commander." He paused. "We also have four JumpShips, two merchant and two military, in holding positions nearby."

Malvina could care less for the local JumpShip resources. They would run within moments. "Has the local recharge station identified us?"

"They would have to be sensor-blind not to notice our arrival," the Star admiral assured her.

On an auxiliary monitor, a senior technician brought up an image of the local station. An *Olympus*, with its tadpole design and the immense solar sail drifting out behind it to capture solar radiation from Skye's sun and convert it to useful power, stored in helium-cooled superconductor rings and held in reserve to beam-charge JumpShip engines. Such stations were not uncommon, placed at the zenith and sometimes a system's nadir jump point as well. Most were very old, bordering on ancient, and replacing them was expensive, as the expertise and technology was now limited to very few shipyards within the Inner Sphere.

"Our IR signatures have been visible for several minutes, and the electromagnetic-displacement shocks must be tripping every alarm they have. Not to mention we have just parked the largest WarShip they have ever seen on Skye's door. They know, Galaxy Commander. They know. And they are already transmitting news of our arrival dirtside."

"There go the two merchants," a sensor technician called out. "We have energy blooms in the military vessels as well. KF drives are charged. They stand ready to jump."

She began to say something, but the Star admiral interrupted her. "Distance checks?" he ordered. "Are we close enough for our own KF drive to get caught in the energy backwash?"

"*Neg*, Star Admiral. Interference will be negligible."

Malvina stifled her impulse to lash out at the admiral. His caution had been appropriate, and under time constraints. "They have had long enough," she decided. "Open a channel to the recharge station."

The Star admiral nodded her request on to his communications tech. "*Gondola Station*," he informed her as the connection was made.

"*Gondola Station*, this is Malvina Hazen of Clan Jade Falcon. You will surrender unconditionally. You will do so within the next thirty seconds."

On the auxiliary screen, the image of the recharge station winked out, to be replaced by a whip-thin Republic naval officer fastening the cuffs at his wrists. His reddish orange hair stuck out to the left, still tousled and matted from sleep.

"This is Commodore Billings aboard *Gondola*. With what forces do you challenge for this station?"

The man sounded almost bored. An insult worse than his attempt at batchall. When the Clans first invaded the Inner Sphere, adopting Clan bidding practices and twisting honor rules had become a commonplace tactic. In effect, the treacherous surats helped the Clans to defeat themselves. Malvina was not quite the student of history that her brother had been, but she knew better than to allow Inner Sphere barbarians any access to such customs.

"If you will look at your primary monitor, you will see what forces I have deployed in challenge. You now have fifteen seconds."

Perhaps the tired officer's mind was still bedded down in his shipboard bunk. Perhaps he simply could not believe what Malvina was telling him, even when the truth stared him in the face with open gunports and sensor lock. "I don't understand. My sensors show no fighter craft deployed. Just . . . the WarShip." He shook his head. "We have six aerospace fighters standing by on—"

"Five seconds," Malvina cut him off angrily. This man would never have made it out of a Clan sibko alive. The Republic should take greater care whom they posted to important positions. She was not here to hold his hand and explain her demands as if to a child. She didn't especially care if he understood or not. She did not need his edification.

She needed an example.

This order did not go to Star Admiral Binetti. Malvina gave it herself, directly to portside gunnery. The man had a hawklike nose and a jutting chin, and a fanatic's light in his eyes as she told him, "Open fire."

The command was relayed through secure systems to the weapons bays, with less than three seconds elapsed between her order and the first naval-grade PPC slashing out with cold, ruthless talons to rake critical wounds across the station's bow. Naval autocannon and a pair of capital-ship Gauss cannon followed, hammering at the *Olympus* with Thor's own fury.

On-screen, the commodore's face twisted itself into a mixture of confusion and fear as his station shook violently.

"Wait," he pleaded, trying to get back on top of the situation. "We can—"

Malvina reached forward and switched the monitor by her own hand from his cowardly visage to a gun-cam view of *Gondola Station*. Air frosted out of a half dozen deep wounds, jets of ice crystals streaming into space as the station bled to death. She saw a body tumble out, blown clear in the rapid decompression, arms flailing about for less than ten seconds. Then another body. This one got caught between the *Emerald Talon* and *Gondola Station*, ripped in half by the next naval PPC, which struck the station amidships in its small fighter bay.

More weapons converged over the thick doors, blasting them into ruin and reaching deep within. No aerospace fighters would launch now.

"We have one military vessel jumping," a sensor tech called out. "There goes the second one as well."

Running for safety. One or both might simply have jumped for the nadir station, where they would recharge and await orders from Skye. They might just as easily flee for the relative safety of another system altogether, spreading word of the attack.

That also was fine with Malvina Hazen.

Sporadic return fire rose up from the recharge station as a few defiant crewmen struck back with light autocannon and wave after wave of long-range missiles. A few particle cannon joined in, late. These were conventional weapons, with pathetic range compared with capital-ship guns, and even worse damage profiles. They barely scratched the *Nightlord*'s armored hide.

"Hit them again," Malvina said calmly. Even though she had never given an order to cease fire, she wanted it clear that she approved of the continuing barrage.

Gunners walked a line of horrific damage from stem to stern, pounding the hapless facility without mercy. As Malvina desired. A few escape pods launched. Some even managed to clear the storm of weapons fire that filled the vacuum between WarShip and station. Nickel-ferrous masses launched by the *Emerald Talon*'s rail guns snapped off three of the station's six jumpsail supports, and several square kilometers of solar sail creased and tangled into its own cables. Capital lasers carved deep into the engineering spaces, darkening *Gondola*'s station-keeping drive.

A few seconds later the flickering power went out for good. The hull-mounted spotlights darkened. No weapons were fired at the attacking WarShip.

There was no further attempt at communication.

Malvina let the assault hammer into *Gondola Station* for another moment, pounding it into unrecognizable scrap. Finally she nodded. "Enough."

The station's corpse continued to bleed air into the cold vacuum of space. A nimbus of scrap metal and bodies tumbled about, caught only in the WarShip's massive spotlights. When Malvina ordered the lights extinguished a moment later, nothing could be seen of the once graceful station except where its mangled bulk excluded the starlight.

Gondola Station was dead.

"I congratulate you," Beckett Malthus said when she joined him on one of the *Emerald Talon*'s secure administrative decks. The two of them entered her shipboard office. "My aides inform me that you allowed one lifeboat and a half dozen escape pods to clear the kill zone. Skye must know all about the attack by now."

Malvina shrugged. Now that it was over, she saw very little point in reliving the moment. It had been vaguely unsatisfying. Not personal enough for her.

"As it was on Chaffee," she said, taking a seat at her desk, leaving Malthus to stand or accept one of the room's inferior chairs. "The survivors are carriers. They will spread their fear to everyone with whom they come into contact. Skye will know what is in store for it."

"And they will have a week to stew while we travel in-system." The WarShip's massive drives burned hot and silent several dozen decks below, pushing the *Nightlord* into Skye's system at just over one standard gravity of acceleration. "Quite an efficient use of terror as a weapon, I would say."

"As an object lesson it will serve its purpose."

"I wonder," Malthus said, taking a seat and leaning forward as if sharing a secret with Malvina. "How will Skye react, do you think, once the *Emerald Talon*'s lasers start probing down from orbit?"

Meaning, what were her exact plans for the WarShip once they reached the world of Skye? Whatever Malthus thought personally of her tactics, he hid behind inscrutable green eyes, but Malvina was no fool. Beckett Malthus cared less for the local reaction than he did for how Malvina planned to further Jade Falcon goals inside The Republic. All the better to position himself as well.

She spread her hands over her spotless desktop, feeling the cold metal burn against her left palm. Against her right, she felt nothing. "We will not use the *Emerald Talon*'s weapons in an orbital bombardment of Skye, except as a final resort. The WarShip will be used only to interdict the world, making sure none escape the Jade Falcons' will."

Malthus ran blunt fingers through his hair, tugged at his deep widow's peak. "You wish to mitigate the damage to Skye itself? Does that not run counter to your plans to instill fear and use it to hold the populace in thrall?"

"This has nothing to do with mitigating the damage. This is about victory and honor. *I* want this world, Beckett Malthus, and I will have it by my own hand."

She raised her right arm, with its false, ebony sheen, and stared at the replacement hand. It was stronger than a true limb. It could crush bone, shatter someone's skull with a backhand slap. But it wasn't real.

"I am no Star admiral. I am a MechWarrior. Skye must and will fall to me through my own prowess if I am to fulfill my role as the Chinggis Khan. People will tremble at the sound of a 'Mech footfall. My *Shrike* will be my avatar."

"And the people will have a face to put to their nightmares. You are most cunning in your foresight . . . my Khan."

Yes. Enough to see how much she had come to rely on the machinations and resources of Beckett Malthus. More so than she had ever relied on Aleksandr for his counsel and his aid, and with her brother she had always been assured of his ultimate loyalty. Not that he would not oppose her—he had—but Aleksandr could be counted on to work by the light of day where she could watch him, always wary.

Beckett Malthus suffered no such personal constraints. And the *Emerald Talon*, for all its implied power, was his. Given to him by the Jade Falcon Khan Jana Prydc, as her way of setting her stamp of approval on the undertaking. No matter how Malvina orchestrated events, with or without Malthus' help, some of her prestige would always bleed back to Pryde if she was not careful, and if she continued to rely on the Jade Falcon flagship.

"I . . . understand," he said.

If he had followed her reasoning through, he just might. The man could not read minds, but Malthus had an uncanny gift for intrigue. She knew she must watch him. Malvina needed him in the here and now. But not forever.

Just long enough to take Skye.

24

Jasek's reception on Hesperus II was everything he could have hoped for. And more than he wanted.

For two days he was toured around Maria's Elegy and the 'Mech factories under Defiance Peak. The city reminded him vaguely of Cheops back on Nusakan, sculpted into the side of several terraced mountains. But Cheops was a poor comparison. The Rises in Maria's Elegy were steeper, grander, than anything on Nusakan. And the heavy reliance on domed construction gave the entire city a glittering, jewellike presence. As if half the buildings were constructed of faceted crystal, throwing around bright spots of color and more than a few rainbows.

He and Joss Vandel were feasted with local fare, which tasted a bit too much of iron for Jasek's palate. Sturdy livestock and hardy plants, he imagined. Wines and delicacies were all brought in from off-world by the ruling Brewster family. Not one item came out of The Republic, or Skye. Not even as a courtesy.

Two days.

Jasek wearied of the constant attention and the ultrapolite refusal of anyone in Duke Vedet Brewster's family to talk business. He never saw Trillian Steiner. His requests for an audience with her went unanswered.

Perhaps his distant cousin felt so far removed from the Kelswa offshoot that she would rather leave him in the generous—if careful—hands of the local nobility.

Caroline Brewster escorted Jasek this evening to what he was certain would be yet another formal dinner engagement, fully scripted right down to the afterdinner conversation, which in no way would touch on events taking place inside the old Isle of Skye. Caroline's skin was ebony black and her eyes had an exotic fold just at the outer edge. She wore pristine white gloves and a gold-colored cocktail dress. A striking debutant, no doubt meant to distract him from his agenda. Perhaps he was being maneuvered into some noble matchmaking as well, a game not unknown in the Lyran Commonwealth, where marriages for social alliances were even more commonplace than the Inner Sphere norm. He resolved to be on his best behavior, and on his guard.

So when Trillian Steiner opened the door herself, with Colonel Vandel standing behind her and Vedet Brewster grazing a nearby table of appetizers, it took Jasek a moment to regain his political feet.

"Cousin," she greeted him warmly, as if they had seen each other quite recently. Trillian leaned in to give him a chaste peck on the cheek. She embraced Caroline with far more familiarity, bussing her cheeks with a leaning hug. "And Caroline. Good eve."

Trillian practically glowed, with long golden hair braided behind each shoulder, and alabaster skin that forced her, here on Hesperus II, to extreme precautions to protect that paleness. Though five years younger than Jasek, she carried herself with a graceful confidence common to only the most experienced politicians. This was a young scion of House Steiner who had embraced everything that Jasek had refused in his own heritage. Position. Privilege. She was her family's direct representative here on Hesperus II, able to charm the local nobility, or stand up to them if the needs of the ruling House diverged from that of the Brewsters.

"You both know Joss Vandel," she said with just the

right timbre of expectation. If she had been a Clansman, Jasek would have expected her to follow up with the rhetorical "Quaiff?" "Joss is an old friend."

Jasek's colonel for the Archon's Shield battalion of the Stormhammers looked perfectly at ease in full Lyran dress, light blue woolen jacket and white stirrup pants, showing off a row of medals won in Lyran service as well as the rank awarded by Jasek. Vandel smiled and half bowed to his commander.

"I was aware that you knew each other," Jasek said. "I didn't realize how well."

Trillian offered her arm to Vandel and allowed the officer to lead her back into the room. There were several guests whom Jasek did not recognize invited to this predinner rendezvous. The most important ones, he felt certain, were within arm's reach.

"Joss Vandel taught a civics class at Tharkad University. Between assignments."

Military assignments, or Lohengrin? Jasek doubted that the intelligence service made available a list of agents, but he was equally confident that very little had been withheld from Trillian Steiner. She was being intentionally vague, playing the old game of "What do you know?"

"Indeed." Jasek plucked a heavy crystal goblet of dark wine from a bed of ice. "I'm sure Colonel Vandel has served the Commonwealth in many useful matters."

Not the least of which was his current role as leader of a Stormhammer unit and a champion of returning Skye to Lyran rule. An assignment he felt certain Trillian would rather be kept concealed from their hosts.

Duke Vedet Brewster shared his niece's dark skin but not her exotic eyes. The man had a plain, honest face that was surely a shield for the plans he harbored within. Balancing a small plate of appetizers in one hand, he walked around the end of the table and joined the conversation. "Interesting, don't you think, that we all find ourselves in the same place just now? Hardly a coincidence, though."

"Hardly," Jasek agreed. Was he supposed to open a dialogue here and now? He sipped his wine, found it delightfully sweet. "I came here for a very specific reason, Duke Vedet."

It was a Skye tradition to apply the noble title to a first

name rather than the family name, creating a more intimate manner of address. Vedet Brewster did not correct his usage. "Hopefully not the same reason that brought you to Chaffee," he said with a touch of steel.

If the duke felt the action on Chaffee had offered the prospect of Republic annexation, he had not been following events inside the Sphere of late. Then again, with Hesperus II suffering under the same blackout as so many other worlds, his wondering what plans were being bandied about in the dark did not count as a major strike against him.

"Chaffee was a gift. To get your attention. I presume I have it."

Trillian preempted the duke with a casual glance in his direction. "It took us the past week to get independent confirmation of the status of Chaffee. Some of us wondered if The Republic was going to claim dominion." She directed a dark gaze at Joss Vandel, who wore a consciously blank look. "After all, it was not the Commonwealth who went to their aid."

"Chaffee is not an old Skye world," Jasek said, putting the emphasis where it belonged, "though certainly we have shared interests several times over the centuries. It was hurt badly when the Falcons used their blistering agent on the population, but at its core the world is Lyran. It belongs with the Commonwealth. Any lingering feelings of abandonment will fade with time and freedom."

He was not referring only to Chaffee, or to the Falcons. Duke Vedet raised an eyebrow as he absorbed Jasek's meaning, and nodded. "I have guests I should greet. Allow me to introduce you."

If Jasek thought that business was finished for the evening, Duke Vedet quickly disabused him of that notion as he introduced senior officers in the Lyran Commonwealth's standing army and several civilian officials. All of them were interested in what Jasek had seen and done on Chaffee, what was going on among the old Isle of Skye worlds, and his take on the Jade Falcon incursion.

"We never believed the Jade Falcon ambassador who claimed their forces were merely on a long-strike expedition to hunt down and destroy the Steel Wolves." Jerome Boxleitner was a senior aide to the planetary administrator, specializing in interworld relations. "But what were we to do? The Falcons' army dwarfed the entirety of what we had in the region, and not even fifty-odd years of relative peace have been enough to make us forget the damaging losses our military saw in the decades of violence between 3050 and 3080."

Jasek nodded in acknowledgment. "But what if the Clanners chose to bypass The Republic and strike here at Hesperus? What if next time they decide to wipe their feet on you as they strike for Terra?"

" 'What if' is a dangerous game," Boxleitner said with a pinched expression. "For example, what if they had actually held to their word and rid your Republic of the Wolves?"

"But they didn't. Far from it. Instead, they struck Porrima, an ancestral holding of House Steiner." Jasek's raised voice drew a few nearby military officers into the discussion. Joss Vandel nodded surreptitiously. "And on Chaffee, your citizens were abused with a blistering agent. Who knows what horror they will visit on the next world they attack? Does it matter if that world is Republic, and not Lyran?"

"Shouldn't it matter?" a young leutnant-general asked.

From his decorations, Jasek saw that he was a sharp-shooter and had received several unit citations on his way up the chain of command. Which was interesting, as the man had no campaign ribbons and—Jasek noted—bore no callus on his hands that would indicate he held a weapon regularly. Or at all. Another social general.

"It didn't matter to me," was all Jasek said. He caught several people nodding, swayed, if not convinced. Yet.

Trillian tapped Jasek on the elbow, extracting him from the small crowd. "I'd like you to try the Sarpsborg shrimp. They just set some out." Her casual approach lasted until they were out of earshot of the crowd. "You're very good when you know what you want." She used a long skewer to place three tiny pieces of curled, pink meat on his plate. "But do you understand what it is you are asking?" She shook her head.

The shrimp tasted bitter. No doubt an acquired taste. "If Duke Vedet thought it would soften the blow for the no to come from family," Jasek told her, sensing a refusal of his appeal, "you should remind him that our relationship is quite distant."

Her blue eyes were the color of a summer sky, and hard as diamonds. "You've made many good points. Likening the Commonwealth to a doormat was an ingenious metaphor."

. "If the muddy boot fits," he said with a forced smile. "Look. The Isle of Skye was a thorn in the side of the Commonwealth for centuries. I know that. But you must still feel some obligation to its people, or we wouldn't be talking."

"Let us say that Duke Brewster agrees to help you. He might, you know. With the resources at his disposal, and the general level of military downsizing since Devlin Stone's Terran Accords, Hesperus has never been better defended. We can afford to be generous. And sitting here on our hands while the Jade Falcons tramp among our worlds does not sit well with anyone."

Jasek did not miss that his cousin had shifted from talking of Duke Vedet to saying "we" and "our." He felt a surge of hope.

"However"—she raised a hand—"if Skye is successfully defended, with or without our help, it may drive the Jade Falcons back into Lyran space. Would you have us go to war in place of The Republic?"

"I wouldn't ask that of you unless Skye was willing to stand apart from The Republic, and at your side."

"Then how can you ask for the one, while not guaranteeing the other?"

Now Jasek did smile. They were getting close to a bargain, and even as an expatriate Lyran he enjoyed a good negotiation. "If that is truly your concern, Trillian Steiner, I believe I can set your fears at ease. If I accomplish what I have planned, the Jade Falcons will not be able to turn their eye on the Lyran state for some time."

"You are saying we'd be risking very little?"

"No, I'm going to ask you to risk quite a lot. But it comes with an insurance policy. Win, lose, or draw, the Falcons will not be coming back into the Lyran Commonwealth."

"How can you promise that?"

Jasek Kelswa-Steiner picked up another glass of wine, took a healthy swig, and told her.

25

The floor of Tara Campbell's New London command post was a poured slab, raked rough and not quite level. Hasty construction. Capped wires stuck out of electrical conduits where power outlets had not been installed. Cinder block walls sweated condensation from a lack of proper heating. The smell of fresh cement mixed with the ozone scent of warm electronics; that, and a low ceiling, made the large, long room feel smaller than it was.

Tara Campbell rocked back on her heels, as if testing the floor's slight tilt, but kept her gaze fastened on the workstation monitor where a sensor technician framed the Jade Falcons' DropShip insertion. An amber band marked the hazy boundary between stratosphere and space. Seventeen red-glowing icons trailed dashed lines to mark the DropShips' progress. Seventeen! Half of them now edged into the amber band.

Conversation in the room was hushed, mostly an exchange of tense, clipped sentences. The weight of the Jade Falcon arrival over Skye sat heavily on the shoulders of every military person in the room. More than a few glanced upward, as if able to see through steel, ferrocrete, and several meters of dirt, and the hundreds of kilometers of atmosphere.

Tara resisted the urge.

"Have we confirmed their targets yet?" she asked the officer on vector mechanics.

Possessed of sallow skin and bloodshot eyes, Leutnant Nicole Barringer obviously spent too much time in dimly lit rooms, staring at computer monitors. But she was the best Skye had, which was why Tara had pulled her for duty. She performed only half of the mathematics by computer, the other half in her head.

"Twelve of the seventeen DropShips have reduced their deceleration burn and are pulling ahead of the pack." She used a stylus to draw a lopsided diamond around their icons, then sketched a golden arc up off the screen, approximating their average insertion angle. Another arc trailed from the bottom tip of the diamond down through the amber band and into one of the color-coded boxes that sat at the lower edge of the screen. Each box represented an insertion path for one of ten high-priority targets.

"It's not safe money, Countess, not yet, but these at least are holding to a tight course. Textbook vectors from their orbiting WarShip, falling straight down at New London."

Nodding, Tara tapped the screen over each of the other five red icons. "And these?"

"No aspect change in bearing or velocity, but . . . I don't know. It looks like New London, but I think they are saving delta-V to make low-atmospheric changes."

Going just as the defenders had predicted. Which bothered Tara a great deal.

"Keep our aerospace fighters well away from their insertion path. Seventeen DropShips and a heavy fighter escort is more than we can bite off." And even if they could, there was the WarShip to consider. Malvina Hazen had already shown her willingness to use it.

Murdering bitch.

Forcing herself to continue a slow pace along the row of workstations, Tara confirmed every detail at least twice and stopped at ground-monitoring stations to check on New London itself. Her skin prickled with gooseflesh despite the warmth of the room, tiny bumps standing out on her bare arms and legs. She was dressed for combat, already in cooling vest and padded shorts. When the time came for action, she didn't want anything to slow her down.

"Have the sirens done their work?" she asked another tech.

"Working, ma'am." He leaned aside to give her a better view of the screens he watched. Prefect Della Brown joined Tara at the bank of small monitors, crowding in at the man's other shoulder.

Silent camera views switched along the many arterials of New London, the green-budding parks, the commercial and industrial centers. For midday, traffic was light and thinning out every minute. No one picnicked to celebrate spring's early arrival. Shopping was limited mostly to frantic purchases of canned goods and urban survival gear: flashlights and bottled water, sweets and cigarettes. Restaurants were closing and nonessential services were suspended for the duration. Sanglamore had been emptied and Prefect Brown's New London Tower operated on a skeleton staff.

After the high cost Skye paid during the last assault by Clan Jade Falcon, with her *Himmelsfahrtkommando* sacrificing hundreds of lives to keep their world free, Tara Campbell wanted no repeat of such a massacre. At least, not when it would not do any good.

The Falcons were back for blood.

"We're not going to make it easy for them," she promised, speaking to herself in a soft whisper.

Della Brown straightened. "In fact," she said, not bothering to hide her unease with the plan, "we are."

Prefect Brown was a tall, svelte woman who had put herself through college by working as a runway model. She had dark hair and stormy gray eyes, and had held her figure well, even if she dressed down with her gray field uniform. She wore little makeup these days, and didn't need to. Her austere beauty and her extra fifteen centimeters of height were just a bit intimidating, though Tara fought back with a mixed package of popularity and vivacity.

"What would you have us do, Prefect?" Tara asked simply.

"Open resistance. BattleMechs and tank columns along

the main arterials. VTOLs to skirt the edge of the city, and infantry dug in at all the hardened buildings we have."

"Blood in the streets," Tara said. "We saw enough of that along Sutton Road and across Seminary Hill the last time. You don't think the Jade Falcons came ready for that? We need to stay one step—"

"Countess!" The woman on vector mechanics was first with an alert. "We have . . . I've lost signal. We have no—that's *zero*—confidence. Some kind of interference pattern I don't recognize."

"Same here." She may have been first, but now other voices around the room called out with frantic need for attention. A major on tactical shouted down some nearby techs. "I have negative feedback on every channel. High electromagnetic interference."

"No feed," someone else complained.

"Wild power fluctuations on— "

"—dead sensors."

Tara and Della Brown had watched as all of the New London cameras blacked out simultaneously. The tech didn't bother with complaints or guesses, but set about working his emergency procedures to acquire data. He toggled for power, ran checks on the local electronics. Everything seemed to be in order.

But there was something coldly familiar about this. A report Tara remembered reading from . . . from . . . a hollow pit opened up inside her.

"Nicole!" Tara jogged back up the line of workstations to the woman on vector mechanics. "What was the last thing you saw?"

"Possible bearing changes across the board. And the lead DropShips, I think they had all poured on harder decel burns, slowing their fall. I was working on confirmation when it all went dark."

"I want a direct camera view over New London." Tara shoved herself away from vector mechanics, trying to remember which station had auxiliary taps into meteorological data. Those were local systems and might be safe from what she feared was happening. "Weather feeds," she called out. Was that on tactical?

No. Aerospace control. A bright-eyed young ensign

waved for her attention, frowning at his monitor. "Whatever this is . . . ," he began.

But Tara knew. So did Prefect Della Brown, apparently, who was at the workstation a step ahead of Tara. The blacked-out sensors and interference patterns. It read too similar to reports from Glengarry, when Malvina Hazen had brought down one of the Stormhammer DropShips. The kind of disaster that Tara had hoped to avoid.

The two women stared at the bright, glowing streaks that smeared the daytime sky like a high-strength aurora borealis.

"That," Tara said with false calm, "is a nuclear detonation."

There was no way to estimate the height, but it had to be a high-atmosphere detonation to get that kind of wide-coverage effect. Ionization covering thousands of square kilometers was reflected back down at Skye and New London by the planet's own magnetic field.

"What's this going to mean?" Della asked, voice low and shaking with barely controlled fury.

Tara held herself up against the edge of the workstation. The cold metal edge cut into her fingers like a dull knife. "Severe ionization and intense magnetic fields which will induce high voltages in power lines, communication towers, and other long-range conductors." Bad. Very bad. "We'll get feeds back slowly, except where electronics might be completely fried from power surges. Fortunately, our most valuable equipment should be in hardened facilities."

"What about our fighter craft?"

She considered. "They should be okay. But we'll keep them grounded or on patrol out of the area regardless. We keep to the plan, and when the Falcons try to move their DropShips after grounding, that's when we hit them."

Della Brown nodded. "I suppose we should feel fortunate that Malvina Hazen didn't take New London right off the map."

"Fortunate?" Tara shook her head. "If the Jade Falcons are willing to spend from their nuclear arsenal and did *not* want New London erased, it's because they have something far worse in mind."

"Like what?"

Tara looked over the various workstation screens. Mostly

static and darkness. "We don't know," she admitted. "That's the entire point. For now, we're blind and deaf.

"And the Jade Falcons are falling right on top of us."

Roosevelt Bridgehead

Missiles shattered armor along the entire right side of Tamara Duke's Eisenfaust, digging sharp claws through the *Wolfhound*'s protection. Elemental lasers raked a pair of narrow red furrows down the side of the BattleMech's "face." One clipped the upper corner of her cockpit's ferroglass shield, and a single drop of molten tears trailed halfway down the transparent screen before carbonizing into a black crust.

She thought she detected the acrid smell of burned metal, and worried for the space of a single heartbeat how deeply those lasers had cut.

It was all the time she had. The Elementals were on her like vermin. Nipping at her legs. Slashing at her with lasers and missiles. A few of them clambered for a good hold somewhere around the *Wolfhound*'s waist. She plucked one from her hip, crushing the suited figure in her "iron fist."

"We're good, Kommandant. Get out of there!"

One of these days, she'd pound it through Vic Parkins' thick skull that he did *not* give her orders.

Of course, this time it could be nothing more sinister than a need for quick communications. Hauptmann Parkins had led a short retreat back toward the Roosevelt bridgehead while she held back the Falcons. His Behemoth was perfect for anchoring a new line. She had the ability to catch up quickly. If he was set, she needed to be out of there, fast!

Kicking out with her 'Mech's left leg, Tamara let the armored infantry get a quick feel of her iron foot. One battlesuit trooper went flying off like a punted football. But his comrades pressed in closer, and she couldn't risk another swarming attack. She slammed down on both foot pedals, lighting off jump jets as she arced backward in a long, flat hop.

More ground lost.

That had been the way of the entire morning, in fact.

Ever since the Jade Falcons had landed an old *Union*-class DropShip and a *Sassanid*-class infantry carrier near Roosevelt Island. Not enough to take Cyclops, Incorporated, away from her Lyran Rangers—not without backup—but enough to put some serious hurt on her company if she once thought of standing toe-to-toe with the assault force.

It was all stick-and-retreat from then on, with the Falcons pushing hard, taking risks time and again as they did everything possible to gain an advantage. Maybe Tamara had moved them out a bit too slowly at one point. Maybe she'd played it all a bit too cautious. Fighting their way back toward the bridgehead, her Rangers had ended up pinched between a heavy line of 'Mechs and vehicles and this ambush of Elementals. The trap cost her company a lot of armor and a few good warriors before they slipped free.

Jasek, she knew, would have done better. She had to prove that she could as well.

Landing alongside her lance, Tamara froze over her controls for a few seconds while a Demon raced up to take care of the lone Elemental who had tagged along for the ride. A Falcon *Eyrie* let fly from long range with its advanced tactical missile system, but the warheads went wide and blew impotent holes in a nearby hillside. When it attempted to race forward, a pair of SM1 Destroyers was able to change its mind and send it fleeing for the safety of the main Falcon line.

A *Vulture* swaggered out to give its smaller cousin some covering fire. Behind both 'Mechs, the Clanners shook themselves into a new order of battle with Elementals fanning out in overlapping scrimmage lines.

The bridgehead wasn't more than a kilometer behind the Lyran Rangers now. It ran out from a rocky slope, tied into the highway system that wound and twisted its way north along the coast to eventually reach Norfolk or speared directly west toward Braggart and Miliano. Truxton Sound lay between the mainland and Roosevelt Island, home to the main factories for Cyclops, Incorporated. The wind-chopped waters reflected back a steel gray sky, exactly the color of Tamara's mood.

She toggled for planetary defense again, not expecting any change, but hoping. "This is Roosevelt Station. We need artillery and aerospace support. Still." Static answered her. "This is Roosevelt Station. Come in, damn it!"

It was Colonel Petrucci who got back to her. Again. "Sutton Road is still off-line, Kommandant. We're on our own. Deal with the situation as you see fit."

Easy for the commander to say. He had the bulk of the Rangers spread out far to the south, covering several large cities, the Hemphill Company sapphire mines, and a host of small preassembly plants for Avanti Assemblies. And by reports he had only a few Jade Falcon reconnaissance lances to deal with.

The *Vulture* dumped out twin loads from its missile racks, and Tamara fell back another two hundred meters to escape their maximum range. Her large laser was equally useless, though. Artillery! What she couldn't do right now with a simple Long Tom or Paladin defense system.

"We can hold, Colonel." Parkins again. He was tied into the Rangers' command frequency. Damn the man!

"We can hold," she agreed through clenched teeth, "but it won't be pretty."

The Elementals were beginning to sneak forward under the cover of the *Vulture*'s missile barrage and the threat of a Kelswa assault tank. She sent her Destroyers out on a quick jaunt, threatening to run under the long-range fire to blast apart the Falcons with their assault-class autocannon.

"You aren't the only one with troubles, Tamara. Wolf is calling for any backup she can get, and only the Steel Wolves are in place to support her. The Highlanders and Seventh Skye Militia report heavy action north of the capital as well."

Alexia Wolf and elements from the Archon's Shield had been charged with holding Miliano. Those troops had been hammered mercilessly by a veteran Falcon force. Tamara had requested the city's defense—let the greenies handle Cyclops!—but Tara Campbell had gambled heavily on the Falcons' being preoccupied with New London, instead. Apparently that ruse had not gone off so well as they'd hoped.

And if the Miliano Basin fell, both Norfolk and Roosevelt Island would be flanked by a Jade Falcon push. She slammed a fist against the arm of her command chair.

"If we pull out and go to their aid, we lose Cyclops,

Incorporated. If we don't, we might lose even more. Will Kerensky assist?''

"She hasn't moved yet. The Falcons threw a little bit her way, but fell back twice as fast when that *Overlord* spoke up with its big guns. Trouble is, pretty much the only officer that woman trusts is Campbell. And her not too far.''

She'd dance to Jasek's tune, if he were here. What would *he* say to convince Kerensky? "Colonel, we can't let Miliano go. Point out what kind of trouble Norfolk will be in if the Steel Wolves don't reinforce the basin. Remind them that Wolf is one of theirs.'' More theirs than she was a true Stormhammer, anyway.

Tamara triggered a laser blast as a Falcon Skadi swooped in too close. The VTOL retreated with a landing skid burned away.

"Tell her . . . tell her Jasek would take it as a personal favor.''

That hurt. Doubly so when Vic Parkins chimed in. "That might do it,'' her exec agreed.

Petrucci thought so as well. "I'll see what can be bargained. In the meantime, Kommandant, keep your head low and your people safe.''

"Safe as we can,'' Parkins promised for them both. His *Behemoth* rolled forward, soaking up some long-range sniping as the Falcons geared for another relentless push.

Not about to be seen accepting cover behind Parkins, or any tank commander for that matter, Tamara Duke throttled her *Wolfhound* into an easy walk and stalked into the open territory between her Rangers and the Falcons. Her large laser sliced angry-bright, cutting at the *Vulture*'s right arm.

She ducked beneath a return salvo of missiles, taking only a handful of them across her back and shoulders. "We do *not* give them the island,'' she told her Rangers, determined not to fall back again. They would keep the bridgehead on this side of the sound, and they'd pluck some Falcons doing it. "We dig in. We hold here.''

She toggled off. But under her breath, she continued.

"And we hope we get some relief forces over this way before the Falcons do.''

26

Sutton Road
Skye
30 November 3134

Tara Campbell sprinted down the short, rough-hewn passageway that led to "the Pen." Already in combat togs, she simply stripped off the headset she'd been using and tossed it onto a maintenance bench as soon as she burst into the cavernous bay her engineers had secretly dug into the face of the Sutton Road bluff.

Sodium-vapor lights brightened the space, and the roar of internal combustion engines competed with the backwash of lift fans that stirred dirt and loose papers into a cyclone. Two Highlander infantrymen finished sealing up in Cavalier battle armor and boarded a waiting Maxim. Ten vehicles, all crammed in fender to skirt, waited for the camouflaged door to open.

Waited for her.

Her *Hatchetman* waited as well, crouched just inside the door where the ceiling had been carved high enough to admit the slender BattleMech. Its ax lay against the floor, covered in a light patina of rock dust. The sloping head tilted down at a restful angle. It took Tara all of two minutes to scale the simple handyman's ladder, button up the cockpit, and pull on her neurohelmet. Leads to the inside of her arms and legs. Coolant line snapped into her vest's socket. Toggles up. Switch on. The fusion engine thrummed awake, breathing life into the forty-five-ton machine. Her computer flashed for attention, demanding security protocols.

"Tara Campbell. Countess Northwind." Her voiceprint appeared on the monitor as a jagged sine wave, filled with a few special dips and peaks uniquely hers.

Still, it was possible to fool neurocircuitry and voice-prints. And MechWarriors tended to be just a little bit paranoid when it came to protecting their ride. As a backup measure, the computer's synthesized voice prompted her for secondary protocol. One wrong word—one anomalous reading in the neurocircuitry—would lock out weapons controls.

Tara adjusted her neurohelmet, wanting good contact with the sensors. She had no time for mistakes. "*Manus haec inimica tyrannis.*"

Latin. One of the advantages of a classical education.

This hand is hostile to tyrants.

"Where are they?" Tara asked as the main door levered open.

A pair of hoverbikes was first out the door, with the lower edge barely clearing the drivers' heads. A low-profile Shandra was next, and then two JES missile carriers. Tara crowded into line and duckwalked the tall 'Mech out into the day's gray light. The balance of her forces followed after.

Della Brown came on the communications line herself. "Still two klicks north along the river. They haven't got you yet."

A good thing, or the command post would have to be abandoned. Tara turned her *Hatchetman* enough to see out of a side-view shield. The rock-faced door was just swinging closed. Higher up, with its commanding view over the Thames and the last battlefield of her Forlorn Hope recruits, was the Sutton Road Memorial Park, where she had attended the press event—it seemed like years ago. No one had even suspected the excavation for the HQ, with all the heavy machinery there to smooth out a new parking area and add acres of sculpted grounds. It was her final advantage in this latest battle for Skye.

"Keep everything dimmed until they've passed," Tara told the prefect as she throttled into a loping run, heading south. "We'll hit them five kilometers below your position." While the Jade Falcons still felt safe.

"Good hunting."

They'd need it. Things were already off to a faster start than anyone had planned. The Jade Falcons had surrounded and entered New London quickly, under cover of the EMP-imposed blackout. Six DropShips all told—grounding at the DropPort and in the industrial sector, and even one massive *Lion*, ninety meters tall and more than seven thousand tons, squatting over what used to be the parade grounds of Sanglamore Academy. Tara had needed no camera to guess the outrage on Malvina Hazen's face when she found the capital all but deserted of every administrator, business leader, and warrior.

Confirming that had taken time, precious hours, and by then reports must have been rolling in that her secondary objectives at Roosevelt Island, Miliano, and Corruscat were heavily defended and bloodying Jade Falcon advance teams.

When the command post finally restored some of their communications, Tara found out that she had guessed right about most places, but not all. Miliano was being held by the grace of God and the tenacity of Alexia Wolf's Strikers.

Colonel Petrucci and Anastasia Kerensky still could not be reached.

And now the first Jade Falcon reinforcements were striking out from the capital, searching for signs of local defenders as they moved on Norfolk and Miliano. They came along a southern valley, following Sutton Road and the Thames in a short column designed more for speedy travel than defense, led by a *Warhammer IIC* and a lightly armored *Koshi*. The *Warhammer* was a real monster, with four extended-range lasers and an SRM four-pack over each shoulder. It caught Tara's breath in her throat, and nearly choked her on it.

Tara had her small company spread out in some nearby trees and hunkered down in a dry wash. She hid her *Hatchetman* as well as she could in a stand of stunted evergreens, her targeting system on passive mode. Hoping to get at least one good shot in on the assault 'Mech before it started ripping apart vehicles.

The Falcons caught on, but far too late. A pair of venerable Pegasus scout craft on the column flank nearly missed half of Tara's hidden company. As it was, they had barely enough time to skate in a circle and run out from beneath the missile umbrella that scattered around their position.

Then a Kelswa assault tank swamped up from a marsh near the river, and its twin Gauss rifles hammered ferrous masses into the side of a straggling APC. The devastating hits crushed in the entire side and rolled the vehicle over, spilling wounded and angry Elementals out like bees shook from a hive. A Hasek MCV rolled clear of the dry wash, dropping Cavalier troopers. Its particle cannon slashed out to rip armor away from the *Warhammer*'s leg.

First blood for her Highlanders and for Skye! "Tallyho!" Tara called out, pushing her *Hatchetman* from the tree line.

The Jade Falcons had made their first real mistake, treating the area surrounding New London as if it were safe. Their own personal land hold. Tara was here to make them pay for that. As high a price as she was able.

Miliano Basin

The Miliano Basin was three-rivers country. Wide stretches of forested hills were cut with sharp valleys in some places and had been hammered down by time into nothing larger than rolling mounds in others. The rivers pushed at their banks with the spring runoff, and in many places flooded lowland bogs. It was an area of fish farms and logging concerns, and a few large agricultural combines.

And today it was another battlefield.

The price had run fairly stiff against Alexia Wolf's Tharkan Strikers. She had held the Jade Falcons back from Miliano, but too often she had been forced to send a crippled 'Mech or vehicle limping toward the rear lines, preserving it for another day. Harder choices forced her to sacrifice machines and men to buy time. To redeploy. To save a larger piece of the Stormhammers who suddenly found themselves in a threatened position. If not for the two elite lances she'd borrowed from the Archon's Shield, her people would already be in a full rout.

"Leutnant-colonel." It was one of her pathfinders, scouting the back trail to make certain they did not fall back into an enemy trap. "We have the city's outskirts in view."

Coming up against a hard wall, then. Alexia dropped her crosshairs over a distant *Koshi* and spread two loads of long-range missiles through the air. Her *Catapult* rocked back under the missile exhaust, then forward as she hunched over.

The missiles slammed down around the *Koshi*'s position, driving it back. But not for long. Not when it was joined just outside of her best range by a pair of Skandas and a *Thor*. All along her thinned line, the Falcons massed in pairs and clumps. They would be coming again. Soon. And the Stormhammers would not be able to stand against them.

She was realist enough to admit it to herself. The Clans raised practical warriors who spent their lives judging very carefully the subtle win-loss percentages of any battle. Failing her Trial of Position on Arc-Royal had reinforced that skill. There she had fought for herself, and that had not been enough. Here Alexia believed she had found a larger cause, but that did not confer on her aerospace support or a company of heavy armor, which was what she needed.

"Light forces roll forward, engage, and skirmish. Prepare to fall back on our main line."

She sent a practiced glance to her HUD, her tactical maps, and the view outside her cockpit ferroglass. She could buy another hour. Perhaps two—no more than two. "Air support. If you can get those Yellow Jackets back in the air, now is the time."

Her VTOLs were the only aerospace forces she had under her command. Or was likely to see. The bulk of Skye's aerospace corps was working to keep enemy DropShips grounded, to prevent the Falcons from redeploying their forces caught at New London.

The problem was, they had hoped to trap a lot more than they had.

It was her own fault as much as anyone's. She had agreed when Tara Campbell judged Miliano safer from attack than

Norfolk or Roosevelt Island. So had GioAvanti, whose family held widespread local interests, and Jasek, who had discussed it with his commanders in meetings before Glengarry and Chaffee. A larger city. More manpower to hold it. Everyone expected the Falcons to spend all their forces against the capital.

Using a high-atmosphere nuclear detonation to disrupt ground forces? Never. Not in the Clans she'd grown up learning about.

The *Koshi* began its run down through the valley that separated the Falcon position from her own, trailed by the Skandas and then the *Thor*. The lighter 'Mech had exceptional scouting abilities; no doubt it was looking for hidden battlesuit infantry or dug-in tanks. She almost wished she'd tried a trick of that nature. The maybes were piling up. So were the bodies, though, and any unit left in the no-man's-land out there was not coming home.

"Forward and engage on my mark," she ordered.

Throttling into a stiff, bowlegged walk, she pulled her crosshairs over the *Thor*. Her plan was to brush through the light machines and try to inflict some heavy damage on the larger 'Mech before being forced to run. It was a good plan. But someone else had it as well.

Twin streams of high-energy particles slashed out of a blind draw on the *Thor*'s left, ripping deep wounds along the BattleMech's side. The machine rocked over on one foot, then teetered back.

For a second, Alexia wondered how one of her inexperienced warriors had slipped behind the enemy line. And had managed to stay hidden.

Then she realized that one couldn't have. If nothing else, she knew she'd not lost track of one man or woman on the field today.

Another savage assault as PPCs blazed out arcing lashes to flail and strip the *Thor* of two more tons of armor. This time the seventy-ton machine went down, falling with a crash that Alexia thought she felt half a kilometer away. A *Ryoken II* stomped into view, its icon lighting up her HUD as it switched to active targeting sensors. That kind of accuracy on *passive* sensors?

More icons popped at nearly the same time, identifying

Demons and Condors and even an SM1 Destroyer. All tagged with Steel Wolf marks.

"Not just for breakfast anymore," a familiar voice crackled over the communications net.

"*Thor*s?" Alexia asked, perplexed at Anastasia Kerensky's comment. Surprised at her very appearance on the battlefield. She didn't waste the happy occurrence, though. Her missiles arced out and fell in desperate waves over the *Koshi* and the Skandas.

"Jade Falcons. In the old days, they would never have come back to Skye for a second bite. I guess somewhere along the way they grew a pair."

And if Kerensky had been impressive coming at the Falcons with her sensors sidelined, as she drew a new bead on the shaken *Thor* she showed a true artist's touch. Her PPCs slashed out in short, accurate cuts, blasting damage in behind each knee actuator and the shoulders as well. In a matter of seconds, she had incapacitated a seventy-ton BattleMech.

Alexia envied the other woman her skill, but did not let it get in her way. She claimed a Skanda and drove the *Koshi* into retreat by slamming a half dozen warheads into the side of its head. The MechWarrior's ears would still be ringing the next day. Turning, she lent savage support to a pair of Stormhammer VV1 Rangers who had corralled a green-painted Demon between them.

Another coordinated assault, and the Demon ground to a smoking halt.

All along her line, machines stomped, rolled, or skated forward. Alexia had no need to tell them to press. They simply did. Lasers sliced angrily back and forth. Autocannon hammered and the lightning of particle cannon struck out with furious insult. In an instant, the battle had shifted in the defenders' favor.

Heavier machines rolling up behind the Strikers' first wave and Steel Wolves on their flank? The Jade Falcon commander knew better than to push a suicidal position. Machines reversed in their tracks, or cut out on long, arcing escape paths. There was no panic. No rout that could be exploited. Chasing them would only open up Alexia's people to a new counterstrike.

She was happy enough surviving the day with what was left of her command. Of Jasek's people.

"We heard you weren't interested," Alexia said, feeling the first drain of battlefield lethargy settling into her aching muscles. "What changed your mind?"

"Oh, you might be surprised the things I've heard in the last few hours. Colonel Petrucci has been yammering reason after reason at me, even while we were under radio silence. But really only one thing he said mattered to me even a little."

"What was that?"

Pause. "It's something that can wait," the Steel Wolf leader said, giving nothing away.

If Kerensky preferred to keep her cards close to her vest, Alexia wasn't in a position to argue no matter how much the Clan warrior interested her. Besides, she wanted to get back to base camp and see to her wounded and her damaged equipment. There would be more battles, harder battles, and she had to be ready with whatever the Jade Falcons had left to her. It wasn't much.

"Fair enough," she said in agreement. "Bargained well and done."

But watching what was left of her Tharkan Strikers limp back toward the city, and how much materiel was being left on the field for the recovery vehicles to salvage, a nagging concern ate away at her confidence. She amended her offer. "Just don't take too long."

Sutton Road

The *Warhammer IIC* was the undoing of every tactic Tara Campbell threw at the Clan warriors.

She matched her Kelswa assault tank against the Jade Falcons' Schmitt. A Destroyer to chase their Bellona, and hoverbikes to harass the Pegasus. Her Highlanders always held an advantage in speed or armor, and usually in firepower as well. She had the majority of the enemy crews flustered and making mistakes. It wasn't the kind of matchup you got very often against a Clan opponent, but then, she had prepared fairly well for this kind of engagement.

What she hadn't been able to do was keep an assault 'Mech on hand at the Sutton Road command post. Her *Hatchetman* was no match for the eighty-ton *Warhammer,* and the other warrior knew it. She couldn't shake him at all. Worse, he cared less for the warriors under his command than she did for hers. When she tried rushing him with her ax, he ignored everything else around him and pushed her back with large lasers and missiles. When she used her jumping ability to grab some maneuvering room, the Clan MechWarrior simply turned his guns into any of the several vehicle duels going on.

It tossed all bets to the wind. It kept Tara coming back at the monster time and again, trading armor for time.

Her company had slowly whittled away at the Falcon column, but without a decisive edge she was starting to lose warriors—Highlanders—to battlefield attrition. Most live bodies had made pickup. But few would be able to escape, thanks to the assault 'Mech's overcharged engine and a top speed rivaling her own.

Wrenching on her control sticks, Tara cut back again into the *Warhammer*'s embrace. Sweat streaked down the sides of her face. She blinked dry, scratchy eyes. Temperatures soared in her cockpit. Destroyed heat sinks. An engine breach. Her poor *Hatchetman* was quite a mess.

It still handled with showroom-level response, except for a persistent limp. She planted one shovel blade foot, twisted, and *ducked*. Two lasers crisscrossed overhead. Another ruby lance speared beneath her left arm. One slashed an angry wound across her waist, and the short-bodied warheads of SRMs hammered in behind it to chip away more ceramic composite from her legs, her arms.

Another telltale lit up with warning red. Leg actuator. Her second.

No hope for it, she decided. Her autocannon hammered away at the *Warhammer*'s chest. A double pulse from her lasers splashed emerald darts from shoulder to hip. It wasn't enough.

"I'm not getting out of here."

Her voice-activated mic picked up the statement. Della Brown was all over her in an instant. "You damn well better get out of there. You *find* a way."

Tara limped the forty-five-tonner backward, gaining only

a temporary respite as the assault machine sensed the 'Mech's weakness and pushed forward at sixty kilometers per hour.

"I have a gimped leg and a supercharged *Warhammer*. We've hurt them, Della, but we can't do much more than lose a lot of good people if we don't find a way to disengage." She took a deep breath. "Call them home."

"Not happening, Campbell. You'll bring them back."

"Not this time." Her autocannon belted out the last few hundred rounds of munitions. "Dry. Not good." She blinked the burn of sweat from her eyes, and focused on the assault 'Mech. Left or right?

"Don't worry," she said. "I'm not going MIA or even POW. I have two hovercraft left out here, and I'm taking them for extended duty. Bring the crawlers home, Prefect. Out."

Left or right? Tara throttled forward, hobbling into the waiting weapons of the *Warhammer IIC*. Her pulse lasers spat out stinging energy. And again. "I want Big D and Jess-two across the Thames now. Disengage and run, run, run! Everyone else, pair up and best paths back to the Pen. Della Brown is taking operational control as of *now*."

And she slammed down on her foot pedals, leaning forward with her ax pulled out to her side.

It would be the left.

Her *Hatchetman* sprang up on jets of golden plasma, diving forward like some alien creature sensing its prey and ready to take a stainless steel bite out of it. Her pulse lasers shredded more armor from the *Warhammer*, with one of them blistering the composite over its left leg. A good omen, she hoped.

A full-chested Highlander war cry rolled up from deep within, and Tara belted it out as she held the flat-topped jump. Even as the other 'Mech blasted into her with every laser it had. Ruby fire cut hard and cut deep. Two of the lances speared right into her centerline, skewering through what was left of her reactor shielding.

Golden fire ate up at the corner edges of her ferroglass shield. Acrid smoke curled into the cockpit.

With a stumble-caught landing she parked her *Hatchet-man* next to the assault 'Mech and swung down her titanium hatchet with all the force the machine's myomer muscles could bring.

The blade bit into the *Warhammer*'s hip. And stuck there.

Alarms clamored for attention, but none so insistent as the wailing siren of a reactor containment failure. The dampening fields were attempting to drop into place. Failing. Heat soared and Tara couldn't breathe through the thick, caustic smoke. She could hardly see.

She slapped at the control panel, found the handle she needed, depressed the plunger, and twisted for all she was worth.

The violent shudder of explosive bolts firing and a reactor containment failure taking place right under her feet threw Tara hard against her harness. The straps dug painfully into her shoulders and across her chest. Then a growling roar filled her ears, and she assumed she was dead—the fire of a fusion reaction swarming up through her cockpit, burning her alive.

Except that she wasn't burning.

Wasn't even as warm as she had been, actually, with cold spring air swirling into the cockpit through what had been ventilation dumps a few seconds before.

The entire elongated head of her *Hatchetman* had detached, and was now rocketing up and away from the exploding reactor on its escape rocket. The roar of the solid-fuel rocket was horrifyingly loud, and never a more welcome sound. It took her up, far above the golden fireball that had been her BattleMech, above the hapless *Warhammer IIC,* which was caught in the blast. It pushed her over the Thames River and high enough to get a good view of distant New London.

Then it began to drop, and Tara overrode the autopiloting system to gently nudge it farther across the river where her hovercraft would find her and make pickup.

Her monitor screens were dark. Communications had been stripped down to a short-range emergency transmitter. But she was unharmed, and her people had a chance to make it back to the Pen with their lives.

Too bad her poor *Hatchetman* had not taken the *Warhammer* with it. As the 'Mech's disembodied head drifted in a lazy spiral heading down, she watched through her plasma-scorched shield the *Warhammer* limping out from a pile of fire and smoke. It was all but dragging its left leg behind it—with a piece of her hatchet still stuck in its hip, it seemed, fused there!—and was going nowhere now but back to New London for repairs.

"Let them wonder about where we came from," Tara said, her voice rasping out of a raw, smoke-burned throat. "They won't breathe so easily around New London for a few days at least." And if she could keep them off-balance, she might buy another week. Maybe two. Enough for Jasek to work whatever magic he was hoping to bring in from the Lyran Commonwealth.

He would be back—of that she had no doubt. He *had* to come back. Sitting alone in the ruins of her cockpit, remembering the size of the force the enemy had landed with, she could at least admit to herself that the defenders needed Jasek Kelswa-Steiner. She needed him.

Today the Jade Falcons had planted their flag on Skye.

It would take every hand available to pull it back out.

27

*Princes should delegate unpopular duties to others
while dispensing all favors directly themselves.*
                    The Prince, by Niccolò Machiavelli

New London
Skye
5 December 3134

White stone steps led up to the columned portico of New
London's Capital House. Noritomo Helmer's polished boots
clipped a steady, staccato rhythm against them as he drew a
straight line toward the magnificent entryway from the Shandra scout vehicle that had brought him and his command staff
from the local spaceport. Lysle Clees followed one step behind him and to his right. Bogart two steps back on his left.

Elementals in full gear guarded the street-level plaza as
well as the upper courtyard. Their emerald carapaces shone
brilliantly under the cheerful spring sun that scrolled across
Skye's fathomless blue. Lysle first noticed the stain of fresh
blood on the infantrymen's mechanical claws, drawing Noritomo's attention to it by catching his eye in the plaza and
flexing her hand into a rigid talon. No carbon scoring

marred their armor and there was no exhaust residue brushing the backpack missile launchers that rode over their shoulders. Which meant these troopers had not yet seen any real fighting on Skye.

Civilian blood. More of Malvina Hazen's terror tactics, meant to cow the locals into unquestioning obedience.

More darkness unleashed from Pandora's box.

Standing between the widely spaced portico columns, Noritomo paused to survey what he could see of New London's administrative district. He found mostly empty streets and only a few sullen government staff workers traipsing in, late, many of them under guard. What little traffic there was kept tangling up at intersections, where traffic lights hung dark and useless thanks to Malvina's electromagnetic pulse. He could only imagine the chaos it had caused on that first day, with widespread power outages and fire-gutted electronics.

"They got off lucky," Lysle said, keeping her deep voice pitched low. She shook her blond dreadlocks back over both shoulders.

Star Captain Bogart looked askance at the two of them. "How's this any kind of luck?" he asked, using the lazy speech patterns with which he'd grown up. "For them, that is?"

Noritomo glanced up into the sky, where only a few spring gray clouds drifted. The high-atmosphere storm was long past, but he had seen video capture of the detonation.

"Galaxy Commander Hazen could have dropped the Alamo into the heart of New London," he answered the free-born armor commander. "The blast would have shattered larger buildings like Capital House and set fires throughout most of the city. People would still be dying from radiation poisoning. Burn victims would be clogging up hospitals in all of the nearby cities." He felt a tightening across his shoulders and shrugged it off. "I half expected to see that anyway." He turned and led the others into the marble-tiled halls.

"What stopped her?" Lysle asked. By rights, she should have accorded Galaxy Commander Hazen full title of rank, but inside the building it was safer to keep their discussion impersonal.

"New London stopped her. Capital House and the Governor's Palace stopped her. She needs a capital from which to rule Skye. Why ruin the city you plan to make your personal throne?"

It was a short answer, though Noritomo knew that nothing involving Malvina Hazen was ever so direct and so easy. After learning of the WarShip assault against the system's zenith recharge station, he had been surprised to discover that Malvina had since used the *Emerald Talon* only in interdiction efforts. The world was blockaded, but it had yet to feel the pounding thunder of an orbital bombardment.

"She wants this fight up close and personal. Her last assault against Skye cost her an arm and a leg, after all." And a brother. "She could have stood off this time, pounding the cities into submission. She did not." Instead, she had opted for a heavy landing outside of New London. He could not fault her warrior's heart. Spoiling for battle, she led the bulk of her forces into the city, ready to meet any opposition.

"And none came," he whispered aloud. What if they threw a war, and nobody showed up? Wasn't that a classic joke he remembered from another of the books he'd smuggled into his sibko barracks?

"Whatever else Galaxy Commander Hazen asks of us," Noritomo said sotto voce to his staff, cautious as they walked the halls among Capital House staffers and Clan administrative personnel, "be ready with options, with force strength estimates, with cut-downs for any bidding that might occur."

Bogart shrugged his arms out in front of him, as if loosening them up before a fight. A few nearby warriors glanced his way sharply, as if expecting challenge, or attack. "You think we'll be included in the fighting?" It had been the question on everyone's mind ever since losing Chaffee.

"I think our leader has someone she is more angry at than us," he admitted. "I think she wants victory more than anything else." He felt the tension bleeding through the halls—could almost taste it. Copperish, like the scent of freshly spilled blood.

"I think," he said, "that things are about to go very badly for Skye."

How badly, though, Noritomo Helmer was not to find out until Malvina Hazen was through chastising him for losing Chaffee.

The taste of blood was very real now as Noritomo recovered from Malvina's right cross, his jaw throbbing and his right eye squinting shut against the pain. He had seen the blow coming, of course, but made no move to defend himself. It required steeled concentration not to react and tempt the Galaxy commander into further rage. This was her right, and his *surkai*—his penance—for disobedience.

Not that it mattered that his newly formed Cluster had been outfought. His orders had been to hold Chaffee for Clan Jade Falcon. By Clan customs, he was expected to fulfill those orders or die trying.

Only the outlander's offer of *hegira* mitigated the circumstances and might—if the Galaxy commander eventually concurred—salvage his honor.

"You present yourself well, Star Colonel." Malvina eyed him coldly, staring at him sidelong with her artificial eye. By most comparisons, it was a perfect match of the other one. Noritomo noticed what it lacked, however. The carbonation, the life that hinted at a soul. This was her dead eye, reserved now for the harshest of judgments.

To their credit, Lysle and Bogart had shown neither surprise nor a reflex to come between their commander and his punishment. They froze into the likeness of statues. Others in the Congressional Hall were not so diplomatic. Civilians recoiled from the sudden violence. Galaxy Commander Malthus stared at him impassively, but more than a few of Malvina's senior warriors looked on with smug approval, and some began clearing back as if expecting an escalation at any moment.

It did not escape Noritomo's notice that the hall was really a wide amphitheater, where Skye's world senators came together in concentric levels, no doubt in the best spirit of The Republic, which doted on such symbolism that could be found in spheres, circles, and round tables. But among the Clans, such a room framed a natural Circle of Equals where Clan justice by combat—might making right—took place. For the same reason he had made his office on Chaffee next to Longview's central, circular park, Malvina had commandeered Capital House's Congressional Hall for its obvious connotations.

And if Noritomo allowed his deserved punishment to escalate into a Trial of Grievance, then he would have to lose. Defending a "right to retreat" was no precedent he wished to visit on Clan Jade Falcon. Let such hairs be split by Wolves and Sea Foxes.

Slowly, grudgingly, Malvina turned her face so that her real eye gazed upon him. Apparently he did present himself well. Her demeanor thawed a few degrees into reluctant acceptance. "Very well, in fact. A lesser warrior would not dare meet my gaze after such a defeat. An insecure one would be demanding a Trial of Grievance, or even Refusal, against the notion that he had shirked his duty." She sounded almost disappointed, as if she wished to fight him. Fight someone.

But given the opportunity to voice his earlier thought, Noritomo merely said, "I am Jade Falcon."

"Perhaps," she admitted, slowly. "Perhaps you are."

With the prospect of immediate violence slipping away, some of the nearby warriors prodded the civilians back to work. The buzz of background conversations warmed up the nearly empty hall only slightly. A tinny echo bounced back from the deeper corners.

Beckett Malthus stepped up to the small group, arms akimbo. "Why did you not return immediately to Glengarry after giving up Chaffee?" he asked, allowing Lysle into the conversation with a direct glance but pointedly excluding the freeborn Bogart.

It was not lost on Noritomo that Malthus had thrown him a possible lifeline, allowing the Star colonel to explain himself in more detail. In front of Malvina, their Chinggis Khan, as well. He divided his gaze between both commanders. There was no doubt who led the Jade Falcon *desant*; that had been very clear since Glengarry. It was still difficult to say who *commanded,* though.

"It seemed apparent to me," he said slowly, "with the raiding attacks against Glengarry and Ryde, and the loss of Summer, that it was my Galaxy commander's intention to concentrate forces for an immediate assault against Skye."

He carefully did not identify which of the two he acknowledged as *his* commander. Malvina would assume it was her, of course, since he was part of her table of organization. If Beckett Malthus read into Noritomo's reply any offer of alliance—*never* against his commanding officer, but only for the greater good of Clan Jade Falcon—then so much the better.

His answer still did not satisfy Malvina. "You did not

jump to Skye. Nor did you report and request orders from Glengarry, *quineg*?"

"Neg," he admitted, "I did not. By jumping through an uncharted system, my Seventh Striker Cluster was able to quickly reinforce the garrison at Zebebelgenubi, leaving us only a short jump from Skye. In this way, I would not preempt my commander's timetable for any assault, but I placed my warriors in position to support any efforts made in that direction."

Lysle had held her peace, knowing it was better to wait for the opportune moment. Now the large woman volunteered some aid. "Jumping to Glengarry, while politically expedient, was a strategic loss. Our JumpShips have no lithium-fusion batteries. We could not have supported a drive for Skye in anything less than two weeks from our arrival. Zebebelgenubi was far more likely to have free docking collars."

Malvina's gaze was dark. "You presume that your forces would be wanted for Skye."

"Aff, Galaxy Commander." Noritomo stepped between his aide and Malvina's potential threat. "But who could predict that The Republic's garrison forces would give up the capital so easily?"

It worked, turning Malvina's ire back against the local defenders. "They gave up the capital," she admitted, "but not the world. We counted on hard-line resistance for New London, drawing as many defenders as possible into the blacked-out city."

And Malvina had planned to crush them mercilessly. Noritomo heard the frustration in her voice. Such a battle would also have led to incredible destruction visited on the local population as the Jade Falcons battled Republic troops street by street. A terrified people might adopt Jade Falcon rule much more quickly if it meant an end to a direct threat on their homes and lives.

The Shadow-Khan turned to a pair of large tables shoved together on the floor of the Congressional Hall, on which a wide, flat-panel base rested. This was Malvina's strategic-command center. A pair of technicians worked tirelessly at the display controls, moving icons over a large map of Skye displayed on the base.

"Our strikes at important secondary targets were all re-buffed," she said. "Even a week later, we've failed to take even one of them. The Shipil cradle at Norfolk. Cyclops, Incorporated. Avanti Assemblies." She pointed out each on the map, biting off their names, then reached over and slapped her hand down on the golden circle that was the planetary capital. "They let us walk right into New London, tying it around our necks like a dead albatross while they reinforced every weapons stockpile and production center that Skye boasts."

Smart. The Republic defenders had stolen a page out of the Jade Falcon invasion book. Control the military and economic strongholds, and you control the entire region. Noritomo rubbed at his jaw, easing the bruise she had given him while studying the strategic situation. "Governor Gregory Kelswa-Steiner remains free. Prefect Brown and Tara Campbell hold every resource they need for a long, protracted campaign."

Lysle stepped up beside him. "And we strain our supply lines back to Glengarry."

"That may have been," Malvina agreed with the two warriors, "but we are about to shift some of that strain back onto The Republic's position."

"A large offensive push at one of the industrial facilities?" Noritomo asked, knowing it was not the answer.

"Eventually." Malvina Hazen looked across the map at him. "With the arrival of your Cluster, we can throw fresh blood into the line and push through the Steel Wolves or these bothersome Stormhammers. We might be able to track and destroy the raiding force giving us so much local trouble. But first"—she smiled—"I believe a small object lesson is in order."

She nodded at one of the technicians, who blanked the large display and then replaced the world map with one that sent a shiver through Noritomo Helmer. New London stood out on the display in impressive detail, with every street and alleyway and park. Malvina Hazen picked up a laser pointer. Wherever it fell onto the display, a gray shadow stretched over that part of the city. She skipped the light back and forth, scribbling over the map with indifferent care, drawing a swath of destruction starting at an industrial sector, stretching through several commercial and residential districts. Finally, she sent one probing line into the heart of New London, covering several city blocks and ending up at the New London Tower.

"There. That should about do it."

Noritomo had seen this kind of swath laid out in front

of him once before. Only then it had been an entire city, and it had not been a map but real rubble and ash sweeping across the streets of Belletaria. On Kimball II. A sharp glance from Lysle told him that she remembered as well.

"You want to destroy New London." He carefully withheld judgment from his voice.

"Decimate it," Malvina corrected him. "The tactic worked on Ryde, at least with the local population. This time it will not be just the people. One-tenth of the entire city is to be leveled, which is about what I expect to have happened if we had fought for the capital as planned. It will hold the entire planet hostage."

"What is one-tenth of the capital's population?"

"Including the outer boroughs," she considered, "five hundred . . . five hundred twenty thousand." She waved off the number as insignificant. "They have been most uncooperative."

And for that, Malvina Hazen sentenced them to die. Yes, it would have the desired effect of mobilizing the capital's work force, putting them back into their jobs and getting them screaming for a cessation of hostilities. They might even embrace the local Jade Falcon garrison once Malvina left the world—if she left the world—out of relief that they had been spared. But that was all short-term thinking. It did not take into account the partisan activity sure to spring up, like that which they had seen on Chaffee and which still continued on Ryde and Kimball II. It did nothing to deal with the hatred that would fester among the populace for weeks, for months, for years. The kind of indiscriminate destruction that could turn star systems and nations against a Clan.

It had happened before, after all. In the original Clan invasion of the Inner Sphere, Clan Smoke Jaguar had visited terror assaults on worlds in its invasion corridor. On Turtle Bay, it had even used one of its WarShips to laze the city of Edo, effectively wiping it off the face of the world. Resistance efforts had never ceased, and when the Inner Sphere finally fought back, it had been with a vengeance. Clan Smoke Jaguar was no more, in fact, having been targeted for complete annihilation.

Noritomo carefully brought up a few of his concerns, dialing back on his personal feelings and simply pointing out how such tactics had backfired on the Jaguars.

"Another time, another place," was Malvina's answer. "The Republic is not the entire Inner Sphere. They are isolated and alone, and are weakened from the disarmament programs instituted by Devlin Stone. They have no spine for such a fight anymore."

Except for here on Skye, he wanted to remind her but did not. Here on Skye, forces from The Republic and Lyran sympathizers and the Steel Wolves had banded together in just such an alliance. And they were giving the Jade Falcons every bit of fight the Clan could want. Noritomo looked to Beckett Malthus, who stared back without expression.

If the Galaxy commander appointed by Khan Pryde would not gainsay Malvina Hazen, what could Noritomo be expected to do?

Once the box had been opened, the evils released could not be put back inside.

"It is slaughter, not battle," Noritomo said, trying once again to push Clan tradition back at Malvina.

"It is controlled and deliberate. And it will. Be. Done."

Noritomo met her gaze, but could not hold it against the fanatic gleam that brightened behind her right eye. The left eye, the dead one, remained cold and impersonal.

"When?" he asked.

"As soon as you can assemble your Cluster," she said calmly. Noting his surprise, betrayed in the sharp glance he traded with Lysle and with Malthus, Malvina smiled. "This is your *surkai*, Star Colonel Helmer. You will prove yourself to me, or be discarded once and for all."

And it would happen regardless. Nothing was going to stand between Malvina Hazen and her perceived destiny. Especially him. Not unless he found some way to raise his standing among the Clan. Damned in either event.

"How is it to be done?" he asked, seeking any reprieve she might allow.

"It matters not to me. Storm through with BattleMechs. Level the area with missiles and lasers. Send Elementals from door to door." She shrugged her indifference. "I make you responsible for this because without my endorsement you are outcast, and I know you could never abide that. You are honor-bound and, despite your past failures, an excellent warrior who knows when it is time to submit."

She smiled thinly. "You are Jade Falcon."

═══ **28** ═══

Roosevelt Island
Skye
8 December 3134

The three-story building was Cyclops, Incorporated's administrative headquarters. Its flat rooftop, tiled and decorated in the style of a wide piazza, often hosted outdoor business parties. Today it was being pressed into service for more sober duty.

Tara Campbell had walked its banistered edge earlier, before anyone else arrived, looking over most of Roosevelt Island. The waters of Truxton Sound washed up on the three sides she could see, separating the large island from Skye's main continent of New Scotland. The fourth side, north of the administrative offices, was hidden behind several larger buildings that Cyclops used to smelt ore, roll armor, and assemble hovercraft APCs and tanks using the components brought in from other factories across Skye.

This site was one of Skye's premiere military-industrial facilities, which was why it had been chosen.

That, and the fact that Shipil's Norfolk dockyards had been lost the day before.

"I do not care for this," Gregory Kelswa-Steiner whispered, not for the first time. "It seems to me we are cutting off our nose to spite our face."

It was against the northern edge of the rooftop that they now gathered. Tara stood with Duke Gregory and Paladin McKinnon amid a crowd of news journalists, corporate officers, and local politicians. Everyone watched the video footage displayed on a small projection unit. Almost everyone. Tara's chief aide caught her eye and frowned toward one side where Anastasia Kerensky talked in a low voice with the Knight-errant newly arrived from Terra.

She sent a surreptitious shrug back to Tara Bishop. There was no telling what the two discussed, though it was obvious they had history together. Kerensky certainly got around.

Other than those two, who were able to hold themselves apart, the mood was dark and angry as the projection unit finished displaying the devastation visited on New London. The footage was only twenty-four hours old, and still punched Tara deep in the gut. A formation of 'Mechs and vehicles followed a line of Elemental warriors who swept ahead to clear any remaining civilians out of the area marked for destruction. Galaxy Commander Hazen later pointed out the humanitarian efforts Clan Jade Falcon had undertaken, this time, to limit casualties. Tara could tell by her frosty demeanor that she cared little for the civilians. For her, a massive wave of displaced residents flooding nearby cities and towns only added to the pressures mounting behind the defenders to do something quickly in order to save Skye.

No one else spoke as the footage played out. Buildings were razed to the ground. Parks were burned. Homes destroyed. In the end, a trio of BattleMechs came at the New London Tower and tore at its hardened walls until the entire structure finally collapsed under its own weight. It was the first major resource to be completely—and intentionally—destroyed in the Jade Falcon onslaught.

It would not be the last.

"This"—Tara Campbell spoke up, raising her voice to address the captive audience—"this is what we are dealing with. A ruthless invader who acknowledges no boundary between military targets and wartime atrocities. Malvina Hazen would have us thank her for sparing lives—*this* time!

But what of the crew of *Gondola Station*? The citizens of Chaffee subjected to blistering agents? Belletaria on Kimball II. Nukes over New London! I'm not sure how much of her generosity we can survive."

She had subtly changed from questioning Malvina's actions to outright condemnation. Given what she was asking of these people, of this world, she needed all of the moral indignation she could raise.

"We have no body count out of New London. Certainly some are dead, despite any 'humanitarian efforts' by the Jade Falcons.

"We know that a significant portion of the city has been leveled. Residences. Offices. Stores and industry. This, in a city we voluntarily evacuated to spare such treatment.

"While we raise the value on every life, resident or citizen, the Clan invaders lower themselves to indiscriminate warfare."

Her spell over the audience was not quite complete. One newsvid anchorman edged forward. "If The Republic cannot match the Falcon ferocity, or is forced to abandon the moral high ground, would you say that Skye is lost?"

He speared his question right at the lord governor. A Herrmanns news agent, looking to score cheap points.

If Tara was worried about losing the train of her argument, she needn't have been. Duke Gregory might question the need to match such terror tactics with a hard-nosed response of their own, but he remained a consummate politician.

"I concede no such thing," Duke Gregory promised. "Skye may be reeling from the attacks on her soil, and before we are done this day it may seem we have entered darker times. But industry can be rebuilt. Cities restored. So long as our people hold true to the ideals of The Republic, they will always be the free people of Skye, and they will never be forgotten or left behind."

The local political leaders summoned to this event raised a cheer for their duke and lord governor. It would play well on camera.

Still, Tara wondered what Jasek might have to say about that. She could almost hear his voice in her head, arguing.

The people of Skye will be truly free only when they are allowed to decide for themselves whether they want to be

Commonwealth citizens or Republic drones laboring for the basic rights every Lyran enjoys at birth.

She understood his argument, but did not agree with it. Citizenship had to be earned inside The Republic, and was it asking so much that a resident give something back to the government that ensured his or her basic freedoms?

Given that her Highlanders were paying the ultimate price nearly every day, it didn't seem too much to her.

What bothered her, if anything did, was how easily Jasek's voice came to mind when she had done everything possible in the last several weeks to forget him, his coffee-tinted skin and his stormy blue eyes. He had made it off Chaffee, but then where had he gone? As the days ticked by, Skye's defenders grew weary and Skye itself seemed to long for the infusion of enthusiasm the younger Kelswa-Steiner had brought with him the first time.

The wind ran chilly fingers through Tara's hair, blowing a few of her platinum blond strands down into her eyes. With a casual smooth from her palm, she pasted them up and back again.

"It is not a matter of matching ferocity or assuming the moral high ground," she continued. "The Republic is beset without and within at the moment, as the HPG blackout continues to allow its enemies *and* its loyal opposition to divide and conquer. House Liao attacks from the Confederation. The Swordsworn rally new forces from within Prefectures IV and V. And here, the Jade Falcons commit unbridled acts of war. Even Landgrave Jasek Kelswa-Steiner would admit that a divided effort will always demand certain sacrifices, and a prolonged struggle."

She had carefully tiptoed around Jasek's status as one of The Republic's potential enemies, a softened approach that drew a glare from Sire McKinnon and a look of uncertainty from Duke Gregory. But Herrmanns and several other news agencies, as they all knew, favored Jasek and his Stormhammers. Tara was not about to open a new front in her own war to save Skye.

Though she would twist the situation with a few flanking attacks as necessary.

Sorry, Jasek.

"The Landgrave, were he here, would also be among the first to agree that we cannot submit to the Jade Falcon terror tactics. His own actions have proven that, by his coming to Skye's aid when it truly needed him and in his selfless efforts to free Chaffee from Jade Falcon oppression.

"Now it is our turn to take a hard stand against Malvina Hazen. For that reason, we are here at Cyclops, Incorporated, on Roosevelt Island. The Jade Falcons are pressing for this facility, hoping to bolster their sagging logistics network by claiming local resources."

She turned and pointed out three of the larger nearby buildings, pausing for the camera so that the news crews could pan out for a wide-angle shot. They knew what was coming next. Everyone present did.

"Foundry. Armory. Assembly plant. Cleared and secured. Mr. Trosset."

Angus Trosset, CEO of Cyclops, Incorporated, looked pale. He was on board for the very simple reason that Tara had given him no choice. His cooperation secured valuable (and private) government concessions from Duke Gregory and, on behalf of The Republic, Tara Campbell and Sire McKinnon.

A lack of cooperation would have brought the same effect, only under martial law and Tara's direct order, which she had been quite willing to give.

Trosset stepped to the edge of the roof and cleared his throat, posing for the cameras. "Cyclops, Incorporated," he said, "will not shield itself behind a profit-and-loss statement while Skye's civilians are subject to such brutality. Our employees have family and friends in New London who are, if they are lucky, alive but without home or livelihood." He pushed his glasses up farther onto his nose. "If this is an example of Jade Falcon stewardship, we would rather save them the trouble."

He pulled a wireless from his belt and spoke one word of command into it. "Cleared."

A deep-throated roar shook the ground only a split second before the first plumes of smoke and stone dust billowed up around the base of the foundry. The administrative building swayed and bounced. A few of the politicians dropped to hands and knees for stability. Most rode it out, watching in fascination as the three-story-high foundry complex crumbled into a pile of rubble and mangled metal beams.

Before the echoes of the first demolition charges faded, a second set blew the foundation out from under the larger armor-processing plant. Millions' worth of steel-rolling technology became near-worthless scrap metal in less than three seconds as the destructive waves tore through the building, shoving the great machines against one another and overturning several before tons of ferrocrete rained down from the caving roof.

"The assembly building will be left standing," Trosset told the cameras, "to continue operations for as long as possible in support of the allied effort to hold Skye. But plans are already in place to shift operations to remote facilities far beyond Jade Falcon reach."

Tara stepped in beside the corporate officer. "Malvina Hazen," she said in brusque, clipped tones, "this concludes *our* object lesson."

She let the scene play out for a few long heartbeats, with the dust clouds rising behind her, then nodded to the lead production crewman, who cleared the lights from green back to red and said, "We're out."

Duke Gregory moved in at once to reassure the CEO that Cyclops, Incorporated, would be taken care of, and to make plans with the local politicos to handle displaced workers and ready the district for the coming Jade Falcon occupation. There was a slim chance that Malvina Hazen would bypass Roosevelt Island now that its usefulness had been cut by two-thirds, but no one was willing to gamble on that.

Tara let herself be immediately drawn aside by Sire McKinnon. "I wish you weren't leaving," she said.

McKinnon's gaze swept around, searching for the Knight-errant who had come to fetch him from Skye. He scowled at the other man's proximity to the Steel Wolf leader, but said nothing about it. "I have to. Events on Terra . . . demand my attention."

"You said the elections were covered." She had tried several times in the last two days to get the news out of him, ever since the Knight-errant's arrival, but he had pulled in on himself, turning as inscrutable as a sphinx.

"What happened? Why is it so important now?" She dropped her voice to a bare whisper. "You know you can trust me."

For a moment, he looked more distant than she had ever seen him. "No. Not with this, I can't. If you wanted in on my level, Tara Campbell, you had your chance for a paladinship. And you turned it down."

Then his rough edges softened just a bit. "I *am* trusting you with my *Atlas*, however. There is no way to get it aboard a K-3 shuttle, and a DropShip might be seen as important enough to be intercepted by that *Nightlord* up there. Treat it well."

"I don't like this." She nodded at the standing clouds of dust that hung over the demolished buildings. "Any of it."

"This was the right thing to do," the venerable Paladin assured her. His dark eyes were cold, cold. "Hazen cannot miss our message. From a military standpoint, Skye can be left as a world not worth having."

"Defend The Republic at any price?" Tara asked. She shivered, free to do so now that the cameras were dead. "I am not a Founder's Movement advocate."

"Perhaps not." He folded wiry arms across his chest. The light breeze tugged at his cape of rank, pulling it out behind him. For all his age and his weathered body, the Paladin still cut an imposing figure. "But I am. And I will cover your back on Terra."

"It's not my back I'm worried about."

"Well, *that* part is in a sling, Countess. No mistaking."

Despite the Paladin's excellent military skills, and her own, they were both hanging out in the wind when it came to the tactical situation on Skye. "We'll give it everything we have, plus ten percent. We can't do any more than that." She wrapped her arms around her sides.

"Desperate times, Tara." He smiled thin and hard. "Desperate measures. Get used to it."

"I'll do what needs doing, but damned if I'll get used to it. It's a slippery slope, David"—Tara saw him startle as she used his given name for the first time—"and if we aren't careful, we truly will make Skye a world not worth having. Then what will keep us here?" She looked askance at him.

"How far do we let desperation push us?"

Miliano

The Avanti Assemblies factory in Miliano was no stranger to military machines. Though perhaps not so many as this, Alexia Wolf decided.

The main floor worked in quality-controlled teams to assemble Kinnol main battle tanks under a recent license from Kressly Industries. Their work area was shrinking with each passing day, however, with auxiliary stations being taken over by the Tharkan Strikers and Lyran Rangers as maintenance and repair docks. 'Mechs and tanks were braced up against the walls, and infantry in powered armor worked alongside astechs in exoskeletons to lend muscle where it was needed.

Military technicians and factory workers shouted back and forth, often with colorful invective, calling for equipment that had been shared. Or borrowed. Or simply taken when no one was looking. Pieces and parts were routinely scavenged from the factory line, and cutting torches flared as armor plating was chopped up and then welded slapdash over whatever holes needed patching.

The stench of scorched metal hung over everything. It was the smell of desperation.

From her vantage point, sharing the crew boss "nest" with the resident manager and Niccolò GioAvanti, Alexia watched as a scarred Kelswa assault tank rolled by. Broken treads slapped against the ferrocrete floor, and gritty black smoke chuffed from the engine compartment. A floor monitor saw this, flagged down the vehicle, and made a throat-slashing gesture. While the crew seemed confident in their ability to drive the Kelswa in, rules were that factory managers called the shots (against the targets they saw, anyway). The tank engine was shut down and the vehicle rigged to be towed the remaining thirty meters to a berth.

A master sergeant in the Lyran Rangers ran up to argue with the manager. Both gestured to the nest, which was raised only two meters over the floor, but the crew boss let it go and for Alexia it was a lower-caste matter. The situation would resolve itself, the tank would get repaired, and her Strikers would be ready for battle again. Soon, she hoped.

There was no need to involve herself directly.

Not until a LoaderMech tried to walk off with a BattleMech gyro.

Alexia saw the IndustrialMech grab the gyroscope's carrying flanges with its vise grip hands, lifting the valuable component and marching it bowlegged over to a waiting truck. A frown creased her brow. Vehicles came into the Assemblies plant to be worked on. Parts and pieces did not go out to them.

She swung down from the nest, feet hitting the ferrocrete floor, wondering what was going on. Then she saw Tamara Duke.

Then she knew.

Striding over to the waiting truck, Alexia did not hurry, but she did not allow herself any distraction either. Sharing the facilities here with the Lyran Rangers had lent itself to several tense days, and far too many bristling encounters with Kommandant Duke. The lack of Jasek's presence, always a calming influence among the Stormhammers, had put both women on edge.

In a Clan military, Tamara would have already challenged for a Trial of Position. Or Alexia would have simply invoked a Circle of Equals to put the other woman back in her place.

Whatever the Inner Sphere equivalent was, it looked about to happen.

Tamara saw her approach, staring at the leutnant-colonel over the noteputer she held in both hands.

"Kommandant," Alexia greeted her with bare civility. "We seem to have a problem."

"No problem." Tamara used a stylus to check something off on the screen. "One two-ton gyroscope. And an actuator and several tons of armor."

It was all stacked up on the flatbed, being lashed down by the crew under her command. Hauptmann Vic Parkins labored alongside another of the Rangers' warriors and half a dozen techs to secure the load. "We have what we need."

"If you have a crippled 'Mech, load it on a recovery vehicle and bring it in. All repairs are handled here."

"With two of your Strikers seen for every one of my Rangers." Tamara turned her back on Alexia, her dark hair swinging across her shoulders, closing a curtain on the argument.

Alexia felt her hands wanting to curl into fists. "This is our operations area," Alexia reminded the other woman, working on a diplomatic solution. Jasek would not appreciate losing one of his best field commanders to a hospital stay. "I agreed to lend support to the Rangers after you lost one of your maintenance depots."

"A maintenance depot, two munitions dumps, and a nighttime attack two days ago that cost us a pair of salvage vehicles." Tamara whipped around to face Alexia, temper coloring her skin. "We're facing the brunt of the Jade Falcon push into this district while your Strikers handle the light loads."

Swallowing back the metallic taste of anger, Alexia Wolf stepped right up into Tamara's face. Quietly, coldly, she said, "You point out one vehicle being repaired in this Assemblies plant, or one of my people laid up in the field hospital, and tell me who is getting off lightly. Kommandant."

In fact, her losses had been staggering. It might be true that the Rangers saw more desperate fighting, but then, her Strikers were quite a bit greener and had nowhere near the level of materiel readiness that had been prepared for the Lyran Rangers. Alexia might share Jasek's favor, but the Stormhammers' commander did not let that interfere with sound military decisions. And neither would she.

She roped in Vic Parkins by eye. "Hauptmann. You will unfasten that materiel and see that it is placed back where it belongs."

With a hard glance toward Tamara, Parkins shook his head. "I'm afraid I can't do that, Colonel." He braced himself up stiffly. "Orders."

This was not the confident officer who had walked the fine line of insubordination a few months before. Alexia wondered how Tamara had finally gotten to him.

As it turned out, she hadn't. Tamara thumbed a new screen onto her noteputer and flourished it in front of Alexia's face. Orders, countersigned by Colonel Petrucci, commandeering specific parts and supplies. In Jasek's absence, and that of Colonel Vandel, his rank held sway among the Stormhammers. Even over her.

"Is there a problem?" Niccolò GioAvanti asked, stepping up at Alexia's shoulder. She wasn't certain if he had followed her over earlier or had just arrived.

"No problem," both women said at the same time. Alexia with a touch of darkness, Tamara smug.

GioAvanti reached in and took the noteputer from Tamara's hands. There was never any doubt in his demeanor that she would surrender it. The man looked calm and well appointed, even in the frantic sweatshop his family's local factories had become. The braid he wore down the left side of his face was tucked back behind his ear, and pale blue eyes skipped over the screen.

"This looks legitimate," he said evenly, drawing hard stares from both women, if for different reasons.

Of course it was legitimate, though Alexia had a good idea how Antonio Petrucci had come to pull rank over her Tharkan Strikers. It was a violation of military courtesy, taking advantage of Alexia's offer to share resources from her operations area. It wouldn't have happened unless someone—a particular someone—had whispered in Petrucci's ear that Jasek would back his play. When the landgrave returned.

If he returned.

"Anything else?" Alexia asked curtly. "Perhaps there is something more that you need, and cannot get for yourself?"

Tamara's face pulled down into a neutral mask. She read between the lines, all right. "More armored plating would be of help."

"Is that specifically requested in those orders?" She knew that it was not. Tamara shook her head. "Then clear that truck out of my area."

"We'll be back," Tamara Duke promised her. Knocking on the cab window, she made a complicated gesture which basically came down to an order to pull the truck outside of the Assemblies plant. Tamara jumped up onto the running board. On the back, the work crew hunkered down for the drive.

"Cut the support we are giving the Rangers by one-third," Alexia told GioAvanti when it was just the two of them left. "I will answer for it when Jasek returns."

Still staring after Tamara Duke's departure, GioAvanti

shook his head. "No. *I* will answer for anything that goes on at this facility." He turned his impassive stare back to Alexia. "And I won't slow the Rangers down any more than necessary. Take an additional maintenance bay and bump back the next Ranger machine by one slot. Skye needs both of you at the best strength possible."

It was a fair decision, and Alexia knew better than to let her personal feelings interfere with intercaste relations. As she had found out at her own Trial of Position, being in the right—even being the better warrior—was not always enough.

"When Colonel Petrucci marches in here and cuts further into our maintenance and repairs?" she asked. "What then?"

"I will do what I can to keep the Stormhammers functioning smoothly," the young merchant promised. "Even if that means letting the Rangers have their head."

From a man who had quietly but confidently supported her Strikers over the last several weeks, the hedging answer seemed a borderline disrespect. "Whose side are you on, Niccolò?"

The man shrugged. "Jasek's," he answered simply.

There was no arguing that. Though Alexia Wolf could not help one last glance at the retreating truck. "So should we all be," she said. "So should we all."

But she was beginning to doubt it.

29

Let no one be deceived by Caesar's glory.
　　　　　　　　The Prince, by Niccolò Machiavelli

Norfolk
Skye
9 December 3134

Jade Falcon forces holding the Shipil Company's Norfolk dockyards had been strengthened until it was the Clan's entire center of operations against the allied defenders.

It had been Noritomo Helmer's Seventh Striker Cluster that first secured the facility, only a day after their terrifying course through New London, and the Star colonel had quickly converted the same set of offices used by the Steel Wolves into his command post. In this room, which had once been an executive dining area, Clan technicians removed high-current vending machines and an array of personal cooking devices, installing in their place a holographic tank and several computer terminals. It made for an adequate tactical planning room if one could ignore the baked-in smells of grease and the seasoned tomato sauce that Skye civilians apparently liked to pour over most food.

He stood inside the holographic display, walking like a titan over the rocky plateau of Bar-Tania where a double lance from his Striker Cluster protected the salvage of a Stormhammers Behemoth. The assault tank was much slower than Jade Falcon warriors preferred, but as losses mounted on both sides, such an asset was crucial to future operations.

For this reason, and this alone, he ignored Malvina Hazen for several critical moments while he used the satellite-imaged map to set a picket line in case the Lyran Rangers should try to double back and rescue their machine.

Wearing a command glove, he drew a circle in the air above a line of jagged, boulder-strewn hills. A white halo formed where he had sketched it. The computer added intersecting lines to turn it into horizontal crosshairs, and then the entire device flashed down to lay itself over the scrub brush and sparse grass.

It changed to a pulsing red.

With one finger, he tabbed open a nearby icon that floated above the plateau like a miniature sun. A dropdown window opened up, listing several communication codes. He chose one, double tapping it with the same forefinger. On his headset, a channel crackled to life.

"Aff, Star Colonel?"

"Bogart. Set a pair of strategic missile carriers out here behind this slope. They will have some protection, and a good range of open coverage."

The freeborn Star captain acknowledged the order, and the circle changed from pulsing red to gold. Forces were on their way.

When Noritomo finally turned back to Galaxy Commander Hazen, it was with a measure of trepidation. Malvina gripped the fencing that bordered the holotank with white-knuckled strength. Bloodless fingers formed claws around the metal rail, and her right eye burned with a fire that was new. She started to speak, twice, and both times found herself unable to use her voice.

Noritomo had seen Malvina Hazen angry. Furious, even. He'd also seen her burning with a cold rage that threatened to consume anyone who crossed her at that moment—and he had been the closest one just then.

But until now, he had not believed her possible of a spitting fury that threatened all reason.

"Your forces," she said slowly, "were in position to move against Cyclops, Incorporated. Why did you not attack?"

He stripped the headset from his ear, tossing it to a nearby aide who would continue to monitor the salvage operation. The command glove he kept, tucking it into his belt.

"I saw no benefit to spending military resources against an impotent target. The Roosevelt Island complex has been neutered. Instead"—he gestured to the holographic terrain around his feet—"we managed to inflict severe damage against the Lyran Rangers as they shifted their base camp."

"The insult behind their televised rebuke is reason enough," Malvina nearly shouted. "Tara Campbell dares take me to task?"

No honor guard, Noritomo noticed then. No Beckett Malthus to restrain the Chinggis Khan's more violent impulses. This was Malvina Hazen pressing her will against Noritomo, and it would be best if there were no witnesses. He nodded a dismissal to his aide, and to several technicians who had frozen in place throughout the small cafeteria.

They left with a hurried relief.

"Tara Campbell has identified our weakness," he said as diplomatically as possible.

"I am not weak, Star Colonel Helmer."

"The Jade Falcon *desant* is," he replied. "For the same reason we identified our primary targets inside The Republic as military-industrial and economic strongholds, we need to capture and stand on the industrial strengths of Skye if we plan to contest this planet over any length of time."

"Reinforcements arrive from Glengarry and Ryde. We have sufficient force on planet to take this world."

"But not to hold it. Not if the allied defenders burn every major production facility behind them as they retreat." He braced himself up, showing no hint of weakness before his commander. "You can bring me into a Circle of Equals for saying so, Galaxy Commander Hazen, but if you continue to match Tara Campbell in this way, you will lose. We all will."

It was enough to push Malvina nearly over the edge. She

pulled down the makeshift fencing, stepping over the fallen rail to confront her Star colonel face-to-face. Her scar stood out in livid color where it hooked down the left side of her face.

"We will *not* lose. What we will do is show this Tara Campbell that her presumption is far beyond her grasp. I want the Roosevelt Island complex leveled. You will take a DropShip and land it on top of the assembly facility, deploy forces, and sweep the entire island into Truxton Sound."

In the face of such vitriol, the only thing Noritomo Helmer could do was keep a calm front. "Galaxy Commander Hazen." He pulled himself stiffly to attention. "If you order an attack on Roosevelt Island, under those priorities, I will be forced to demand a Trial of Refusal. My people are better employed elsewhere."

Malvina's dark glower piled up like warning storm clouds. "And where do you believe you are better *spent*, Star Colonel?" Her emphasis was not to be missed. Noritomo was walking a knife's edge.

"Securing Skye for Clan Jade Falcon. Taking down victories on the battlefield."

"Then you could bring me a victory over Roosevelt Island's garrison force."

"I could." She still had not ordered him. Not yet. He found that interesting. "I believe it is a wasteful effort, however. If you are committed to such a path, blow it to hell from orbit."

Far from being insulted, though, Malvina actually smiled. There was no humor in her eyes. "We do think alike, occasionally. That was my first choice, Star Colonel. In fact, if the *Emerald Talon* had been in position, I would have done so yesterday in hopes of catching Duke Gregory and Campbell at the location."

He sensed there was more. "And?"

"We detected the infrared signature of an arriving JumpShip at the L3 Lagrange point. I diverted the *Talon* from high orbit and sent her after the contact." And there was not much a *Nightlord*-class WarShip could not handle.

"Republic reinforcements trying to sneak in?"

"Perhaps," she admitted. "But with the *Talon* guarding the way, the captain of that relief team is very foolish."

"Or very confident."

Reluctantly, Malvina allowed him a sharp nod. Then her eyes narrowed. "I could say the same thing about you, Star Colonel. Three times now, I should have ordered you killed for failing me. Kimball II and Chaffee, and your deliberate perversion of my orders concerning New London. Three times."

"It is within your power to order me into a Circle of Equals at any time, Galaxy Commander." He paused. Certainly it was in keeping with her somewhat erratic behavior since losing her brother. Yet the more he clung to the Way of the Clans, the more she tolerated his actions. Well, it was only the two of them now.

"Why have you not?" he asked.

"Would you really like to know?" Her tone suggested not. But she did not give him time to debate. "I believe that it is just what Bec Malthus would like for me to do." He must have looked alarmed, despite wrestling a mask over his features. "It is nothing personal. I do not think Malthus cares one way or another if you live or die. But it matters to him whether or not I do it."

Because Galaxy Commander Malthus wanted her isolated by her own hand. It wasn't enough that Malvina had lost her brother through their competition with each other. Whatever his plans for—with—Malvina Hazen, and they could be big, he wanted her off-balance and ready to strike out at anyone.

She had been right. Noritomo had not wanted to know this. Being privy to the secret struggles taking place between your betters was not conducive to a long and glory-filled career within the Clans.

He swallowed dryly, then forced a calm over himself. "May I assume at this time that you will not be demanding my death, and that I am not being directly ordered to attack what is in my eyes a worthless target?"

"Assumptions are a dangerous thing, Star Colonel. But yes. You may. *At this time.*"

"What *are* the Galaxy commander's orders?"

She waved a hand dismissively over the holographic tableau. "Salvage your toys and equip your warriors. Take down these Stormhammers if you can. But stand ready, Star Colonel. The next time I call for someone's head, you will deliver it." Malvina Hazen stepped back, allowing him some personal space in which to finally relax. "Or I will have yours."

"Bargained well," Noritomo agreed. "And done."

The formal words were out of his mouth before he thought better of them. It was tradition, after all, and the Galaxy commander had proposed a bargain that he would have had to live with regardless. Her humorless smile, though, and his memory of her earlier words haunted him.

When the time came for her to call out that name, it might very well be Becket Malthus'. And then how much would his life be worth?

DropShip *Himmelstor*
Over Skye

"We are at plus six and looking at occlusion in one hour," Eduard Goran reported to the *Himmelstor*'s bridge.

The radio signal was faint, broken up by the proximity of Skye's moon, Luna. It helped that Jasek knew the time-table as well as the spacer, even if he didn't understand all of the intricacies. His breathing was labored under the 1.8-gravity burn that thrust the *Excalibur*-class DropShip at Skye. He drew in a deep breath, pushing at the bands of steel tightening around his chest.

"Brevet Kaptain Dawkins is about to roll us over for deceleration burn," he said. Isaiah Dawkins was Goran's first officer aboard the *Himmelstor*. Red hair, cropped short, spacer-thin, and far, far too young, the leutnant was eager to prove himself in this difficult planetary insertion. Maybe too eager. "I am beginning to wish you had remained aboard."

"Your idea," Goran reminded him, frowning from the screen. He hadn't liked the idea of remaining aboard the JumpShip.

Jasek swallowed the lump in his throat as the DropShip cut its main drives and swung end for end on attitude jets. Gravity pirouetted sickeningly through the entire operation, and he gripped his chair's armrests with panicked strength. "Your expertise is needed over there. Bring them in safe, Eduard. Only you can do it."

"Just be sure to draw a few of that *Nightlord*'s assault shuttles after you." The captain scowled, not liking the need to wish assault vessels after his lord and master or after his ship. Maybe both. "If this doesn't work, we're going to spend a week or better hanging around in system with our pants down around our ankles."

"If this doesn't work," Jasek said as gravity pressed him once again into the seat, "we're all going to have our asses hanging out in the wind. You've got to come through."

Goran grunted. "I'll come through. But then it's all on the Lyrans." He paused, checking sidelong off the screen at some incoming readings. "Looking at the monster coming at us, I'm thinking this is going to take a miracle."

"It's coming up on Christmas," Jasek reminded the elder man. " 'Tis the season of miracles." He cut the connection with a nod and a difficult motion to the communications officer, then settled back for the bone-bruising run they were about to make for Skye.

Malvina Hazen, he decided, was due an early Christmas present.

30

In seizing a state one ought to consider all the injuries he will be obliged to inflict and then proceed to inflict them all at once so as to avoid frequent repetition of such acts.

The Prince, by Niccolò Machiavelli

LCS Yggdrasil
In Transit
9 December 3134

Eduard Goran considered that jumping into a Lagrange point—the same one twice inside of twelve hours—was likely the most ordinary task he was going to perform as part of Jasek's Operation Lodestone.

His first time was easiest, aboard Jasek's command JumpShip as it dropped the *Himmelstor*. The JumpShip's lithium-fusion batteries allowed for an immediate second jump once its position was well hidden behind Luna. A shuttle transfer and a new set of calculations, and here he was again jumping into Skye.

Hopefully—if that was the word for it—into the path of the *Emerald Talon*.

Not that the Stormhammers didn't have some powerful force on their side now as well. If everything held to plan, Goran would have a ringside seat to the first WarShip naval battle of the new century.

Kommodore Goran, given the honorary promotion to prevent any conflict with Kaptain Lionel Brionns, occupied second seat at Navigation on the WarShip *Yggdrasil*'s spacious bridge. A bit rusty, the WarShip and crew, but still serviceable despite any rumors. Goran's job was to facilitate the safe arrival of the *Mjolnir*-class WarShip into the near space around Skye. With so few WarShips surviving the Jihad, and even fewer kept in fighting shape as the Inner Sphere powers repaired their damaged economies, it was history in the making to help bring the grand fighting dame to war. And having come up through the service as a navigator, running time and again through the system, he knew every back-alley route and Lagrange point Skye had to offer.

But none of those points had ever been guarded by a fast-approaching Clan *Nightlord*.

Most space travelers reported sensing some kind of passage of time while in jump, even though the clocks all stopped between seconds and no voluntary movement was possible. The time slip ratcheted up from a simple eyeblink to the mind-bending effects of Transit Disorientation Syndrome, which landed people in sick bay for days after. Goran had never suffered from such a debilitating state.

There was only a slight twist in the back of his mind, which let Goran know reality had shifted in that heartbeat between suns, and the stars displayed on the main viewing screens jumped to new positions.

"Battle stations!" Kaptain Brionns shouted, though his men had been rung into position before the jump had ever begun. "Break loose the assault Drops."

A metallic clanking, the sound of DropShip docking collars being unlocked, carried through the *Yggdrasil*'s hull and announced to the bridge officers even before news came by communications that four assault-class DropShips had severed their connection to the battle cruiser. A pair each of *Overlord-A3*s and *Union-X*s. The *Union*s took up station trailing the *Yggdrasil*. With their heavier armor and weapon systems that could worry even a WarShip, the *Overlord*s moved up forward and flanking.

"*Nightlord*-class WarShip approaching hard," Sensors reported. "Twelve degrees off our starboard ventral beam."

"She's launched her ready-fighters." This from the tactical officer, a distant cousin of Duke Brewster, Goran recalled. "Forward Gauss cannons . . . firing . . . missed!"

Goran had tried to preserve the *Yggdrasil*'s orientation, bringing them in exactly where the JumpShip had been only eight minutes before with its nose pointing at Skye and the approaching *Nightlord*. Off by twelve degrees wasn't so bad, considering. The battle plan had rested on hopes that the Clan WarShip would not be so quick to respond, though, as an unarmored JumpShip swapped out for the Commonwealth's flagship.

"We won't get that lucky next time," Brionns said, tightening the harness that held him into the 360-degree rotational captain's chair. "Helm, swing us around. All engines full ahead. Forward batteries commence fire—fire at will."

On the forward-facing screens, a hardpoint swung into view as sunlight gleamed off the distant *Nightlord*. The *Emerald Talon* looked no more threatening than a small comet, except that this comet had teeth.

But then, so did the *Yggdrasil*.

From extreme ranges, the heavy naval-grade Gauss and particle projector cannon could deliver staggering damage. Lights on the bridge actually dimmed as the rail gun capacitors dumped their charges into the acceleration coils, creating a cascading magnetic field that grabbed half-ton ferrous masses and charged them at the *Nightlord*. Screens flickered with a static wash as the NPPCs joined the fusillade.

There was no avoiding the readied crew's marksmanship. Streams of particle energy softened up the *Emerald Talon*'s nose, with the railed masses slamming in afterward, caving in several compartments just to one side of the main weapons bays.

"First blood!" Brionns crowed, taking superstitious glee in the light damage done to the *Nightlord*. His bridge staff cheered.

For Goran, unused to the idea of WarShip combat, he felt less like cheering and more like throwing his arms up to shield his face as the *Emerald Talon* answered back with a combination of lasers, PPCs, and Gauss cannon of its own.

The storm of destructive energies hammered into the *Mjolnir*, shaking the entire ship with a mastiff's fangs. The forward screens went white with static and then black for a moment, flashing back to a new angle on the approaching *Nightlord* as Sensors routed new camera eyes to the bridge displays.

Goran swallowed dryly, hands clenched at his sides as he relegated himself to the role of observer for the hard-slugging match.

The vessels powered at each other, still probing with their farthest-reaching weapons. Fighters spilled out of bays on both sides, and the *Overlord*s started dropping naval-class missiles into space with impressive regularity.

The *Mjolnir* battle cruiser shook again under heavy weapons fire. And again.

WarShips, heavily armored as well as impressively armed, were designed to take a great deal of damage. The *Mjolnir*, the second-largest WarShip ever built by the Inner Sphere and largest to survive the Jihad sixty years earlier, carried fifty thousand tons over the *Nightlord* with thicker armor and an equal weapons load-out. On paper the match looked good, even slightly in favor of the Lyrans. But that didn't take into account the ships' captains. How the vessels were fought could make the difference between victory and sucking on vacuum.

And when the *Yggdrasil* lost Kaptain Brionns on the next exchange of salvos, it kicked Goran in the gut.

The *Mjolnir*'s battle bridge was buried under several decks, but once the vessels thrust into broadside range, all bets were off so far as maintaining positive protection. The *Nightlord* turned first, cutting out its massive drive flare and putting momentum in charge as attitude thrusters turned 1.2 million tons of destructive power on its long axis. Brionns matched them only a split second later, losing gravity on his ship along with the thrusters. As the vessels closed on intercept paths, both brought their huge spread of weaponry to bear.

"Missiles away!" one of the bridge officers shouted. Four AR10 launchers could spread a good dozen capital-class missiles between the WarShips before the first set even approached its target. Naval-class autocannon now joined in to the attack as they acquired target lock. Smaller, point defense weapons concentrated on holding off the aerospace fighter runs.

Then the *Nightlord*'s weapons hammered in, concentrating on the battle cruiser's tower with uncanny targeting. The navigation bridge near the very top of the tower was gutted out by naval-grade shells. More tracked down the port side, chewing through bulkheads and frames, opening up a large scar in the *Yggdrasil*'s side.

Rail gun strikes found that scar, drilling a ton of hypersonic mass deep into the vessel.

A scream of tortured metal rang through the battle bridge. The floor bucked, and in one place an errant girder thrust through like a spike. It missed skewering the communications station, and the comms officer, by half a meter. Air whistled out through the split in the deck, finding its way toward vacuum.

Overlapping deck plates shifted and buckled. One unlucky wrinkle thrust up beneath Brionns' seat. The chair broke away from its mounting, spinning up into the overhead and slamming the unfortunate kaptain into the ceiling.

Marines, stationed on the bridge and highly trained in zero-G operations, caught the chair within seconds, getting lanyards on it to fasten it to a stanchion. Medical personnel rushed to their commander's aid, while damage control teams used slapdash patches and a hardening sealant to make the bridge airtight again. The chaos lasted for half a minute—an impressive display of battle reflexes. But in that time, the two WarShips had drifted several klicks and were quickly coming up on point-blank ranges.

And there was no captain to command the *Yggdrasil*.

The ship's executive officer, a leutnant-kaptain, commanded from Central Control deeper into the WarShip's bowels; the division of command prevented the ship's two officers from being incapacitated at the same time. But from that position he was more effective in leading damage control teams and supporting orders from the bridge than fighting a pitched battle.

Goran expected the chief weapons officer to take local control, perhaps even Duke Brewster's relative, who could leverage political clout into the chain of command. But every station had its hands full dealing with the bridge damage or the approaching *Nightlord*, or worrying for the kaptain.

Only one station had the presence of mind to continue calling out information, and that was Sensors. And he directed it to the next senior rank on the bridge.

"Kommodore. We are at five hundred klicks and closing fast."

Goran was part of the chain of command. Technically. Brionns had inserted him when making him second seat at Navigation. But to bring him forward in battle to command a vessel he'd never set foot on before today?

Part of command was being decisive, and five hundred kilometers was not much to work with in space. There was no more than a heartbeat's hesitation before Goran dialed his headset over to the general command channel, patching in to Central Control.

"This is the bridge. Kaptain Brionns is injured. Leutnant-kaptain Franklan, respond."

Nothing.

"Comms have been severed to Central," the communications officer yelled out. "We're working on a bypass."

"Keep up heavy fire against that *Nightlord*." The most obvious order Goran could think of, perhaps, but it filled the void where panic too often started, even among the best crews. He scrambled mentally for a plan of action. If he'd been fighting DropShips, he'd default to his gut reaction. So be it.

"Helm, roll us onto our back relative to that battleship. Weapons, ready a switch from port broadside to starboard."

"They'll have our belly, Kommodore." This from Helm.

"Better than cutting off our head," he snapped. There was no more argument, and he felt gravity shift as the vessel began to roll.

"Three hundred klicks," Sensors called out. "Passing within ten kilometers."

So close? Brionns ran a tight ship and fought a close battle, it seemed. Good Lyran tactics. Walk a big gun up to your opponent, and fire when you can't possibly miss.

"Helm. Can we use thrusters to put us on direct intercept?"

"S-sir?" The *Mjolnir* trembled with new damage being spread along her underside.

"Collision course. Scrape the paint and wake the ghosts." He saw the uncertainty on the officer's face. "Do it, man!"

"Aye, Kaptain."

Goran accepted the change in ranks with a grunt and a nod, his attention focused on the flickering main screen and the magnified display of the *Emerald Talon*. No captain in his right mind would stand for a collision in space, especially at the speeds at which the WarShips closed. Goran wanted the Clanners thinking about it, though, and worrying about something other than how to inflict more damage on the struggling *Mjolnir*.

Except that his fast-to-action plan did not seem to be working. The *Nightlord* rolled top-over as well, never presenting its underside but putting fresh armor between the two vessels. There was no attempt to move out of the way. The other captain either couldn't or wouldn't believe that Goran would go through with it.

More traded weapons fire. This time the *Mjolnir* got off light as several volleys concentrated on one of the *Overlord*s. Maybe the missile barrages were starting to wear on the other crew.

"Two hundred kilometers, passing within five . . . make it four . . ." Sensors sounded uncertain. "It's going to be close, sir."

Close would have to do. Jasek Kelswa-Steiner had counted on Goran to bring the *Yggdrasil* into Skye. One way or another, it was going to happen.

Hopefully, not as a fireball plummeting through atmosphere.

"Bridge, Central." The voice was reedy and distant, but there. "This is Franklan. Status, Lionel?"

He thumbed open his circuit. "This is Kommodore Goran. Brionns is injured and being attended to. I have assumed temporary command. Leutnant-kaptain, are you capable of assuming full control of this ship?"

A new aftershock shook the entire ship, and blanked comms for several crucial seconds. Then—

"I show a collision course and port-for-starboard roll, with massive damage on the lee side?" Franklan asked.

"One hundred klicks . . . ," Sensors let them both know.

"We've brought a fresh side around," Goran acknowledged. "I'm trying to make the other commander flinch. I'm cutting this circuit in ten seconds, sir. Is Central capable of running this fight?"

To Franklan's credit, he considered it for less than five. "Keep the ball," he ordered. With one hand over his mic, his voice barely discernible, he ordered Central, "Ring for collision. All hands, brace for impact."

"Fifty klicks. Sir, I think . . . she's rolling, and thrusting down!"

In his mind's eye, Goran saw it coming together. The two vessels approaching broadside, both turning belly-up to bring them back on a relative plane. But as he committed the *Yggdrasil* to an upward drift, relative to the plane of the system, the other captain had no choice but to thrust down.

Main drives would not help at this point. Not without spinning the ship and risking a T-bone collision. The worst you could have, threatening to break your vessel in half.

Which put Goran above the other WarShip, attacking at its belly and then slashing back at the wounded side it had rolled away.

"Roll twenty degrees over, maintain upward thrust. Light off the mains and get ready to swing around! All weapons save for missile launchers, hold for her wounded backside. Missiles continue to fire at will."

In the time it took to relay his commands, the WarShips were rolling over each other on parallel bearings.

Weapons stabbed out from each, and fire blossomed silently on the outer hulls as oxygen burned off into space.

Fighter craft flashed between and over both ships, adding their needle teeth to the raw damage being dished out by naval-class weapons bays.

The *Overlord*s absorbed damage against their triple-reinforced hulls, threw out another brace of missiles each. One of them took another desperate salvo, lost its main drive, and tumbled out of control deeper into the system.

Inside the ships, the damage translated into a violent shudder that seemed as if it would never stop. A rumbling call growled through the bridge. But all the while Weapons called out the volleys. First strikes.

Second.

Third.

Then the vessels were past. They came within two kilometers of each other, at normal magnification looking like a far throw but point-blank by space-faring distances. The *Union*s brushed over the *Emerald Talon* in one last-ditch effort, and then they were past and in the clear as well.

Gravity returned as the mains lit off, and damage reports flooded the bridge, passed along from Central where Leutnant-kaptain Franklan rode herd over the worst of them. Sensors reported the better news: how much pain they had inflicted on the Jade Falcons.

"Aft Gauss bays, silenced. Portside autocannon seem out of commission. There is a hydrogen fire glowing on her port ventral . . . I think that's a blowout! She's lighted off her mains, but it looks like she's only getting half thrust out of them. Kaptain! You sliced her engineering spaces!"

Which gave the *Mjolnir* a distinct advantage. Weapons continued to trade off as the ships sped apart, but with less intensity than before. That was going to change in a hurry.

"Leutnant-kaptain, your presence is required on the bridge." The fight wasn't over, and this crew deserved a seasoned WarShip captain. Goran had done what he could.

Though maybe he could do a little more.

"Helm, bring us around on an intercept arc. By the time Franklan arrives, I want us ready for a second pass. Angle in at her aft, and ready all weapons. Here's where we grab the Falcons by the scruff and kick them in the ass."

He had done his part, breaking the Falcons' death grip on Skye.

The rest was up to Jasek.

31

Norfolk
Skye
12 December 3134

Jasek Kelswa-Steiner let a pair of wheeled Demons and a towed Long Tom artillery piece take the Norfolk Bridge.

Slogging his *Templar* across the river on its north side, chased by a pair of Pegasus hovercraft and a Maxim heavy hover transport from his Archon's Shield battalion, he dropped his crosshairs on one of the converted SalvageMechs that held the opposite bank, but held his fire. Listening to the comms chatter, sensing that his full line was not quite in place, he hesitated, stalling his push forward and leaving himself open to attack. The SalvageMech's light autocannon chipped away at his armor, striking sparks from his BattleMech's shoulders, its chest. Earlier there had been a *Shadow Hawk IIC* stalking his flank, using its jumping ability to threaten Jasek's advance forces, but it was hiding in the tree line now or had moved to another part of the wide-front battle.

Instead, a Kelswa assault tank with a hastily painted Jade Falcon crest on its side rolled forward from the cover of a stand of tall ponderosa pines to anchor the enemy position.

Two Cardinal VTOL transports followed, popping over the tree line, belly flopping into a clearing where Elemental battlesuit troopers jumped free.

The Kelswa's Gauss rifles flashed telltale blue discharges, and a pair of nickel-ferrous slugs skipped across the river. One dived beneath the water, raising a large sheet that sprayed across Jasek's ferroglass shield. The other crushed into his right-side armor, stripping away most of his protection.

"Heavy massing south of the Norfolk Bridge," Colonel Vandel reported, his Praetorian mobile HQ breaking onto the western shore about half a kilometer downriver from Jasek's position.

Jasek could read by his own HUD that Joss Vandel faced a trio of Skanda light tanks and paired JES II strategic missile carriers.

Beyond his sensor range to the north, Vandel's top kommandant, Leslie Hoarus, reported much the same. "Rangers. Elementals. Damn!" Static. "One Kinnol main battle tank with a *way*-too-accurate PPC."

All up and down the river the scene was repeated as the Jade Falcons fought to repel Jasek's forces. The Clan warriors obviously thought they had a good chance to hold off the Stormhammers.

They thought wrong.

Jasek had borrowed a page out of the Jade Falcon manual for his assault on Shipil Company's Norfolk dockyards. He followed much the same battle plan as the Clanners had in their raiding assault on the local area before he left Skye.

DropShip grounding near the North Inlet.

A solid drive spearheading his column through a gap in the western hills.

Heavy woods along the river's edge had broken the battle up into small-unit engagements as the Stormhammers pushed for the river, the bridge, and Norfolk, which now lay only a few kilometers away. So far, the enemy had seen only a pair of BattleMechs with perhaps slightly higher-than-average supporting forces. Heavy tanks and fast hovercraft. Artillery. VTOL support. Jasek planned to reeducate them.

It came a moment sooner than expected, with two MHI

amphibious APCs and a Manticore II splashing into the river just above Jasek's position. All three vehicles bore the clenched-gauntlet crest of the Lyran Commonwealth. The Manticore II heavy tank looked fresh off the factory floor, with its pristine armor and gleaming polish to its PPC barrel and its missile launcher. It likely was, given that Hesperus II produced the veteran fighting vehicle, and Duke Brewster had promised Jasek some of his best.

Best seemed to be a relative term as the Manticore crew couldn't hit an *Overlord* at five hundred meters. Its particle cannon lashed out with brilliant firepower, exploding through a magnificent elm just beyond the Kelswa. It might have provided cover for enemy forces—Jasek gave them that.

Its missiles arced overhead but fell short. Water burst up at the river's edge in a line of geysers. At least they got the Jade Falcons wet.

"Weapons free." Jasek gave the command as the Kelswa slammed a Gauss slug into his chest. It staggered the eighty-five-ton machine, but did not drop it.

His thumb mashed down on the firing stud. A particle projector cannon in each arm arced new lightning at the Kelswa. Both struck the vehicle along its front, carving away armor, splashing it across the ground in large molten puddles.

The Pegasus scout craft pushed past him, throwing back long rooster tails as their drive fans kicked them up toward ninety kilometers per hour in their short sprint across the river. They guarded the Maxim, only slightly slower, which turned near the water's edge and pulled up short. Gull wing doors flew up, and Stormhammers Gnome infantry leaped out to trade laser fire with the Clan Elementals. The Gnomes bore the brunt for several long seconds, until the MHI craft drew close enough to the opposite bank that Fenrir troopers could begin to bail over the sides and splash through the water on their own.

The quadruped battle armor made all the difference. With one squad bearing medium pulse lasers and two more backpack mounts of three small lasers, they were a serious threat at range and decimating up close and personal.

Turning their attention on one of the hovering Cardinals, the pulse laser squad blasted through its light armor. Sooty, gray smoke roiled out of its engine compartment. Both craft banked away, racing back for the Shipil dockyards. The wounded VTOL hardly made it a hundred meters before it crashed down into the trees, swallowed by the forest.

Meanwhile, both of the close-in Fenrir squads had joined Jasek's Gnomes in routing the Elementals. The genetically engineered Clan infantry were fearsome in their own right, but they weren't so foolish as to push a losing position against superior firepower. Bounding away on their jump jets, they gained the safety of the trees with only minor losses.

Which left a lumbering SalvageMech and the Kelswa.

Jasek let the SalvageMech go, concentrating his fire on the assault tank as he waded free of the river. But the SalvageMech pilot was not about to be ignored. In a display of battlefield triage, the awkward IndustrialMech plodded forward into Jasek's line of fire, protecting the more valuable assault tank. Jasek's particle cannon ripped it up one side and down the other.

The Manticore II had all but disappeared beneath the water as it crossed, but came plowing out like some submarine monster looking for victims. It missed again as the SalvageMech stumbled out from beneath its sights. Jasek made up for it with double strikes from his energy cannon. Temperatures soared as the fusion reactor spiked to meet the power draw. The cockpit began to smell like a sauna.

The SalvageMech toppled over onto its side, the left leg severed just below the knee. Fenrir infantry swarmed over it while the Pegasus craft formed a defensive line, ready to bloody any attempt by the Falcons to rescue their man or salvage the 'Mech.

There would be no attempt. As Lyran ground forces broke cover along the river's edge to bolster the Archon's Shield battalion, the Clanners gave up the eastern bank as lost and fell back toward Norfolk.

The Stormhammers and Lyran forces paused only briefly to pull together inside the forest, and then they chased after.

"Why are we seeing such light defenses?" Vandel asked over his private channel to Jasek. His crew tucked the command crawler in behind Jasek's *Templar*. "Norfolk is supposed to be the center of their operations locally."

True. Tara Campbell had transmitted the intel to them as they made planetfall. But it was also clear that the central line of communications between the disparate elements of Skye's defenders was haphazard. At best.

"If their forces aren't here, it's because they were needed elsewhere." Jasek blinked sweat back from the corners of his eyes, cycled his weapons back to standby to let them cool. Temperatures inside his cockpit dropped slowly.

"Take the gifts where they come, Joss. It doesn't happen this way too often."

And it wasn't going to be so easy on the other side of the forest. They broke out of heavy cover to find themselves rolling into several square kilometers of planted saplings. A fairly young tree farm that Jasek had seen before. Now there were leaves budding on the slender branches, and new grass, but he could see the damage left from the previous fighting in the scarred ground and burned swaths. The Shipil Company dockyards waited directly in Jasek's line of march. Norfolk spread away from the tree farm south and east.

Here the Jade Falcons had found time to mass up in front of their DropShip. An *Overlord*, painted green, standing thirty-plus stories tall and dwarfing the Shipil dockyards with its empty "nest," it straddled the tree farm and a portion of the dockyard parking area. With its heavy array of weaponry, equal to any combined-arms company, a DropShip was no small advantage in battle. Provided you were willing to risk such a valuable piece of technology.

Jasek would make certain they did.

Long barrels flashed with high-output energy as lasers and particle cannon speared out from the sloped sides of the vessel, drawing lines of destruction down toward the tree line where the Stormhammers and their Lyran allies began to emerge. Missiles dropped on falling arcs, and fireballs blossomed among the saplings as well as over the top of a Stormhammer VV1 Ranger. The vehicle erupted into flames, turned instantly into a charred husk. The soldiers inside never knew what hit them.

"Stormhammers, press the ground forces back. Always concentrate fire on the forwardmost units. Lyran command, work over that DropShip."

Fortunately, with its weapons bays distributed equally

around its massive bulk, the *Overlord* could bring only five or six of its primary weapons to bear. It evened the odds, but was not necessarily tipping the battle in favor of the Jade Falcons.

The Clan warriors had formed up in a double line fronting their DropShip as service trucks and salvage vehicles formed a steady caravan carrying personnel and salvage from the Shipil Company facilities to the waiting *Overlord*. The Falcons were not conceding the battle, but they were preparing for the worst-case scenario.

The Kelswa assault tank Jasek had chased from the river crawled up to the Jade Falcon fore, taking a place alongside the *Shadow Hawk IIC* he had seen earlier and an eighty-ton *Warhammer IIC*, which he hadn't. Nacon armored scouts and Skanda light tanks formed the bulk of the Falcon armor command, wheeling about in short, sharp circles, waiting for Skye's defenders to press forward, but Jasek also counted strategic missile carriers and a Schmitt among their numbers. Skadi swift attack VTOLs, a limping MiningMech outfitted with a missile system, APCs with Elementals clinging to the sides.

Still not enough.

Jasek pressed forward in a slow walk, his PPCs ramming out one bolt of man-made lightning after another. Vandel's mobile HQ hung out just inside the tree line, but by rank and column the Stormhammers' Archon's Shield unit pushed with him, adding to his firepower, savaging the Falcon line with autocannon, missile barrages, and the red spears of laser fire.

A Gauss slug *spang*ed off Jasek's shoulder, close enough that he saw the silver blur through his ferroglass shield. He swallowed tightly and continued on, establishing a beachhead for his emerging forces. Two *Storm Raider*s leading their own fast-armor contingent. A Behemoth II, which was the equivalent of most any BattleMech. Demon medium tanks. Maxim hover transports. Then came the Lyrans with a trio of Manticore II heavies and their MHI transports, Pegasus scouts . . . and finally the *Zeus*.

It was the Lyrans' ace in the hole, which he had kept hidden from the Jade Falcons on the entire drive forward. An eighty-ton assault 'Mech, also produced on Hesperus II. And also fresh into battle.

The first Manticore let fly with missiles and energy cannon, striking far wide of the massive *Overlord*. Jasek merely nodded, having a very good guess which team crewed that tank. It actually did miss an *Overlord* at five hundred meters. Its brethren made up for it, though, slicing PPCs into the DropShip's armor-plated side. Missiles pockmarked and cracked into the hull as well. When the *Zeus* added its own PPC and lasers into the attack, the Lyrans were giving back nearly as good as the DropShip could dish out. What they lacked in skill they certainly made up for in heavy firepower.

Evened odds. Jasek had lost both of his aerospace fighters to an assault-class DropShip on the insertion run, so he had no way to counter the Jade Falcon VTOLs that came springing forward, their nose cannon blazing long streams of fire, but he was not totally without aerial support.

"Sergeant Maxwell, give them the silver hammer," he ordered over a combat frequency.

Jasek had left his Long Tom artillery piece back at the bridge. A good stable platform under open sky. He couldn't see Jergen Maxwell worrying over the elevation and angle as the artillery team levered the large barrel into place, but he could well imagine the man's beefy hand grabbing on to the hammer of polished silver that the sergeant had custom-installed on the firing mechanism. Rock it forward, disengage safeties. And *pull*.

Three seconds later, a large fireball erupted next to an enemy Skanda, flipping it into an aerial roll that eventually dropped it onto its side.

Another blast tore the back end off a missile carrier. Missile loads exploded in sympathetic detonations, creating a fireball that dwarfed even the massive artillery round. Jasek felt the tremor through the ground and his *Templar*'s thick legs.

"Correct by point-two degrees. Lower elevation." An artillery spotter, safe and secure inside Vandel's mobile HQ. "Bring it home!"

Jasek traded his PPCs with a quartet of ruby-bright spears that slashed at him from the *Warhammer*. Autocannon pounded around him, hammering armor as well as the dirt around his feet as the *Overlord* added a portion of its own firepower to the Clan BattleMech's. The Falcons had obviously identified him as the Stormhammers' point leader.

Fair enough. "Primary units, slash at their front," he ordered. "Secondaries, transfer fire to the *Warhammer*. Now!"

In a well-coordinated strike, half of Jasek's line leaped forward, suffering the VTOLs' line of death, and turned all weapons against the *'Hammer*. Less than half hit, at the ranges they traded fire at, but it was still enough to set the Clan MechWarrior back on his heels. The BattleMech teetered and swayed, but held to its feet. The Long Tom dropped an artillery strike only sixty meters behind it, crushing a Nacon scout like a tin can, and no doubt worrying the Clanners a little more.

"Transfer all fire to the DropShip. If you can get an angle on it, work over the main ramps. Let's clip their wings."

The last of the noncombat vehicles had lined up for entry. Two of them fell under heavy attack and erupted in flames. A Gauss slug from the Kelswa clipped Jasek's knee and nearly sent him sprawling. He corrected with a foot planted ahead of him, turned, and sliced at the tank in a cross-body shot.

By luck more than design, one PPC found a flaw in the assault tank's armor, cutting deep over one tread well, severing the chevron-shaped belt and anchoring it in place.

As the concentrated firepower began to work over the ramp area in earnest, it was enough for the Falcons. In good order, the main units began to fall back for emergency boarding. Jasek's artillery piece kept working over their lines, but the Falcons got some of their own back as VTOLs continued to pounce on any vehicle that strayed too far forward.

The *Overlord* shook with unleashed fury as its main drives lit off, blasting the ground beneath it with a bright plasma flame. Smoke and steam curled up around its sides and hid the main ramp from view as the *Shadow Hawk* and the *Warhammer* were last to board.

The VTOLs spun about and shot off to the southeast, running for the safety of their closest stronghold.

Knowing the kind of damage a drive flare could do if the DropShip decided to hover and drift over his line, Jasek scattered his units back. Most of them took cover at the forest's edge. A few found safety inside the near fringes of Norfolk.

Jasek waited on the field, confident in his ability to out-maneuver such an ungainly—if powerful—craft.

The DropShip tried nothing spectacular. It lifted straight off, setting fire to a new ring of saplings as it drifted slightly off center, but doing little more damage than it had already caused on its landing. Within moments it was a bright star in the sky.

"Good riddance," Joss Vandel said.

Jasek nodded. "But not good-bye. They'll be back." He had almost hoped for a longer stand-up fight, giving him the chance to inflict heavier damage on the Clanners. But the Falcons had learned from their earlier mistakes, it seemed. They were far more ready to retreat and re-form.

They were in this for the long haul as well.

"They'll be back," he said again, though this time in a whisper quiet enough not to activate his mic. Louder, he ordered, "Get some men into the facilities, Joss. Battlesuits sweep through first, then combat engineers. Make certain that it's safe—then we'll see what kind of mess the Falcons have left for us. And send out the call."

"Everyone?" Vandel asked.

"All of them. If they're not needed or supporting a current firefight, I want the Tharkan Strikers and the Rangers to begin gathering here at Norfolk." He bared his teeth, knowing what it was about to cost them. "It's time for the Stormhammers to draw a line in the sand."

And then they'd see just how badly the Jade Falcons wanted Skye. If it was enough to stand, and to die, for.

32

Miliano
Skye
15 December 3134

A late frost still dusted the pale grass and rimed Miliano's streets where trees and buildings cast their protective shadows. Skye's sun, drifting higher every morning as local winter gave over firmly to spring, beat down out of a perfect, cobalt sky to melt what it could reach. Here, ice crystals glittered. There, wisps of steam rolled over paved, damp-black surfaces.

Cold one moment. Sweating the next.

Tara Campbell understood that sensation very well.

Riding with Duke Gregory Kelswa-Steiner in his stretched hover-sedan, Tara stared out of the mirror-tinted window and attempted to catalog reasons for her unease. The streets and side lots surrounding Avanti Assemblies looked nearly deserted compared with her previous visits. She had expected to see military vehicles swarming around the facilities, with damaged 'Mechs and tanks waiting in a long queue for their time in the maintenance bays. Battlesuit infantry patrolling the streets. Support vehicles bringing in salvage and the wounded. An armed camp bursting at the seams, preparing for siege—that was how she had characterized Miliano last time.

All erased in less than five days, since Jasek's return to Skye. Under his direction the Stormhammers responded much more smoothly, rotating refit units into the field at a much quicker pace.

It also appeared that he had pulled half of his troops out of the city. Tara had yet to count one vehicle bearing the crest of the Tharkan Strikers. Lyran Rangers were all that appeared to be left.

Another corner and Duke Gregory's motorcade—with full military escort, of course—flashed through the gated entrance without so much as a nod to local security. A squad of hoverbikes leading, a pair of VV1 Rangers marking perfect time behind them, and then the black hoversedan with Tara and Jasek's father seated in back. A Fox armored car followed, where Legate Eckard had taken the one passenger jump seat.

Tara saw Jasek standing outside the main factory, attended at the moment by his civilian adviser and a Lyran general. Jasek looked ready to jump into combat at a moment's notice, wearing the gray utility jumpsuit most MechWarriors pulled on over their battle togs. She shifted uncomfortably on the leather seat of the armored limousine, feeling more than a bit pretentious with her formal arrival. It didn't help when she saw Jasek shake his head and lean over to whisper something to GioAvanti. She could only imagine.

"Sometimes I wonder if we would do better without Jasek." These were the duke's first words in the last quarter hour. He sat next to her, staring through the tinted glass at his son, stroking his beard thoughtfully.

"We need his Stormhammers," Tara reminded him. The blood price they had laid down for Miliano, for Roosevelt Island, argued for itself. Even the lord governor had to admit that by now.

Apparently he did. "But do we need Jasek?"

Something in his tone caught her attention. "Why?" She glanced at him sharply. "Is there a reason we would lose him?"

"Apparently not, if he is able to leave the Commonwealth for our company." If there had been a suggestion hidden in his words, it had clearly been pulled back. It was simply a tired politician and a disappointed father who sat next to her.

The motorcade pulled up in perfect parade formation. She was out of the sedan the moment it drifted to a stop, never waiting for the driver to get out and open the door for her. The sun warmed the back of her neck, but her ankles felt the dampness of a frost-touched breeze that blew out from the shaded alley between two buildings. Gooseflesh tingled on her arms, and she wrote that off to the chill in the air.

And the pleasant warmth in Jasek's hand clasp. That was just body heat.

"Good to have you back," Tara let him know right off.

She wanted no argument between father and son to interfere with firming up the bridges she had built with the Stormhammers' leader before Chaffee, before Hesperus II. First, be appreciative. Second, take control.

She needed to greet the Lyran representative as well, a young leutnant-general with a fresh-pressed field uniform, and preferably before the lord governor insulted the man. Duke Gregory's comments inside the sedan had been less than complimentary. But Jasek was not so eager to release her hand. He held it in a firm grip, pulling her back around to meet his stormy gaze. Dark blue eyes, so nearly indigo. Why did he distract her so easily?

"What?" she asked.

He'd brought his other hand up, and now cradled her hand in both of his. The way he shifted from one foot to the other. His hesitant glance toward his father, and then toward Niccolò GioAvanti. He looked nervous, like a man about to propose.

Far from it.

"We got word about two hours ago," he said calmly as his father and Legate Eckard approached. "Jade Falcons overran your hidden command post outside of New London this morning. An assault Trinary."

The facility she had built into the bluff, below the Forlorn Hope memorial. Where she had overseen the response to the Jade Falcons' landing assaults.

"We didn't have more than a lance . . . maybe two . . . of light vehicles left there."

And twenty-two personnel, several from the staff of her

own Highlanders. Tara Bishop had been sent back there! And Della Brown. Niccolò and the Lyran general refused to meet her eyes, leaving this to Jasek. She swallowed hard. "How many escaped?"

"An assault Trinary," he repeated, and let the silence stretch out uncomfortably.

"No one escaped," Niccolò GioAvanti finally said. He tugged at the braid lying down the left side of his face. His pale eyes caught each of the new arrivals in turn. "No one was taken prisoner. Prefect Della Brown is dead. The staff is dead."

"Well, that tears it," Duke Gregory said. "We need to take back New London."

Jasek shook his head, finally releasing Tara's hand. "That would be a bad idea."

"It might cause some military hardship," the lord governor snapped, "but it's a political and a *command* necessity. We swore—each in our own way—to put the people of Skye and the men and women under our care first and foremost. We're failing them all, boy."

Visibly calming himself when Jasek did not contradict him, Duke Gregory placed a hand on her shoulder. "It was a fair gamble, Countess, letting them occupy New London, but I'm not going to watch while that murdering bitch takes Skye apart one piece at a time."

GioAvanti studied his fingernails as if looking for flaws in his manicure. " 'Fortune is a woman,' " he said, his eyes finding Tara, " 'and in order to be mastered she must be jogged and beaten.' "

Duke Gregory physically recoiled from the GioAvanti scion. The Lyran officer frowned his disapproval as well. But Tara recognized that far from making a sexist comment, he quoted from an ancient political text. And it did seem to match the Clan philosophy of mating military might with political gain, and of aggression in place of caution. On the face of it, GioAvanti seemed to be agreeing with the lord governor that rash action was needed. But she also knew the context in which that quote was nested.

" 'She runs her course only when she is not contained by proper safeguards.' " She nodded, and turned the small group toward the nearby facility.

"We either trust our original plans or abandon Skye's fortune to a coin toss. Duke Gregory, I've lost as much or more in this recent setback." She winced as memories of Tara Bishop threatened to flood to the surface—of all her Highlanders to lose . . . "And I still believe that we must hold to our position."

"There are not that many positions left to hold," he twisted her words around. Glancing to his left and right, he studied the light defenses surrounding the Assemblies plant, shook his head.

Too few vehicles, Tara agreed. Stepping inside the shadowed interior of the facility did not raise hopes. The main floor continued to work on assembling a Kinnol main battle tank, but fewer than half of the converted maintenance bays were busy with repairing allied war machines.

Again, that feeling of abandonment. Or maybe it was the ghosts of so many Highlanders. Tara shivered, but then, it was cooler inside the building, out of the sun. A few of GioAvanti's people crewed a beverage table just inside the doors. She accepted an insulated mug of black, black coffee when it was offered, as did the Legate.

The beverage was bitter and burned-tasting, but at least it was hot.

Duke Gregory refused the offer. "It appears we are preparing to give up Miliano next," he said with a frustrated glare toward his son.

"That will not happen, Lord Governor."

Ignored for the last several minutes, the young leutnant-general now stepped forward to introduce himself. He looked more than a little out of place, his Lyran dress uniform standing out against the field dress of the other officers present. His woolen jacket was light blue. Red piping trimmed the cuffs and the outside seam of his white stirrup pants. His shoes were polished to a reception-quality shine.

"Hiram Brewster, of the Lyran Guards. My forces are set in a picket line just south of Miliano. We can hold against a Jade Falcon push."

Tara had her reservations, having seen battlerom footage of the recent recapture of Norfolk. Also, she had spotted a *Zeus* being worked on in the facility's large corner bay. Technicians were busy ripping out a mangled gyro, to be replaced from valuable local stores, no doubt. If the white horse's head painted on its leg was an indication of ownership, Hiram's 'Mech was currently sidelined.

Still, beggars couldn't be choosers, she reminded herself, and shook the offered hand in a quick, neutral clasp. "We appreciate the offer of Lyran assistance." She had worried about Duke Gregory, but apparently for nothing. He stepped forward with a hand outstretched as well. She breathed easier, for about two seconds.

"My son may have warned you of my feelings against bringing in the Commonwealth, and he was right." Tara drew in a sharp breath as the two men shook hands. "But for Skye I welcome you here. So long as we understand each other."

"Father," Jasek warned.

The leutnant-general did not seem to mind. "I think we do, sir."

"I hope so. Because in this manner I do not speak for the Exarch, whoever it turns out to be. Jasek wants you here. Tara Campbell approves. So be it. But the minute I believe your Archon is trying to open the door for an invasion of The Republic, I'll sic the hounds on your heels."

Tara winced. Losing Paladin McKinnon had been a hard enough blow to the defense of Skye. If the Lyrans decided to pick up their toys and go home, whom did that serve?

Brewster's face darkened only a touch. "I don't make or discuss policy, Lord Governor. I enforce the will of the duke of Hesperus. And that will, currently, is to render aid and assistance to Jasek Kelswa-Steiner and to Skye."

Good answer. He was a better politician that Tara would have given him credit for, or was a good enough soldier to simply fall back on his orders.

"I'm sure frustrations are running high on both sides of the border," she said in an attempt to mollify both men. She warmed her hands on her coffee mug. Her eyes begged Jasek for help, even though she hated herself for the need to do so. "Sniping at each other does nothing to solve our immediate problems."

Jasek stood just inside the large doors. He nodded to Niccolò, who invited Legate Eckard to the supervisor's station, where the most recent estimates on the facility's repair capability were being discussed. Tara had no doubt that several necessary questions would be answered regarding logistics support.

Which left Jasek to deal with his father.

"It remains," the younger Kelswa-Steiner said, "that Miliano is in no immediate danger. I've ordered Kommandant Duke to Norfolk, which sits in the path of any Jade Falcon push out of the New London area. Colonel Petrucci is pushing back a Jade Falcon expeditionary force with half the assets left to the Lyran Rangers."

"And the Tharkan Strikers?" Tara asked, noting that he had not volunteered their whereabouts. Duke Gregory glared harder with every use of Lyran rank and mention of the Stormhammer units.

"What's left of them pulled out on their own two days ago, moving to the aid of the Steel Wolves. Anastasia Kerensky was in trouble, forced into the coastal lowlands outside of Second Bristol. Between them, they forced a rout of the Falcons' Seventh Striker Cluster."

Jasek's seizing Norfolk behind the Falcons' position had had a great deal to do with that as well, Tara guessed. Just like he had pressured the Jade Falcon WarShip by bringing in the Lyrans' fabled *Mjolnir*. Both WarShips were circling out near the zenith now, holding each other back from Skye. On the face of it, Jasek seemed to be doing everything in his ability to throw off the Jade Falcon occupation.

So why did Tara assume he was holding out on her? The voice of experience whispering to her? Or was it the attraction she felt and wanted nothing to do with?

"The Seventh Striker Cluster." Duke Gregory glanced sidelong at Tara. "Is that the unit you let walk from Chaffee?" She could have thought of a better way to phrase it. "If you had hit them harder, there wouldn't have been as many to reinforce the Falcon offensive."

"There wouldn't be as many of my Stormhammers either." Jasek shrugged. "But I doubt that means as much to you."

"They were my subjects before they became your renegades. They are still sons and daughters of Skye. Most of them. Their lives mean as much to me as . . . as . . ."

"As mine does?" Jasek smiled without humor. "A stunning endorsement, Father."

"Against the survival of Skye and the prefecture," Duke Gregory said coldly, flushing into his beard, "all resources must be measured with a critical eye."

"Which brings us right back to where we were." Tara

stomped into the middle of the father-son battle, grabbing the conversation with both hands and wrestling it back on topic. "Deciding what is best for Skye. We've lost our best advance post at New London and some very good people. Our forces are stretching thin, gentlemen." She included Leutnant-general Brewster's force in the assessment, shooting a pointed glance at his wounded *Zeus*. He nodded reluctantly. "Jasek has retaken the Shipil Company facilities at Norfolk, and we still hold Cyclops, Incorporated, as well as Miliano. How do we use that?"

"We reinforce our position," the lord governor of Skye said at once. "Bring at least half of the Tharkan Strikers back to Miliano. Let the Steel Wolves guard what's left of Cyclops on Roosevelt. We dig in and hold, and make the Falcons pay for every meter."

Hiram Brewster considered, and gave the duke a reluctant nod. "Sounds right," he said. "Fortune favors the defenders."

"Strategy favors the offense," Jasek replied. "A defensive posture is nothing more than a waiting game. Can we get reinforcements out of Prefecture X before the Falcons draw from their garrisons on Glengarry, on Ryde? Can we use local industry to make up for increased losses—which we will take if we surrender the initiative?"

Tara sipped at her coffee, letting it warm her. She tore Jasek's plea apart word by word, analyzing it with a cold eye rather than letting his charisma sway her. "What would you have us do?" she asked.

"Miliano is the key to the continent's lower seaboard, but Norfolk is the key to Miliano. Unless the Jade Falcons are willing to risk a nonstop DropShip brigade to tie two remote areas together—and we have better aerospace assets than they do without their WarShip in place—they need to control the ground corridors. We mass our forces at Norfolk. Stormhammers. Highlanders. Militia. Lyran." He nodded to Brewster. "Everyone. Malvina Hazen will come at us, and we will have our chance to break her."

"What's to stop her from seizing Roosevelt Island or Miliano when our backs are turned?" His father sounded skeptical.

"If she does, and wants to safeguard New London, she

does so without enough force to hold them. Whatever we lose, we can take back."

"You'll turn our most important cities into battlefields. No." Duke Gregory shook his head. "We play the long game."

There it was again. A hard mask slipping over Jasek's face. Something . . .

Tara Campbell looked from one leader to the other. Father to son. Politician to faction commander. Jasek's plan had a strength of audacity behind it, much in keeping with the younger man's own stunning personality. Tara felt herself drawn to it, convinced, ready to take a stand and defend The Republic as well as avenge her fallen Highlanders, Prefect Brown, the people of Skye.

But at what final cost? She was not part of the Founder's Movement. Her charge was the defense of Skye, and to uphold the security of The Republic. A desperate gamble was not in her nature. In the long run, she believed, the side that remained truer to its ideals would win out. And in that, the Lord Governor had the stronger position.

She remembered her vow. The Republic first, in all things. It was the only way she could continue to do her job, and live the life she'd chosen after Terra. So be it.

"We hold our lines," she said. "Norfolk is a tactical strongpoint, but gives us no strategic advantage in the long run. Not like Miliano does." She saw the disappointment flare on Jasek's face, but quickly buried her feelings. "I'm ordering my Highlanders forward," she said, "but to secure this city and hold Avanti Assemblies. With some adjustments to our supply routes, we can make this the focus of our logistics network."

"Excellent," Brewster congratulated her. "I'll rotate in our damaged vehicles as soon as my *Zeus* is back in prime condition."

"Prime condition?" Tara shook her head. "If it can walk and has armor, it's good enough for the field." She caught Jasek's gaze, held it. "You will have to defend Norfolk with what you have. Can I count on you?" She'd meant to say, could she count on his Stormhammers?

He nodded. His ego had not been caught up in his proposed plans. Jasek folded his hand with grace, and accepted her lead. It made her feel worse instead of better. "We'll give our best," he promised. "For the long game."

"For Skyc," she reminded them all.

And felt a pang of loss when Jasek refused to meet her gaze.

33

Clouds over the Norfolk area were thick, leaden gray, heavy with the promise of rain, though not a drop had fallen. Dry thunder occasionally rolled over the forested wetlands and brush-covered hills, put to shame by the constant, heavy echoes of artillery fire that shook the battlefield from one horizon to the other.

Jasek Kelswa-Steiner strained at the controls of his *Templar*, riding the tide of battle that swept him up a long hillside. A single squad of Hauberk infantry followed, losing themselves behind a pile of old snags, waiting for their chance. Farther along, a broken lance of Demons and Pegasus staggered around a bend in the narrow valley below, pulling back to regroup. Getting out from under the Jade Falcons' heavier weapons.

Dawn was several hours past, though still newer than this Jade Falcon assault, which had begun a few hours past midnight. Muted light crept across the overcast skies. The brightening day drew back morning's haze like a blanket of gauze being stripped away layer by layer. Jasek had a good idea what it revealed. BattleMechs stomping across ridgelines, pushing their way through stands of dark green pines and yellowed alders. Heads thrust toward the sky, masters of the battlefield. Their spade-shaped feet scarring the earth beneath them with deep prints chewing into dark, loamy soil. Vehicles and battlesuit infantry cutting back and forth over those tracks, racing forward to press an advantage, falling back as the enemy responded.

It wasn't lost on him that his Stormhammers were doing more falling back than racing forward. And from what Joss Vandel's command staff had gleaned from reports by Tara Campbell and Anastasia Kerensky, they were seeing much the same as they tried to hold the allied flanks. Precious kilometers were lost with each burning vehicle, every life spent.

Even without reports from his senior officers, Jasek knew the Jade Falcons had pushed forward stronger forces than anything the Stormhammers had seen in the last week. Seven days over which Jasek basically slept in his Mech-Warrior togs, rising to fight, finding time in which to review losses, and then grabbing a few hours' rest before the next alert.

He'd called for help from Tara Campbell, and she'd sent him what she could, he knew. But it hadn't been enough. Not with the thin spread of men and materiel trying to safeguard Miliano, Second Bristol, Norfolk, and a half dozen other important sites.

And with the allied defenders holding on by their fingernails, Malvina Hazen had obviously chosen to push her people for all they were worth.

This could be the day, he decided, eyeing the toggle on his communications board.

As a new threat pushed back against the Stormhammers, Jasek's *Templar* rocked beneath a blistering attack of laser and autocannon fire. Sidestepping into some red cedars, shearing away thick tree limbs with wet greenstick fractures, he dodged away from the worst of the damage. A few new pits and pockmarks covered his BattleMech's arms and shoulders. An angry red weal slashed across its left hip.

A *Gyrfalcon* had slashed in with Skanda light tanks and a hoverbike squad as escorts. They held the narrow valley between two hillsides, cutting off Jasek from the lance he'd pushed up the opposite slope. Two JES strategic missile carriers and a Hasek MCV, and a Maxim with Gnome armored infantry.

"Reverse track, Epsilon-four," Jasek ordered his wayward crew. He alternated his left and right particle cannon, holding his heat curve to tolerable levels. "Push back to the south and regroup at grid four-two-five."

"Landgrave. There's a 'Mech in our way."

"It won't be there long," Jasek promised. And hoped he could deliver.

Skating along the edge of the tree line, Jasek used his particle cannon to grab the Jade Falcons' attention. If it had been Noritomo Helmer in the *Gyrfalcon*, his job would have been much easier. Helmer had to be spoiling for a rematch after Chaffee. But this 'Mech had darker green paint and the blue eyes painted on its chest that he had come to recognize as an emblem of Malvina Hazen's warriors. Jasek would have to convince this one to follow.

The PPC shots he whipped over two hoverbikes did the trick. As the open-air vehicles tumbled into death rolls, the Clan *Gyrfalcon* leaped forward on jump jets to suddenly set itself between Jasek and its own support force.

Its paired weapons, extended-range lasers over ultra-class autocannon, chewed up the forest surrounding Jasek. One stream of angry bullets hammered into his shoulder, spoiling his aim as he tried to flail more of his artificial lightning among the Skandas.

A Kelswa assault tank rolled into the valley behind the *Gyrfalcon*, brought up to plug the gap.

"Hold, damn it. Epsilon, hold."

Frustration and more than a little concern chewed at his confidence as he spent another PPC against the *Gyrfalcon*. Not only did the assault tank make it impossible to recover his trapped people, it had come up from the east where Joss Vandel was supposedly holding forward of Jasek's position. Supposedly.

Now a pair of Skadi swift attack VTOLs chased in behind the Kelswa. The armored helicopters buzzed up the opposite slope, discovered Jasek's armored lance, and began hammering down at them with heavy autocannon and lasers.

Recognizing the immediate danger, Jasek's Hauberk infantry broke cover and swarmed toward the *Gyrfalcon*. Missiles chopped out from their backpack launchers. Their light arms flashed ruby darts at the fifty-five-ton 'Mech. It bought the Stormhammers' leader a few seconds' distraction. He dropped his crosshairs over the Kelswa, reaching at long range with both PPCs at once. His targeting computer made the shot possible, adjusting automatically for the deflection angle. Ionized particles cascaded into twin streams of energy, snaking down the hillside and carving deep wounds into the Kelswa's thick armor.

It was like waving a red cape in front of a bull. The Kelswa's turret swiveled around, and twin pulses of bluish energy punched out two Gauss slugs that smashed in near Jasek's position. One blew a cedar's trunk into kindling, toppling the majestic tree which fell near Jasek's right side with a ground-shaking crash. The other Gauss slug dug into the ground right at the *Templar*'s feet, spraying dirt clods high enough to patter against Jasek's cockpit shield.

The *Gyrfalcon* followed up with more autocannon fire, walking a hailstorm of slugs from Jasek's left knee to his shoulder. Its lasers had already driven the Hauberks back, into the forest.

Jasek retreated deeper into the autumn camouflage as well, teeth grinding together as his trapped unit called for help. He toggled for one of his private command circuits. "Colonel Vandel! If you aren't holding in sector eighteen, regain control now."

No response. Joss Vandel had to have his own plate full.

He saw just how full a moment later. Pushing back farther as the Clan MechWarrior chased up to the forest edge with weapons blazing, Jasek crested the hill and was able to look down into three different valleys where his Stormhammers fought to hold off the Jade Falcon offensive. The forested cover bought Jasek time. Seconds only, but enough to measure how the battle was progressing.

Not well.

On his right, the Archon's Shield had all but surrendered initiative to a long column led by a *Shrike* and two converted SalvageMechs. To the left, Tamara Duke bridged the gap between Jasek's position and the balance of Colonel Petrucci's Lyran Rangers. Tamara was trading a great deal to hold that position. Jasek counted four . . . five . . .

six vehicles burning on her side of the battlefield. Half that among the Falcon lines.

He already knew what lay in front of him.

He sensed the pressure building along the entire front. Messages that made it over his command circuits were short and often frantic. From his vantage point, he saw tall pillars of flame lancing skyward as missile barrages spread destruction in indiscriminate patterns. Autocannon chopped at the air, and jewel-bright colors flashed as laser fire mixed among the brilliant lightning strikes of particle cannon. And it was starting to look a little too one-sided.

"Shield!" Jasek called again for Joss Vandel. "Push those Falcons back. We have forces trapped on the back side of"—he checked his tactical-map display—"hill four-three-alpha."

"Landgrave," Vandel finally reported in. "The Highlanders and Hiram Brewster's Guard have folded back on our far eastern flank. I'm getting pressure from two sides now."

It wasn't an excuse. Jasek could see that his senior colonel was throwing units forward again, trying to cut off the *Gyrfalcon's* position from further reinforcement. But it *was* a warning. There wasn't enough left to the Archon's Shield to stand up against the Falcons for much longer. They were spread too thin from so many hours of feints, stands, and forced retreats. As were all the Stormhammers. Spread thin and spending themselves to meet wave after wave of well-coordinated assaults.

It was a hard call to make. The hardest he'd been pushed to yet for Skye.

"Artillery, lay down staggered fire at grid four-two-four. Three by three," he ordered, calling for sets of triple strikes. "Then give our people sixty seconds to clear the area before you hammer that valley with anything you can. Epsilon-four. You know what you have to do."

It was a suicide run. Straight down the hill toward the waiting Falcons, and hope a few of the vehicles could break through to the rally point. But the Jessies were too slow, and Jasek knew it.

So did the missile carrier crews. "We've swatted down one of the Skadis," one of them reported. JES-47. Jasek couldn't remember the man's name, and suddenly felt a deeper loss because of it. "We're going to hunker down and give missile support to the others as they make their break."

Jasek slammed a fist against his chair's armrest. "You can't stay on that hill."

"Landgrave, sir. You know we can't make that kind of push. Not in these beasties."

He nodded reluctantly. "And we can't come back for you." Not without losing twice as many vehicles as they'd gain.

"We're POW anyway you look at it. We'll take it on our terms. Holding at the bottom slope and spreading out an umbrella that'll make the Clanners think the sky is falling in on them. Luck."

"Godspeed," Jasek sent them. Snarling, he pushed forward to bring the *Gyrfalcon* back into range. Line of sight was tricky with all the trees, but not impossible. His PPCs danced through the forest, scourging the Falcon machine with lashes of blue white energy.

Jasek slapped at the emergency toggle on his communications panel. "This may be it. Ready Operation Lodestone, but wait for my order." Throttling into a forward walk, he tied in his personal command frequency and called up the Hauberks as well as the two Pegasus scout craft.

Niccolò GioAvanti was on the other end of the channel. "Acknowledged. Where will you be?"

"Giving these men every chance I can," he said, and severed the connection.

North Inlet Coastal Ranges

Noritomo Helmer planned to give his warriors every chance possible.

He stalked his *Gyrfalcon* down the draw. Arms lowered. Targeting system off. Trying to ignore the alarms of multiple target locks that rang loudly in his cockpit, drilling sharp holes into the side of his head. Every impulse in his body—his instincts and twelve years' experience of duty—screamed at him to snap the toggles over, bring up his crosshairs, and drop them onto the wide-shouldered outline of the *Ryoken II* that waited for him at the end of the sloped canyon.

"Formality always has its place in Clan tradition," he

whispered to himself, careful of his voice-activated mic. He sounded as if he was trying to convince himself of the idea. "She wants me to blink first."

Anastasia Kerensky, leader of the Steel Wolves, had refused long-distance comms to arrange this batchall. "I want to see your face," she'd said, as she had every time in the last thirty-six hours.

This was their third meeting, always on her territory with her warriors backing her up. A *Mad Cat III* and a pair of SM1 Destroyers were arrayed behind Kerensky's *Ryoken*. Ready to fire at the first sign of his treachery, or *as* the first sign of hers.

The narrow draw, with its high, shadowed sides, and the gunmetal gray sky hanging overhead left Noritomo feeling a bit claustrophobic. As if he walked his fifty-five-ton 'Mech down a very large barrel. Fifty meters was close enough that the two MechWarriors could stare at each other through ferroglass shields. He throttled back, bringing his *Falcon* to a wide-legged stance, and dialed in a common channel. Unsecured transmission.

"I am Star Colonel Noritomo Helmer. I have added two of your warriors to my codex list of kills since our last batchall. With what forces do the Steel Wolves defend the North Inlet Ranges?"

A jaunty wave saluted him from the other cockpit. In a way, he thought that Kerensky was somehow casually mocking him. *Hi, Noritomo.* "I am Anastasia Kerensky of Clan Wolf and the Steel Wolves. Star Commander Yulri will defend the North Inlet mountains."

Behind her, the *Mad Cat III* made a half-step bow.

"He has chosen two SM1 Destroyers and a pair of Demon medium tanks to fill out his Star."

A hard-hitting force, and totally unexpected. Noritomo knew that Kerensky's forces still had several tracked crawlers available, which were far better suited to the mountains than hovercraft and the wheeled Demons. He had anticipated a strategic challenge of position, playing heavy, slower forces against each other. By opting for fast-hitting firepower, she threatened to destroy anything he sent into the coastal ranges after her.

Trying to get something back for the Stormhammers, perhaps. Or, just some good old-fashioned posturing. The collapse of the defenders' line near Norfolk had left the Steel Wolves exposed on the western flank. While the Stormhammers retreated to a new rally point somewhere north of Miliano, Kerensky fought tooth and nail to hold her unit together in the face of his superior force. So far she had made each small engagement costly, but a high price paid with small units beat a medium price paid by his entire Cluster.

And a victory was still a victory.

Still, something pulled at the back of his mind. Something dangerous that he had taken to heart from his hidden books. *He whom the gods would destroy, they first make complacent.* He swiveled his camera views around, pulling the *Mad Cat* and the two Destroyers in closer on video. One of the SM1s had different markings!

"Anastasia Kerensky, one of your Destroyers bears the Stormhammers crest." Not all of the Stormhammers had retreated after Jasek Kelswa-Steiner?

"Why, yes, it does. So do both Demons, if you must know. But since they were bid in as Star Commander Yulri's supporting forces, their pedigree is subservient to his. How they were lent to me, and how many more I have"—which was the real question she let hang between them for a moment—"is for you to discover."

If he'd been a betting man, Noritomo would have guessed they were from the Tharkan Strikers, who had given Kerensky an earlier assist. Green troops, or close enough to make no difference. So she was conserving her own forces as well. So what?

"Aff," he agreed. "And I will."

He throttled into a backward walk, never turning his back on the enemy. Wolves were never so dangerous as when they felt cornered. "Bargained well and done. You will meet my forces soon."

Sooner than she expected. Noritomo had already brought forward the Star he intended to personally lead in this Trial. They were a touch slower than he would have liked, but one thing he *had* learned under Malvina Hazen was better a constructive blow struck quickly than a well-matched blow struck too late to do much but glance off a shield.

Noritomo gave Kerensky's people sixty seconds to clear the

area. They retreated out of the canyon's far end, spreading onto the small plateau his scout VTOLs had warned him about. "First Star, forward and attack," he ordered.

A Defiance Industries Schmitt and two Jousts, both captured in the Jade Falcon drives against other worlds, rolled forward. With them came a Cardinal transport, hovering overhead, ready to deploy Elemental infantry. Careful, so as not to outpace the slower tracked vehicles, Noritomo tucked his *Gyrfalcon* in behind the Jousts and followed them back down the draw, targeting system active, searching for his first victim.

He whom the Gods would destroy . . .

"Alert! Forces in near vicinity of draw's exit!"

The VTOL had jumped above the cliff face, taking the high road to come down on the other side. But without an express order to lead the charge, they too had hung back, and so their warning came late, just as the Jousts cleared the draw and piled into the cleared grounds where Kerensky and her forces had met him for batchall.

Both of her SM1 Destroyers had circled back to flank the exit, and they used their assault-class autocannon to drive hot metal into the flanks of both lead vehicles. Armor, chiseled away by twelve-centimeter slugs, littered the ground. The Jousts slewed over, the forty-ton tanks rocked nearly off their treads by the hard-hitting assault.

Sooner than *he* had expected, as it turned out.

But Noritomo had not brought his people through unprepared. Stepping out right behind the Jousts, he levered both arms forward and rammed several hundred rounds of eighty-millimeter slugs into one Destroyer's front. Following up with lasers, he sliced deep, angry wounds into the hovercraft.

The Schmitt rolled out behind him, turning in to the second Destroyer while both Jousts hooked back to slash with their own large lasers.

The battle looked to be decided right there. But Star Commander Yulri had not expected easy prey, and he had known better than to sacrifice his assault craft. From a nearby stand of ponderosa pines, his *Mad Cat III* leaned out to stab lasers in Noritomo's direction. Missile launchers belched gray smoke, dumping twin flights of long-range missiles into the air. The warheads hammered down around his position, chewing rock into gravel and sand, slamming into his *Gyrfalcon*'s chest and shoulders.

One pair of warheads rang a one-two punch into the side of his head, shaking him against his harness, leaving him disorientated for several critical seconds.

Enough for the Destroyers to power up their drive fans and skate for the safety of some rocky, scrub-covered hills. The Schmitt continued to pound at one of them, using its rotary autocannon to strip away more armor, but then the weapon jammed and fell silent and Noritomo had nothing able to catch the hovercraft, except for his *'Falcon*.

Lighting off jump jets, he side-skipped over in front of one SM1 Destroyer—the Stormhammers' Destroyer as it turned out—taking its best punch and forcing it to swerve back in toward the Jousts. Still rattled from the missile strikes as well as the assault cannon, he eschewed autocannon and laid into the Destroyer with lasers alone. Both weapons sliced into the vehicle's skirting, slowing it as the fender dipped down to drag the ground.

Which brought the hovercraft directly under the Jousts' main weapons. More laser blasted out with angry, ruby knives, carving though the damaged skirt and fouling the lift vanes beneath.

The hovercraft bottomed out as its cushion of air spilled free, and what was left of the spinning blades spent themselves against the rocky ground in a catastrophic release of kinetic energy.

The tank jumped up and spun, tossed like a petulant child's toy. Through luck, it came down right side up, striking sparks between metal and stone as it ground to a halt.

Noritomo saw the steering rudders slam over to the left. Knew that the hovercraft's main drive fans were still turning. But in his mind's eye, he had already written off the Destroyer as scrap. Maybe salvageable. Maybe not. So he was just as surprised as his Joust crew when the drive fans had enough push left in them to turn the SM1 in its final slide.

A few degrees to the right was all it needed. Turning in fits and starts as if mounted on some kind of turret-style base.

Turning directly into the face of the lead Joust.

A long tongue of flame licked several meters out of the

Destroyer's barrel, flaring into a burning rose as the autocannon vomited out lethal streams of high-velocity metal. Twelve-centimeter slugs tipped with depleted uranium slammed into the Joust, and then again as the crew hot-cycled the weapon and just kept pouring on the damage. The cannon fire ripped the nose right off the Joust, pummeling it into unrecognizable scrap. The left-side track spun off the drive wheels as a hail of bullets severed the treads. The damage walked its way right up the side, pounding into the turret with such force that it tore off the missile launcher.

What was left could hardly be called a vehicle, much less a military machine.

"*Neg, neg!*" Noritomo tried to bring his people back under control as the remaining Joust and the Schmitt hammered again at the crippled Destroyer. He actually had to wade his *Gyrfalcon* into the line of fire, taking a few scattered shots before he was able to save the Stormhammer crew from being torn to pieces.

The *Mad Cat III* dumped another double load of missiles over the party, then ducked away to catch up with the escaped Destroyer.

Noritomo weathered the missile barrage with hunched shoulders and a careful hand on the control stick. "Stay out of its angle," he ordered. "Transport, drop two Elementals on top of that tank and bring me the crew alive!"

He'd have bondcords strapped to their wrists before the day was out. Such effort! Perhaps they would not care for the Clan practice of claiming warriors, but if they could be educated, they would make fine additions to his Cluster. Bogart, freeborn himself, would train them well.

Seeing the mangled wreck the Destroyer had made of his Joust, Helmer reaffirmed once again it would take a great deal of cunning and practice to keep his force in any kind of shape as they continued to push back Skye's defenders.

"It can be done," he said, promising himself as much as anyone. "But carefully. Carefully." A Joust for a Destroyer was a good trade on any tally sheet, but armies could not take and hold cities with tally sheets.

"These Steel Wolves and Stormhammers earned some breathing room with this battle," he whispered.

"Just enough time for them to contemplate the end."

34

The brush fire spread over several kilometers, dancing bright licks of flame along the ground as it jumped from brambles to bush, skated among the dry grasses. Sooty wisps of smoke gathered into patchy clouds. Dark streamers of ash spiraled into the overcast sky.

Vehicles charged from one dark island to another. Sometimes they rolled over flaming debris, sending up bright swarms of sparks that immediately drew attention. Other times, they skirted around such obstacles in an effort to keep their course from being seen.

Armored infantry also used the darker sworls of ash and smoke to hide behind, covering their advances, their retreats, always ready to leap out in ambush.

BattleMechs, though, could not hide.

Tara Campbell certainly could not, at the controls of McKinnon's *Atlas*, drawing the attention of every Jade Falcon in range. Her Gauss rifle and pair of extended-range lasers were a threat to man, vehicle, and 'Mech. Heavy armor protecting the one-hundred-ton assault 'Mech gave her a presence of invulnerability that she did not feel, but that most enemy warriors assumed and so tried to chip away at every chance they found.

Light autocannon rang hollow against the side of the *Atlas'* chest. Demon fast tanks used their lasers to work over her lower legs, while a Falcon *Uziel* probed and pounded at her with its twin PPCs.

Still getting used to the assault 'Mech, a large step up from her poor *Hatchetman*, Tara pulled crosshairs down over the *Uziel*, too slowly, and had to shift them over to an M1 Marksman when the fifty-ton machine slipped back out of range. Her lasers burned large, red-tinged wounds into the Marksman's side armor. The Gauss slug punched in behind, rocking the machine up and then slamming it back down again with incredible force. The turret barrels sagged. More smoke littered the air. On her HUD, its red icon faded from the cluttered battlefield.

Not too bad, she decided, grading her performance.

Then a brace of long-range tactical missiles punched the *Atlas* in the chin, sending her stumbling back, arms wind-milling for balance.

Not too good either.

Fighting against gravity, Tara planted one foot behind her and kept the *Atlas* on its feet. Her vision was hazy and her ears rang, but already she was searching for the new threat. Too late again.

The *Eyrie*, which had tagged her so easily with its ATMs, used its jump jets to rocket away from her, dancing through the air with a ballerina's grace. It landed in a light crouch, as feather softly as thirty-five tons could fall out of the sky.

Far beyond her limited mastery of the assault machine. She half expected to see the *Eyrie* try a handstand next, maybe a cartwheel. The image garnered a grim smile. Such tricks were the province of circus stunts and monster 'Mech rallies, not intentional battlefield tactics.

She throttled forward, drawing a bead on the distant *Eyrie*, and put a Gauss slug into its left thigh. At extreme range, it was one hell of a shot. Enough to give the other warrior pause, and send the light 'Mech stumbling back for the safety of the main Falcon lines.

"Highlanders"—she opened a channel to her force—"prepare to swing back and around again on my mark. Anastasia, where away?"

"Pulling . . . under new . . . Falcon drive." The return call came full of crackling distortion. Short-lived. Interference from particle cannon fire, Tara guessed. "If that smoke we see is a good . . . of your position, call it ten kilometers. Lyrans are much closer."

Tara nodded to the empty cockpit. It was getting harder to hold a clear picture of the battle in her head. Her Highlanders and elements of the Skye militia spread over two dozen square kilometers, fighting a series of small, desperate battles. Overlapping offensive waves as the Jade Falcons never gave the defenders much time to regroup, rearmor, and rearm. Lyrans mucking things up on her flanks. Stormhammers rallying somewhere to the south, having given up the main route from Norfolk but hoping to rejoin.

With Miliano now under Jade Falcon threat, it fell to her Highlanders and Kerensky's Steel Wolves to collapse the flanks inward, forming a new defensive line before the Falcons split them for good. The running battle had taken hours to coordinate and pull off, but finally they were within range. It seemed.

She had to trust Hiram Brewster not to fumble the ball as he tied the two flanks together.

She had to trust Anastasia Kerensky to be there.

She hated trusting them. Putting the fate of Skye in hands not sworn to The Republic. Of course, if she had looked more carefully at Jasek's plan to use Norfolk as a thrust into the belly of the Falcon position, trusted him as everything inside her said she should, they might not be on the verge of losing Miliano and possibly Skye with it.

More laser fire cut at her through the smoke, flashing in bright scarlet and stuttering darts of emerald green. She wrenched her targeting reticle over and slammed lances of energy into an encroaching Scimitar. It backed off, and Tara searched for a new target.

Her ferroglass shield was streaked with sooty grime. It was hard to tell at a glance where her forces ended and the Jade Falcons' began. Even in places where the smoke cleared, most vehicles were blackened by fire and ash. Emerald green or Highlander blue were both muted into shades of gray. Crests had been scorched off. She recognized a few units by their force composition—the *Arbalest* and two Jessies blazing a forward trail were hers, and that trio of Condors protecting the MASH trucks—but so many vehicles had changed hands recently she couldn't say for certain that a Hasek mechanized combat vehicle wasn't now Jade Falcon property, or that a Skanda light tank wasn't one of the two her Highlanders had pressed into their own service. Her HUD was a tangle of icons and identification tags, and she had no time to worry them out in her head while trying to fight a battle at the same time.

There was one good way to help sort things out.

"Mark!" she commanded. "Jersey Swing!"

In practiced coordination, every Highlander vehicle turned away from its opponents and raced back to the southeast. The few Stormhammer stragglers attached to her command were slower, taking one last laser shot or throwing out missiles to cover their ass, but followed quick enough. Her *Atlas* and a Highlander Behemoth II guarded the exercise with weapons blasting into any Jade Falcons who gave thought to chase. Then they too turned and powered into best-speed retreats.

How the maneuver earned its name, Tara wasn't certain. All she cared about was that it worked. Punch them in the nose and then hook back to the southeast, followed by a turn westward with every unit pushing for all it was worth. It was usually good for a handful of kilometers.

VTOLs spotted for them, picking out the best paths and warning of enemy pathfinder units. They cleared the brush fire, even though the prevailing winds drove it right at their backs. This time her maneuver headed the Highlander main force right into the flank of a Falcon advance, shearing off the tip of the Falcons' spear like a scythe took the heads off grain.

Tara laid out a lightly armored *Stinger* with her lasers, and spent one of her few remaining Gauss slugs into the belly of a troublesome Skadi. The VTOL burst into flame before it hit the ground. More fires spread out from the burning wreckage.

It set the Jade Falcons back on their heels, throwing them into disarray. Tara's instincts told her to push forward and drive them back. Chew several large pieces out of the enemy. But her head warned her that she had too far to go still. Instead, she opened comms again and ordered a second swing right on the heels of the first.

"We're running."

Tara's whisper was low and with barely any strength behind it, but in her own ears the words echoed loudly as she admitted them to herself for the first time.

They were collapsing the flanks, forming a new defensive line. They had pushed across several dozen kilometers in a handful of hours, making the Falcons pay desperately for every meter gained, every machine taken. But they were, in fact, running. Running toward Miliano, where the Stormhammers were putting together a last-ditch effort to stand and hold Skye. Many Highlanders would not see the end of the race. Not with their machines and equipment. Some of them, not with their lives.

And now she was trusting Jasek Kelswa-Steiner to have something worthy of the sacrifice her people—all of the defenders—were making.

A deep bass rumble shook the ground as the *Union*-class DropShip lowered itself onto the blockaded highway north of Miliano. Tamara Duke felt the trembling underfoot, glanced south. As late afternoon rolled toward twilight, the white-hot flames that pushed out beneath the DropShip flared brighter even than the nearby glow of Miliano's city lights. An afterglow reflected back against the underside of the spheroidal vessel, lighting up the Highlanders' banner crest, then darkened as the engines were finally banked to standby mode.

"Third landing in an hour," she said to Jasek, who had caught her on the way back to her Eisenfaust. Farther south, along the highway, the *Himmelstor* and an *Overlord* rose up like majestic mountains dropped by a giant's hand.

"The highway makes for a good ad hoc landing field. Cleared land. No fires started by the drive flares."

But there would be crushed and fusion-slagged ferrocrete, making a major thoroughfare impassable for days. The defenders had been pushed beyond caring about such minor infrastructure concerns. Tamara nodded, noting that he hadn't answered her question.

Then again, it hadn't really been a question.

"You're thinking we may need to relocate. Fast."

"We *are* relocating," Jasek said. He stared north, where the glow of wildfires could be seen against the dark cloud cover, and the battle still raged between the Jade Falcons and Skye's defenders. He seemed about to say something more, then shook his head.

Tamara had done little else but watch Jasek after he came limping in with maybe a ton of armored protection left to his battle-ravaged *Templar* and the two vehicles he had escorted out of the kill zone being formed by the Jade Falcons. A Hasek MCV and a Maxim heavy hover transport, each with half their loads of infantry.

Amazing that any of them had gotten out of there alive, but especially Jasek, who had been the last man to run. The Falcons had ripped through Vandel's unit, and then split the Stormhammer lines between the Archon's Shield and the Lyran Rangers. Split it right next to her unit, actually. The Clanners had pressed forward strong advances, then cut in from each side to form a box. The containment had held long enough to inflict serious casualties.

Fortunately, the Landgrave had not been one of them. Tamara had no idea what she'd do if Jasek was lost to the Stormhammers.

To her.

"Look," he said, regaining a measure of command posture. "You'll be on my right flank as we head north. Petrucci is sidelined, so it's your unit. And I want you to hold what I told you right up front."

"Secure the Highlander position," Tamara recited. "Protect Tara Campbell. Do *not* let our forces get split apart again."

It could have been much worse. She could have been sent to safeguard that she-wolf. If Alexia Wolf wanted to spend her people in aid of Anastasia Kerensky, that was on her head. Tamara wasn't going to spend good Lyran lives pulling the Strikers out of the fire.

She had to be a mess. Twenty hours in combat togs. Sweaty and sore. Hair matted down by her neurohelmet, and a nick in her shoulder where shrapnel had burst through her cockpit's ferroglass shield. Blood stained her arm and the side of her coolant vest. A quick meal of field rations, some new armor for her 'Mech, and now it was right back into the fray.

None of that mattered to Jasek. Or, perhaps more certainly, it all mattered to him. He placed a hand against the side of Tamara's face. She could feel his heat burning her cheek.

"I depend on you. You know this."

"I do," she said. On her more than anyone.

He left her with that parting gesture, ever the gallant commander. So close, and still held apart. But maybe not for much longer. Tamara had plans. Long-range plans. They certainly included Jasek Kelswa-Steiner.

Staring past Jasek's retreating form, she caught Vic Parkins, her company's exec. Parkins was talking to Niccolò GioAvanti near the Kelswa assault tank he'd crew into battle. Gone was his Behemoth II, lost in the last Falcon offensive. He hadn't the good graces to die in his command chair, though. No, he was still there, one step behind her, still chumming up with the brass—or at least the brass's best friend.

Some of her plans included him as well. It didn't matter that Parkins had performed his duty fairly solidly since his aborted court-martial. She knew, if no one else but maybe Jasek did, that the man had something on his own agenda.

Parkins did not look exceptionally happy talking with GioAvanti. His shoulders slumped heavily and he shook his head quite often. But when GioAvanti offered his hand, the two shook on whatever they'd been discussing. Then Vic shrugged into padded togs and joined the Kelswa's crew at the side of the tank. He saw her staring, and tossed her a hesitant wave.

Tamara turned her back on him, and broke into a trot toward her *Wolfhound*. Parkins would keep until later. She wouldn't turn her back on him, certainly, but she had larger concerns than any deal he'd struck with GioAvanti.

Right now, she had to live up to Jasek's expectations. And her own.

35

A prince must have no other objective, no other thought, nor take up any profession but that of war, its methods and its disciplines, for that is the only art expected of a ruler.

The Prince, by Niccolò Machiavelli

Miliano Basin
Skye
23 December 3134

Green bright flares held aloft on parachutes and steel cabling pushed back the night as the Jade Falcons advanced on Miliano. Wind gusted violently across the basin, first from the west, then the north, spinning the flares beneath their silken canopies. A light rain—more a heavy mist—swirled over the struggling forces, often blown sideways or even back up into the air.

Noritomo Helmer studied the battle that raged before him, around him, behind him, through a ferroglass shield streaked with mud and ash. His *Gyrfalcon* stalked the forward western edge of the Falcon drive, tangled among Stormhammers and Steel Wolves and even a Lyran Manti-

core, which had done more damage ramming into the side
of a Kinnol main battle tank than it ever had with its PPC.
Armored infantry swarmed over the ground in rogue packs,
forming and breaking in haphazard patterns that could not
be anticipated. Light vehicles paired up when possible,
charging from one firefight to the next. Assault tanks
claimed good locations, holding them to form brief islands
of security, moving only when artillery fire walked in too
close.

Jade Falcon BattleMechs all but ignored the chaos surrounding them, holding themselves above petty squabbles
as they trudged forward, seizing new ground and pulling
the battle lines with them.

Still it was not enough for Malvina Hazen.

"Star Colonel Helmer. Dress up your lines. Shore up my
flank. You are . . . falling back again."

He pulled his *Gyrfalcon* up short as lasers cut back and
forth in front of him, crisscrossing in deadly volleys. The
too brief flare of missile exhausts gave only a few seconds'
warning before a trio of warheads slammed into the
'Mech's right leg, throwing a hitch into his stride.

Dropping crosshairs over a fleeing Scimitar, he sliced
ruby lances across its rear. A solid kick in the ass that
should keep it moving.

"Helmer?"

"Aff, Galaxy Commander."

Noritomo checked his map screen. Hazen's command
worked the point of the Jade Falcon spearhead, and had
pushed far forward of the main lines. Dangerously so. It
would have been better—smarter—to await reinforcement
by Galaxy Commander Malthus, who pushed down from
the northwest, crossing behind Noritomo's position. Malthus rode command in a Tribune mobile headquarters, slow
but certain, and had an assault Star for escort. A strong
"swing" of force strength.

More missiles cascaded over his position, erupting
around him in fire and shrapnel. Noritomo tied the *Gyrfalcon*'s autocannon into his triggers and spread more destruction along the confused lines.

"A few loose ends which need tying up," he said.

"If your flank collapses . . . it is your career . . . we will
be tying up." She was panting. Overexerting herself as she

drove forward against Tara Campbell's Highlanders and the small Lyran contingent.

"We will hold," Helmer promised.

He traded weapons fire with a Joust. His cut deeper, harder, slicing down through diamond tread and snapping the belt. A double squad of Hauberks moved up to support the crew, buying them time to evacuate the ruined vehicle. Some Elementals jumped in too quickly and paid for it as they were overwhelmed by strength of numbers.

"We need more than that, Helmer."

The Falcons needed more? Or had Malvina adopted the royal *we*? And did it matter, at this point?

"I have a fresh Trinary ready to swing in behind your position at your order," he offered, damning the need. He toggled a switch, calling them forward.

His Cluster retained nearly seventy percent of its operational status due to his judicious bidding and constant resupply, but that force was now spread over too great a distance to leverage its full strength. He had this one Trinary he had hoped to use to shore up against any counterthrust. His entire reserve, built from those careful expenditures as he drove back Kerensky and her Steel Wolves. The damage his warriors had inflicted on them in the last week was impressive, but like her Black Widow namesake, the woman seemed to have the lives of a cat.

Malvina did not care for the hows and whys. "Send them to me. It looks like we are facing—*stravag!*"

The Clan curse was all the warning Noritomo received. Malvina cut out in a burst of static, and he was still trying to patch back through to her when the Stormhammers struck from a nearby wood.

Four . . . five lances. More, possibly. Threat icons littered his HUD in a tangle of red identification tags. Light tanks and personnel carriers hammered into his front, slicing across to separate his battle Cluster from the besieged Steel Wolves and Tharkan stragglers. Heavy armor and a few limping 'Mechs followed.

A *Catapult*. An *Ocelot*.

A converted ForestryMech.

A pair of Fox armored cars skated up on their drive fans, slamming in on either side of a wounded Kinnol and pinning it in place. Their light weapons could only pick at its armor. An SM1 Destroyer powered up after, slid around behind, and gutted the Kinnol with two savage blasts of autocannon fire.

Another team tried that with him, spreading a line of Infiltrator battlesuits around him, jamming two Demons in against his legs. The *Ocelot* raced forward with a JES tactical carrier in support. Noritomo kicked out violently, caving in one Demon's cockpit with a well-placed foot. His weapons spat long streams of death at the *Ocelot*, pairing up autocannon and lasers. It staggered the thirty-five-ton machine, but did not drop it.

Then, hearing the metal strikes of armored claws grabbing into his armor, Noritomo lit off jump jets and rocketed up and out of the potential trap.

He carried a pair of swarming Infiltrators with him, the infantrymen clinging desperately to his 'Mech's legs. One fell off just short of the ground, and was buried beneath the *Gyrfalcon*'s left foot as it landed. The other was peeled away by a pair of nearby Skandas, using their lasers like surgical scalpels. Noritomo held a small island of sanity in the growing chaos. A few tanks and a *Shadow Hawk IIC* rallied to him as his reserve Trinary slammed into the fight behind him. He pulled in a Condor as well, and some Elementals.

He could hold. He felt that in his bones. He'd prepared for this. But the Jade Falcon spearhead looked as if it had been blunted as well. Comm traffic among senior warriors was frantic. On his tactical map, he saw identification tags for Malvina's command roll backward, several of their icons fading as battle damage took its toll.

Her *Shrike* held up, it seemed, but no telling for how long.

If Malvina Hazen fell, the Jade Falcon *desant* fell with her.

Lasers and particle cannon flared around him, spearing into and out of his small formation. A JES strategic carrier rolled up, added its four-pack of LRMs into the mix, spreading overlapping waves of fire and destruction over a Stormhammer Hasek MCV. Return fire was just as savage all along his battle line, but discipline held. These were his people, his warriors whom he'd readied for battle and promised honor as well as glory.

And now Noritomo Helmer had to abandon them.

"Bogart, rally and *hold*. Lysle"—he spotted her bright tag circling in on his left on his heads-up display—"gather two points of Elementals and load them on the fastest APCs you can find."

He read off a list of warriors, gathering in the *Shadow Hawk*, the Condor—not the JES carrier—and some Skandas. Also a pair of nearby hoverbikes he could use as pathfinders. He sent the hoverbikes, moving fast and furious, out in front and then led the column charge himself as he broke from the battle and pushed northeast.

Only to find a *Ryoken II* and a *Catapult* blocking his way, holding the entrance to a shallow river valley.

The *Ryoken* was familiar enough, even through his streaked ferroglass shield. Anastasia Kerensky. The *Catapult* bore markings from the Stormhammers' Tharkan Strikers. So did the small handful of tanks that gathered around the feet of the avatars.

Before weapons had a chance to fly, Kerensky's voice tripped over the open frequencies. "What forces challenge for this valley?" she asked in mocking tones.

Stravag woman. She was toying with him, obviously enjoying herself as she sought to batchall in the middle of a firefight. She could certainly hold him up. And would have, except for Beckett Malthus.

"Galaxy Commander Beckett Malthus issues challenge," the Falcon leader said calmly, his command crawler edging up behind Noritomo's massed troops. He brought a *Warhammer IIC* and a trio of assault tanks with him. Their very presence seemed to enforce an eye of calm in the battle's maelstrom. The main firefight pushed slightly to the southwest as the assault Star formed up. "Face me, Anastasia Kerensky, or not. But Star Colonel Helmer is passing through."

"Bargained well and done!" The *Ryoken II* wasted no more time in formalities. It leaped forward on jets of plasma, particle cannon streaming out, attacking the largest threat, which was the *Warhammer IIC*.

"Ignore them!" Noritomo ordered, watching as the *Ryoken* arced overhead, leaving him an easy run for the valley. The *Catapult* might slow him, but it could not stop him. "To the Khan!"

It was the first time he had used Malvina Hazen's adopted title. It brought with it a shiver, and the desired effect. With the defenders' attention divided between his force and Malthus' assault Star, there really was no chance of stopping him. His small force slammed through the Stormhammers like a sledgehammer through brittle wood. Hardly a fair fight—with little honor to be gained for sure—but against the danger to Clan Jade Falcon as a whole, he could let that go.

It cost him one Skanda. And it left an open path to Malvina Hazen.

Noritomo Helmer had unfinished business with the Stormhammers' leader, it seemed.

Tara Campbell's *Atlas* staggered to one side, crippled by a Gauss slug that hammered in over its left knee, crushing the joint and the lower-leg actuator.

Bending her wounded knee down against the ground, she saved herself from a nasty fall. Pulling her crosshairs from the fallen *Shrike*, she grabbed the Kelswa assault tank and fed it back a Gauss slug of her own and followed up with paired lasers as well as a six-pack of short-ranged missiles.

The desperate salvo ripped armor from the length and breadth of the ninety-ton assault vehicle. Then a squad of Lyran Rangers bulked forward, spreading a line of Infiltrators around the wounded tank while two Rangers escorted an engineering unit. The struggle was short and fierce, and left the Stormhammers in control of the wounded Kelswa. The Infiltrators escorted it back while the Rangers took one pass each at the rising *Shrike*.

Then they got the hell out of the way of the assault 'Mechs.

"Tara, fall back. Rally to Miliano!"

Jasek had all but thrust her small command lance aside as his Stormhammers took over the central line. He was insistent. He was also beginning to annoy her.

"Not . . . finished. Yet." Her breath came in ravaged gasps as her fusion reactor spiked yet again and drove the cockpit temperatures up another few degrees. Sweat poured from her face and ran in heavy beads down her bare arms and legs. Only the cooling vest kept her going, lowering her body's core temperature.

Jasek's *Templar* struggled forward against a blistering

Jade Falcon defensive line. Mostly medium lasers and light autocannon, but when rallied against a single target, it could do a great deal of damage. A pair of Manticore II tanks and a Hasek mechanized combat vehicle chased after him, prodding at the hole he opened up in the Clan lines.

"You're not going to do anyone any good by running that *Atlas* into the grave. Tamara, take care of this!"

Tara levered her BattleMech up from the ground. It swayed dangerously. He was right, and he wasn't, all at the same time. There wasn't much fight left in McKinnon's *Atlas*. Armor was shredded, and damage to the engine shielding was making it a walking bomb, ready to be lit off by one solid core shot. But without her, the Falcons would collapse around Jasek and tear him apart. Hiram Brewster's *Zeus* and elements from the Archon's Shield held Jasek's immediate left flank. But the Rangers were spread thin on the right, with Tamara Duke's small *Wolfhound* holding the integrity of the allied lines in its iron fists. Instead of shielding Tara's Highlanders from the pressing Falcon advance, the Stormhammers had simply shoved aside the point of the spearhead. It brought some relief, but not enough.

Not while Malvina Hazen continued to stand.

"Live with it," Tara gasped out. "Going . . . to stay."

Damning her heat curve, she cut loose with a savage alpha strike yet again. Her next-to-last Gauss slug took the *Shrike* in its right arm, snapping it back and spoiling some of its return fire. Her lasers missed wide as the heat stress on her electronics caused a failure in her targeting system. The power draw spiked her reactor's centerline temperatures, and waste heat bled through her BattleMech's chest.

Too much. And she was a heartbeat too slow on the override. "Heat safeties engaged," the synthesized computer voice warned her. "Shutting down."

"No, no, NO!" Tara slapped again at the override, knowing it would do no good.

Her targeting system winked out, followed by her monitors and the holographic heads-up display.

No targeting reticle. No power draw for lasers.

Her indicators on the reactor's status slowly levered down to zero as its deep thrum stifled to a whisper, and then nothing.

Even over the thunder of artillery and exploding missiles, the chopped roars of autocannon, she heard the pinging sound of cooling metal. Like seconds of a clock, ticking away, as she waited for heat levels to drop down far enough for a safe start-up. In a dark cockpit, Tara Campbell gripped dead control sticks and stared out through her misted ferroglass shield, into the night, waiting.

Waiting for the end.

When Tara's *Atlas* went dark on his HUD, Jasek knew a moment of pure panic that had nothing to do with being a military commander and everything to do with personal worry for Tara Campbell. Thinking the 'Mech had been destroyed, he twisted his control stick against its limit stop and wrenched his *Templar* around to see.

The machine stood there, frozen and silent.

Powered down on a live battlefield.

Malvina Hazen's *Shrike* paused for a long heartbeat, as if considering the dead 'Mech a ploy. Then she drilled long pulls from both of her autocannon into the immobile target. Jasek's crosshairs swung around far too late to stop her.

At short range, against one hundred tons of standing metal, there was no way for her to miss. If she'd been thinking clearly, she would have taken the head clean off the assault 'Mech. Her rage or her recent fall had shaken such an idea from her, though. Instead, the streams of lethal metal tore into the *Atlas*' left arm, shoulder, and chest. It shoved the entire side back at an awkward angle, tipping the machine off-balance. No working gyroscope, no myomer control to shift an arm or bend forward against gravity.

The *Atlas* fell back in a lazy spin, crashing down onto its already damaged left side.

Which was painful enough to watch. More painful a few seconds later when the Jade Falcons rallied around fresh reinforcements and blistered the *Templar* with lasers and missiles and hammering autocannon that shook the 'Mech as if it had fallen into a cement mixer. Twisted about, distracted, Jasek felt the *Templar* start to go over, and worked his arms beneath him as he rode gravity to the ground.

"Jasek!" Tamara Duke's worry was clear in her voice. "Parkins, forward and shield!"

She sent her exec's lance up to give him some covering support. Another lance was peeled back to guard the *Atlas* as well. Jasek pictured it in his mind, and thought about how vulnerable Tamara's position was with her *Wolfhound* and a short lance to support it.

There wasn't a lot he could do about it, though, as he worked the controls to pick his *Templar* up from the ground. He had more pressing business with the *Gyrfalcon* that had shoved its way forward, and the fresh Star of mixed vehicles that spread out behind it. There was never any doubt in his mind that Noritomo Helmer had arrived. Even under the green light cast by the hovering flares, he knew this 'Mech. After their run-in on Chaffee, it had come to a rematch on Skye.

But this time Jasek did not stand alone. Vic Parkins stepped up into part of the hole Jasek's *Templar* had left, and threw his Kelswa in front of a Falcon *Shadow Hawk*. Twin Gauss rifles flashed a blue discharge and railed nickel-ferrous masses into the 'Mech's chest and shoulder.

The other warrior held his ground, and stabbed back with powerful red lances. Add in the fat-bodied ATMs that corkscrewed down at the wide-bodied tank, and Parkins had taken about equal to what he'd dished out.

A line of Stormhammers vehicles staggered forward, some disgorging infantry onto the field. More weapons traded back and forth. More molten composite splashed over the damp ground.

From a half crouch, still trying to get his feet fully beneath him, Jasek traded weapons salvos with the *Gyrfalcon*. His PPCs lashed out with a furious wash of energy, blasting away armor. Lasers and missiles chopped in afterward, but did little more than carve away more protective plating.

Helmer had the better end of it. His lasers cut like surgical tools, opening up the left side of Jasek's chest, destroying his targeting computer. Autocannon walked hard-punching slugs from his right knee up across his hip, stripping away more armor, throwing a shake into his gyroscope.

Jasek staggered, nearly fell again.

The intense firefight, point-blank and bloody, was taking its toll faster than anything they had seen in nearly twenty-four hours of combat. A missile barrage scattered several

Stormhammers Infiltrators across the ground, lifeless and still. Their Hasek MCV roiled smoke into the air, tinted a sickly brackish green by the overhead flares. In minutes, two Falcon Skandas lay burning and overturned, and the *Shadow Hawk* had lost an arm thanks to a second Gauss strike in the same shoulder.

Malvina Hazen's *Shrike* bulled its way forward, crashing streams of lethal metal into Tamara Duke's *Wolfhound*, trying to move it aside. Tamara's lasers were no match for the assault 'Mech, but she stubbornly refused to budge. She raced to her left, then right, but never once took a step backward.

"Another minute," Jasek said, being pummeled from three sides while he struck again and again at the *Gyrfalcon*.

"We'll hold. Parkins, back to me. Parkins!"

Without his targeting computer, Jasek's *Templar* and Helmer's 'Mech were nearly evenly matched. The *Templar*'s stronger armor was mostly nonexistent by this point. Helmer was not taking advantage of his greater mobility. They slugged at each other, both running dangerously into the red. Taking a warning from what had happened to Tara, Jasek dialed back on some of his lasers to preserve his heat curve.

As if thinking of the Highlanders' commander sparked some kind of reaction, the *Atlas*' icon warmed back to life on his tactical display.

"Parkins," Tamara shouted her order. "Acknowledge!"

Jasek blinked sweat from his eyes, ignoring the burn as he quickly collated HUD and tactical monitor.

There was Hauptmann Parkins' *Kelswa*, holding a patch of ground with no enemies around it. But the man did not fall back.

Tamara's *Wolfhound*—her Eisenfaust—starting to lean his direction, away from Malvina Hazen's *Shrike*. But too late. Too late.

And a gold triangle. The identification tag read AS7-K2(TC). Tara Campbell.

"I might . . ." Tamara's voice wandered. She sounded weak, possibly wounded. Her beloved Eisenfaust took numbing hits from the *Shrike*. One stream cut from shoulder to shoulder, across the face of the *Wolfhound*. "Parkins . . . need . . ."

Jasek throttled forward, slammed himself up against the *Gyrfalcon* with cannon stripping away armor and myomer flesh. It staggered Helmer, forcing him to step back. The Kelswa assault tank drove forward at his side and shoved aside a smaller Condor, then turned away from Tamara Duke to punch a Gauss slug into the *Gyrfalcon*'s side. More particle cannon fire splashed out to strip away myomer and cut at supports. The *Gyrfalcon*'s left chest sagged. Its left arm fell straight and hung down limply at its side.

"Jasek?" Tamara's voice was soft. Lost.

"No!" Tara's shout was right there, behind it. "Not her . . . me!"

The comms chatter pulled Jasek around, away from Helmer. He saw Tara's *Atlas* rising, levering itself up on one arm. He saw Tamara Duke in between them, alone, holding position in her *Wolfhound*.

Not budging an inch as the ninety-five-ton *Shrike* limped up into her face.

Two gem-bright lasers and several hundred rounds of autocannon fire braced up the *Wolfhound*, ripping into its chest, its guts. Jasek waited for the *Wolfhound*'s head to detach and blast away. Maybe the ejection system had been damaged. Maybe Tamara never reached for the lever. Golden fire bled out of several cracks in the 'Mech's reactor shielding. Then it burned away in a bright, angry flash of plasma as the reactor exploded and the *Wolfhound* disintegrated into a ball of fusion-fed flames.

The shock wave staggered the *Shrike* and flipped over a Condor that had skated in at Malvina's side. It shook the ground worse than any artillery strike. Jasek held to his feet, struggling forward against the wall of flames. There was no need to search the air for an ejection rocket. It wasn't there.

A heartbeat later, neither was the *Shrike*. Tara's final Gauss slug cut into it at the back of its wounded knee, snapping the limb off with a violent twist. The assault machine toppled, and thrashed against the ground as it struggled in vain to right itself.

The *Wolfhound*, and Tamara Duke, were gone.

What was left of the Stormhammers and Tara Campbell's Highlanders was in desperate straits. The Rangers appeared thunderstruck, hardly firing at all as they took in what had just happened. The Jade Falcons were rallying to Noritomo Helmer, who held a great advantage as he formed up a new offensive charge. And now Jasek's timetable—his plan—was shot to hell. Tamara Duke was dead. No telling what was left among the Steel Wolves and Alexia's Tharkan Strikers. It would be a long, hard fight back toward Miliano.

Or did it have to be? Jasek hadn't planned for such a drastic and violent disruption, but he could use it. In the same way he had let Clan traditions weigh in on his side on Chaffee, he could let those traditions work for all of them now.

"*Hegira*," he transmitted on an open channel. One he knew the Jade Falcons monitored. Limping his *Templar* into a shuffling turn, facing Noritomo Helmer and the Jade Falcon line, he cut his targeting system and dropped both arms to his side.

"Star Colonel Helmer. I formally request *hegira*."

36

Tara Campbell supervised the technicians racking David McKinnon's *Atlas* into one of the *Himmelstor*'s 'Mech bay stalls. She had been able to crawl the assault 'Mech off the battlefield under its own power, and so it fell into the salvage exception granted to Jasek Kelswa-Steiner under his deal with the Jade Falcons. Tara felt good for that, at least. She still had hopes of returning the hundred-ton monster to Sire McKinnon.

Someday.

Turning from the alcove, she dodged around a lifter, its forks stacked high with a pallet of supplies, and went looking for Jasek. The bay was a hive of activity, with people rushing around in this last hour of safety. It smelled of blood and soil and nervous sweat. There was so much left to do. Equipment to store, machines to slot into the crowded bay, and people to find some corner where they could ride out what would hopefully be a short trip.

Skirting the edge of the *Excalibur*'s cavernous main bay, Tara wove between rows of hoverbikes and then a trio of

MASH trucks. The mobile-hospital vehicles had been jammed together to form a small medical center right along the curved outer bulkhead. The wounded had been first priority with Jasek, and he had not bothered to separate out Stormhammers or Highlanders or Steel Wolves. Like the machines crowded into the DropShip, many of the wounded had fought under different crests and insignia but were treated with equal attention.

There would be time enough for sorting out the different commands later, after the evacuation. Tara approved. In fact she approved of much—most, even—of what she'd seen from the landgrave.

When she found him at the foot of the DropShip's secondary ramp, directing the final stages of traffic as three different lines of vehicles converged and jockeyed for position to be included in the retreat, she nodded at that too. He had triaged them fairly well, bringing up military vehicles and flatbeds piled with the salvage the allied defenders had scraped up. The moving vans and the civilian pickup trucks flooding out of Miliano, carrying parts and materiel unloaded from the Avanti Assemblies plant and warehouses—these Jasek had peeled away to one side where they could be unloaded by hand. Now he simply pulled the last few up after the military line, no time left.

When he saw her, he handed the finale off to a master sergeant. One of her Highlanders, as it turned out. Jasek trotted behind a slow-moving J100 recovery vehicle and joined her at the side of the ramp. "Ten minutes," he said, glancing at his watch.

Tara looked out into the gray afternoon drizzle. She couldn't see the Jade Falcon line, holding several kilometers back from the cluster of DropShips. But she could sense them out there. Waiting. "You don't think Helmer will give us a little room?"

"I wouldn't want to risk lives on it."

He paused as a long peal of rolling thunder smashed into the conversation—a fusion drive lighting off. From the side of the covered ramp, the two looked north to find a *Union* blasting off from where it straddled the highway. The next-to-last vessel. It rose slowly at first, then gained speed. In less than a minute it had lost itself among dark gray clouds.

"Actually, if it was Noritomo Helmer, maybe I would,"

he finally admitted. "But I won't gamble anything on Malvina Hazen."

Tara nodded. "It still seems too easy. We ask to be allowed to pull back, and they just say okay. Too simple."

"Nothing's ever that easy, even if it seems like it to us. The Clans have centuries of effort behind their traditions. Maybe it did work against them this time. But having seen how Helmer kept his force intact in the face of such a long drive, I think they might have the right idea."

Her agreement was grudging. "Still, they have to know we'll ready a new line and they will have to come at us again. At Roosevelt Island or Cyclops, Incorporated."

"Well, we have DropShips there as well," Jasek said, obviously hedging. "Also at the Avanti Armory in New Dublin."

The two of them followed the final cargo truck up the ramp. Even before they reached the head, the ramp began to retract.

"But why?" she asked. "They seem the best points for a rallied defense of Skye."

"I agree. They would be."

Tara almost began to argue, then remembered her own admission on the battlefield. "We're running," she whispered again. Then looked to the Stormhammers' leader. "Jasek, where are you taking us?"

The landgrave looked out at Skye. Fondly. Sorrowfully. The main doors to this bay were beginning to fall, ready to seal it against atmosphere and vacuum. He stared out into the drizzle and the gray, at the fusion-scarred landscape the retreating DropShips were leaving behind, and nodded once, decisively.

"Nusakan," he told Tara then. "We're relocating to Nusakan. All of us." Too late for her to do anything.

Even if there truly had been nothing left to be done.

Standing atop Galaxy Commander Malthus' Tribune, wary of the company he kept, Noritomo Helmer watched as the final DropShip blasted free of Skye. Fire and steam rolled out in large plumes. The white glare of the fusion drive lit the *Excalibur*'s underside in a harsh backsplash. The ground shook and Malthus' mobile HQ swayed on its treads. Noritomo flexed his knees, cautious. The three senior officers waited very close to the forward edge of the crawler, almost two stories up. Beckett Malthus folded arms over a broad chest. Malvina paced along the very edge, as if daring fate to push her over.

Noritomo waited just between them. Trapped.

No one spoke as the artificial thunder continued to crash over them. They waited. A light rain pattered down around the trio, dripping off their emerald green foul-weather ponchos and beading on black, knee-high boots, splashing against wet-black steel. Everything else was drowned out by the throaty rumble of the rising *Excalibur*.

Jasek's DropShip. He knew it down in his bones. The Stormhammers' leader would be the last man away.

"You have a lot to answer for," Malvina Hazen finally said.

Noritomo pulled himself up to strict attention. "At the commander's disposal."

"Aff," she agreed. Stopping her pacing, she stood balanced on the balls of her feet, with her heels hanging out into space. "And I should have disposed of you several times over. Your list of failures grows impressive, Star Colonel Helmer."

And yet both Malthus and Malvina Hazen had entered brief commendations into his codex for rescuing the final battle for Skye. An interesting conflict.

"I stand by my decisions," he stated formally. He would defend them as well, if it came to that, in a Circle of Equals.

"As do I," Beckett Malthus offered, stepping up next to the Star colonel. His impassive stare let nothing of his personal feelings show, but his words, at least, melted away a small measure of Noritomo's concern. "Your forward thinking and your adherence to the Way of the Clans earned your reprieve last night."

The soft-spoken man looked him directly in the eye. "I would have forbidden any punishment against you, Noritomo Helmer. You should know that I did not have to do so."

Surprised, Noritomo looked to Malvina Hazen, who nodded with something resembling reluctant admiration. "Galaxy Commander Malthus pointed out, and I agreed, that you have done as my brother would have. You held to your personal ideals and honor, and you *possibly* saved the entire assault on Skye. Certainly you made it happen faster than per our original plans. For that, I am forced to admit that my brother's ways may not have always been incorrect."

Grudging, left-handed, but an impressive admittance by Malvina Hazen regardless. "I am honored."

"You may be yet. We shall see."

It felt like vindication. Though not without a small price. In the battle, Noritomo had unbent enough himself to recognize Malvina Hazen's value to the *desant* and how her way of unbridled war could be properly applied at the right time. Such as his quick-and-ruthless push past Kerensky's roadblock, subordinating his own honor to that of Beckett Malthus in order to accomplish his goal.

It was a small step to make toward a meeting of philosophies with Malvina Hazen. But a critical one.

"I am Jade Falcon," he said.

Malvina lifted her obsidian arm, rubbed the knuckles of her artificial fist along her jaw. Coming to a decision, she nodded. "And you will remain on Skye. With me. Galaxy Commander Malthus will oversee matters on Glengarry for the time being, coordinating with our outlying holdings while we rebuild our forces here.

"Your duty, Star Colonel, will be to keep my brother's spirit alive among our forces. You will continue to challenge me." Her smile was thin and humorless. "Until you prove yourself wrong or I simply get tired of your incessant meddling."

One foot in a minefield. The other on slippery ferrosteel. Noritomo could almost wish for an insignificant garrison post. But Clan warriors did not back away from a fight.

"Aff, Malvina Hazen. I understand completely."

He gave her a short bow, then stepped forward to let the toes of his boots hang out over the crawler's edge. Purposefully, he did not look in her direction. If she decided to shove him over, let her try it. He would respect the Chinggis Khan, but he would not be afraid of this woman.

In fact, he decided, he might accomplish a great deal should he remain alive long enough. Today, perhaps, he had pushed some of Pandora's evils back into the box. Enough that he could once again stand proudly as a Jade Falcon warrior. It would be a struggle, keeping that lid on, but he welcomed the challenge.

He glanced back to nod his appreciation to Beckett Malthus, wanting to thank the man for his support and shore up the bridges he had made into that camp. But Malthus was gone, back down the open hatch and into the belly of his Tribune command vehicle. Noritomo had indeed been left alone with Malvina Hazen, for better or for worse.

He stood by her side, silently, watching as the *Himmelstor* lost itself in the clouds.

Epilogue

Leaving Niccolò next to the elevators, Landgrave Jasek Kelswa-Steiner joined Alexia Wolf and Tara Campbell. Both women were watching the Steel Wolf exodus from the comfort of the Cheops DropPort observation tower. He placed a hand on Tara's shoulder, and the three stood together for a moment in front of the bronze-tinted windows as vehicles and 'Mechs, infantrymen and technicians, all gathered by columns and ranks on the tarmac. Steel Wolf forces straggled in from the *Himmelstor* as well as from three other DropShips. Some were towed behind heavy trucks. The half-gutted shells of several ruined tanks and a *Mad Cat III* rolled in on the flatbeds of J100 recovery vehicles. All in all, if they were returning to Seginus with half their initial strength, he'd be surprised.

"I'd hoped Anastasia would join us," he said, staring through the tinted ferroglass. The warmth of Nusakan's summer sun barely filtered through. "We owe her a great deal."

Alexia had made the trip from Skye to Nusakan aboard the Steel Wolf JumpShip. "She preferred to remain in orbit." A sly smile played on her lips. "Said that she did not want you charming her into another futile stand. At least, not until she's had time to re-form and rest her people. She did extend an offer for you to visit Seginus, if you have any personal time to spare." Alexia held up a hand as Jasek startled, pulling away from Tara. "I told her you would refuse. That you . . . *rarely* work that way."

Tara glanced from one to the other, obviously not following the exchange, but choosing not to intrude. "Seginus will not be receiving much in the way of aid and resupply," the countess said. Having had a few weeks in transit to acknowledge the loss of Skye, she had already begun planning a new defensive stand for Prefecture IX. "She would do better to stay close."

Frowning, and without looking away from Alexia, Jasek nodded. "Think you can talk her out of it?" he asked Tara. Almost hoping.

"There is a remote area, with old militia facilities, on Nusakan's southern continent. The Steel Wolves could occupy that."

"I will pass that information to the commander," Alexia offered.

He heard the finality in her tone and accepted that the Steel Wolves would not be staying. Neither would Alexia. "This war is not over," he reminded her. "Will you ask the Steel Wolves to at least keep open a line of communication?"

"I will see to it," she promised. Leaning in to him, Alexia Wolf put an easy hand around the back of Jasek's neck and pulled him down for a kiss. There was no desire in it, no strength. It was soft and sorry, and then it was over.

"Thank you for everything," she told him.

She nearly left on that, but paused to size up Tara Campbell with a quick glance from head to foot. "You win," she said, as if casting a vote of confidence. A half smile. "I did not think it was possible."

Tara gazed after Alexia with a confused look. She turned to Jasek, and brushed her platinum blond hair back with a quick sweep of slender fingers. "That looked suspiciously like a good-bye."

"It was." Jasek steeled himself against showing how much the loss hurt him. As a commander losing one of his best officers, more than as a man losing his lover.

He nodded after her. "Alexia is leaving with Kerensky and the Steel Wolves," he said. "We were always a temporary stop for her. Now that she's proven herself as a warrior, it's time for her to follow her original path. I hope she finds what she is looking for with them."

First Tamara, who held such hopes for Jasek, even though he had been casually committed to another. Now Alexia. It wasn't a surprise. But was she leaving so soon because of her desire to "return home" with the Steel Wolves, as close as she could get to being among the Clans, or because Jasek had allowed something far more serious to come between the two of them? Her parting comments seemed to indicate a measure of both.

"And the rest?" Tara asked, not letting it go. Like a terrier getting her teeth into a bone, she'd worry it until it cracked. "What did I win?"

"I think she meant . . . me," he offered with a small smile.

"How's that again?"

Clasping hands behind his back, hiding his nervousness, Jasek turned away from the window. Tara's bright blue eyes studied him warily. She knew. And she was just as obviously scared for what it might mean. "On Chaffee and again on Hesperus II," he explained slowly, "I kept hearing your voice in my head. It stuck with me, Tara. I couldn't shake it, and didn't want to. From the first day we met, I've felt an incredible attraction for you."

He paused, stepping forward. "And I've flattered myself into thinking you felt something for me."

For a moment, Jasek believed that she did. He saw the softening around her eyes, and the cautious smile most women displayed when they'd made a decision about their feelings. He would have sworn he saw her rise up on the balls of her feet, ready to lean in to him.

But then Tara pulled back. Her eyes shone with resolve as she stepped away. She shook her head.

"I'm married to The Republic, Jasek. It's what I promised myself, and that's the way it has to be."

Duty before all. Jasek understood that, even if it tore at him. By the pained look on Tara's face, her decision was costing her too.

"You'll change your mind," he said, turning back to the window. She had to change her mind. For everything else he'd given up in the last two years, and everything he'd lost, she was the one thing he no longer was certain he could stand to be without.

"Don't count on it," she shot back at him quickly.

But she stood beside him a moment longer anyway. It felt very comfortable until she cleared her throat nervously. "Take care of yourself, Jasek. All right? I *would* like to know that you're . . . safe." Then she too left.

It was a very awkward parting, and he nearly went after her right then. Maybe she wanted him to. Maybe not. He let her go. There was time enough for such pursuits, he told himself. This first day back on Nusakan, there were other priorities that needed handling. His father, for one. Spreading out the Stormhammers' intelligence network again, for another. Whatever was happening back on Terra, they needed to know something as soon as possible.

And then there were the new allegations against Vic Parkins to investigate. Whether the hauptmann abandoned his superior officer on the battlefield or had been engaged and truly unable to respond. Nicco had repeatedly advised Jasek that Tamara's romantic loyalty fostered a potential discipline problem, but still, she deserved better.

So much to do. Tara Campbell would have to wait. She wasn't going anywhere.

He hoped.

Niccolò had waited by the elevators. The doors on Tara's car were barely shut when Jasek walked up, his face solemn. "Bad day at the office?"

"We're back on Nusakan, and most of us are alive, if a bit battered." Jasek had little doubt his friend saw how much he was hurting. "It's a good start."

"We knew going in that Skye was lost," Niccolò reminded him. "Had to be lost."

Jasek said nothing. He summoned a new car.

"Fifth Rise?" the GioAvanti scion asked. It was where Duke Gregory waited. It would be a necessary stop.

"Yes," Jasek agreed, hardening himself to the difficult decisions he now faced. The Isle of Skye was about to go through very hard times. The Stormhammers had to be ready to cushion the blows.

The elevator arrived, heavy doors rolling back quietly. Both men stepped inside the waiting car.

"There is nothing more difficult to plan, more uncertain of success, or more dangerous to manage than the establishment of a new order of government," his best friend said. "And that is exactly what you are trying to accomplish, Landgrave."

"But not alone," Jasek whispered as he watched the doors roll shut. "Not alone."

At the mansion residence on Fifth Rise, Jasek Kelswa-Steiner found his father standing on a small balcony just off Governor Paulo's drawing room. A glass of dark red wine sat forgotten on a nearby bistro table. Hands clasped behind his back, hair shining glossily under Nusakan's sun, the lord governor stared out over Cheops, given a commanding view of the sculpted city as it flowed down the mountainside.

"It's a beautiful city," he said, sensing Jasek's arrival.

Jasek joined him at the railing. "But you won't be staying."

"No. Nusakan is your world, boy. Lyons will make a better home for my lord governorship in absentia. It's a strong world, and they hold fast to The Republic there."

At least it was said without the usual rancor. After seeing off Alexia and with Tara's uncertain good-bye, Jasek had no strength for another fight. A strained silence fell between them as they tried to enjoy a moment of peace. Such moments came so rarely. Jasek listened to birdsong and tasted the sweet fragrance of cherry trees wafting from Governor Paulo's nearby orchards. The sun warmed his skin. Shielding his eyes, he stared down Cheops' five Hills and Rises and saw the distant DropPort, where large vehicles crawled like ants among gray spheroidal hills.

It reminded him too much of what he'd recently lost.

"Would you rather have been left behind?" Jasek asked after a moment. His father had not been a willing participant in the evacuation, after all. He'd not even known about the bargain of *hegira* until the DropShip carrying him had left Skye's atmosphere.

"I would rather have been given the choice. Not pulled out of Second Bristol by your storm troopers."

"I sent Nicco."

"And a squad of Hauberk." The duke scratched absentmindedly at his beard. More steel gray had crept in at the edges of his mouth, his sideburns. "It was all very smoothly done, and no doubt planned for some time. My Ducal Guard did not even tumble to it until we were already inside the DropShip."

This civility was murder. Jasek began to wonder if he would feel more comfortable with his father flushed red and ranting. "I'm sorry we could not save Skye." But his words fell flat.

"You never meant to save Skye, no more than you meant to give me a choice in leaving." His father turned away from the view, and there was a bite of steel in his voice again. "I'm not a fool, boy. You played this your way from the start. Media attention. Lyran involvement. And the fall of Skye. Admit it."

Jasek shrugged, rested his forearms on the balustrade. "I would have taken a victory over the Jade Falcons if there had been one in the offing, but you and I both know that it wasn't going to happen. Not without substantial support from Prefecture X. Exarch Redburn left you—left Tara—fighting a losing battle."

He shoved himself away from the rail suddenly. "You told me—you *taught* me—to play the long game. Well, I have, Father. Nicco and I saw months ago that the Jade Falcons held too many advantages. All that was left was to choose the final battlefield, and I forced it on them. They are stuck now. Stuck holding Skye. Now *we* move where *we* will, and attack at our convenience, because they can't afford to give it up. It's been tied around their necks like a millstone."

His father nodded. "And whoever frees Skye earns the undying gratitude of the people. Even if he comes bearing the Lyran fist. Well, it might work. If it's you who succeeds and not I." He turned back toward the city, large hands gripping the balustrade's stone rail. There was still a great deal of strength in them. "But that's only going to happen over my dead body."

"And vice versa, I'm certain," Jasek said deadpan, even though it tore at him to admit it. His father seemed to have no difficulty with the idea, though. "Tara warned me, you know."

His father grunted in response, but Jasek waited him out.

"If it was going to happen, it would have already."

"And here I've been looking over my shoulder for the better part of two years waiting for the attempt. Why didn't you?" he asked, throat tight around the words. "Why didn't you have me killed when I broke from you?"

"Don't think I haven't come close a time or two," his father admitted calmly, as if discussing the pleasant Nusakan weather. "But there were always . . . considerations."

"Such as?"

"Even though you think you are playing the long game, Jasek, you aren't. In fact, you've barely made it out of my sight. You're impatient. You're reckless. Time will do the job for me, if you don't come to your senses first."

Jasek nearly smiled, hearing his name from his father's lips. If the darts flung behind it hadn't felt so accurate and so sharp. "What if you're wrong?"

A shrug. "Then you are still blood of my blood. And in the end you may be all the Isle has left."

He considered that for a few moments. It sounded almost like an admission of respect. But he could not forget his father's adamant declaration in their last, bitter conversation before Jasek first left Skye with the Stormhammers.

Skye will never need your kind of leadership.

We'll see what Skye needs, Father.

Neither of them would know the answer until one or the other stood victorious in the Isle.

"We'll see," he stated flatly, then turned from the cityscape view, toward the balcony door.

"And you'll continue looking over your shoulder, won't you, boy?"

Jasek stopped in the doorway. It took great strength of will not to look back. He imagined his father leaning against the stone railing still, but had the old duke turned to watch his son depart? If Jasek glanced over his shoulder, just one last time, would they each see the other searching for some kind of common ground?

Or would he only feel foolish for surrendering another round to his father?

He stepped through the open doorway, leaving the duke and lord governor of Prefecture IX to himself. The battle for Skye was just beginning, Jasek knew. There would be other days to measure themselves against each other. Better days, he hoped. Though maybe, he acknowledged, this was all that was left between them. Soft words and hard feelings.

And the blood of the Isle.

About the Author

Loren L. Coleman grew up in the Pacific Northwest. An avid reader, he became infatuated with stories and the art of storytelling at an early age. He wrote creative works when he was as young as twelve years old, and began to write actual fiction stories in high school for a creative-writing class, but it was during his enlistment in the U.S. Navy that he began working seriously at the craft. Discharged in 1993, he went to work as a freelance fiction writer and eventually became a full-time novelist.

His first novel, *Double-Blind*, was pubished in 1998. He has since explored the universes of *BattleTech, Magic: The Gathering, Crimson Skies, MechWarrior: Dark Age*, and *Star Trek*. Around the time of this printing, he has written and published fifteen novels and a great deal of shorter fiction, and been involved with several computer games. Currently, he is working on a new trilogy set in the Conan universe.

When he isn't writing, Loren plays Xbox games, collects far too many DVDs, and holds a black belt in traditional Tae Kwon Do. He has lived in many parts of the country. Currently he resides in Washington State with his wife, Heather Joy, two sons, Talon LaRon and Conner Rhys Monroe, and a daughter, Alexia Joy. The family owns three of the obligatory writer's cats, Chaos, Ranger and Rumor, and one dog, Loki, who like any dog is just happy to be here.

His personal Web site can be found at www.rasqal.com.